Romy Hausmann was born in East Germany in 1981. At the age of twenty-four she became chief editor at a film production company in Munich. Since the birth of her son, Romy has been working as a freelancer in television. Her thriller debut, *Dear Child*, became a number one bestseller in Germany, was published in twenty countries and has been adapted into an internationally successful Netflix series. *Anatomy of a Killer* is her third thriller. Romy lives with her family in a remote house in the woods near Stuttgart.

Also by Romy Hausmann

Dear Child
Sleepless

ROMY HAUSMANN

Anatomy of a Killer

Translated from the German by
Jamie Bulloch

QUERCUS

First published in the German language as *Perfect Day* by
dtv Verlagsgesellschaft mbH & Co. KG. München, in 2022
First published in Great Britain in 2023 by Quercus
This paperback edition published in Great Britain in 2024 by

QUERCUS

Quercus Editions Ltd
Carmelite House
50 Victoria Embankment
London EC4Y 0DZ

An Hachette UK company

Perfect Day by Romy Hausmann
© 2022 dtv Verlagsgesellschaft mbH & Co. KG. München
English translation copyright © 2022 by Jamie Bulloch

The moral right of Romy Hausmann to be
identified as the author of this work has been
asserted in accordance with the Copyright,
Designs and Patents Act, 1988.

Jamie Bulloch asserts his moral right to be identified as the translator of this work.

A CIP catalogue record for this book is available
from the British Library

PB ISBN 978 1 52942 240 5
EBOOK ISBN 978 1 52942 241 2

10 9 8 7 6 5 4 3 2 1

Typeset by CC Book Production
Printed and bound in Great Britain by Clays Ltd, Elcograf S.p.A.

Papers used by Quercus are from well-managed forests and other responsible sources.

For you, Papa.
For your humour and your strength.
You are Iron Man.

The power of fantasy can be comforting.
Or deadly.

It's a Thursday when Ann dies – the most miserable of deaths. She lies on her back, her legs stiffly outstretched, pressing her trembling hands to the gaping wound in her chest. The men have removed her heart; they just cut it from her body and took it with them. She wants to scream but can't, as other sounds are coming from her throat: gurgling, wheezing. Lights explode on her retina – it's a strain, such a terrible strain, and she just wishes it were over; she can't cope anymore. And so she lets go, she falls, closes her eyes, ready . . . Behind her closed eyes, it's a better place. There the sun glistens, the sky is blue and she sits on her father's shoulders, waving her arms around as if she could fly. It's long in the past – she's seven and Dad calls her his 'Beetle'. He holds her tightly and securely by the legs; she doesn't have to worry, not anymore.

So this is what it's like, she tells herself. This is death.

And it can happen so quickly.

A moment ago this Thursday was just a Thursday. They were waiting for their dinner, a pizza delivery from Casa Mamma. Dad had put some music on, a Lou Reed record from the 1970s, before Ann was born. A time when her father was young, reckless and foolish. She would grin when he said such things. Dad, foolish? Never! How preposterous was that? But all the same she liked the record, which he must have played more often than any other; it was a backdrop to Ann's childhood. Wood was crackling in the fire and it smelled as if Dad had lit it with paper. Ann hated this smoky tang with its hint of acute danger. As if the entire house could go up in flames at any moment.

'Where's our dinner?' came the typical whinge from Ann, which Dad poked fun at.

'While we're waiting, why don't you make yourself useful and fetch some more logs?' he said, handing her the wood basket. Ann pulled a face. When she was hungry, she wasn't in the mood for banter.

In the garden, November had created shapes that looked even stranger in the shadowy glow of the terrace lamps. The bushes, bent under the weight of the snow like hunched old ladies, seemed to be heading for the mountain beneath which her old trampoline was hiding. Ann trudged over to the woodshed, tossed a few logs into the basket and returned to the house.

That was when the dying began.

First the light shooting through the window from the other side of the house, the front. Blue circles suddenly dancing in the room. Ann, standing there in bewilderment with the basket, and her father, joking about their pizzas now being delivered express by the emergency services – the restaurant must have sensed how distraught his Beetle got when she was hungry.

But then . . .

The front door bursting open and the men storming in. Throwing themselves on Dad and wrestling him to the ground.

There must have been a whole lot of shouting because Ann saw wide-open mouths. But she heard nothing; all of them were bellowing silently under the high-pitched tone that filled her head like tinnitus. The men yanked her father, yanked him to his feet, yanked him towards the door. Ann clutched her wood basket. She saw Dad flounder backwards and turn to her. His utterly empty face. Then they took him away, out into the night. Two of the men stayed inside the house, trying to explain to her what had just happened. Their words sliced into Ann's chest, gouging deeper and deeper until they finally reached her heart. She fainted. The basket fell to the floor. The thudding of logs was followed by the clunk of her skull. Ann's body began to convulse, to twitch; she wheezed, whimpered, and it felt really bad until she got here: the world behind her closed eyelids, where her heart is still intact, where it's summer and with Dad's help she can fly. She's seven years old, his 'Beetle', and Lou Reed is singing about a perfect day.

'We need a paramedic!' An unfamiliar voice cuts in from somewhere, getting louder. It orders Ann to breathe: breathe in on one, out on two, and to stay calm, as calm as possible.

'Here, the asthma spray!'

She feels her head being moved. Rough fingers force open her mouth and push something hard inside. Her throat turns cold, her chest relaxes. Sluggishly she opens her eyes. Someone is bending over her.

'It's good to have you back,' the happy fool says. He has no idea of hell.

3

NEW LEAD IN BERLIN RIBBON MURDERS CASE:
55-year-old arrested after thirteen-year manhunt

Berlin (JW) – On Thursday evening a 55-year-old man was arrested in relation to the series of dramatic murders dating back to 2004. The man is suspected of having abducted the victims, whose ages range from 6 to 10, taking them to various remote locations in the vicinity of Berlin and then killing them. The suspect left red ribbons to ensure the bodies were found. Most recently, the body of schoolgirl Sophie K. (7) was discovered in a cabin in Königswald. The week before, the girl had been kidnapped from a playground in Berlin-Schmargendorf. The police revealed that a witness statement led them to the 55-year-old.

ANN

It's as if the city has been cleared out; I can't see a single car or person, not even a stray dog. The shop windows are black, the entrances obstructed by roller shutters. Berlin is dead, everything is. Except for me. The last survivor, the only person left after the end of the world. Only me and Berlin and the festive lighting hanging everywhere, which flashes deceptively in rhythm, as if the city did have a heartbeat, after all, a last hint of life.

I'm in a hurry; my steps are rapid and ungainly. Slush splashes up to my knees. So what? My trousers ought to have been washed a while ago. I used to be vain, but that's in the past now. Zoe changed the locks to our flat and just left a small travel bag for me on the landing. From time to time I imagine her sitting at uni in my dark red velvet jeans or wearing my golden sequin top on a date. It's okay, or, as Saskia E.'s father recently said in an interview: *The pain threshold shifts.* At some point, things that used to hurt like a flesh wound only feel like a scratch. Saskia E. was victim number seven, murdered three years ago at Christmas 2014.

5

I quicken my pace, chasing away shadows and footsteps that aren't there. Sometimes there's a splash of blood instead of snow. Saskia's father was right about this too: *Inevitably you go a bit mad.* He does the rounds of the media as a distraction. I have a distraction too, but it's work. Although I've no idea who's going to drift into a grubby fast-food joint like Big Murphy's today of all days – they would have to be very, very lonely. The truth is, the city isn't dead. It's still alive, of course, and how. It has merely withdrawn into its warm, lovingly decorated sitting rooms. It's sitting at tables laden with food, folded napkins and the best cutlery. It's giving each other presents and revelling in eyes that light up. It's happy, this city, and the only ones left out today are those at the very bottom. It's Sunday. And Christmas Eve.

'There you are! Finally!' Behind the till Antony flails his arms about. He's Cuban, just turned twenty-one, and he's been in Berlin for two years all on his own, without his parents or four siblings who still live in Moa, an industrial city on the north-east coast of Cuba. He needs the money he earns at Big Murphy's to finance his studies and his room, but most of all for the transfers he sends home every month via Western Union.

I close the glass door behind me and look around. A single table is occupied, by an old man whose face appears to be nothing but eyes and a beard. He's wearing a dirty brown coat, and as he bites into a floppy burger, I can see fingerless gloves full of holes. Ketchup drips out of the bun like thick, red tears.

'Yes, thank God, given the rush on here,' I mutter as I wander past him and into the changing room.

My uniform consists of a short-sleeved, green polyester shirt and brown trousers that open at the sides: ventilation slits. You come to appreciate them when, in the cramped kitchen, oil at 180 degrees is bubbling in five deep fat fryers at once.

It's not the best job in the world, but it was almost criminally easy to get. No written application, no references, no CV. Just a phone call and the next day a job interview using my dead mother's maiden name. The manageress liked me at once; I came across as uncomplicated. Working hours, overtime, even the salary: I didn't care. All that interested me was having my wages paid in cash. And that was fine so long as I signed for it. After some rudimentary training in hygiene, infection control and accident prevention, I was shown the ropes.

Today there are only three of us here: Antony, who's looking after the till and the drinks; Michelle, who's preparing the burgers in the kitchen; and me, who right now is helping her, because nobody's coming to the drive-in that I'm responsible for. Of course not: it's Christmas Eve.

'You all right, Ann? You're so quiet today.' Dear, sweet, simple Michelle. How concerned she sounds. She's in her mid-forties, her hair dyed a yellowish colour, and she's always plastered with make-up, which at the start of her shift makes her look at least five years younger, but later, when it has gathered in the wrinkles around her eyes, has the opposite effect.

'Sure, everything's fine,' I say, for no reason poking my finger into the container with the tomatoes.

Michelle nudges me in the side to cheer me up. 'I find Christmas depressing too, if that's what's bothering you. For three whole days, everyone behaving as if all was right with the world. Peace, love and light a candle. Yeah, right.' Michelle is a single mother of two teenage boys and a grown-up daughter. Her eldest hasn't celebrated Christmas with her for years, and the boys are with their father this year. 'What about yours?'

She means my daughter. I'd called her Diana, because I couldn't think of anything better when I was put on the spot. Diana, after the Roman goddess of hunting – not, as Michelle thinks, after the dead princess. But basically it doesn't matter what my daughter's called. She happened when I was eighteen, happy-go-lucky and naïve, one of those silly young girls who's just careless. Now I'm twenty-four and I have to earn money for her, just as everyone here at Big Murphy's has to earn money for someone. All I say is, 'With her father too,' and fiddle with the tomatoes again. I don't want to look at Michelle.

'What are you giving her?' is the next question, and the first thing that comes to mind is: 'A trampoline.'

Just like the trampoline I got for Christmas when I was Diana's age. The box the frame came in was brown, and so huge that it would have needed several rolls of paper to wrap it up. So my father simply tied a large red ribbon around it. As soon as it was spring and the sun had sucked up the last of the dampness the snow had left in the soil, he would construct it in the garden with his fingers that were all thumbs, the touching clumsiness of an academic. He would position it so that when he sat at the desk in his study he only had to peer out of the window to see me jumping. I liked my present, I really did. But then, in the depths of winter, I couldn't do anything with it. So I asked him to take the metal rods out of the box, then I climbed in and put the lid on. My father found this interesting, astonishing,

strange. With that look of his which reflects his need to analyse everything, he asked me what was going through my head
when I lay in my box, as quiet as a mouse, perfectly still and
with my eyes closed. He thought it might have something to do
with my mother. And that I was trying to find out what it was
like to lie in a coffin.

'But Dad,' I countered, 'this isn't a coffin. It's just a box and
I'm lying in it.'

'Great!' Michelle looks really excited, then a second later her
face assumes a touch of sadness. I know she's worried her sons
might take after their father, who's already twice served time for
assault. 'Enjoy it while Diana's still young.' Sighing, she wipes
her sweaty brow with the back of her hand. 'The moment they
get to twelve, they don't want to know you anymore and start
stealing from your purse to buy weed.' When she takes her hand
away from her face I see brown streaks and her left eyebrow is
slightly paler than before. Now she's laughing again, like she
always does when she realises that frying oil is the best make-up
remover. But maybe she's also laughing to hold back the tears.
I know the feeling, but I'm ashamed nonetheless. So many lies.
Perhaps Michelle would understand if I explained. Perhaps she
wouldn't judge me; she is a good person, after all. On the other
hand, that's what I thought of Zoe too.

'Earth to Ann. Ann, come in, please!' Putting on a voice,
Michelle speaks into her fist as if it were a radio. I suppose that's
what mums are like. When their children are young they get used
to doing silly things they never grow out of.

'Sorry, I was lost in thought.'

9

'I noticed.' Grinning, she points to the monitor showing the pictures from the drive-in. A car has just pulled up. 'Customers.'

I hurriedly slip on the headset and take a deep breath before pressing the button that connects the microphone to the intercom outside.

'Happy Christmas and a warm welcome to Big Murphy's Burgers and Fries.' I can't believe how friendly I sound, how unfazed. It seems that, like my headset, I've also got a button, an inner button, that switches me into a different mode if I press it hard enough. *You just function*, Saskia E.'s father said in the newspaper, and he's right.

'May I have your order, please?'

I can only hear static at first.

'Hello?'

Puzzled, I stick my head out of the window. The intercom is five or six metres away. Only when customers have given their order do they move up to the serving window. From this distance, however, all I see is the silhouette of a car, its headlights stamping two bright circles in the late afternoon darkness.

The static goes silent and a man's voice crackles, 'You didn't really think you'd get away from me that easily, did you?'

Frite. (Ann, 7 years old)
a frite is like when you get an electric shock. your hart jumps up and when it goes back down again its still beating faster than before and sometimes it hurts. theres buzzing in your ears and you feel so cold that you shiver, then the frite nose its worked and maybe it stops. but sometimes a frite is just a joke and you get scared for no reason, then you have to larf because you were silly and fell for the frite.

'You muppet!'

I laugh hysterically. Jakob, it's only Jakob, sitting outside in his car, having given me one hell of a fright via the intercom. Jakob, who's laughing too now.

'That's no way to greet your customers. I think I'm going to have to complain to the management.'

'To get me sacked at Christmas? Charming.' Seeing the look on Michelle's face, I whisper, 'Jakob.' She grins and raises her left, unpainted eyebrow. I'm embarrassed that she knows about us, even though there's actually nothing to know. I adjust the microphone in front of my mouth and stick my head out of the serving window again. I still can't see anything but the car in the darkness and two circles of light.

'What are you doing here, Jakob?'

'You said you hate Christmas and don't want to celebrate. And I said I couldn't allow that.'

'I guess you're right.'

That was yesterday. I was on the till when Jakob appeared at the counter and ordered a 'Big Murphy's Mega Meal'. He comes in often, almost every day. I even arrange my breaks to coincide with him. We sweep the snow from the bench in the Big Murphy's car park and sit there, a coy distance apart like two people who'd really like to arrange a proper date. But they don't; the woman has her reasons and the man clearly has sufficient tact to realise that she'd give him the brush-off. He thinks she's studying German and working at Big Murphy's to cover her rent. And he probably finds her a bit prim too. So he tries to lighten the mood by telling her funny anecdotes about his work at a recycling centre in Kreuzberg. She likes the idea of him helping people get

11

rid of their relics. Their bulky rubbish, worn-out clothes, empty paint tins, cardboard boxes, batteries, garden waste. Most of all she likes the idea of him climbing on to the overflowing paper skips and jumping up and down until the mountains of paper sink beneath his weight, making room for more. His gangly arms whirling in the air, his short, dark hair dancing up and down and his blue eyes gleaming with boyish exuberance. She finds him so carefree, so unencumbered.

'Well, and that's why I thought we might . . .'

I sigh. Today, of all days, Jakob seems to have decided to narrow the distance between us.

'I can't, I'm afraid.'

'But you don't even know what—'

'I've got to work.'

'That's not a problem. I'll wait for you.'

'My shift doesn't finish till nine.'

'Doesn't matter.'

'No, that's too late. Anyway, I'll be exhausted and stinking of frying oil.' Tugging at a greasy black hair in front of my eyes, I look at it and wonder if I had a shower before going to bed last night. I can't recollect taking one. All I remember is an insipid microwave dinner, collapsing on to the sofa like a sack of flour and watching E.T. the Extra-Terrestrial because I wanted to cry as a release, out of emotion for once, rather than pain. 'Another time, okay?' On the monitor, I see, to my relief, another car turn into the drive-in lane behind Jakob. 'Now you have to place an order or move on.'

I hear him mutter something unintelligible, then he drives past the serving window – speedily and without glancing in my direction. I close my eyes briefly and take a deep breath. Pressing the button on the headset as well as my inner one, I smile and say, 'Happy Christmas and welcome to Big Murphy's Burgers and Fries. How can I help you?'

Do you remember . . . ?
– 22 December 2014, Christmas three years ago.
– What's wrong with our tree?
– It's plastic, Ann.
– It's a tradition, Dad. We've had this tree ever since I can remember.
– That's even worse.
– What now?
– I know a place in Blumenthal woods . . .
– Are you going to chop one down? You're joking, Dad. With an axe?
– No, I'm going to gnaw at the trunk until I've bitten it all the way through. Of course with an axe!
– Do you remember when you tried to put my trampoline up? You drilled into your finger.
– Did I end up sorting out the trampoline?
– Did we end up in A&E?
– Come on, my Beetle. Where I'm going to take you is a wonderful place. And we'll have a proper Christmas tree like normal people do.
– When have we ever wanted to be like other people? Quite apart from the fact that you can't just go marching into the woods and take down any tree you like. Imagine if everyone did that!
– We'll just be careful not to get caught.

– You're crazy.
– And you're my daughter, so welcome to the club!

And that's precisely what we were, wasn't it, Dad? A really exclusive club, just the two of us, ready to confront the rest of the world if necessary. You comforted me whenever I cried about Mum. Left me to it when I hated her and wished she were in hell. You plaited my hair and told me goodnight stories. You told me about womanhood, gave me tea for my cramps and chocolate when I was ravenous. You covered for me when, heartbroken for the first time, I scratched Nico's 125cc because he'd been fooling around with my best friend Eva.

His mother came knocking at our door.

'Are you trying to tell me my daughter did that?' you said to her. 'Never!'

'But I saw her with my own eyes yesterday evening. Hanging around in our street. And the damage was there this morning. Do you know how long Nico saved up for it?'

'Look, I'm really very sorry, but you must be mistaken. My daughter was at home all evening. We were playing chess.'

And you always let me win at chess, because you didn't want me to feel like a loser. You know me so well, Dad. And I know you.

That's why it's a shock every time.

Pixellating the face doesn't make it any easier.

They write about you and seem to be so sure of what they're saying.

I'm halfway home, standing by a newspaper dispenser, staring at tomorrow's edition of one of the largest Berlin newspapers, lit up by a streetlamp. The front page carries a report about how the E. family is planning to spend the Christmas holidays, now that the suspected killer, the man who is presumed to have done all those terrible things – *you!* – is finally in prison, or at least in custody. They will be putting up a Christmas tree for the first time in three years, Jörg E. (43) says. He is crying and smiling simultaneously, the editor adds. At the bottom it says: 'Continue reading on page 3.' I don't know if I want to. Recalling this episode from 2014 is enough. The first time you wanted to have a real tree and were planning to go to Blumenthal woods to cut one down. That same year was the first Christmas the E. family spent without their 'darling little Saskia (8)'. She'd been abducted a few days earlier by an unknown person. She was found dead in a hut in the first week of January. In Blumenthal woods.

A coincidence, I know, Dad.

You're not a killer.

They're so dreadfully mistaken, but they refuse to see this. They'd rather keep spreading their lies, their godawful lies.

Anger. (Ann, 7 years old)

anger is invissible like air and creeps into you when you get very angry. you start with a lump in your throat and you breath like a bull. your hart starts beating very fast and you grind your teeth so you calm down, but it doesn't work because anger is stronger than you and it explodes in your body and because you cant cope you start moving your arms and legs and hitting and kiking. thats the only way to get the anger out of your body and to be left in piece. I was angry once at my MUMMY but I didnt hit her because she was sik. you mustnt hit someone if there sik. shes dead now sadly.

Someone shouts, 'Ann!' and puts their arms around my waist. I'm swept off my feet and I kick at thin air, where before there was the newspaper dispenser. All the same I keep kicking. I'm not going to stop; I can't stop. I'm determined to destroy the lies, even if all I can do at the moment is target a newspaper dispenser.

'Ann!' the voice calls out again and the grip tightens around my waist. 'For Christ's sake, what are you doing?' I'm spun around. 'Stop it!'

I'm going to do nothing of the sort; I mean to fight, destroy. Metal crunches, plastic shatters and paper tatters. Until I gradually lose my strength.

'It's okay, it's all right,' the voice says. Jakob's voice – Jakob again. He gently releases me from his grasp, now that I've finally calmed down. In silence we first look at each other, then at what used to be a newspaper dispenser. The frame is bent, the box is battered and there's a crack in the acrylic viewing window. The newspapers lie shredded in the slush.

Exhausted, I shuffle off to the nearest porch; I need to sit down. The steps are cold and wet, but I don't care; I'm sweating and panting as if I'd just completed a marathon. In the cycle lane in front of me is Jakob's red jeep, the driver's door open. He sits beside me. Judging by his expression he wants to know what just happened, but doesn't have the right words on his lips. I've no idea what to say either. How can I explain this outburst, this other Ann he's never seen before, who attacks newspaper dispensers like a madwoman? Apart from telling him the truth, of course. Have you ever wondered whether the man in the paper, the one they call the 'monster', has any family? Yes, he does, Jakob. Me. I'm the daughter of the supposed ribbon murderer, who is alleged

16

to have abducted and killed nine little girls over the past thirteen years. I was there when they arrested him. I was visiting him that Thursday evening, six weeks ago. We'd ordered pizza and opened a bottle of red wine. When the doorbell went we thought it was the deliveryman. But it was a SWAT team, a dozen men at least. They pounced on my father, handcuffed him and took him away. They were going to take me too and have me give a statement, but I had an asthma attack. And what was I meant to tell them anyway? He's innocent, you fools! He's been in custody ever since and they're linking up their ludicrous chain of evidence, which is supposed to end in a noose around his neck. That's why I'm so furious, Jakob. I'm furious and I'm absolutely terrified.

I don't say any of this; I say nothing. Because it's pointless. Zoe didn't understand either, even though we've known each other for three years and even lived together. It's not that she thinks my father's guilty, she says, absolutely not. And she's really sorry, but she's just got this bad feeling about it. It won't be long before the journalists pitch up and lay siege to our flat, she says. All the whispers at university and the fact that she's got two younger siblings around the age of those girls who were killed. *Please, Ann, don't be cross with me.* No, Zoe, not at all, it's fine.

'Are you all right now?' Jakob asks.

I mumble something.

'Okay, good.' He puts out his hands and straightens the collar of my old, thickly padded denim jacket. It's Dad's jacket and I can sink in it, not only physically. Sometimes, when I take it off the hook, I imagine he's just removed it and hung it up there. And when I put it on, I fancy I can still feel a residue of his bodily warmth.

Instinctively I knock Jakob's hands away.

'Sorry,' he says, startled. 'I was just trying—'

'No, no, it's okay. I'm sorry. I'm just a bit sensitive today. What are you doing here, anyway?'

He shrugs.

'I drove past Big Murphy's again, hoping you might've changed your mind. But I saw your colleague, who said you'd already left. So I headed back home, and then . . .' He nods at the road – presumably to indicate he'd driven past by chance – and then at the wreck of the newspaper dispenser.

'I don't know what came over me. Maybe a bout of Christmas depression that got slightly out of hand.'

I try to distract him with a smile, but Jakob remains uncomfortably serious.

'You lied to me, Ann,' he says. His words are like a bucket of cold water in my face.

I blink frantically. 'What?'

'Your daughter.'

'My . . . ?'

'It's what your colleague just told me. She sent you home a little earlier so you could set up the trampoline before your daughter gets home from her father's tomorrow.' As if in slow motion, his gaze wanders to the pile of shredded newspapers with their headline about the murders.

It suddenly hits me.

My aloof manner. My neglected appearance – unwashed, dyed black hair, and clothes full of stains. My pale face, the bags under my eyes from the sleepless nights. This angry outburst. And, most of all, a daughter I never told him about. As if she didn't exist – *anymore*.

US

You're like a song that's planted itself in my head, a stubborn melody. You're expertly arranged, a perfect harmony of beauty and innocence. Every one of your notes goes to the centre of my heart. I purse my lips and hum to myself, softly, very softly, because nobody must hear you. I don't want to share you. Ever again.

I arrived silently, like a ghost, like a shadow in the night. A screwdriver and thirty seconds was all it took the shadow to force open the window on the ground floor. On a standard window you only need to use a screwdriver in two places, as the shadow learned from an information film the police – the police! – had put online to warn people of the tricks burglars use, and to encourage the use of security windows. Idiots. I climbed in, crept my way through the building and found you sleeping like an angel. The moonlight on your face – how beautiful you were, so lovely, lovely.

'Wake up, princess,' I whispered softly, and you opened your eyes. You looked at me as if you'd long been expecting me to come. And you had, hadn't you? I could read it in your face. You didn't have to say anything; I could hear your thoughts, as loudly and clearly as words.

'Take me with you,' you begged. I carefully lifted you in my arms. Your head lay peacefully on my shoulder; you let yourself be carried away just like that. We disappeared via the window I'd come in through and hurried to the car I'd rented. I wrapped you in the warm, cuddly blanket that was lying ready on the back seat. It was winter after all, and I didn't want you to freeze.

'Go back to sleep, my sweetheart,' I said. 'And don't worry. When the sun comes up, we'll be somewhere different, far away where nobody will find us.'

I kept my word, didn't I?

Nobody's found us, nobody has a clue.

You and I, or death. It's as simple as that.

ANN

BERLIN, 25 DECEMBER 2017

At first there's just the hissing in my ears, then comes the stabbing pain in my skull. I try to open my eyes, but in vain. My eyelids are heavy, my lashes stuck together. I'm lying softly, but uncomfortably. I move gingerly, first stretching my legs out, then placing a hand on my head where the pain is raging.

What happened?

Yesterday evening . . .

Jakob was asking about my daughter. I realised there was a dreadful misunderstanding. He thought I was the mother of one of the victims, who'd flipped out when the newspaper reminded her that she'd never again celebrate Christmas with her child. I felt like leaping to my feet and making myself scarce. But I suspected that would only make it worse. And that Jakob was the sort of guy who'd come running after me in a situation like that. So I had no option but to admit that I'd merely invented my daughter.

'I thought a bit of sympathy couldn't hurt, seeing as I had no other qualifications to bring to the job. Everyone at Big Murphy's is working to look after children or family, you know, and it creates a sort of bond between them. They're different from me.'

'What are you like, then?'

I shrugged. 'Complicated, I reckon.'

'Really?'

'Well, what I told you about my German studies is roughly true. I mean, I was studying until recently, at least. I just need a break at the moment, you understand? So I can think about my life and that.'

'A minor crisis, then?'

'That sort of thing.'

'What about the newspaper dispenser?'

'Okay,' I conceded. 'Maybe it's a slightly bigger crisis. Christmas really grates.'

Jakob sighed. 'Come on, I'll take you home.' He got up and offered me his hand. 'Don't worry, this isn't a date, just a lift. I mean, all manner of nutters could be roaming the streets at this time of night.'

My eyes automatically darted to the left and right across the deserted Christmas streets. There was nobody here. Nobody apart from him and me. But I got into his car and, instead of letting him drop me off a few streets further down and disappearing into the entrance of any old building, I unthinkingly directed him to our house.

This is where I grew up and this is where I moved after Zoe booted me out of our flat. My home, although since the police were here, it's no longer what it once was. For three whole days, officers turned the whole place upside down in search of potential evidence, and their approach was anything but gentle. They even broke one of the photos from the mantelpiece; now there's a big crack in the glass, behind which my father and I are grinning in front of the Eiffel Tower. Every time I catch sight of the picture now, it breaks my heart.

Jakob didn't have a clue about any of this when he parked his car in our drive last night. 'Wow, what a lovely house!' he said, but that wasn't true. Without Dad there, it was just empty and dark, like an ugly black hole in the middle of the neighbouring houses, all lit cosily. All of a sudden I didn't fancy getting out anymore.

'Tell me about your idea,' I said.

'What idea?'

'You know, the one you were going to surprise me with at Big Murphy's this afternoon.'

He grinned. His idea was two six-packs waiting behind the passenger seat . . .

I blink. In a blur I can make out our coffee table, on it a dozen beer bottles, some of which have toppled over. The crystal bowl, which still had chocolates in it on the evening Dad was arrested, is overflowing with cigarette butts. The absurd idea of getting up and sorting out the chaos before Dad comes home shoots through my mind. He'd be especially upset by the cigarette butts. Although my asthma isn't that bad, I still have it. I sit up, prop my elbows on my thighs and bury my head in my hands. Construction work is going on inside my head: hammering, drilling, sawing and planing, all at once. I can also hear the clatter of crockery coming from the kitchen, and soon afterwards the hum of the coffee machine.

I can't believe it. Not only that Jakob now knows where I live, but that I actually invited him in, him and his beer. We spent the evening and the night together. And he's still here.

'Good morning!' as if on cue, somewhere amongst the din of the building site in my head. I hear the clinking of glass on glass, Jakob clearing the coffee table. Several times he goes from the sitting room to the kitchen and back again. I stay where I am until the table is clear and there's a cup of coffee on it.

'How are you feeling?'

'Hungover.'

'Surprise, surprise,' he says, laughing. 'I stopped counting when you got to your sixth bottle.'

I reach for the cup, not so much because I need a slug of coffee, but more to distract from my embarrassment. Jakob sits opposite me on the coffee table, so close that our knees are almost touching.

'What's the time?' I ask, after a while spent blowing on my coffee and trying to get my head right. I need to be in Moabit at eleven. I'm allowed to see my father, but only according to the strict rules of custody visits: 1. Discussing the crime is forbidden. 2. A prison guard will be present throughout the visit. 3. Everything will be recorded on video.

'Just gone nine,' Jakob replies, pointing at the clothes I had on yesterday and slept in too. 'So you've got plenty of time for a shower beforehand.'

Beforehand – it takes a moment for the word and its meaning to settle. But then they do and I put my cup back on the table in horror. Coffee sloshes over the rim.

'Don't worry, Ann. Nothing happened last night. You slept here and I slept over there,' he says, nodding to the second sofa opposite mine, separated by the table. But I know at once that this isn't true. Something did happen last night. The worst. And Jakob knows it too. A sense of unease spreads, as if the entire living room were being flooded by a viscous liquid, the level rising and rising continually until it comes up to our chins.

'I'm sorry. I didn't mean to embarrass you. I can imagine how dreadful the situation must be for you. Actually, no . . .' he says, shaking his head. 'Actually, I can't even begin to imagine. It's just . . . if you need a friend, I'll be there for you.' He raises his hands and adds, 'No ulterior motive, I give you my word.' I don't feel reassured.

Yesterday evening.

The images in my head are hazy and shaky, as if they'd been taken by an ancient camera. The sound is like it's canned. Lou Reed is playing on the record player. Bottle tops are popping. I'm being silly and want to dance. I want to be normal again, totally naïve. Let go of everything for a moment. I'm circling like an aeroplane in a blue sky; the sun is shining. Here it's much nicer than outside in the cold, black orbit. Here it's warm and I'm not on my own. I want to break free, rid myself of all my baggage. Slurring my words, I confess to him that the story of the German student with an existential crisis is only half the truth. That the real reason I'm working at Big Murphy's is because I'm terrified of going mad if I surrender to my misery. That I invented a child out of cowardice and pure egotism because I want there to be at least one place – even if it's just a grubby fast-food outlet – where I can be someone else apart from my father's daughter.

Who they say is a murderer.

Who they say has a scheme. Little girls and red ribbons that lead to their bodies.

They make a half-hearted attempt to disguise his face then

print it in their rags and write about deep cuts and huge pools of blood. I don't believe a word of it, not one of their despicable lies, and yet . . . it's so painful, so unbelievably painful. It's a pain that tears at all my limbs, trying to dismember me alive. A pain that puts my heart out of sync and drives my head mad, and I don't want this anymore, I can't go on like this, I really need a break. So, Lou Reed, sing, sing for me, sing louder, just let me dance and forget it all. And you, Jakob – my only friend, even though we haven't known each other that long – I'm so glad you're here, for everyone else has gone. I don't have Zoe or anyone else anymore. Thanks for dancing with me and giving me strength. Because tomorrow's going to be a difficult day. I have to be in Moabit at eleven, where he's being held on remand, but soon, after the trial, he'll be transferred to Tegel where he'll remain, like the proper criminals, the real monsters, permanently, for life, unless a miracle occurs and they realise their mistake. Come on, Jakob, let's dance some more. Give me a moment elsewhere. Just you and me and the beer and Lou Reed . . . and then the film snaps – it all goes black. My memory of the rest is hazy: Jakob carrying me to the sofa, covering me with a blanket and maybe whispering some nice words in my ear: 'Goodnight, Ann. Don't worry, everything will be fine.'

That was yesterday evening.

I sniff – a really pathetic sound. It suits me. 'I didn't mean to tell you everything, you know.'

'I realise that.'

'You have to promise me to keep it to yourself. Enough people know already. The university, the neighbours, friends – or should I say, those who used to be friends.'

'What? How? Your father's name has never been published.'

'But the police questioned everyone who knows us. And these people aren't exactly stupid. Of course our friends recognise his photo in the paper, whether or not he's got that ridiculous black bar over his eyes, which is supposed to preserve the last remnants of his supposed human rights. I'm just waiting for the moment when one of them decides to talk to the press, thereby unleashing the entire mob on me.' The sensation-seeking, the vindictive. The press pack camping outside our house and following my every move. Parents like Jörg E., the father of little Saskia, who will try to track me down and make me pay for the alleged crimes of my father. Merely thinking about it makes me shudder.

His gaze sweeps our living room. The dark green velvet sofa I'm sitting on, the other one he spent the night on, and between them the small mahogany table. The fireplace and all those framed pictures on the mantelpiece: pictures of us, Dad. It's a little journey through time in photo format, with changing shades and styles of hair – you turn greyer and I more colourful; you seem to shrink as my body stretches; fashions change, everything changes, apart from one thing: in each of these pictures we're laughing and very close.

The floor-to-ceiling bookshelves, three metres wide: Schopenhauer, Seneca, Nietzsche and Camus; Munch and Macke prints on walls painted dark red with distemper. So that's how he lives, the alleged killer. This is where he brought up his daughter, who claims she wasn't aware of any of the dreadful crimes he's accused of.

'Maybe you should consider living somewhere else for a while,' Jakob says when his eyes finally come to rest on me. 'I mean,

27

you're right. At some point you'll become the focus of press interest, seeing as you're his daughter.'

'No, that would be like making a statement. If I moved away, everyone would think I'm trying to distance myself from him. And I don't want to do that, not at all. I mean, I know he's innocent.'

Jakob looks pensive. 'There's another option.'

'What?'

'Instead of waiting for the press to come at you, you could make the first move yourself. Seek out a trustworthy journalist and give them an exclusive interview with your version of what happened. You'd be the one pulling the strings and you'd set the parameters.'

'Trustworthy? Yeah, right.'

'Ann.' Jakob sighs. 'You can't hold it against people for wanting to know what happened. Let's face it, nine girls have died and somebody is responsible.'

'But not my father, that's for sure.'

'He's the one who's come to the police's attention, though.'

'Because he was unlucky! Really bloody unlucky, Jakob!'

'Look, with these investigations, I mean . . . it's not like they just pick out some name at random from the phone book when looking for a suspect.' It takes both of us a moment to grasp what he's just said. 'Oh God, I'm sorry. That was silly of me. I wasn't trying to—'

'Imply that my father's guilty? Hurt me? Forget it, your opinion doesn't bother me. You're just some guy from the recycling centre. What do you know?' I've no desire to continue this discussion, and my watch says I don't have to either. 'I should take a shower now, otherwise I'll be late.' I get up from the sofa. 'Thanks for the beer. I'll see you out.'

'It's all right, Ann. You don't need to.' The tone of his voice. And the expression on his face. I can still feel his disappointment long after the door has closed behind him.

Sadness. (Ann, 7 years old)

its not true that when your sad you always have to cry and your nose is runny. Sometimes sadness is much deeper inside and blocks the tears from coming. It feels very cold and dark like sitting in a tower, like the old tower Rapunzel sits in in my book of fairy tales, but without windows. And also theres no door. your really frezing and the cold makes you very tired. You want to get out of the tower becaus you know that the sun is shining outside. But you cant go out becaus youve forgotten where the exit is.

As he sets out the latest findings, my father's lawyer, who was waiting for me in the meeting room, speaks softly, staring at his hands clasped on the table rather than looking at me. Larissa Meller is the latest finding, an unsolved case from fourteen years ago. Soon after my father's arrest, they were already speculating that her death might be linked to the series of killings of young girls, but now the police are certain. Larissa was ten when, one June afternoon in 2003, she set off on her red bike from her home in Hellersdorf with a friend and never came back. A few days later, someone out walking found the bike near the ponds in Hönow; three months later a body was discovered in a wooden hut. Although the hut was only a few hundred metres from where the bike had been found, it was so overgrown that the police had missed it in the course of their large-scale search of the area. They immediately suspected the body might be Larissa's, but it took weeks for a definitive identification. That June had been hot but very rainy too, and so the body was in a terrible state. They also found size 42 footprints, which were made in the rain then dried and preserved by the subsequent heat. At the time, the investigation stalled through a lack of further evidence, so of course it's handy my father also happens to have size 42 shoes. Now Larissa is said to have been the first victim in the series of killings. Only in her case there were no ribbons leading to her body.

'The police are speculating whether Larissa was the reason why the killer used red ribbons later. Maybe he felt bad that the mother had to see her child in such a state.' He's still avoiding looking me in the eye; instead he's kneading his hands so firmly that the skin is turning red in places. 'At any rate, neither her nor any of the other victims show signs of sexual abuse, which means the killer must have been driven by a different motive.'

Having listened silently in disbelief to the term 'the killer' being used as a synonym for 'your father', all I can think of saying is, 'You're his friend, Ludwig.' It sounds like a question.

Ludwig Abramczyk used to be one of Berlin's top lawyers. He's sixty-two and has actually been in retirement for three months, which he's spending at his hunter's cabin in the Polish forest. He's returned in his smart, tailor-made suit specifically for my father's sake, and thus slipped back into his old role. To *help*.

'That's precisely why I'm here, Anni. But he's being very difficult. If you ask him what he was doing at any of the times in question, he either says nothing at all or just comes out with his philosophical stuff.'

'Come off it. As if you could remember what you were doing some afternoon in June fourteen years ago.'

'But he's not even getting worked up about the charges, let alone making an effort to rebut them! He's confronted with nine murders – ten, now, assuming that Larissa's death is part of the series – and all he does is sit there in silence.'

'Because he's distraught! Clearly not even his best friend seems to think he's innocent.' I can see my accusation explode in Ludwig's face. His friend Walter, with whom he spent endless summer nights on the terrace, or by our fire in winter, brandishing their whisky glasses, cracking jokes and having discussions. There was always a topic. Ludwig, who in his work as a defence lawyer had come face to face with so much human wickedness, and my father, who as a philosopher and anthropologist was fascinated by this wickedness, its motives and mechanisms. Barbecues in our garden. My father, often in his own world mentally, letting the sausages burn, and Ludwig, grabbing the tongs to take over just in time. And me, Walter's daughter, little Anni who he's known ever since she took her first wobbly steps on her chubby baby legs. Who he watched grow up, raised by the most loving father you could imagine. His goddaughter, now sitting opposite and who's utterly disappointed in him.

'Please don't be unfair,' he says, after I've said my angry piece. 'You know full well that I'll do everything in my power. But the longer he keeps quiet, the trickier it gets.'

I look up at the ceiling and see cracks in the concrete. Like the cracks in the photograph on our mantelpiece after the police search. Cracks that have marred our entire life. *Because he was unlucky*, is what I said to Jakob this morning. Unlucky that he happened to bump into an acquaintance in the Königswald just before the last body was found. Soon afterwards this very same acquaintance came across one of the notorious red ribbons, which the media had talked about so often in relation to a number of murders, and then the hut where the lifeless body of a seven-year-old girl lay in a huge pool of blood. Of course the man immediately called the police and, when asked if he'd met anyone in the woods, gave my father's name. This in itself probably wouldn't have been enough to arrest him. But there was also that fricking lecture he'd given a few years ago at the university, and especially the newspaper articles he'd used as a basis for discussion. Then the sighting of a dark Audi A6 near an earlier crime scene, and a black Audi A6 parked in our garage which is registered to my father . . .

'Why?' I ask Ludwig. 'Why should he have committed those murders? I mean, he has a daughter himself, and you know I'm his whole life. He always loved and protected me, and would have been beside himself if anything bad had happened to me. As he would be now. So why should he, of all people, inflict such pain on other parents?'

'I don't know.'

'But isn't that precisely the point? Isn't it always about a motive? Evidence can be misinterpreted. It's even possible to cobble evidence together maliciously if you're out to harm someone, isn't it?'

Ludwig nods, slightly reluctantly, it seems. Whereas I shake my head. 'It wasn't him. There was nothing in the world that could have made him do something like that.'

'Oh, Anni.' Over the table, Ludwig reaches for my left hand and turns it so the palm is facing upwards. Then he pushes my watch strap so he can stroke the little scar on my wrist with his thumb. I was very little when I hurt myself there. 'All of us get the odd scratch and scrape over the course of our life. And not every one is visible on the outside.'

I yank back my hand, speechless.

'You can never see into someone's mind, my child. Not even the mind of those you think you know best. All I want is for you to be prepared for everything. The clues—'

'The clues! Are you listening to anything I'm saying?'

'Anni—'

'You're all so fixated on him that you've become blind to another possibility.'

'What's that?'

'You know, another killer! Are the police investigating every angle? No. It was Dad and that's that, case solved. And if I say that this can't be right, I'm treated like an idiot who can't handle the truth.' I begin chewing my bottom lip. 'Maybe I ought to give an interview after all.'

'What? For God's sake, get that out of your head at once.'

'But if the public understood what kind of a person he really is, it might put pressure on the police to be more thorough in their investigation and so find the real guilty party.'

'No, no, no!' Ludwig says, emphasising each word. Then comes a long speech. The press are an unruly mob. Very few journalists these days feel like they're on a mission, still keen to uncover the truth and look for facts. On the contrary, most just go for the entertainment value; they're out for blood and drama, circulation figures and ratings. This – and only this – is what drives them. If I were to speak to them, Ludwig warns, I might only make things worse. 'You'd be the most help to your father trying to keep your own life under control. That way you'd take a lot of worry off his mind.'

I roll my eyes and utter a drawn-out, 'Blah, blaaaah . . .' but this time Ludwig is unfazed.

'And you would help me by appealing to his conscience and getting him to cooperate.'

'I thought it was forbidden to discuss the charge.'

'And you shouldn't do it directly. You should only say what's necessary to make him aware how serious the situation is. The department of public prosecution knows the reason for your visit, so don't worry, okay?'

I nod, even though I don't have a good feeling about this. Something doesn't seem right.

US

I know you're used to better. The big beautiful house. The lovingly decorated children's room in the attic extension. The big garden with the pool ... You're a real water baby, aren't you, princess? In summer I watched you wearing your plump armbands, splashing around in the pool and squealing with pleasure. Your lips had turned slightly blue; perhaps one ought to have been stricter, made you get out of the water and wrapped you in a thick towel. But seeing your enthusiasm, that innocent, genuine liveliness which only a child can display, made me forget my misgivings and plunged me into the moment. No, I didn't have to worry about you; you weren't stupid. You would get yourself out of the pool when you began to freeze and no longer felt comfortable. I secretly hoped that wouldn't happen for ages; I wanted this moment to last for ever. The sun laying itself over all the colours like a filter, making them rich and vibrant. Your unrestrained joy. Drops of water flying through the air as if in slow motion. I felt as if I were watching a film; I was desperate to press 'pause' and for ever freeze the image of you looking so happy.

Now we're here and I know you don't particularly like it. You're the princess from the big beautiful castle; you don't belong in this dump. But sometimes you simply don't have the choice, and surely the most important thing is that we're together. Just as you are everything for me, I am everything for you. Only through me can you stay alive; if I abandon you, you're dead.

ANN

BERLIN, 25 DECEMBER 2017

Meeting my father – in this concrete room with the neon ceiling light that flickers nervously and the sparse furnishings, a table and two chairs; in this bloody cold, bleak place where he doesn't belong – feels like being crushed under foot. Mentally it wrestles me to the ground, this feeling; it assaults me with blows to the stomach so overpowering I can barely stop myself from retching. Opposite me, slouched, is a man who used to sit upright, his back always straight. He was tall and dignified, his short grey hair neatly parted and combed.

'I'm so pleased to see you, my Beetle,' a stranger says with sunken, narrow shoulders, hollow cheeks, messy hair and vacant eyes. It doesn't sound as if he's pleased; there's no trace of emotion in his voice, monotone like a machine's.

I say, 'Dad,' and start to howl because I'm so horrified at what's left of him. Only then does his dead face stir.

'How are you?' he asks. 'Tell me. No need to be brave.'

I shake my head because this isn't about me. *I'm* not the one who's been framed and locked up. *I'm* not the one being accused of ten counts of murder. 'Ludwig told me you're refusing to cooperate. You're not saying where you were when the crimes were committed, nor are you making any effort to explain the evidence. But you've got to, Dad. Listen to me!'

I look around uncertainly. This isn't the first time I've seen my father since his arrest. But we've never met without a prison warder in the room. Today, though, I'd be grateful for a reprimand or at least a clearing of the throat when I step on to forbidden territory. I'm not allowed to talk about the charge, but I've got to try to make my father break his silence. I don't want to do anything wrong, especially as all conversations between prisoners and visitors are recorded on video. 'I know it all seems so stupid. You must think it's ridiculous to have to clear yourself of something so absurd. But please believe me, your pride isn't going to get you anywhere here. On the contrary, you *must* tell the police you're not the killer, you just *have* to.'

'Oh . . .' He gives a feeble shrug. 'They're not interested in protestations of innocence here. They've made up their minds, they've got a clear picture. Like the prisoners in Plato's cave.' Again something darts across his face, maybe the memory of how only six weeks ago he was still giving lectures, trying to make the great philosophers accessible to his students. He taught at the university for thirty years, was invited to all the big conferences, and received countless international accolades. He's a luminary in the field of philosophical anthropology, a branch of the philosophy of human nature. Professor Dr Walter Lesniak, the former renowned anthropologist, who since his arrest has seemingly been paralysed with shock, and has forgotten one of the basic human skills: speech. The ability to explain yourself. To protest.

'Dad, for God's sake,' I say, grabbing his hands, which feel limp and cold. He lets me take them without squeezing mine back. 'Don't you understand what your silence is doing? They see it as an admission of guilt! You've got to help Ludwig refute the evidence! He can't do anything for you if you won't cooperate. For Christ's sake, make a bit of an effort, however hard it is for you.'

He stares at me through narrow slits, as if on drugs, an understandable feeling. I've often felt like I was on a bad trip recently. But his eyes are unnerving. They're both dreamy and somehow piercing.

'What about you, Ann? Are you making an effort? Or are you still frying burgers instead of going to university?'

'I've already told you, Dad. We've got other problems to deal with right now.'

Ten other problems, to be exact. Ten girls that the killer kidnapped and took to a variety of secluded spots in the Greater Berlin area. He brought them to woods, industrial sites or abandoned construction sites, where there was always a hut, a shed, a cellar or some deserted room that was ideal for his purposes. Ludwig said the girls died of blood loss from deep cuts, according to forensics. I don't know any more than that; Ludwig's keeping the details from me and there's no more to be got from the papers. They say only that the police are withholding certain details for reasons related to the investigation.

'Dad, there's a killer running around freely out there. All he has to do is change his methods or hunting ground and he'll be able to continue committing his crimes unchecked, because you're in prison for him, and for the rest of your life too. If you don't cooperate, the truth won't come to light and—'

'*Truth*. Most of us experience the world only in the way that their own perspective allows. "Man is . . ."'

'". . . the measure of all things." Protagoras, I know.' Now I understand Ludwig's despair. Time for another attempt; I'll try him with a mind game. More girls are going to die because he's obstructing the investigation with his silence. 'They're wasting their time on you when they ought to be hunting the real killer. Do you realise what that means?' My father doesn't react; his drugged expression drives me crazy. 'It means you'll be complicit if another girl dies.'

Nothing.

'Please, Dad! I know it's hard. But if you don't want to talk to the police or Ludwig, then at least talk to me. I'm still your Beetle, aren't I?'

He gives no more than a faint smile. A smile that's unfamiliar, as if he'd copied it from someone else because he's forgetting how to do it himself. He must be dreadfully exhausted by all this. Where are you, Dad? I want to ask the stranger. And: don't you remember us?

Walter and his Beetle.

That's not just the plaits and goodnight stories, tea and chocolate to help with tummy aches, or an alibi when a moped has been scratched. It's Walter explaining to his Beetle why she hasn't got a mummy anymore like the other children do. Treating Beetle's wounds and not allowing her to lie torpidly in her cardboard coffin. Teaching her how to be happy again. Walter, who has always been there for his Beetle, and Beetle, who now realises it's time to return the favour. Because they're a team, an exclusive club – lined up against the rest of the world if necessary.

'I'm sorry,' a prison officer interrupts us as he enters the room. 'Your time is up.'

My father has to go back behind bars. Hugging him as tightly as I can, I whisper, 'I love you, Dad.'

'In that case, stop frying burgers, Ann,' he replies with that crooked, unfamiliar smile. 'You've got the rest of your life ahead of you. Don't throw it away on my account.'

I nod and I mean it. Don't worry, Dad. I've got another job now. I'm going to get you out of prison.

Ditermination. (Ann, 7 years old)

Ditermination means you really want something bad. You feel it tingling in your body like if you had ants under your skin. And your hart beats fast and exsitedly. But its not bad and it doesnt hurt. Your hart is just exsited about what will happen if your ditermination works. Becaus then you get what you want and your happy.

I don't know what to do with myself, only that I need to move, bring my body into line with the activity of my brain. So I stomp around in circles in the prison car park, waiting for Ludwig who's having another conversation inside. He's offered to drive me home after meeting Dad, which I'll happily take him up on as it'll save me having to take the underground. I never used to notice how many people use the time on public transport to read the newspaper. But I do now, as my father's on every other front page.

The fact that the suspect in custody is a university professor has leaked out and the press are using it to make sensational comparisons. They've already made reference to the Russian Oleg Sokolov, a highly respected historian who specialised in the Napoleonic era. Sokolov taught at St Petersburg University before he chopped up his young lover and disposed of the pieces in the Moyka. Or Hannibal Lecter, who isn't even a real person, quite apart from the fact that he's a psychiatrist rather than a professor. And he ate his victims, for heaven's sake. Nonetheless, in every case, it's the same killer profile, one which merely makes the crimes even more sinister. It's a man of intellect and prestige. Not a degenerate killer who acts on impulse, who doesn't know what he's doing, but a highly intelligent monster with a sophisticated plan. 'Professor Death!' one newspaper proclaimed only a few days ago, its article speculating about barbaric experiments and not shying away from making the most vulgar parallels to concentration camp doctors.

All this is absurd, of course, but ubiquitous too. The craving for sensationalism is eating its way through the city like acid. It's corroding people's eyes and reason, and with every day, the calls get louder to publicly unmask the man disguised in the photo and finally bring him to court.

'I hope you didn't have to wait long!' Ludwig hurries over to me. His left hand is swinging his briefcase; his right is already feeling for the car keys in his coat pocket.

'Only a few minutes.'

'That's good,' he says, opening the car and putting the briefcase on the back seat. 'Get in.'

'There's something I wanted to ask you,' I say as we drive out of the car park.

'Go ahead.'

'Are you doing any deals with the department of public prosecution in the background?'

'What? What makes you think that?'

'Well, you said the DPP already knows that I've discussed the case with Dad. That sounds to me a bit like you're in cahoots.'

'They would have found out from the video footage anyway, so, yes, I thought it better to straighten things out in advance. And before you ask, it was also agreed that you should be able to meet your father without supervision today.'

'Why?'

'Call it my Christmas present to you both. Before I retired, the public prosecutor and I used to play tennis together on Tuesdays. This brings the odd benefit from time to time.' Ludwig shoots me a brief glance. 'But, to return to your question, no, I'm not making any deals.' He indicates to turn on to the Strasse des 17. Juni. The metronomic clicking synchronises my heartbeat.

'Ludwig?'

'Yes?'

'I'd like to see the police files. Or at least your documents.'

'What?'

'I feel I could help if I had a more detailed understanding of things, especially because Dad ...' I break off when his face flashes before me. Those empty eyes and the strangely unfamiliar smile, which he forced himself to make for my sake. 'I think he's given up.'

Ludwig doesn't respond.

'I have to know what happened to the girls,' I add. 'And I mean everything! I need the details.'

'Believe me, my child. There are good reasons why the police are keeping certain pieces of information under wraps. People are going crazy enough as it is. Ribbons are being auctioned on the internet, supposedly from the original crime scenes. And did you read about the desecration of that grave?'

I shake my head.

'One of the girl's graves, not long ago,' he says. 'Those responsible stole all the decorations – candles, flowers, everything that was there – leaving it as empty as an abandoned field.' He puts his indicator on again, this time to enter a petrol station.

'Who'd do a thing like that?'

'Souvenir hunters, Anni! The same sickos who auction the ribbons. It's hard for the police to go after these people too. They can barely keep up.' He stops behind a red jeep. *Jakob*, I immediately think, but it's a young woman who's just come back from paying and is getting into her car. Ludwig waits for her to drive off, takes her place by the pump and switches off the engine. 'Do you want anything? You used to love those caramel bars.'

'No, thanks.'

'All right. I promise to be as quick as I can.'

In the wing mirror I watch him put the nozzle into the tank and look around innocently. I wait tensely until I hear a plop. Ludwig returns the nozzle to its holder, closes the fuel cap and pats the sides of his coat in search of his wallet. Then he goes into the kiosk, and I'm betting he'll buy me a caramel bar anyway. He wants to cheer me up like you do a child – with sweets and some affection. He ought to know that I was never that easy – a bit of sugar and a pat on the head: risible! I was a difficult child, with a few difficult phases. The first was after my mother's death, the second in puberty. At fourteen I was really bad, always getting caught when I was up to no good. Smoking weed with the older boys behind the dining hall instead of going to lessons. Slitting open the mats in the gym. Locking my friend Eva in the girls' loos because I wanted to stop her getting to the drama club auditions on time . . .

'Right, then,' Ludwig says a few minutes later. He flops on to the driver's seat and closes the door. 'You can eat it later if you're not hungry now,' he says, smiling, as he hands me the caramel bar. I smile too – I knew it – and tear open the colourful wrapping at once. I'm really not hungry, but I don't want to open the rucksack on my lap and put it in there.

Yes, at fourteen I was permanently getting into trouble. But sometimes not. My maths teacher, for example, never worked out who stole the answers to a forthcoming test from his briefcase.

Unlike yesterday, when the city looked extinct, there's an extraordinary amount of traffic today. I wonder where everyone's going. My guess is that they're paying festive visits to relatives, or taking minibreaks, which is reassuring, but at the same time feels horribly unfair. There are some little lives the world is indifferent to; it keeps turning as if nothing were happening.

Only when we're close to home do the roads get quiet again, dead in that typical Christmas way, and I realise that this upsets me just as much. Ludwig stops outside our house. The usual phrases. If I need anything. If there's anything he can do. I say no to everything; I'll manage. Big Murphy's is closed today and tomorrow, and I just fancy having a rest, a sleep, watching films and eating pasta with ketchup and cheese.

'But don't forget,' he says, putting his thumb to his right ear and little finger to his mouth. 'You just have to call, anytime.'

I thank him and get out of his car as fast as I can.

Walking to the house, I realise how dirty the ground-floor windows are; the rain and snow of the past few weeks have left crazy artworks of speckles and smears. We used to have a cleaning lady but she doesn't come anymore. Soon after Dad was arrested, she called to say she'd have to stop until further notice for health reasons – her back, her hips, etc. I guessed at once that the police must have gone round to question her. But I didn't probe; I didn't want to know. Instead I thanked her for all the years she'd worked for us, for having tidied up my squeaky baby toys and picture books, and for always bringing me a cake for my birthday because Mum's illness meant she couldn't bake me one. I asked her to put the house key in the letter box whenever it suited her; she did it less than two hours later.

'Happy Christmas, Ann!' I hear at my back, just as I'm about to unlock the front door. I don't bother turning around; I know the voice is that of our neighbour, Elke Harbert. Elke also uses the same cleaning lady, the only difference being that she's still working for the Harberts despite her supposed aches and pains. Sometimes, when I'm making my morning coffee, I can see her through our kitchen window, ducking as she scurries past our hedge to get next door.

'You too, Elke,' I rattle off flatly. I know full well what's about to come. Since the arrest, Elke and her husband, Caspian, have been turning up at least once a week, trying to get me to come to dinner. But I don't have to accept their invitation to know how the evening would unfold: uncertain looks and awkward silences over an aperitif, then by the time we're on to the main course and the third glass of wine, the first questions would be fired at me. *Is it really true . . . ?* Of course not! Have you gone mad? *But the* papers . . . Lies. *And on the telly they said* . . . No, thanks. The mere thought of it is quite enough for me.

'I was going to ask whether you'd like to come and have goose with us tonight.'

'Thanks, that's very sweet of you, but I've got something else on.'

A brief pause, then: 'You're making a big mistake, Ann.'

Now I do turn round. The way she stands there, in the middle of our snowy drive, in her light jeans and pink blouse, which immediately repulses me because it's ironed so perfectly. Not even the faintest crease has the courage to rebel against the immaculate appearance. 'I'm sorry. What mistake?'

'Shutting yourself away like this. I'm really worried about you.' She kneads her hands; it's cold today and she isn't wearing a coat over her thin blouse. I wonder if she thinks I'm embarrassed about my father. That this is the reason why I'm avoiding going over there. The anger is back, welling up inside me; I feel like grabbing Elke by her starched, pink collar and yelling, 'How dare you, you stupid cow! If I'm ashamed of anyone at all, it's people like you who've been our neighbours for over twenty years and bloody well ought to know better!'

But I keep my cool. After all, Elke isn't a newspaper dispenser, she's a human being who could be seriously hurt. I assure her that everything's okay and thank her politely – for whatever. Then I unlock the front door.

'Eva's coming too.'

I flinch, as if she'd just given me a slap. Eva, probably the only – albeit major – crease in the otherwise impeccably ironed life of Elke and Caspian Harbert. Their daughter, who took flight

47

the moment she'd finished school. Away from the strict mother and her lapdog of a husband, away from a house full of scatter cushions and the stench of Dettol, away from the pressure to achieve and the feeling of never being good enough. I can't recall her ever visiting her parents since, not at Christmas nor on any other occasion. Dream on, Elke.

'All I'm saying is . . . the two of you used to be inseparable.'

We were. Until Eva abandoned me as well as her parents, absconding with Nico, the boy whose motorbike I'd scratched the previous year out of jealousy. There were rumours that she might be pregnant by him, and even more rumours when Nico returned to Berlin alone only a few months later.

'Send her my regards,' I mutter, before dashing into the house and locking the door behind me. I close my eyes and take calm breaths until I start hearing noises coming from upstairs. A chair scraping across the old floorboards, then footsteps creaking. Finally I hear the door to the study and my father's voice. 'Beetle? Is that you?'

Who else could it be, Dad?

'How was uni?' The footsteps come closer.

Boring as usual. German isn't exactly the thing for adrenaline junkies.

'I could have told you that straight off.' The stairs creak beneath his lively tread. Now he's beside me, saying, 'Shall we have a coffee first? You look like you could do with one.'

I smile and open my eyes. But there's nobody there – of course not; it's just my imagination. A few moments that are lovely to begin with, then painful as they fade. I slip the rucksack off my back, take off his jacket and then the boots, which have left a brownish puddle on the light-coloured floorboards. It doesn't bother me. I want to go into the kitchen to make some coffee and also to fetch the cup from the living room that's been on the table since this morning – save resources, the dishwasher is full. Although I go straight past the windows that lead on to the terrace, I don't see it at first, not until I'm grabbing the cup and look up by chance.

Just my imagination again, is my first thought.

I blink a few times, to be certain. But no matter how often I open and close my eyes, it's still there: the red ribbon tied around a branch of the dead oleander on our terrace.

RECORDING 01
Berlin, 7 May 2021

– To be honest, I'd imagined you to be quite different.
– Really? How?
– Well, I mean, I've seen photos of you, of course, but . . . I thought you'd have some evil aura about you. I thought it would be tangible somehow. Do you understand?
– Oh dear!
– Yes, silly, isn't it?
– Oh well, I suspect you're rather nervous. You have been after me for years, I suppose. So am I right in my assumption that this is going to be the grand finale? You and me and all our cards on the table, hmm? The end of the hunt, the hunter trapped.
– Is that how you see yourself? As a hunter?
– No, as a matter of fact, but I get the impression you like a bit of drama. People like me are supposed to have difficulty

reading others. But do you know what? I always had a good inkling of my opponent's needs. You learn what people want, their longings, fears, desires – basically all of these are mere templates you can interpret according to a fixed pattern.

– So you're more of an actor, then?

– Yes, and I think a rather good one at that. By the way, does your mother know what you're doing here? Isn't she worried about you?

– My mother? I don't know what my mother's got—

– Calm down. You want me to share my secrets with you. It's not something one does with any old person, is it? I'd like to get to know you first.

– I . . . All right, I don't have a mother anymore. She's dead. But if she were still alive, I'd tell her she needn't worry.

– *(grins)* But I'm a killer. And I've got nothing to lose.

– Are you threatening me?

– Is that how you feel? Threatened by me? Intimidated? Inferior?

– *(audibly swallows)* I didn't come here to play games, but because I wanted to know who you are.

– 'Wanted'? Are you saying you do know now? Well, that was quick, I take my hat off to you.

– No, I . . . I mean . . .

– Good God, why don't you relax, and let's get this done with a modicum of dignity. It is the grand finale, after all! It would be a real shame if, after all the effort you've put in, you failed now, wouldn't it?

ANN

BERLIN, 25 DECEMBER 2017

It's like a scavenger hunt, only there's no treasure at the end, only the discovery of a dead child. Red ribbons pointing the way to the bodies, and now a red ribbon tied to a branch of the old oleander on our terrace. For a few seconds I just stand there, rigid, staring and unable to comprehend. It's like a tsunami: all my thoughts and feelings retreat into the distance, where they gather and tower up to come surging forth and crush me.

Then I suddenly realise: the killer.

He's free and he was here.

He's left me a sign.

Slipping from my hand, the coffee cup crashes to the floor and breaks. I stagger, check my balance on the armrest of the sofa, then teeter backwards until I feel the wall behind me – a cold, hard wall that offers support, its firmness reassuring.

Nonsense, it's all nonsense. Now I've thought it through, of course the ribbon murderer wasn't here, that's absurd. What would he want from me? Why would he provoke me, given that he must be thrilled my father's in prison in his place? No, what must have happened is what I've been fearing for a while: my father's identity has been revealed. He's no longer a disguised face in a photo by the name of 'university professor (55)'; now he's Dr Walter Lesniak, a verifiable individual with an address and a daughter who's being tracked down. Maybe by Jörg E., the man who's always doing the media rounds, father of little Saskia, victim number seven. It was him, or another father, mother, grandfather. Someone who's lost a child to the serial killer. Who's now found me and wants to torture me just as their own child was tortured. Because I'm someone's daughter too. *His* daughter. An eye for an eye.

I tense my jaw; fear and helplessness give way to blazing anger. Marching to the terrace door, I yank it open and inspect the red ribbon. It looks new, barely touched by the weather, as if it's only just been tied there. My eyes flit around. Footprints, definitely a man's. I follow them through the snow; they lead from the rear garden door to our terrace and back. Suddenly I find myself standing on the little path that runs behind our garden. The footprints are mingled with countless others; lots of neighbours go walking here or take their dogs out. It's impossible to work out where the intruder came from or in which direction he fled. I turn around a few times, wheezing alarmingly. I ran out without any shoes on and now my socks are soaking up the wet. The cold, the distress. If I don't calm down, this is going to end in another attack. Breathe, no matter how. Cautious movements, back inside the house. I don't know if I've shut the terrace door properly; I can only think about my asthma spray. A reverberation of the cold pulses in my feet, niggling me. But it's no good, I lurch into the hallway, over to my rucksack. Only in emergencies, the doctor said. Shake the cartridge, put the mouthpiece between your lips, lean your head back, breathe in slowly and deeply while pressing the spray button, then hold your breath for five seconds. 5 – 4 – 3 – 2 – 1. I breathe a sigh of relief. I'm all right again; I don't suffer as badly as others. My asthma is more like a rubber band that can be stretched and stretched and stretched until it finally breaks. I drop to the floor; I want to sit down, just for a moment, until the rubber-band sensation has eased a little. Then I put the spray back into the rucksack and take my mobile out. My first attempt goes straight to voicemail; the second time Ludwig answers immediately. From the background noises I can tell that he's still in the car. I try to sound as composed as possible: the red ribbon on the oleander, the footsteps in the garden, someone was here.

'What? What are you talking about, Anni?'

Once again. The red ribbon, the footsteps.

'They've found me, Ludwig!'

'Who's found you?'

'Some relatives, I imagine! Don't you get it? We need to inform the police!'

'I fear there's very little they'll be able to do. Nothing has been damaged, nor has anyone physically assaulted you. Trespassing on private property – no more than that.'

'Are you being serious?'

'Listen. I understand you're shaken up, but the situation is like this: someone was in your garden and tied a red ribbon to the oleander—'

'The message is: we have found you.'

'Anni—'

'Are you saying I just ought to accept it?'

'Once again: someone was in your garden and tied a red ribbon to the oleander. Nothing else actually happened. At most, the police will tell you to be circumspect and get in touch if anything worse happens, if the person comes back or if you feel threatened . . .'

I hang up in consternation. But Ludwig's probably right; calling the police won't help. They'll only think I'm being hysterical and deal with me exactly as he said: monitor the situation, get in touch if something *really* happens. A *really* that's based on more than just a state of mind, the oppressive feeling that, in crossing the boundary to their property, someone has also violated a personal boundary. My home, the place where – at moments in my imagination, at least – everything can be as it used to be. My old home, it's all I've got left. I slip my mobile into my trouser pocket and take the grey cardboard file from the rucksack.

I've got to be quick. It won't be long before Ludwig realises that something important is missing. He'll run back over the day and soon remember that he left me alone in the car at the petrol station, alone with his briefcase on the back seat. He'll also recall that only a few minutes earlier I'd asked if I could see these papers.

This isn't the only reason why there's no time to lose. Somebody was here, if only in our garden this time. All the same, this person is one of those I have to convince of my father's innocence as soon as possible, before they go further next time and I find myself in serious danger. Who knows what desperate people are capable of when they believe they're in the right and become impatient? Who knows if the red ribbon isn't just a means to pressurise the man that they believe to be the killer to finally break his silence, having refused to make a confession till now?

*

Dad's study. Where he prepared his lectures and wrote his papers. Where he was inspired and we weren't allowed to disturb him. A room the real world had no access to, a place that seemed to be from another dimension. Maybe I'm secretly hoping that something of the particular intellect enveloping this room will rub off on me as I climb the stairs with Ludwig's file and another cup of coffee. The room is at the end of the landing, beyond the bedrooms and the two bathrooms. Its windows look out on to the garden, offering the perfect view of me as a child, whooping and roaring as I leaped around on the trampoline down there. The perfect view if the intruder were to return.

I always find it painful to think of the police storming into this room during the course of their search. At first they only wanted to because the door was locked. I tried to explain the rationale behind it, tell them that this room was especially private, as intimate as an organ or a thought you don't share, which belongs to you alone. They didn't understand this, of course, and threatened to break down the door if I didn't get them the key immediately. In the desk they then found the fricking newspaper articles; I bet the public prosecutor jumped for joy. An entire folder of reports on the ribbon murderer – of course this must be some sort of trophy collection. But that wasn't the case. I know the file and also know that my father kept the articles for a lecture on 'The Dark Side of Human Beings'. These cases were clearly a perfect way to underpin the often very theoretical discussion with true-life events. His students – most, at least – loved their professor for not torturing them with pure theory. At home we discussed the cases a few times too, most recently on the evening he was arrested.

On the kitchen counter was that day's edition of a newspaper in which Jörg E., Saskia's father, commented on the death of another girl.

'Do you think the children realised that they'd die?' Dad asked me. 'Do you reckon their immature brains could comprehend this fact?'

'No,' I replied. 'I think they hoped for a miracle right up to the last moment. Everyone would do that, wouldn't they? No matter what age. Just think of Mum. Until the very end, she said, *I'll be all right.*' I shook my head. 'But it's good to have hope, if only to counter the fear. Something you can cling to before you enter oblivion.'

'Oblivion? I thought you believed in God?'

'I do. Well, God or something else – a higher power, yes. I just don't believe we get a second round in the hereafter, so to speak. I believe in this one life, and when the lights go out here . . . well, they stay out.'

'Or maybe they don't. Euripides said, "Who knoweth if to die be but to live, and that called life by mortals be but death?"'

'To establish this beyond doubt I'd have to sacrifice my own life, so no, thanks. I'm far more interested in finding out where the hell our pizzas are. I'm about to die of hunger here . . .'

The pizzas didn't come, but the blue lights did. The police. They took my father away and searched the house, including this room. I don't want to think how their mere presence defiled it. I want to think that there's enough of my father here still to hold and guide me. Just as I sometimes can feel his residual warmth in his jacket when I put it on.

Having fished the key from the large vase that stands on a

console table at the end of the landing, I unlock the door almost devoutly. And it is really true. Apart from the fact that documents and books torn from the shelves still lie scattered on the floor, and the drawers are wide open – I haven't yet felt able to tidy the chaos left behind by the search team – I only have to take a deep breath. The smell of old paper. The wood of the desk. The leather of the sofa. Something comfortingly stale, and dust dancing in the sunlight – a huge amount of dust, because even our cleaning lady, who kept the rest of the house clinically clean, didn't have access to this room. I breathe and sense his presence. Hang in there, Dad, just a while longer. I'll find something to exonerate you. I'll get you out of prison, I promise.

Confidens. (Ann, 7 years old)

Confidens is a bit like hope but that you know for sure that something is going to be good and your looking forward to it but with hope theres also the possibility that something wont be good. Like when I hoped MUMMY wood get better but she died. This means that confidens is better than hope and if you have the choice you shud always chose confidens.

I begin by tidying up – superficially, at least. The books go back on the shelves and all the paper into the drawers of the desk. I find a folder with short essays in which Beetle recorded her feelings in spidery handwriting, and a tatty wooden box. Inside is my old school ID card, a rosary with broken links, the torn ticket to my leavers' ball, a sewing kit from a hotel on the Baltic, a few mussel shells and a flat, triangular stone that Dad gave me many years ago to remind me I'm strong enough to

overcome the worst. My old talisman. I place it in my palm, feel
its cool, smooth surface and trace its pattern. I'm confused as to
how it could have ended up in this mishmash of meaningless
things. Was I not going to keep it on me at all times? I ought to,
especially in this situation, which has completely redefined 'the
worst' as a term. I finish by sorting out the pen holder, and put
the chair back in its place, not too far under the desk, but so that
Dad could immediately sit on it if he came into this room right
now to work. I've done it; I've created some order, both around
me and inside me. My head is clear, my mind alert, my heart
beating a nervy staccato. I sit cross-legged on the floor and spread
out the contents of Ludwig's folder in front of me. First there are
the copies of all the documents – witness statements, résumés,
forensic reports, summaries of the presumed circumstances of
the crimes and the current state of investigation, including all
the evidence – merely words, technical-speak lacking all feeling.
But then come the photographs, beginning with those that the
parents must have given to the police when their daughters were
still classified as missing. Photos of animated girls in a variety of
everyday situations, all of them with one thing in common: in
every image they're laughing. I start hearing it, only very softly
at first, as if from a memory. But it doesn't stop at that. I can see
them as if they were real: a little blonde girl, dancing through
the study in her tutu. Another, with brown plaits, holding up her
huge cone of sweets as she gives me a proud smile, revealing the
gaps between her teeth. A third, suddenly sitting on the leather
sofa, with a puppy on her lap. That's Saskia. I recognise her at
once because her picture is always printed alongside that of her
ubiquitous father. The room fills, the laughter growing louder

and more real. I realise how badly mistaken I've been. These aren't just ten 'problems' as I still thought this morning, but real people with names, families, interests and a future that's been stolen from them. No first kisses, no first heartbreak, no finishing school, no becoming adults. Just a big black nothingness. Tears flow. Such injustice. Who's responsible? Who played God and what gave him the right? Why should someone like that be allowed to live, to experience what he's maliciously stolen from others?

I thought you believed in God?

Not in moments like this, I'm sorry.

Leaping to my feet, I run into the bathroom to throw up, retching so loudly that the noises echo off the tiles. Noises that capture and drown out everything. Even the footsteps on the stairs. The footsteps along the landing. The footsteps that stop outside the open bathroom door. I simply didn't hear them, and only realise when a shadow looms in the corner of my eye.

US

Now don't look so sad, my sweetheart! We talked about that yesterday, didn't we? I realise you'd rather have had a proper Christmas, with a tree and lots of presents like you're used to. Last year, for example, you got a pink bicycle with a Princess Lillifee pennant that stuck up from the pannier rack like an antenna. You were so thrilled, riding up and down the snowy drive. I almost cried watching your unsteady legs on that bike, and every time you pedalled, the pennant would move above you like a dodgy windscreen wiper. But we have to be grateful for what we've got, and we are, aren't we? Yes, we are. We've got us – and Cosmo. Look, Cosmo's here! Your favourite teddy with a button in place of his left eye. Listen to what he has to say: 'Hello, little princess, it's me, your Cosmo. I don't think our new home's bad at all.' And Milly, I even thought of your little Milly. Can you hear her purring? She feels happy here too ... No? You don't want to smile? Not even a teensy-weensy little bit? But you've got such an enchanting smile ... Oh, I know! I know what'll cheer you up! Let's give you a bath, my angel. We'll give you a bath and make you pretty! Brush your sweet locks and put on an especially beautiful dress in honour of the day. I'll make us something delicious and we'll eat together, by candlelight. How about ravioli with tomato sauce? It's unhealthy and gooey, but what the hell. We make our own rules here, don't we? Aren't we happy? Yes, we are, my sweetheart, we're unbelievably happy.

ANN

BERLIN, 25 DECEMBER 2017

Her.

The shock is like a blast, a violent inner explosion. I try to jump up but my body is sheer chaos; my legs just twitch and my hands can't get a hold. By contrast, she stands there in the door, tall and superior, a faint smile on her lips. She's not saying anything, which is the worst thing. I want to ask her how she got in. What the hell she thinks she's doing here, in our house and in general, after all these years. Maybe I'd ask too whether she's real or just a hallucination like the girls in the study. Only my mouth feels blocked and my throat constricted. And she, she's making no move to help me and resolve the situation herself. She seems to be enjoying the fact that I'm squatting beside the loo, looking surprised and incapacitated. I manage no more than an 'Eva', but even that's too much. It feels as if I were opening the door to a storeroom that's been piled high with rubbish for years, eventually getting so full that I had to press against the door with all my body weight to close it. Now I've opened it again and its entire contents come spilling out, battering me. Years, images, memories.

'You still remember me, then,' she says, her grin getting wider.

Of course I do, even though she's changed a lot. Her hair, once long and strawberry-blonde, has now been dyed dark brown and only comes down to her chin. She looks pale, as if made from porcelain. She's also lost weight – too much, in my opinion. She's thin like one of the lines on her wide pullover and her narrow jeans. But she's genuine, real, I can't blink her away. Eva, the ugliest, meanest person on earth. She broke my heart when she went off with Nico back then.

I try to restore some order to myself, starting with my body. Bracing my feet on the floor, I reach for the rim of the sink and pull myself up. I hope she doesn't notice that every fibre of me is trembling. I don't want her to think of herself as my wound; I've been taken by surprise, that's all, and she's not even a scab anymore.

'What are you doing here? How did you even get in?'

She shrugs. 'Your bell seems to be broken, I tried a few times . . .'

I nod. I switched the bell off a while ago now. Nobody ever came who I wanted to let in anyway. Usually it was Eva's mother inviting me to dinner yet again.

'. . . so I wandered around the house, like in the old days, and saw that the terrace door was open.' The terrace door – I must have forgotten to close it properly after being completely thrown by the red ribbon on the oleander. 'You should really be more careful now that you're here on your own.' The amused look, the supercilious tone; she's trying to provoke me, and she's succeeding too.

'What about you, Eva? Do you think it's normal to march into a strange house?'

'In case you don't remember, this house was never strange to me. Quite the opposite – for a long time I felt more at home here than with my own parents.'

'How touching.'

She gives a slightly forced laugh. 'I see you still bear a grudge for what happened with Nico.'

'Rubbish! I'd just like to know what you think you're doing in my house.'

'My mother sent me in the hope that I'd be able to swing it and get you to come to dinner after all. She doesn't want you spending Christmas on your own.'

'Tell her you tried everything.'

'As you wish,' she says, turning to go. I put my hands up and massage the sides of my head. Listening to Eva's footsteps, I'm relieved to hear them get further away. Until I realise they're heading in the wrong direction. I rush after Eva, but don't catch up with her until she's already in the study, in the middle of all the papers and photographs of happy little girls.

'Holy shit!'

'Yes, exactly: holy shit. What do you think you're doing, Eva? Just get out!'

'What's this?' she says, bending down to one of the pictures. 'Where did you get all of this?'

'Doesn't matter, leave it!' I try snatching the photo, but she turns away with it.

'Do you know I never actually came into this room? I spent half my childhood in your house, but this door was always closed. We knew we weren't allowed to disturb your father when he was working, even though he never actually said that to us.'

'Are you deaf? I want you to leave. Now!'

She looks at me – the face she presents today is swimming once more with childish features. Eva, my Eva, part of me for so many years. My fury writhes, flattened by the feelings from the storeroom jammed with rubbish.

'You just left,' I hiss between clenched jaws. It sounds pitiful and feeble.

The photograph in her hand begins to tremble faintly; it's as if her smug smile has been wiped away. Has Eva got a storeroom like mine? Things she's locked away for her own protection?

'I know,' she says softly.

'You didn't think I was worth a goodbye, an explanation.' I purse my lips; I don't want to sound like an injured bird, make myself small and vulnerable before someone who's shattered my ribcage and squashed my heart.

She nods uneasily. 'It was an emergency, wasn't it? You were my second family, my better family.'

'Is this something that's only occurred to you now? After more than seven bloody years ?'

'I buy every newspaper that reports on the case.'

I shake my head. 'I don't. It only makes me angry.'

'At your father or the journalists?'

'What? The journalists, of course! Come on, Eva, you know my dad! Surely you can't believe he's got anything to do with it.' I point at the carpet of documents at our feet. 'Somewhere in all of this there's a mistake and I'm determined to find it.'

'Ann . . .' Now she's the one sounding feeble. 'Maybe—'

'No, not *maybe*. Go, get out of here. You're no longer welcome in this house. When you packed your bags to bugger off with Nico, you discarded us and your past life like a redundant tool.'

Eva doesn't budge an inch. Her gaze penetrates me effortlessly; my skin is made of cellophane and I'm transparent. Because the fact is, I don't really want her to go. I've never stopped missing her. And I'm longing for support.

'Who's that?' she asks warily, meaning the girl in the photo she's holding. I crane my neck. It's a portrait; the little girl has red hair and freckles.

'I don't know,' I reply, moving my index finger in a circle. 'Turn it around; the names are written on the back.'

'Larissa Meller,' Eva reads out.

I nod discreetly. Larissa was the girl Ludwig told me about, the most recent development in the case. 'She was ten when she disappeared in June 2003 on a bike ride,' I say, repeating what I remember. 'Her body was found three months later in a hut by the Weihenpfuhl. The police reckon she was the ribbon murderer's first victim.'

'How exactly did he . . .' Eva falters, but it's obvious what she wants to know. It's the question whose answer is still hiding in Ludwig's folder, deliberately sealed in a large brown envelope. An answer whose details are known by very few. Not even Jörg E., Sakia's father, who doesn't usually omit a single detail, has ever spoken about it; presumably the police have made him swear to keep quiet on this matter, because, according to Ludwig, they've got their reasons for withholding certain details. When questions are asked as to exactly how the girls died, the vague line is that they bled to death from their cut wounds.

'There are photographs of that too,' I say quietly.

Eva's eyes grow large. 'Do you really want to see them?'

'I have to. So . . . thank your mum for the invitation. Or tell her she knows where she can stick her sympathy. Whichever you consider more appropriate.' I essay a smile, but Eva shakes her head.

'Forget it. I'll tell her to make us up two plates. We'll eat here.'

She's out of the study in a flash, so quickly that she forgets to give me back the photo of Larissa. I can only hope she realises before she gets home and Elke catches a glimpse.

It's a good half hour before she comes back. I'd almost given up on her and felt angry at myself for being taken in by her again.

'Sorry,' Eva says when she's at the front door, carrying two plates covered in tinfoil. After she went, I carefully locked the door to the terrace and switched the bell on again. 'I had to have a bit of a discussion with Mum. She couldn't understand why we wanted to eat here instead.' She hands me the plates and takes off her boots.

'Did you tell her?'

'Are you crazy? You know my mum.'

'True.' With my head, I indicate that she should follow me upstairs. One half of me has already put cutlery, napkins, two glasses and a bottle of wine on the desk, whereas the other half is just shaking its head. How can I get involved with Eva again so quickly after everything that happened? Maybe because, amongst all the emotions in my inner storeroom of rubbish, there was always the secret hope I'd see her again one day. Surely I still mean something to her; it must be true or she'd never have come back.

When Eva lifts the foil from one of the plates, the goose leg with its red cabbage gives off a Christmas aroma, an illusion that immediately feels wrong to both of us.

'We could eat later,' I say, ashamed of the wine and glasses, which seem just as inappropriate, as if I were trying to exploit a dreadful occasion for my own benefit. Two former friends, toasting with Chardonnay their reunion in the shadow of ten dead children. I pour the wine anyway, and I'm happy to see Eva empty her glass in one go.

'While you were at your parents', I started looking at some of these documents, especially the evidence that's been gathered.'

Eva holds her glass out to me, a silent prompt.

'And the photos of . . .' she begins, but can't say more than, 'you know.'

'No, not yet.' We drink in sync, both eagerly and quickly in the hope it will give us the necessary courage for what's in store. 'Did you bring the photo of Larissa back? I have to return the folder in its entirety when we're done or I'll be in even more trouble than I'm already in.'

Eva puts her empty glass on the desk then reaches behind and pulls the photo from her waistband like a gun. 'Here.' She gives it another close inspection before handing it back to me. 'She'd be our age now.'

'True.'

'Where do you think she was going when she disappeared that June afternoon?'

I shrug. 'Maybe nowhere in particular, maybe she was just exploring the area. Would that be so odd?'

At Larissa's age, Eva and I often went out on our bikes. Our trips sometimes took us far, down farm tracks, through woods and marshes, and to an old gravel pit which we fantasised was a sea. The best fun we had was when Eva could stay the night at ours and we didn't have to keep an eye on the time to ensure she'd be back home punctually for dinner. Elke was reluctant to allow sleepovers; she was worried my father wouldn't much care whether we ate healthily or went to bed on time. In one respect she was right: my father did give us a lot of leeway. Not because he was ignorant, but because he wanted to see us happy. He pumped our tyres up – clumsily, but he did it – before we set off, gave us money so we could buy ice creams on the way, and told us to have fun.

Fourteen years later Eva and I are on a journey again together. Ten stories take us through the entire Greater Berlin area, each ending at the moment the crime scene photographer pressed the button on his camera. The girls were called Jana, Kati, Olivia, Laetitia, Hayet, Jenny, Saskia, Alina and Sophie. We find them in woodland huts, cellars and warehouses, where they lie before us, their faces pointing upwards or tilted limply to the side. Some have their eyes closed and look as if they're sleeping. Others stare horrified into the void. And then there's Larissa – all that's left of her is an unrecognisable black something with matted red hair.

Eva cries bitterly; she can barely speak. But I don't want her to either. I'm the one with a clear head; I have the overview, the plan.

'It's essential we find out the significance of the gaps between murders. He kills in 2003, 2004, 2005, 2007, 2008, 2011, 2013, 2014, 2016, 2017. What sort of a cycle is that? And what's with the years 2006, 2009, 2010, 2012 and 2015? Nothing happens in those years. What's the killer doing during this time? Is he ill? Is he in prison for other crimes? Or is he abroad seeking victims there?'

When Eva swallows, I ignore it. My mind is in overdrive.

'Whoever killed those girls must have a few gaps in his CV that relate to these very years. My father doesn't. He was never ill for a long period, let alone ever in prison. He's never even run a red light in his life, but nobody's interested in that.'

Eva makes a noise again; the sight of the dead girls must have really unsettled her. But it's what she wanted. She wanted to help with the research and the photos are part of that.

'They just come up with their arbitrary evidence, and, in all honesty – I want to hear you say it, Eva – it really is arbitrary, isn't it? Size 42 shoes and a dark Audi? I mean, how many other men in Berlin fit the bill? Must be tens of thousands at least.' I point at the papers, including the document listing the evidence. 'Otherwise all they've got is a partial fingerprint – smudged so it's useless – and a few textile fibres, probably from a shirt. What they don't have is any DNA or mobile phone data to prove my father was in the vicinity of the crime scenes. Nothing certain.'

Eva shakes her head as if I'd asked her a question. Her face is so contorted with pain that her tear-stained mascara is running in oddly crooked lines.

'And okay, then there's the acquaintance who ran into my father on a walk near the last crime scene,' I continue breathlessly. 'But that could have been a coincidence, couldn't it? Turn it round and you could also say my father ran into this acquaintance. So why isn't he under suspicion? I admit, the newspaper articles in his desk give the wrong impression, but he'd kept them for his lecture series, for God's sake! He was analysing these articles as part of his research, because that was his specialism: "Evil in humans as an anthropological, cultural and historical constant, and philosophical views of death". I was always really impressed by the weightiness of the topic. And very proud of him because his lectures and seminars were in great demand. Most students found his approach cool, apart from this one girl, a prissy nerd . . .' My thoughts are racing at such speed that my speech can hardly keep up. 'She complained to the dean because she thought what my father was doing was disrespectful, verging on abuse of the dead children for' – here I make air quotes – '"study purposes". Discussions with the university management ensued and the complaint was officially recorded. But that dozy woman – I expect she'd watched too many serial killer documentaries – she only had to go to the police too, didn't she? My father was questioned, and of course he was able to point out to the officers that science *has* to use material from real life to produce findings that can be taken seriously. It was relatively easy to convey this to the police. Back then, at least. And finally, there's the photofit image that was put together from details provided by a woman who claimed to have seen Saskia with a strange man.' I thrust the picture above my head. 'This is a joke, isn't it?' I say, waving it around so it rustles noisily in the air. 'Look at the nose: far too small and broad. Then this bloated chin and the close-together eyes. It looks more like your dad than—'

'Please stop!'

'Or Ludwig, that would be a great Ludwig, wouldn't it? Do you remember Ludwig? He used to come here often—'

'Ann! That's enough!'

I recoil and blink as if I'd been dreaming. Eva wipes her eyes with the back of her hand, smearing the lines from the mascara that's run. Her face now looks sooty, as if she'd just escaped a major fire in the nick of time.

'I'm really sorry,' she whispers.

'So am I, Eva . . . We can't change the fate of these poor girls. But we can—'

'I'm sorry for you.' Without taking her eyes off me, she pulls up the left sleeve of her jumper as if in slow motion. 'You saw it too, Ann. The same thing ten times, each girl.' She puts her right index finger on her wrist and traces an invisible line to her elbow. My heart is vibrating; I no longer feel individual beats, just a pervasive tension.

'But . . . but that's crazy.'

'Really?' She grabs my left hand and turns it so my wrist is facing upwards. We both look at my scar. Now we know how the girls were killed. It wasn't the photographs from the crime scenes that showed us – it was difficult to make out anything in them due to all the blood – but the other pictures in the brown envelope. Small, stiff bodies, their wounds cleaned, lying on cold metal tables in forensics labs.

The killer slit the girls' wrists.

I was six when my mum died of leukaemia. My mind doesn't have more than a few flickering images of a bald woman lying in a bed. I remember she was always weak, jittery, and had to take a mountain of medicines. Sometimes she let me tip out the contents of her pill box and then rearrange them again. We'd pretend that I was Cinderella sorting through the peas. I nonetheless loved her very much – not for what we did together, for that wasn't much; our world played out in a hospital room – but for the feeling she gave me. Because she was so sick that each new day seemed to her like a miracle, she treated me as if I were one too. It was very different with my father back then. Not that he was cold or unapproachable. But there was something mechanical about him, which is probably quite normal if you've got to function all the time. And he did. He bore the responsibility for a terminally ill wife and a little child.

But then it was just the two of us. He told me stories from the other place Mum was now – happy and healthy – a wonderful garden beneath a permanently blue sky. I tried to imagine her going for walks there amongst knee-high flowers with blooms the size of cabbages, and her having long hair again, long blonde hair that glistened in the sun. I'd never seen her like that in real life; for me she was only ever ill and bedridden. All the same, I didn't cry for my mum. I didn't admit to myself that I missed her, or was angry because I felt betrayed by a version of her I'd never had the chance to meet. In fact, I showed no emotion at all, until the point came when I didn't feel anything either. Noticing that something wasn't right with me, my father got very worried. He took me off to child psychologists and bereavement experts, and kept asking me how I felt. He wanted to know everything in great detail, wanted me to describe at length what was happening inside me, every tiny nuance. But there wasn't anything. One day – it was summer and very hot – I fell off my bike on the gravel path behind our house. A large, sharp stone dug into my left wrist. Eva, who was there, immediately started screaming and ran off to get my dad. I just sat there, watching the blood run down my arm, marvelling at the pain I felt. After all those months I'd spent as if numbed, this was like a release. I didn't want it to subside, the pain. I wanted to scream and cry and explode with this feeling. I twisted the stone deeper into the wound. At that moment Eva came back with Dad . . .

'Are you out of your mind?' I jerk my hand away. 'My father almost lost it because he was worried his six-year-old was a suicide risk. It took him years to finally realise that it was just a stupid, one-off thing. Do you imagine he'd do something that reminded him of this? Of one of the most traumatic episodes in his life?'

'Those are your words,' Eva says, making a dismissive gesture. 'All I did was point out that your wrist was cut too, once.'

'But it wasn't my father who did that, it was me!'

Eva doesn't respond. Her mascara-smeared face makes me aggressive.

'Just say something!'

'Okay.'

'Okay?'

'I can see we're not going to get anywhere like this. So let's leave your dad out of it for the time being and take a neutral approach.'

'Meaning?'

'We'll start at the beginning. With serial killers, the first victim often plays a crucial role. Later, the choice of victim may be random, but the killer often has a close connection or even personal relationship to the first one.'

'You mean Larissa?'

Eva nods. 'What do we have on her?'

Together, we sift through the documents that are explicitly about Larissa. I want to divvy them up and get cracking, but Eva begs me to make her a coffee. The wine and all the emotion have made her quite woozy. When I come back from the kitchen, she's sitting on the floor, deep in piles of paper.

'Right, Larissa lived with her pregnant mother, one-year-old half-brother and her stepfather in a block of flats in Hellersdorf. As you know, she'd been missing for three months when her body was found by the Weihenpfuhl. Apart from size 42 footprints, there were no leads, so the official investigation was soon called off. But the stepfather believed he had a lead. He suspected a friend of the family . . .' She puts out her hand and wiggles her fingers. I don't understand what she's getting at to begin with, but then realise that I'm still holding her cup of coffee.

'Oh, sorry,' I say, giving it to her. 'What sort of friend?'

Eva takes a sip. And another. I'm getting nervous. I grab the top sheet of paper from the pile in her lap and skim the statement made by Larissa's stepfather. At a party a few months before Larissa disappeared, he caught the said friend sitting with Larissa on her bed and brushing her hair.

'A site manager by the name of Marcus Steinhausen,' I read out loud.

'Not so fast,' Eva says, putting her cup down and picking up another piece of paper. 'Although the stepfather voiced his suspicion to the police right after Larissa went missing, Steinhausen had a watertight alibi. When Larissa's body was found, the stepfather, who'd never stopped suspecting Steinhausen, went through the roof. He went to see Steinhausen and badly beat him up, which earned him his first spell inside. Two years later, he had another go at Steinhausen, fracturing his skull. When he recovered, Steinhausen moved away, but it's unclear where he went. At least there's no new address in the documentation.' She puts the piece of paper down and looks at me sympathetically – why, I don't understand.

'What we've got is a lead, Eva!'

'What? No! What we've got is a stepfather who became so obsessed by his hunch that he ended up in prison. Not to mention an innocent man who almost lost his life as a result.'

'You think this Steinhausen is innocent just because he was able to come up with an alibi? That sort of thing can be organised. We should talk to them.'

'To who?'

'Larissa Müller's family. There must be a reason why the stepfather is so—'

'Meller.'

'What?'

'You made a mistake. It's Meller, not Müller. But I don't think—'

'Meller,' I repeat. A name that sparks something in me. Just a hazy feeling, like a mist. When I check it in the documents, the mist is no more. It doesn't thin out, it doesn't lift gradually – it's gone in a flash, as if at the flick of a switch.

'My God!' I pant. 'I know her!'

US

You really must have liked that, my angel. Just look at your dress, it's got all dirty. You sweet, clumsy little thing! We're going to have to get you changed right away, but it doesn't matter. It's late anyway and time you were in your pyjamas. Come on, I'll carry you to the bathroom . . . You know, I've been thinking. It's Christmas, after all, and, well . . . you've every reason to be a bit disappointed. But something has occurred to me, the ultimate present for you, princess: a friend! How about that? Shall I get you a friend, a real, flesh-and-blood friend, just for you? I've even got an idea who it would be. Her name's Sarah. She's a bit older than you, but I think you'd get on famously. I've been watching her for quite a while, watching her very closely. Her expressions, my angel. I can read her face: she's longing for it too. Life isn't that great for her at home; her mother's a dragon who doesn't deserve such a charming, lovely daughter. And it's not fair on Sarah that she's not appreciated. Do you want her to visit us? Should I go and fetch her? Yes, I think I should. But not until tomorrow. It's too late today, we have to go to bed. Come on, my angel, off to bed. We'll snuggle up really close, just as you like it. I'll hold you as tightly as I can and cover your head with a thousand kisses until you've fallen asleep.

ANN

'You knew Larissa?' Eva's eyes are wide open.

For now all I can manage is a vague movement of my head. The surname – I can't believe it. Ludwig mentioned it during our conversation in the prison and I remember being overcome by a feeling of unease. I thought this was because I was worried he might be in cahoots with the DPP. But maybe it was the name gnawing away at me. And then Eva read it from Larissa's photograph. So far I must have heard Meller at least twice without really registering it. Even though for the past few weeks I've seen the name on an almost daily basis, stitched on the chest pocket of a green polyester shirt. And Larissa's file confirms it.

'No,' I say. 'But I know her mother.'

'You know . . . ?'

I skim once more the information I find on Larissa's family. Her mother's first name: Michelle.

'It must be her, it all fits.'

My colleague Michelle, who told me on Christmas Eve that her grown-up daughter hasn't spent Christmas with her in ages. Michelle with an ex-husband who's twice been in prison for

78

GBH, and two sons who are now teenagers. Michelle who, as I may have suspected, sometimes laughs only to stop herself from crying. But I've always believed those tears were a result of the stress of being a single mother and the additional burden of the job. Now it dawns on me why she always wears so much make-up. Every morning she stands at the bathroom mirror, and paints on a mask, from behind which she feels able to face the world.

Eva's getting impatient; I fill her in.

'Wow!' she says, unable to say any more either.

I think out loud. I need to speak to Michelle if I want to find out what significance her daughter could have had for the killer. But there's a problem: she knows me by my dead mother's maiden name, as Ann de Groot, and thinks I'm a single mother too.

'Are you saying the woman doesn't have a clue who you really are?' The expression on Eva's face speaks volumes. As if she supects I might have deliberately applied to Big Murphy's to work side by side with the mother of one of the victims. She's wrong, but I don't want to waste any time explaining myself, having to justify myself over a coincidence.

'I have to call her and ask for a meeting!' I pick up my mobile and scroll through my phone book.

'You've got her number?'

'Of course. We're work colleagues, we need to be in touch about shifts.'

'You must be crazy!' Eva snatches my mobile away. 'The poor woman has no idea what's coming to her. You can't wake her up at one in the morning and out of the blue confront her with the worst nightmare of her life.'

Bloody hell, of course I can't. 'Okay, but tomorrow morning then.'

'There's no guarantee she'll want to talk to you, you'd better bear that in mind. Some people would rather block out things like that. Quite apart from the fact that you're the daughter of the main suspect.'

She's right. To make Michelle realise the urgency of my concern I'd have to take off my mask, regardless of the consequences. I don't care that it might lose me my job at Big Murphy's. But what if Michelle flips out, goes to the press and I end up being accused of harassing one of the victims' mothers? A headline like that definitely wouldn't help my father. My thoughts are interrupted by a gentle snapping: Eva deep in contemplation, nibbling at her thumbnail.

'I have to risk it, Eva. You'd understand if you'd seen him in prison. He's completely changed, so empty, so strange. As if part of him had died and been replaced by mechanical components.'

Eva slides over and embraces me for a long moment. Then she offers to come with me if Michelle does agree to a meeting.

'I'll think about it,' I say.

The rest of my night is sleepless. Eva's gone home and I can't think of anything else but my forthcoming conversation with Michelle. I fetch a knife from the kitchen, switch on the terrace light, put a chair beside the pot with the oleander and sit there, wrapped in a thick blanket, with all my thoughts and the miserable hours until morning before me. How do you speak to a grieving mother about the murder of her child? How do you ask her for help when you're the daughter of the main suspect?

I work out phrases, rework them, pondering individual words, searching for those that seem most sensitive: suitable packaging. Yet with each new attempt, I merely arrive at the same conclusion: in a situation like this, there's simply no way of approaching it delicately. I'm going to shock, horrify and agitate Michelle, no matter how carefully I try to formulate my sentences. The content always remains the same.

I begin to cry. The things I've got to deal with now. How dramatically my life has changed. On this very day last year there was a party in this house, an over-the-top cheesy Christmas party where everybody had to wear ugly festive jumpers and flashing plastic antlers on their heads. Everyone was there: Dad, Zoe and many, many others I'd regarded as friends or at least good acquaintances. I've often wondered why none of them has yet spoken to the press in return for a nice little remuneration. Now I think I know. It's the fear of what the whole affair might say about themselves. They've happily spent a lot of time with an alleged killer. They've enjoyed his company and drunk his wine, and if the accusations turned out to be true, they'd be complicit for having been so stupid and blind. This risk isn't worth a little remuneration. They're cowardly and fake, the lot of them. I ought to be grateful that this thing with my father has enabled me to see their true faces. I wipe away the pointless tears; everything can spur you on, even hatred.

Picking up my mobile, I open the browser and type the name 'Marcus Steinhausen' into the search engine. Nothing. How is that possible? If, as the files say, Steinhausen worked as a site manager, it must be possible to find a few of the projects he worked on. I try 'Steinhausen', 'Berlin' and 'construction' in all possible variations – still nothing. I'm frustrated. And tired. And maybe a bit paranoid, seeing as beside my chair a kitchen knife is close to hand, with a blade that must be twenty centimetres long. I almost wish that the man who tied the ribbon to the oleander would come back. Now, right now, on this night that feels as if it's never going to end. I'd have every right to defend myself and no scruples about doing so, the realisation of which horrifies me. But it's the truth. I shake my head. One year ago. It may have been phony, but it was fun. We laughed and danced and kept coming up with new excuses to gather under the mistletoe hanging from the chandelier in the hallway.

I close the search for Marcus Steinhausen and open my address book instead. Three hundred and sixteen contacts. The last number I saved is Jakob's. He gave it to me when we were sitting on the bench outside Big Murphy's and said I should ring it when I got the chance so he'd have my number too. He still doesn't have it. I go to my messages. The most recent is from Zoe, five weeks ago. *Please don't be angry with me.* I haven't replied, until now.

I miss you, despite everything, I write.

I miss you all.

Loneliness. (Ann, 8 years old)
Loneliness is not a nice feeling. I imagine it has a sharp knife and can cut you off from the rest of the world with just one cut. Then you float away out into the universe. Eva thinks its nice in the universe because of all the stars. But thats not true. Its just cold and black and you dont have any air to breath. Without air you will die so loneliness is a very dangerous feeling too.

'Hello?'

Michelle sounds sleepy, which isn't surprising as it's only just gone half past seven – and it's Boxing Day. I ask if I can come over; I really need to talk to her. She wants to know what it's about, but of course I can't tell her, or she might hang up. So I just stammer something about a supposed emergency and resort to saying 'please' as often as I can.

'To be honest, you're beginning to frighten me.' In her voice I can hear an anxious smile.

'No, no, that's the last thing . . . it's just . . . please, Michelle . . .'

'It's all right, calm down. I'm at home all day, you can come round whenever you like.'

I'm out of the house less than ten minutes later. Last night I wasn't sure whether I would actually take up Eva's offer to accompany me. Out of concern for my father, we'd patched things up for a few hours – a provisional stitch job. I've no idea how long it will last until it bursts open, nor what's beneath it. And yet now I'm at her door, ringing the bell. Maybe because loneliness is more painful than anything else.

It's Elke who opens the door, in a pink fleece dressing gown and with a pale, puffy face. She looks as if she's had little sleep, or even none like me. Eva appears briefly behind her mum's shoulder before I hear her clattering up the stairs, presumably to get dressed.

'Come in,' Elke says. 'We can have a nice leisurely breakfast together.'

Gratefully I decline, as ever. 'Eva and I have something planned.'

I evade her obtrusive attempt to find out more by stepping a few paces back and pretending to stretch my legs. But Elke stays in the doorway and watches me. It's very uncomfortable.

'Ready!' Eva calls, pushing past her mother.

'Would it be okay if we took your car?' Without waiting for an answer, I head straight for the passenger side of the Mini with its Frankfurt number plate. I haven't got behind the wheel of a car since I hit a deer two years ago. Sometimes I still dream of the huge, terrified eyes of the roe staring into my headlights, not to mention the plates and screws in my jaw. Eva knows nothing about this, but she doesn't ask any questions either, just takes the keys from her coat pocket to unlock the car.

'If I were her I would've moved away,' she says, putting the address Michelle gave me into her satnav. She still lives in Hellersdorf, in the small flat she shared with Larissa. 'I mean, I can understand it if your daughter's missing and you remain tied to a certain place by hope. But when you know for sure she's dead, and there'll never be a *one day*, when she's suddenly standing outside your front door . . . No, I couldn't hack that.'

'Because of all the memories, you mean?'

Eva concentrates as she reverses the Mini out of her parents' drive.

'Memories are only lovely when there's hope,' she says. 'After that they destroy you.'

We say nothing for a while until I find the silence uncomfortable.

'So, you're living in Frankfurt now?'

'How do you know that?'

'Your number plate.' I smile. She doesn't need to know that I often looked for her online, especially in the first few years after she left. Without success. No Eva Harbert on social media or on any company or college websites. She seemed to have vanished like a ghost and I couldn't even find out from her mother where she was. Although, till yesterday, I'd thought Elke didn't know herself and had only not said so because she was ashamed. What would people have thought of her? Similarly, I keep it to myself that I even tried talking to Nico. He took off with Eva and came back on his own a few months later, albeit only for a while. He told me to forget it. Eva didn't want any contact, and I felt as if I'd hit a sore spot. Maybe the rumours were indeed true that he'd got her pregnant and they'd eloped in a flight of romance, but soon realised that they weren't right for each other.

Eva nods. 'Of course. For a long time now – in fact, since the beginning. Nico's got relations in Frankfurt. We stayed with them for a few weeks after leaving Berlin.'

I flinch. Although I'd just been thinking about Nico myself, hearing Eva utter his name feels like a sting.

'Go ahead and ask me,' she says, after a quick glance in my direction. 'Ask me whatever you want.'

'None of my business.'

'But you're interested.' She laughs. 'We were together a long time, even if Nico popped back to Berlin for a spell. His father was undergoing chemotherapy and Nico had to help his mother with everything for a while. Then he returned to me in Frankfurt.'

'I see.' I swallow a stone. It's only small, like a pebble from the shore that the tide has smoothed down over the years, and yet I can feel it. I clear my throat. 'People were speculating you'd become pregnant.'

'So typical.' She laughs again. 'No, in truth I wasn't pregnant. Nico and I were very much in love and wanted to put all the crap here behind us. It lasted until a few months ago.'

'That *is* a long time.'

85

'Eight years.' For a while we fall silent again, then she asks, 'What about you? Anyone in your life?'

'Yes, but . . . this isn't probably the right time.'

'To be happy with another person, you first have to learn to come to terms with yourself.'

'Amen.'

'What else? When you told me yesterday about Michelle and the burger joint, you mentioned you were studying again.'

'Yes: German. Fourth semester. We'll see if and when I continue. Maybe I'll change uni or abandon it altogether. I don't know yet.'

'Fourth semester?'

I shrug. 'I took a break after the first two years to travel around France and then I changed subjects. It happens, doesn't it? Not every CV is without its gaps.'

'Yes.' Eva sounds pensive.

'What?'

'Talking of CVs without gaps, yesterday you worked out that there were years without any murders. What if that isn't the case? If the killer was active but the victims escaped before he could murder them?'

I shake my head. 'Well, they would have gone to the police, don't you think?'

'Adults, the parents might have gone to the police. But we're talking about children here, Ann! What if they didn't tell their parents anything because they didn't understand what had happened to them? If they thought it was something else or they were ashamed because they thought they themselves were to blame?'

'I don't know, Eva.'

86

'Why not? Do you think a child can't feel shame? Do you think a child wouldn't wonder what they might have done to deserve it, or whether they'd provoked someone?'

'Sure, it's possible, but . . . I think it's more likely that the killer didn't keep going merely because he couldn't. If we get too complicated in our reasoning, we'll end up overlooking the simplest solution.'

Eva mutters. Neither of us say anything else until we park outside Michelle's house. 'Should I come in or wait out here for you?'

'Wait,' I decide. 'I don't know how Michelle will react if I turn up with someone else unannounced.' I get out. 'But thanks for your support, I'm really grateful,' I add before closing the passenger door.

I wander along the path to the door as if to the scaffold: with heavy steps, tense shoulders and bowed head. To my right is a playground covered in snow. Maybe Larissa used to play here. Scarcely has that thought crossed my mind than my imagination effaces the snow and a green meadow sprouts in its place. Larissa is dangling her legs from the swing and squinting into the sun, when, against the light, the dark silhouette of a man looms menacingly before her. I shake my head and the image dissolves. The playground is as it was: in the grey snow of the early morning and without Larissa.

When I get to the front door, I look for a bell beside the name Meller. There are twenty flats in this ugly, bright yellow block. I have to ring several times before I hear a buzz and push open the thick, streaky glass door. When I get to the seventh floor, Michelle is already standing in the doorway. She's made up as ever, but her dyed blonde hair hasn't been styled. She's wearing grey tracksuit bottoms and a light top with dots on it, which seems to be part of a pyjama set. I get the impression her tentative smile is wavering between uncertainty and a hunch.

'Come in,' she says, stepping aside. I thank her and take my boots off on the mat.

Even the hallway gets to me. The walls are hung with photographs, almost all of them showing Larissa in every stage of her life, from infancy to her school induction.

'I hardly took any photos of her in the last few years,' Michelle says, shutting the door to her flat. I turn around to her in shock.

'That's why you've come, isn't it? Because of Larissa?'

'I . . .'

'Only a couple of days ago there was this newspaper article, an interview with Saskia's dad. It said the alleged killer also has a daughter.'

Two days ago – now it flashes through my mind: *Continue reading on page 3*. An article I was so keen to avoid I demolished the newspaper dispenser instead. I give an indecisive shrug. There are lots of daughters in Berlin, hundreds of thousands of them.

'What's more, two days ago you signed your cash receipt at the end of your shift with "Lesniak" instead of "de Groot" like usual. You were so all over the place that day you didn't even notice, did you?'

I purse my lips and my heart begins to gallop. How could I have made such a stupid mistake? At least I've been saved the trouble of having to gently let Michelle know who I really am. But I'm even more ashamed. How must she have felt when she realised her work colleague had been deceiving her all these weeks?

'Do you know what comes up first when you search for "Lesniak" and "Berlin" on the internet?'

I nod apprehensively. My father – that's what you find. Walter Lesniak, a university professor, just like the alleged killer who's in custody. 'So you put two and two together.'

'I wasn't completely sure. But when you called this morning, so upset and so early, I knew, yes.'

'And even so, you're prepared to help me?'

'Looks like it. Come on.'

She takes me into her sitting room. It's small and untidy, and here too there are lots of photos on the walls. Only some of them show Michelle's sons: two boys, redheads like Larissa, looking grumpy. Michelle removes an overflowing washing basket from the sofa and invites me to sit down. She remains standing and looks down at me, her jaw muscles twitching.

'About four weeks ago I was told that Larissa's death was probably linked to the series of killings, and a few days ago this was confirmed as definite. I should be shocked, no? But I'm not. It's as if I suspected this long ago. Only I can't make out where you come into it. How's it possible that the daughter of my child's alleged killer gets a job in the very place where I work? I mean, it can hardly be a coincidence.'

Although I'm still wearing Dad's thick jacket, I suddenly feel cold. I can understand Michelle's mistrust and yet I don't have another explanation except for the fact that it's just that: a coincidence. A totally crazy, unbelievable coincidence of the sort that only fate can cook up when hatching plans for people. When two paths have to cross.

Set on being honest with her, I tell Michelle about the weeks since the arrest. That I didn't want to go to uni anymore because I was worried about the looks I'd get and the gossip. But that I couldn't sit around doing nothing at home, where my despair and memories were on the verge of driving me crazy. This was why I looked for an undertaking, something to attach me to the real world, to give me a reason to get up in the morning. An undertaking that I found in the job at Big Murphy's. I don't know if she believes me, but at least she doesn't immediately ask me to leave.

'I dream about it almost every night,' she says instead, wandering over to the window and peering out. 'I see my little girl running through the woods, desperately trying to escape her pursuer. She stumbles, trips and keeps hitting her shoulder because she can barely see anything in the dark. In her thoughts she's calling for her mummy, but I'm not there. She's all on her own. Eventually she gets so tired that she slumps to the ground behind a thick tree trunk. She makes herself as small as a mouse, just like when she used to play hide-and-seek here at home, always squeezing herself into the gap between the back of the sofa and the wall. She knows she has to be very quiet to not give herself away. Maybe he'll give up if he doesn't find her, or at least he'll go off in another direction. And in fact she *is* lucky: from somewhere in the distance comes a loud crack that catches his attention. He follows the noise and moves away from her. She gets to her feet and keeps running; she's so brave – Mummy's big brave girl. Then the miracle occurs: the woods end in a road. She's made it, she's escaped from him! And there's something else, two shining circles, getting bigger and bigger: a car. She sets off on a final sprint, flailing her arms about, her whole body screaming for attention. Sitting in that car is someone who can help her. Someone who'll take her back to her mummy. The driver stops the car right beside her. The door opens – but it's too late. It's him: the man who chased her through the woods. He drags her to the car and locks her in the boot, where it's cramped and stuffy, and just as black as it was in the woods. She feels they're driving on a bumpy road. She knows it leads back to the hut, where terrifying tools hang on the wall. Old screwdrivers, an axe with a rusty blade and a saw with sharp teeth. The car stops. When the man lifts her from the boot, her body is completely limp, abandoned by all hope, no fighting spirit left. She allows herself to be carried back to the hut. In her head she sings herself a lullaby. *Goodnight, Mummy. I love you anyway . . .*'

Michelle, who was standing at the window with her back to me, turns around so abruptly that I jump. Black trickles of mascara are running down her face; it's hard to look at. Feeling uneasy, I shift my position on the sofa Larissa used to love playing hide-and-seek behind, and try to find the right words. There was nothing in the forensics report to suggest that she did try to flee before her death and almost managed to escape the killer. But I can understand that it's painful for Michelle not to know how the abduction took place and what really happened while Larissa was at the mercy of her killer. All she's got is the outcome: her dead child, murdered by a stranger and left for months in a remote woodland hut until there was scarcely anything left of her apart from a rotting black body and her dishevelled red hair. I assume that Michelle's subconscious is trying to fill the gaps in knowledge in its own way, and making her suffer from the never-changing reality that, as a mother, she wasn't there when her daughter needed her most.

'I'm so dreadfully sorry, Michelle,' I say softly. It's stupid, banal and worthless – I realise that. But I can't think of anything better to say.

'It's not your fault,' she says, sounding composed again, and sits on the arm of the sofa at some distance from me. 'No child can be held responsible for what their parents do.'

'But that's precisely why I'm here, Michelle! It wasn't my dad! There's no proof, just a few tenuous leads, most of which are based on coincidence.'

'Nobody gets thrown in custody just because of a few coincidences. What kind of state would we be living in if that happened?'

'The problem is, he simply won't say anything, which the investigation team take as an admission of guilt.' Craving understanding, I look at her, but her eyes return to the window.

'After Larissa's death, everything fell apart. I was pregnant with Ben at the time and Toby had just turned one. I was good for nothing, I spent all day crying in bed. I couldn't even cook for Toby. Rainer, my ex, couldn't watch this happen. He was almost manic in his attempt to find out what had happened to Larissa, especially who did it to her.' She gives me a sympathetic smile. 'You remind me a bit of him.'

I ignore her comment, but it's good that she's the one to bring up the subject of her ex-husband. 'At the time he suspected a friend of yours: Marcus Steinhausen.'

Michelle nods. 'Marcus was an odd guy, highly educated, very polite and obliging, but ... hmm.' She thinks for a moment, as if she doesn't know exactly where to begin. 'So, he was a site manager, in a completely different league from my ex, who was just a simple labourer. Despite this, he was crazy about Rainer, desperate to be friends with him. Rainer used to be very sociable and was always a happy soul. Marcus must have liked this and Rainer loved the attention. It wasn't long before he brought

Marcus home, and he was . . .' – she appears to be searching for the right words – 'so eerily perfect.' She nods in satisfaction. 'Yes, there's no other way to describe it. For each of us, he seemed to be exactly what we needed at any moment, able to switch roles at the press of a button. With Rainer, he drank beer and told dirty jokes, only to appear in the kitchen a few minutes later and lend a hand with the cooking. He helped Larissa with her homework or rocked Toby in his baby bouncer. In time, he started paying for stuff. To begin with, it was just bits of shopping, like when he'd noticed we were running out of milk or beer. Later he paid for Rainer's car to be repaired – actually Rainer borrowed the money from him, but Marcus refused to be paid back and got really angry when Rainer tried to do so.'

'Didn't you think it weird that a stranger suddenly muscled his way into your life?'

Michelle sighs. 'In retrospect, yes. But at the time . . . somehow we just got used to it; it became totally normal. Especially as we never had much money and were for ever having to budget. Marcus's contributions were very welcome indeed.' She looks at me. 'That sounds like he had to pay for our friendship. But it wasn't like that. We never made any demands or asked him for anything. He just did it as a matter of course, as if he really was a member of our family.'

'Didn't he have any family himself?'

Michelle bursts out laughing. 'Now we're getting to the nub of it. Marcus came round to ours almost every day after work, but he rarely stayed later than eight o'clock. You could set your watch by it, for at that time the calls would begin. We would hear him try to placate his wife, who clearly wanted him to come home.

He told us he was married and had a daughter too. But Rainer and I felt that things weren't great at home, at least as far as his marriage was concerned. Once when I talked to Marcus about the situation, he showed me a photograph of him with his family, looking very happy, which was at odds with the phone calls, and especially with the fact that he was always at ours rather than at home. But I didn't say anything, and Rainer thought it was just a male thing. Then came the evening when Marcus left punctually but forgot his mobile in our flat. Rainer decided to drive it over to his. He knew where Marcus lived because he'd dropped him off there once. A nice little house in Lichtenberg, a bit old-fashioned, with a garden complete with gnomes, that sort of thing. So Rainer went there, but rather than Marcus opening the door, it was a grumpy old woman. Marcus still lived with his mum, you see, and she kept him on a short leash. There was no wife and daughter. It was the mother who always rang when he was late. At that moment, Rainer lost all respect for Marcus, but I sort of felt sorry for him. He must have spent his whole life in his brother's shadow – at least that was the impression Rainer got from chatting to the mother. Every sentence she began with Marcus ended in a comparison with his brother, and Marcus never came off well. Sure, his brother had an even better job, his own house and a real family. But ultimately it was Marcus who gave up so much to look after their mother. I understood why he liked talking to people about a life he wasn't leading. I mean, imagine it. He'd even shown me a photo of what he claimed to be him and his family! As it turned out, the photo was actually of his brother with wife and child.' Michelle shakes her head. 'But I don't need to spell all of this out, do I? You ought to know what it's like when reality is so hard to bear that you begin inventing a different life for yourself.' Touché – I look at the floor. Luckily Michelle doesn't prolong this uncomfortable moment any longer, and continues, 'I felt sorry for him, yes, I felt really sorry for him. So I invited him to my birthday party, but that day something happened. Rainer caught Marcus brushing Larissa's hair on her bed. That was weird enough in itself! She was also telling him she was upset because yet another baby was on the way and she already got so little attention because of Toby. Marcus told her she didn't need to worry, he would look after her if necessary. Rainer blew his top. He threw Marcus out of the flat and forbade him from ever turning up here again.'

'And after that you didn't have any more contact with him?'

'Well . . . in the first couple of weeks after my party, we saw him a few times through the kitchen window,' Michelle says, pointing over her shoulder. 'He was hanging around outside and occasionally he'd leave chocolates or flowers at the door.' She shakes her head. 'That stopped a good while before Larissa went missing. But Rainer was obsessed by the idea that Marcus could have something to do with her death. When, in 2005, the body of another small girl was found – as it happened, on a construction site where Rainer and Marcus had worked together a few years earlier – that was that, as far as my husband was concerned. It couldn't be a coincidence.'

'But you thought it could?' I ask doubtfully, and the only answer I get is a scornful look. I suppose only ten minutes ago I was the one trying to convince Michelle of another crazy coincidence. 'I'm only saying because—'

'It's all right,' she interrupts me. 'Of course I thought it was strange to begin with. But Marcus had a watertight alibi for this too. Rainer's refusal to believe it saw him end up in prison for GBH. Which left me sitting there with two small children – and without my Larissa.' An awkward smile darts across her face. 'You know, I wasn't a particularly good mum to her. And not just because I let her get abducted and killed.' Again she points over her shoulder, towards the hallway. 'The last photo I took of her was on her first day at school, more than three years before her death. But I just took it for granted that she was there, and then I met Rainer and, well, you know. It was wonderful to be newly in love again, after Larissa's father had dumped me soon after she was born. With Rainer I had the chance to start from scratch again. We got married quickly.' Another brief smile, then she looks bitter. 'I had to get the photo the police used for their search from my parents. Can you believe that? What sort of a mother am I who has to phone around when she's asked for an up-to-date picture of her daughter? But you wouldn't know about that.'

'No,' I say quietly.

'No,' Michelle echoes. 'You know nothing about motherhood, nothing at all. He slit her wrist. But because she was the first and there were so few clues pointing towards a violent crime, for a long time the police entertained the theory that she might have done it herself. How bad must a ten-year-old's home life be if she commits suicide? That's the sort of question they ask you, and they treat you like a monster. They even look into whether the other two children are okay and whether they might not be better off in a foster family.'

'I can understand you're angry, Michelle.'

'No, after fourteen years, I'm not angry anymore. I'm just tired, in every respect. I always thought I'd want to look the killer in the eye and ask him why he took my girl. Now that I know Larissa was only one of many, just a child who happened to be in the wrong place at the wrong time, I realise I wouldn't get a satisfactory answer. They should put him away for the rest of his life so that more children don't die, nor their families in a different way.' She gives me a searching look. 'But it makes no difference if I tell you this or not. You can't understand it because you're not a mother. You only said you were one to get a job at Big Murphy's and wangle sympathy from your colleagues.'

I nod, embarrassed. Michelle's probably had enough of me being here so I've got to get more information out of her as quickly as possible. 'Do you think I could have a word with your ex-husband?'

'Rainer?' The noise she makes is something in between amusement and resignation. 'He's been drinking himself stupid these last few years. Every time the boys come back from him unscathed, I'm delighted. I'd happily give you his address. But I doubt you'll hear more from him than his absurd conspiracy theories about how sloppy the police were.' Getting up from the arm of the sofa, she goes over to a chest of drawers and takes out a notepad and pen.

'What about Marcus Steinhausen? The police file says he moved away, but doesn't give his new address.'

'No idea.' Michelle laughs. 'But I bet Rainer's got a few theories about that too.' She turns around and holds out a piece of paper with her ex-husband's address. But when I try to take it she doesn't let go. 'I don't want to condemn your father before he's found guilty, Ann. But if it was him who did it, he can only hope he's locked away for the rest of his life.'

Is that supposed to be a threat? I open my mouth, but don't have the courage to ask.

Then Michelle does let go and immediately gives me a hug.

'Be careful, girl,' she whispers in my ear. 'It's a dangerous world out there.'

US

Good morning, princess! Did you sleep well? I've been up a long time – I was tormented by a bad dream. I was running through the woods, looking for you everywhere. I was calling your name, so distraught that my voice cracked and tears were streaming down my face. I knew you just wanted to play hide-and-seek, but I couldn't find you until I came to a clearing. People were there, walkers and a hunter with a shotgun. They stood, heads bowed, in a circle around something. Around *somebody*. I knew at once that something bad must have happened, something to do with me. I pushed my way through the people and saw you there, lying on your back, arms outstretched like wings, your palms facing upwards. Your body was untouched and as beautiful as ever, but your eyes, princess. Your eyes were two black holes with worms crawling out of them. I sank to my knees. My tears ran and I touched my face. But they weren't tears, they were worms, like the ones on your face. I opened my mouth to scream, but no sound came out, only black butterflies. At this point I woke up. What was that, princess? A dark premonition? A warning? I realise more clearly now that we have to safeguard our happiness. I'm not going to let anything bad happen to you, do you hear me? Nobody's ever going to separate us again. Here, my sweetheart, take Cosmo and your fairy-tale book with the pretty pictures. That'll keep you occupied till I'm back. We'll do what we usually do when I leave the house: we'll lock you securely in your room and I'll take the key with me. It's better that way, sweetheart, you know that. We'll lock you away like valuable treasure in the safe. And you've got to be a very good girl, okay? I can't say how long I'll be. Or even if it'll work tonight. It's still Christmas, after all, when people stay at home playing families. Even those that aren't really proper families. Oh, they make me sick, I hate them so much! I'd rather not think about it as it only makes me furious. Can I have a cuddle? Yes, that's good – you see, I'm calming down already, I'm already feeling better. And maybe we'll be lucky, maybe it *will* work today. If it does, that's your Christmas present from me: your new best friend Sarah. Isn't it exciting? I just hope she's as well behaved as you when I get her. Just imagine if she started screaming and kicking because she wasn't so quick to understand how lucky she was. Yes, that would be a real shame, especially for her.

ANN

BERLIN, 26 DECEMBER 2017

We're on our way to Rainer Meller's place in Marzahn. Outside, the Landsberger Chaussee flies past, almost entirely swallowed up this morning by the grey fumes from laundry extractors. It's hard to identify the street signs, tower blocks and trees on either side of the road, and it's only possible at all if you're familiar with the area. It seems almost symbolic. Like my father's innocence, shrouded by a thick fog of prejudice, police ignorance and his own silence. But I know these streets and, more importantly, I know you, Dad. I know that the truth lies behind the fog.

'Marcus Steinhausen told Larissa he'd look after her.'

Eva sighs. 'My God, sounds like a total loser with an excessive longing for family.'

'Or a deranged paedophile!'

'The children weren't sexually abused.'

'That doesn't mean he didn't intend to when he kidnapped them!'

'Are you saying he then backs down because he thinks sexual abuse is a step too far? But murder isn't?'

I shake my head. 'Oh, I don't know. Let's just have a chat with Rainer Meller. Maybe we'll be wiser after that.'

'In three hundred metres you will have reached your destination,' the satnav announces, at which Eva slows down and searches for a parking space. I examine her profile. She looks like her mother, a slimmer, almost bony Elke Harbert, without pink blouse and pearl necklace, but with a paler complexion, hair dyed dark, and chewed fingernails. I wonder what it must be like to take after someone you despise. When every morning you see that person in your own reflection. And I think this is the case. If Eva wasn't pregnant and so didn't leave home for fear of her parents' reaction, it must have been Elke who drove her away. Elke and her obsession with cleanliness, her high demands, her plumped-up sofa cushions, her entire being which is nothing but a façade. I recall Eva once being grounded when we were in the sixth class because Elke thought she hadn't revised enough for an English test. Grounded for a whole week because she got a C. I rarely came home with better marks than this at the time, and my father would merely shrug.

'All school does is teach you to learn things by heart,' he said. 'What really counts is that you learn to think independently, to feel, to question things. Only then can you understand the world.'

I miss him so much.

'Can I ask you something, Eva?'

'Sure.'

'Why did you come back? Now, after so much time, to your . . .' I break off, out of politeness.

'. . . parents, who you basically can't stand?' Eva finishes my sentence, laughs, then at once turns serious again. 'Apart from

102

the fact that I'd read about your father's arrest in the paper, it would've been the first Christmas I'd have spent alone, after splitting up with Nico. The idea of it sort of gave me the creeps. It's ... you know, I haven't been feeling great these past few weeks. I have bad dreams, I'm permanently tense and nervous, I just can't relax anymore. I keep wondering whether it was right to have run off like that. Whether the path that seemed easier at the time turned out to be the harder one in the end.' She turns to me and looks sad. 'As for my parents, well, parents always try to do their best, but the best isn't always good.'

I nod; I feel sorry for Eva.

'How about you come along this time and we talk to Michelle's ex-husband together? It'll be like the old days. You and me ...'

'The best team,' she says, finishing my sentence and smiling. 'Why not?'

Apart from the colour – a dirty green – Rainer Meller's block is scarcely different from the building in Hellersdorf where he used to live with Michelle. An ugly box offering no more than functional living space. Here there's no playground, but a larger car park with tyre tracks snaking through the slush. For a public holiday it looks shockingly empty. This confirms my theory that people might live here, but they're never really at home. After ringing several times without any luck, we're about to turn back when a window opens on the third floor.

'What?' a man bleats down at us. It must be Rainer Meller, who even at a distance seems quite a bit older than Michelle. Either he *is* older, or he looks worn out from the worry of the past few years.

'Hello,' I reply, waving. 'Herr Meller? We've come from your ex-wife and we urgently need to talk to you. About' – I lower my voice because I think it's inappropriate to shout her name out here – 'Larissa.' For a second or two his expression freezes, then he slams the window. Defeated, I look at Eva, who raises her eyebrows and turns around when we hear a buzz: Rainer Meller has opened the door.

'Are you from the youth welfare office?' he asks as soon as we've got to the third floor.

'No,' I say, surprised.

'Police? Press?' Clamped between his fingers is a cigarette he must have just lit.

I shake my head and am about to explain, but Eva gets there first: 'We're private investigators and we've got a few questions.' I don't know what to make of this lie at first, especially as it seems so ridiculous and blatant. But then I see the enthusiasm in Meller's eyes and suspect that Eva has hit the right nerve to stir his readiness to talk.

'I knew it! Come in, come in,' he says excitedly, stepping aside for us.

Apart from the fact that the flat is very smoky, it's almost excessively tidy. The shoes form a guard of honour in the hallway, the coats hang from hooks at absurdly regular intervals and the lino, although it squeaks with every step, is shiny and neutralises the stale smoke with a strong smell of beeswax. Meller has a grey crew cut and an olive-green shirt with a stiff collar, which makes him look more like an army general reject than a construction worker. As we go down the hallway, we pass an open door giving on to a children's room. Michelle and Rainer Meller's two sons are sitting at a computer with their backs to us; I hear shooting and swearing. Their father shuts the door and shows us into the sitting room.

I'm dumbstruck. The furniture – sofa, coffee table and sideboard with a television on it – has all been pushed into a tiny corner, while the rest of the room is set out like a private detective's office from a cheap TV series. A computer monitor sits on a huge desk, beside it an opened bottle of schnapps. Stuck to the wall behind are countless newspaper articles and printouts of photos, some already slightly faded, as well as a spider's web of connections made from woollen threads, which at first glance look unfathomable.

'Shit,' Eva mutters quietly.

I nod.

The photos are blurry, but they all seem to be of the same man from a distance in a variety of situations: getting out of a car, entering a house, mowing the lawn, pushing an old lady's wheelchair, standing by a grave with his head bowed.

Meller doesn't bother with any preamble. 'Marcus Steinhausen, born 16 August 1971 in Beelitz.' He smiles, revealing teeth yellowed from nicotine. 'I knew one day someone would come help me convict him. I've tons of material about this wanker,' he says, making an extravagant gesture at the wall. 'And I also realised you wouldn't come until most of the donkey work was done. That's just what you cops are like, isn't it? You keep your arses stuck to your office chairs for as long as you can, but the moment things start moving, you can't wait to get in on the act. Just like the fucking papers. How often have I called up editors to tell them my latest discoveries? Either I'm told they'll only work with reliable information from the police, or they keep me hanging on until the line eventually goes dead.' He takes a nervous drag on his cigarette, then emits the smoke with a hoarse laugh. '*Reliable information!* All they care about is interviewing Saskia's dad! These days that bloke can turn on the waterworks at will!' Meller shakes his head in resignation, then his face at once brightens. 'But I knew it!'

Eva and I exchange uncertain glances. We're still flabbergasted by the set-up of this ludicrous detective agency and Meller's chutzpa. Eva's the first to snap out of it.

'What did you know?' she asks Meller, who's looking at us expectantly.

'Well, that poor bloke you've been dragging though the media these last few weeks is nothing but a fall guy, because you had to come up with someone to keep the public happy! But it wasn't him. No, it wasn't him and I knew that at once. One of those university eggheads! I've worked for blokes like that plenty of times. They can't even tie their own fucking shoelaces without looking at a book to see how it's done! And he's supposed to be a killer? Bollocks!' Now Meller shakes his head so vigorously that his whole body starts moving and the ash from his cigarette crumbles to the floor. He leaves the room as if slightly drunk, only to return immediately with a dustpan and brush.

Eva looks away when he bends down to clear up the ash, as if it's something very intimate she doesn't want to intrude on. 'But, as I'm sure you also discovered, there *are* leads that point to this man.'

'You call a few little coincidences leads?' Meller stands back up and with his foot clatters the dustpan and brush to one side, a noise that makes Eva spin around and grab my arm. The broad-chested

Meller towers before us, menacingly pointing his index finger. 'Look, what I showed you about Marcus Steinhausen – now *those* are leads! For fuck's sake, do you win your police badges in a lottery? How come your shitty outfit only seems to employ useless fuckers?'

'Once again, we're not from the police, we're private investigators,' Eva says firmly.

Meller looks at us as if this is the first time he's heard it.

'Who are you working for?' he asks, with narrowed eyes.

'I'm afraid we can't tell you that,' I chime in circumspectly. 'But you can be sure we're keen to find out the truth. Just like you.'

Meller holds up his thumb and forefinger, barely half a centimetre apart. 'I'm that close,' he growls, nodding to reinforce his claim. Then he goes over to the desk, unscrews the top from the schnapps bottle and takes a sip.

I look at Eva, who suggestively raises an eyebrow and nods at the sitting-room door. But I don't want to go. As strange as Meller is, I'm thrilled to have finally come across someone who shares my belief that Dad is innocent.

'That would mean that Marcus Steinhausen has given the police a number of false alibis,' I tell him.

'Couldn't be more false!' Meller says, wiping his mouth and putting the bottle back on the desk. 'Those so-called friends who've given him alibis – he's bribed them! I'm one hundred per cent certain of it! You see, one of the boys worked with us on the site. He was never friends with Marcus, he just kept borrowing money off him. Marcus had no friends apart from me!' He pounds his fist on his chest. 'I was his only friend! And how did he thank me?'

'Did you tell the police that he might have bribed the witnesses?'

'Of course! They questioned the guys on site too, but the wanker denied it all.'

Eva opens her mouth, but I get in first. 'Do you have an idea where we could find Marcus Steinhausen?'

Meller comes over to us. His face is contorted into a peculiar grin that makes me shudder. 'I told you I've already done most of the donkey work.'

RECORDING 02
Berlin, 7 May 2021

- I'd like to talk about Larissa Meller.
- Why her in particular?
- For two reasons. First, I met her mother, and so it feels – how should I put it? – personal. And then Larissa was the first. It's said that the first victim plays a special role for the killer.
- Is that so?
- It's proven, yes.
- (grins) What other clichés have you got up your sleeve? The killer who had a difficult childhood, a strict father or no father at all, an indifferent mother or a controlling one, and who started torturing small animals at primary school? A loner, always a bit odd, who later had problems with women. None would let him near them, but little girls couldn't defend themselves, he was able to dominate them.
- But that's often the case.
- (laughs) Tell me about your childhood.
- My . . . ?

- Why not? It doesn't look like we need to bother with my story. You seem to know it all already.
- No, I've just . . . I've looked into the topic and read up on it.
- I'm not a topic, I'm a human being, just like you.
- With respect, you can't compare us. It's never crossed my mind to abduct little girls, slit their wrists and watch them bleed to death.
- Have you read up on this too? What do you say to a bit of biology? The human body contains between three and seven litres of blood. If a person loses more than one and a half litres, they become weak, thirsty and start to freeze. At this point the loss of blood must be stopped or the brain won't get enough oxygen and the person will lose consciousness. Death occurs shortly afterwards. When exactly depends on how big the injured vessel is . . .
- I don't think I want to hear this.
- If the aorta is damaged, for example, it's often only a matter of seconds. It's more interesting when veins or smaller arteries are damaged. Then it can take hours.
- *(clears the throat)* Back to Larissa.
- Two hours and thirteen minutes.
- Jesus, I didn't mean that.
- I got used to timing it, you see? Some girls, even though they were younger, smaller or more delicate, took longer to die. This must have partly been down to the fact that the cuts I made were always slightly different. I mean, I'm no surgeon and I didn't have a scalpel either. All the same, an artery's an artery, you'd think. Anyway, I came to the conclusion that dying isn't just a physical process. Of course, when the body's started

dying, you can't stop it. But I often got the impression that internal resistance was definitely able to prolong the whole thing.

– And the sight of this – a defenceless girl struggling against death, all that blood – excited you?

– Excited? Good God, I beg you. I don't like the term, it always has a sexual connotation. And it's empty too, so empty that it doesn't even begin to express what I felt.

– What did you feel?

– Everything.

ANN

BERLIN, 26 DECEMBER 2017

That he's already done the donkey work.

What does that mean?

He couldn't tell us, he had to show us.

Okay.

We left the flat in Marzahn together with Rainer Meller. Beforehand, he told his two sons he had to go out for a while, and promised them pizza for lunch.

On the way to the stairs we don't speak. Meller's in front; behind him Eva and I go down side by side. I try to catch her eye a few times, but in vain. She looks withdrawn; perhaps like me she's pondering what Meller has said. That he's already done the donkey work. Surely all it means is that he's tracked down Steinhausen – address unknown – off his own bat. I know this, it's obvious. And yet I have to be careful not to form a picture in my mind showing Meller at night with a shovel, at his feet a hand sticking out of the dug earth begging for help and mercy. I know it's absurd and that I ought to be happy to have an important lead thanks to Meller. Marcus Steinhausen, the oddball who pretended to his closest friends that he had a wife and daughter, even though he still lived at home with his mother. Who bought himself alibis for good reason. Assuming, of course, what Meller told us is correct. Well, we're about to find out, and the mere thought of that makes me feel what could almost be described as elated. I still can't quite comprehend what lies ahead of us, but I sense we're on the right track. We follow Meller across the car park to his grey Volvo, a classic family car.

'In you get,' he says after unlocking the vehicle, and I'm just about to pull the handle of the passenger door when I feel Eva's hand on my arm.

'We'll follow you in our car, Herr Meller,' she asserts, pulling me along with her.

'Have you gone mad?' is the first thing I hear her say when we're in her Mini and she starts the engine. 'Were you seriously going to ride with that nutter?' The car sounds disgruntled when she brusquely puts it into reverse.

'It doesn't matter how we get to Steinhausen. The main thing is that we get there at all.'

'You're wrong, it does matter! Meller is a very sick man.' She guides the Mini to the car park exit behind Meller's Volvo and indicates. Right, although I only notice this when she turns the steering wheel to the right too.

'What are you doing?' I thrust my hands to the side, ready to steer the other way. Meller's Volvo turned left. Eva brakes so abruptly that the seat belt cuts through my thick jacket and into my chest. Deeply shocked, I let go of the wheel and point at the Volvo that stops by the side of the road a fair distance away. Meller must have seen in his mirror that we'd stopped. 'Drive! He's waiting!'

Eva shakes her head. 'No way are we wasting any more of our time with this guy. I could smell the booze on his breath when we arrived.'

I roll my eyes. 'For God's sake . . .'

'Come off it, how can you not see what his problem is? It's so obvious.'

'He wants to find out the truth, just like us! Honestly, Eva, what's wrong with you? We've finally got a lead and you want to pull out?'

'No, Ann, what the hell is wrong with *you*? What was it you told me about those photos at Michelle's? That she didn't take another one of her daughter after her school induction and had to ask her parents so she could give an up-to-date picture to the police? Do you want to know how I interpret that? I'll tell you. The moment Meller entered Michelle's life, Larissa was completely ignored. It's irrelevant that he adopted her after the wedding – she never got anything out of him except for his surname. Michelle and he had their fresh start as a couple, had their own child, the next was already on its way, and Larissa was merely a millstone around their necks. But then she was murdered and the two developed their own mechanisms for coping with their feelings of guilt. Michelle tries to function while Meller gets bogged down in completely fanciful theories . . . I mean, you were in that sitting room too! You saw the pinboard with the newspaper cuttings and that crazy web of woollen threads! And all the photos of Steinhausen! He's persecuted him!'

'And yet with all of this, he's got further than the police. He found out that Steinhausen had no alibi, but he did have a motive. Think about—'

'No, that's precisely it!' she interrupts me. 'He *thinks* he's found out that Steinhausen didn't have an alibi. Do you really believe the police wouldn't have checked it out in such a serious case? Meller's a serious alcoholic who suffers from delusions!'

'For a man who's so disturbed, it's astonishing how well he keeps on top of his flat, don't you think? Everything is clean and tidy, suggesting someone who's still got a hold on reality.'

'This outward obsession with order can also be an unconscious counter-mechanism.'

I burst out laughing. 'What are you now, a fricking psychologist?'

'Yes, Ann, that's exactly what I am!' Incensed, she slams the palm of her hand on the wheel, catching the horn. 'I spent eleven fricking semesters studying psychology! I did my fricking master's, and for the past few months, I've been working in the fricking psychological counselling centre for victims of crime and their relatives at Frankfurt University Hospital! I know people like Rainer Meller! I work with them on a daily basis! They look for their own ways to deal with the pain and feelings of guilt, and do you know what? Sometimes these ways lead them straight into the psychiatric clinic.'

I'm silenced. I stare at her, stunned. And somehow time stands still. It's as if Eva had punched me in the face without warning. This pale, thin girl with the chewed fingernails is apparently an expert, way ahead of me, still floundering in my fourth semester. In her analysis of the situation, in her knowledge – which with a CV like hers must be well-grounded – in everything, in fact. I feel small and betrayed once more. Time is moving again, trickling away in an embarrassing silence.

'Let's not argue,' Eva says eventually, her tone gentle. Then she gives a start and a curt scream. I flinch too. Rainer Meller is standing by the passenger door, peering in at us.

'Everything all right?' he asks, his voice muffled by the closed window.

We nod in sync.

'Let's be off, then!' he says impatiently. 'What are we still waiting for?'

Marcus Steinhausen is a gaunt type. Very different from the photos in Meller's sitting room, in which he looks healthy and well groomed. He has greasy, ash-blond hair that hangs in thin strands down to his chin. Hollow cheeks, pimply skin. Most striking of all are those dark, almost black, penetrating eyes. He's living back in the house in Lichtenberg he used to share with his mother. She's not there; she must be in a care home or dead. He doesn't seem happy to see us or Meller at his door, but he lets us in all the same. Eva and me, at least. He tells our escort, who's almost beaten him to death twice, to get lost. Meller's about to make a fuss, but Eva manages to calm him down. Of course she does, she's a psychologist, after all, and knows how to deal with relatives who are practically mad with rage and pain.

Now the two of us are in the sitting room, on armchairs upholstered in reddish-brown velvet, with crocheted cushions as headrests. More cushions on the tiled coffee table. The air is dusty and stale; it smells of an inability to shake off the past in the wake of a serious problem. Although his mother is no longer around, it seems as if Steinhausen doesn't dare change even the smallest thing here. We hear him clattering crockery in the kitchen. After inviting us to take a seat, he said he was going to make coffee.

Heavy, ruched curtains with a flowery pattern hang in front of the windows. They could be grey, beige or merely yellowed; it's impossible to tell because they're drawn and make the room so dark that, without the light from an ornate brass lamp on a small table, we wouldn't be able to see anything at all. After my eyes have become accustomed to the dimness, I allow my gaze to wander. It alights on a piano. I imagine Steinhausen taking lessons as a child, and his mother rapping him on the knuckles whenever he played a wrong note while practising. On top of the piano are photographs.

'Ann,' Eva hisses when I get up to take a closer look. 'Don't! He'll be back in a sec and think we're snooping around!' But that's exactly what we're doing, that's why we're here – so I ignore her warning.

The photos.

Two toddlers, on either side of their mother, holding her hand. One is Marcus Steinhausen, the other must be his brother. Michelle was right: they really do look similar. It's winter; they're wearing thick clothes and staring into the camera with serious, deadpan faces. The next photo is of the mother sitting stiffly in one of the armchairs, the headrest framing her head like a halo. Marcus and his brother, now teenagers, are on the armrests, again wearing those serious, careworn expressions that look as if they'd never experienced the slightest moment of joy or happiness. Another portrait of Frau Steinhausen on her own, sepia-toned and as if from a different time. And then another family photo, this time of the Mellers. Michelle and Larissa as I know them, but Rainer Meller's face has Steinhausen's stuck over it.

'Oh Jesus!' I splutter, and that's all I say because the pattern repeats itself: the next photo is of Larissa in the arms of a man whose face has also been replaced by Marcus Steinhausen's.

'Get away from there!' Eva sounds anxious. Without saying a word or turning around, I wave behind my back to get her to come over to the piano.

Now a photo of Larissa on her own. It looks like she's on holiday; she's wearing a bathing costume and holding an ice cream.

'Eva, you've really got to—'

A cough. A cough and someone's breath on the back of my neck. I recoil and spin around.

Right beside me is a grinning Steinhausen. 'Well, Ann. Find what you were looking for?'

I instinctively throw my hands up in defence.

Resounding laughter rains down on me, big hailstones of cold, biting sounds. 'You must know that old proverb? Curiosity killed the cat?'

I recoil again. 'What?'

'I asked if you knew the proverb.' Eva glances to the side. 'Curiosity killed the cat. It's what my grandma always used to say.' Feeling palpitations, I put a hand to my chest. No, we're not in Marcus Steinhausen's sitting room, we're still following Rainer Meller's Volvo. Although the journey did go via Lichtenberg, where Steinhausen used to live with his mother, we're now more than twenty kilometres away, and with every kilometre, I realise the horrific vision I've just fallen into is only getting crazier.

'All I'm saying,' Eva continues – she hasn't realised my imagination's been playing games with me – 'is that I've experienced this myself. Sometimes it's not a good idea to dig too deeply. It can change your entire life.'

I can't help laughing. 'I thought you were a psychologist? Isn't your entire profession all about digging as deep as you can?'

'Yes, but afterwards it's also our job to teach people how to deal with what they've found.'

'Really, Eva, I don't understand you. You stay up half the night with me, supposedly because you're as keen as I am on finding out the truth. But the moment things get serious and we actually have a lead, you suddenly start getting obstructive. What's that all about? What was yesterday for you? Just a game, like when we were kids and used to play detectives, following some mysterious animal tracks on the edge of the woods? Just a game to escape the boredom of your family dinner?'

Eva shakes her head and briefly takes a hand off the wheel to point at Meller's Volvo, which right now is taking the turn to Henningsdorf. 'We're going too far here. God knows where he's taking us.'

'You can offer to give him therapy when you get the chance. But before that let's see what he wants to show us.'

'A building site?' Stupidly, Eva blinks a few times, as if there were a chance her eyes were playing tricks on her. 'What on earth are we doing here?'

'That's what we're about to find out,' I say, annoyed. I unclick my belt before she parks the Mini beside Meller's Volvo at a construction fence, which separates the huge site on the southern fringes of Henningsdorf from the access road.

'Ann, please . . .' It sounds like she's imploring me, but I'm already out of the car. Behind the fence is a space, covered in snow, that ends in a huge crater. Around it are a handful of weather-beaten construction trailers, and behind them, the half-built shell of a tower block. I can't see a crane or any other construction machinery, but the walls of the shell are already covered in plenty of graffiti, some of which has already faded. Work seems to have stopped on this building site some time ago. Kati comes to mind. The nine-year-old girl whose body was found in a place just like this back in 2005. What was it Michelle said? *When, in 2005, the body of another small girl was found – as it happened, on a construction site where Rainer and Marcus had worked together a few years earlier – that was that, as far my husband was concerned. It couldn't be a coincidence.*

It couldn't be a coincidence echoes around my head.

Meller has come up to me. He's holding a torch. 'In 2000 they built a trading estate in the north of the city, but soon after the construction work began, it proved to be too small.' He nods at the huge area of wasteland, even more desolate beneath its covering of snow. 'Everything here was supposed to be bigger, more modern, but scarcely had we got going than we ran into problems with environmental protection. Apparently it's a nesting area for red kites, which was never on anyone's radar before . . . What's happened to your colleague?'

I follow his eyes to Eva's Mini. She's still sitting in the driver's seat. 'Hang on a sec.'

A moment later I'm knocking on the side window, while silently mouthing, 'Come on!' Eventually she gets out.

'I think this is the building site where Kati's body was found,' I whisper to her as we follow Meller, a few metres behind him. 'He hasn't said as such, but it would fit.'

'And what are we actually doing here?' Eva whispers back. 'Did he give you any idea when you were chatting just now?'

'No, but think about it. If this really is the building site in question, then perhaps Meller has belatedly discovered something else here to link Steinhausen to Kati's murder.' Although I'd been assuming that Meller would take us to Steinhausen, I'm happy to go along with this scenario if it helps exonerate my father.

'Mind how you go!' Meller calls out over his shoulder. 'There's all sorts of building rubble and metal bars lying around here that you can't always see because of the snow.'

I raise my hand to signal we understand.

'Where the hell is he taking us?' Eva whispers, but I can't answer that either.

Until we get to the shell.

Until, under Meller's supervision, we've squeezed through a makeshift entrance hung with a stubborn tarpaulin and made our way down what seems like endless corridors into the underground part of the building. Until we've arrived at a basement room sectioned off by another tarpaulin and also blocked by an upright old mattress. Until we enter the room and Meller waves around the torch he switched on to make it easier for us to find our way in the darkness down here.

Now we're hit by the realisation of where Meller has brought us: to the place he's keeping captive the man he believes killed his stepdaughter. To Marcus Steinhausen, who's sitting on a chair in the middle of the room. His hands are behind his back, probably tied to the chair, and his ankles secured to the legs. Marcus Steinhausen with a bloody gag in his mouth. The left-hand side of his face bruised and swollen around the eye. A scabbed-over cut on his forehead and brown stains on the inner thighs of his jeans. All of this makes it obvious that he must have been down here at Meller's mercy for a fair while. He lifts his head feebly and blinks lethargically with his sunken eye into the torch beam.

Eva clutches my arm. I look at her, she looks back, her eyes wide in horror and her mouth agape, speechless. I freeze – my heart has stopped beating and I'm no longer breathing. This can't be true, it's fake. Reality has been ruptured and I'm just having a bad dream, like I did in the car earlier.

Light!

We jump when the room is abruptly flooded with brightness. Meller has switched on a construction lamp that hangs by a long cable from one of the metal ceiling girders. As it swings it makes a freaky interplay between light and shadows. Rumbling and buzzing at the back of the room, a box has come to life. It looks like an outsized chainsaw, only without the blade – a generator, I assume. To our left another chair is against the wall, an empty half-litre bottle of cola on the seat and a pizza box on the floor beside it. I try to picture Meller sitting on this chair opposite Steinhausen, enjoying his pizza in front of a man who's been going mad with hunger and thirst down here for God knows how long. But I can't. Not even my imagination, which effortlessly concocted the horror story of the doctored family photos for our meeting with Steinhausen, is capable of that.

'Right then, ladies.' Meller's voice drones over the hum of the generator. 'Let's get this fucker to talk.' He checks the pockets of his anorak in turn, but evidently doesn't find what he's looking for. 'Shit. I'll be right back.' Before we can react, he's left the room.

Steinhausen is writhing in his chair. Although the sounds he's making are muffled by the gag, he's clearly panicking. It seems as if he knows the fate that's awaiting him. Eva comes to her senses first. Letting go of my arm, she hurries over to Steinhausen. It's only when I realise she's trying to untie his hands that I shudder and follow her to have a go at the cable ties binding his ankles to the legs of the chair. My fingers are sweaty and shaky, and the acrid smell of all the excretions that have collected in his trousers makes me turn away briefly every few moments. The teeth of the cable ties are still not budging.

'I can't do it, Eva! I can't get him free!'

'You have to, for fuck's sake.' I don't know whether that's aimed at me or her, now that she's likewise realised we need some scissors or a knife to set Steinhausen free. The fact that neither of these are to hand has an even more unthinkable implication: any minute Meller will be back and then we'll have to watch him . . .

I pause in my thoughts.

Steinhausen, who may be the reason why my father's in prison, being presented to all the world as the ribbon murderer.

'Ann!' Eve must have noticed my hesitation. As has Steinhausen, who also realises that time's running out, and now that my hands have stopped fiddling with the cable ties has started waggling in his chair and shouting louder into the gag.

'No chance without scissors,' I say, slowly getting up again to remove the gag, which is sodden with blood, snot and spit.

'I'm calling the police!' Eva says, whipping the phone out of her coat pocket.

Steinhausen gasps for air like a fish out of water. His top lip is swollen and sore, his bottom one seems to be one big scab. 'Thanks,' he mutters, barely intelligibly.

'No reception down here!' Eva.

'Is it true?' Me.

Steinhausen blinks with one eye; I look at him as if he were a work of abstract art. He's no longer the gaunt man from my vision with straggly longish hair and penetrating black eyes. He looks like he does on Meller's photos: shockingly normal. A perfectly normal, nondescript man with short blond hair and freckles beneath the swollen eyes that almost make him appear friendly.

'I'll try upstairs!' Eva says, running past us. Now we're alone, Steinhausen and I.

'Is it true?' I repeat, more insistently this time.

He cries, he begs. 'Please . . . home . . . my wife . . . daughter . . .'

Before I've formulated my next thought, my hand shoots forwards and catches him flat on his left ear.

Steinhausen howls.

'You're lying even now?' I hate the way my voice is quavering. How it betrays my uncertainty and my horror that I've just slapped a man that someone else has already beaten half to death. My left ear begins burning too, like a phantom pain; it's probably the shame. I've crossed a boundary – I'm no better. Eva is better than me, Eva's doing the right thing. She's calling the police, who'll come and arrest Meller and rescue Steinhausen. The police, who'll no doubt allow him to roam free while they keep sinking their teeth into my father instead.

Steinhausen mumbles something, but I don't hear him. I hear my father, who can sense my dilemma and is trying to reassure me.

'You're a good person, Beetle.'

Am I, Dad? Am I still a good person if I want a little more time alone with Steinhausen before the police arrive?

'You can forget that!' I'm rattled by the thunder of Meller's

123

voice. When I turn around he's pushing Eva back into the cellar room. He's confiscated her mobile and an iron bar is wedged in the crook of his arm. Eva stumbles over to me. 'Your colleague felt it was her duty to call the cops to – how did she put it? – *protect a badly injured, innocent man from rash behaviour on my part.*' He spits out a beastly laugh. 'And of course to protect me from myself!' Taking hold of the iron bar, he brandishes it in our direction like a dagger. 'No effing way!' His eyes move from me to Eva, they fix on her as he flings the mobile phone to the floor, where it shatters noisily. 'Did you hear me? It's neither your duty nor your fucking right! This here is my mission, mine and mine alone!'

Eva raises and lowers her hands gently, as if trying to tame a crazed animal. 'Herr Meller, the police will be here soon . . .'

'No,' the animal growls. 'I'm not going to let you fuck everything up when I'm so close.' With the iron bar he forces us into the far corner of the room, while Steinhausen starts yelling for help. Meller drops the bar and lands a punch on his chin. Everything inside me winces – since my car accident a couple of years ago I know what a jaw breaking sounds like. Tiny drops of blood fly as if in slow motion, a fine spray that looks black in the makeshift light of the construction lamp. Steinhausen's head flops limply on to his left shoulder. An overpowering silence grips the room, the unspoken question being if Steinhausen is unconscious.

He is – in the best-case scenario.

And maybe he is. Meller makes sure by grabbing Steinhausen's hair, yanking his head back and putting his hand under his nose to check for breathing.

He definitely is, thank God; Meller nods at us.

'I've put this fucker in hospital twice already,' he says. 'And

I went down for it. Six months the first time – utter nonsense. The judge realised my head was a fucking mess and so accepted there were extenuating circumstances. But when I got out I saw Steinhausen was behaving as if nothing had happened. He was still living in Lichtenberg, going to work, cutting the hedge, pushing his mother around in a wheelchair.' I think of the photos on Meller's pinboard, showing Steinhausen in different everyday situations; they might date from this time. 'Then little Kati was killed – here!' Meller opens out his arms. 'I tried to beat the truth out of him, but the problem was, I was just a touch too keen. A few kicks and the tosser had a fractured fucking skull. Which meant he was back in hospital and I was back in the nick. Five years this time, no more mercy from the judge. So I was inside when Steinhausen came out of rehabilitation. He made use of his chance and did a runner. But not only that!' I see blobs of spittle fly from his mouth. 'Or don't you think it's strange that no children were kidnapped while this wanker was in hospital, licking his wounds? I read the paper every day when I was banged up – nothing! No children murdered when he was out of action! Am I meant to believe that's a coincidence?' He shakes his head and I copy him, as if hypnotised. 'At any rate, for years after I came out, I couldn't for the life of me find out where he was. But then, a few weeks ago, his mum died and I knew that now, now he'd come back like the dutiful son he is . . .' Meller is a wild beast, prowling around this basement room as if he were cooped up in a cage. He moves from left to right and from right to left, menacingly entranced, describing how Steinhausen lurked at the funeral. He photographed that too, I realise. Steinhausen standing beside his mother's grave. But this time he intended to be smarter, Meller continues. Instead of nabbing Steinhausen at the cemetery, he followed him to his new home. 'He was awarded compensation for his injuries – a tidy sum. His lawyer was a real crafty bugger. Together with the money he had already put aside, the fucker was now able to afford a fancy bungalow in the leafy suburbs! And there's me in my shitty little room in Marzahn, agonising over what had happened to Larissa.' He spent days watching Steinhausen, driven by a vague hunch that something was about to happen, something fateful, something incontrovertible. 'And it did happen.' Meller breaks off abruptly and gives us a triumphant look. 'One morning I followed him to a primary school. It was 22 December, the last day before the Christmas holidays. He was hanging around the playground, ogling a group of little girls while they were having a snowball fight. They were laughing, giggling. Alive.' His face darkens. 'For now.'

He doesn't have to say any more. Both Eva and I know this was the moment when Meller pounced, overwhelmed Steinhausen and dragged him to this basement.

'Originally I was going to take him to the hut by the Weihenpfuhl, but the terrain there's so rough that I couldn't have driven with Steinhausen in the boot. And nobody ever strays out here.' His gaze sweeps the room, coming to rest on Steinhausen, who's still unconscious. 'I would have already finished the job, but it's Christmas and I've got my boys to think of.'

I look to the floor in embarrassment when I grasp another piece of the puzzle that is the Meller family tragedy. A father who, by all appearances, is devoted to solving the death of his stepdaughter, and yet interrupts this – his most important mission – to offer some normality to his sons, at least at Christmastime.

'What? Why are you gawping like that?' Meller's voice

thunders like a sudden storm. I frantically wipe my eyes. 'I've treated the tosser far better than he deserves!' In a flash he's hurried over to a canister beside the entrance, which I hadn't noticed before. He's jittery as he turns the red screw top, and then he empties the contents in Steinhausen's face. As if on cue, Steinhausen comes to, flouncing and gasping in panic, like a drowning man.

'It's true, isn't it, Marcus?' Meller says, bending down to Steinhausen. 'I've treated you far better than you deserve during your little stay down here. But now's the time to put an end to the Christmas charity.' Dropping the canister, which clunks on the floor, he stands up and takes a mobile out of his jacket coat pocket. This must be why he left the basement earlier: he'd forgotten his mobile. Which he now needs – 'Showtime, arsehole!' – to record Steinhausen's confession. 'And you're going to tell all, every little detail. About what you did to Larissa and all those other girls. And why . . .' All of a sudden he starts shaking; first just his shoulders, then his entire body is quivering with pain. 'Why?' he repeats. A *why* which this time seems to be referring only to his stepdaughter and perhaps is questioning more than just the murder itself. Why did it get to that stage? Why didn't he look after Larissa more when she was still alive?

'. . . It . . . it . . . wasn't . . . wasn't . . . me . . .' Steinhausen mumbles with his badly swollen lip, then howls. This only gets Meller more worked up. Slipping the mobile back into his coat pocket, he bends down to pick up the metal rod.

Eva takes a pace forwards; I hold her back. Meller isn't going to kill Steinhausen. He only wants answers. Just like us.

He takes a swing.

No, he's not going to kill him, absolutely not, no way. Not even here, in this strange space where reality has sprung a leak.

The rod swishes through the air.

Meller's bluffing. Just before the metal comes into contact with Steinhausen's skull and shatters it, he'll stop – I'm sure about that.

And I'm right.

Meller doesn't kill Steinhausen.

He kills Eva.

RECORDING 03
Berlin, 7 May 2021

– You must have wondered about killing at some time or other.

– Of course. That's why I'm asking you about your emotions. I can imagine that you sort of – how can I put it? – get into a different state of mind. A kind of intoxication, ecstasy. And fury, fury must be in the mix too, because you need strength to kill like you did. Either fury or a profound conviction. Something, at any rate, that gives you this strength.

– Hmm. I think it's more likely the latter. I'm not an angry person. How about you? Do you have angry outbursts?

– I can get angry, sure. I mean, everyone does, don't they?

– Not me.

– Maybe you just don't realise it.

– That's possible. *(grins)* But, to be honest, it didn't require that much strength, at least not to overpower the girls. They were in a state of total shock. My attacks came as such surprises that very few of them put up anything like resistance. I threw them to the ground and sat on them, clamping their arms with

my knees. That's not hard when their bodies are so small and
delicate. Only the cuts required a bit of strength, that's true.
Human skin is very elastic. It's like pigs' skin, did you know that?

– Yes, I think I've heard that before.

– Indicative, isn't it? Humans, pigs. Continue.

– Continue?

– What do you imagine it's like to kill? Come on, make a bit of an
effort!

– Well, I assume it might have something to do with power too?
That . . . oh, I don't know, you feel like God when deciding about
another person's life?

– Careful, you're slipping into cliché now.

– Isn't it right what I'm saying?

– Is that how it would be for you? Would you like to play God for a
time?

– Not in this way, no. *(clears throat)* Can we talk about Larissa now?

– In a minute. There's one thing I'd like to know first. Who would
you kill if you knew there would be no consequences . . . ?

– I don't think—

– Come on, be bold. You've got a free pass.

– Do you want to hear me say I'd kill *you*? Make me realise that
everyone's capable of murder? That's ridiculous.

– It is. Particularly as I wouldn't have to make you realise it, you
know it yourself. And you feel caught out. I can see it in your
face and in the way you're clenching your fists. Are you here
because of the murders? You want to know how and why it all
happened? You've had so much time to prepare for me – and
what do you do? You get distracted and ruffled like a little girl.
Like *those* little girls. How did the killer manage to keep abducting

129

children without anyone noticing? I'll tell you: just like that! I didn't have to go hunting children, I could pluck them like apples from a tree. Be friendly, tell them a story or promise to buy them an ice cream or show them a special place. You distract people by giving them your undivided attention, making them feel that everything is about them. Some people are flattered, others unsettled, but either way it always leads to the goal.

– How did you lure Larissa?

– Larissa? With an excursion. I told her I was going to the Weiher but couldn't remember the way. She agreed to show me and asked if we could take her bike. You see, she didn't dare ring the bell at home to put it in the hall, as her mother was just having a siesta. But she didn't want to leave it outside, either, because her old one had recently been stolen, which got her into big trouble with her stepfather. Poor girl.

– A poor girl you took advantage of.

– I see it differently.

– How?

– Give and take. We helped each other.

– Are you trying to suggest that you did the girl a favour by killing her?

– For heaven's sake, what a silly thing to say. I'm sure she would have liked to go on living if she'd had the choice. But . . . are you all right? You look a bit pale and we haven't even started talking properly yet.

– It's fine, no problem.

– Are you sure? Okay. Then give me your left hand.

– My . . . ? What for?

– You wanted to know everything in detail, didn't you?

ANN

BERLIN, 26 DECEMBER 2017

I'm acquainted with death. I've seen its workings a few times. It launched a ruthless attack on my mother's face, twisting her eyeballs upwards and wrenching open her mouth into an eternal, silent scream. It came for my grandfather while he was asleep; he was still smiling as if he'd just had a lovely dream. My uncle, who died of a brain aneurysm, looked surprised, as if he couldn't believe it. Nine girls, mercifully from photographs only, who the killer left behind as if they were dolls fallen from a shelf; and Larissa, who was no longer recognisable. Now death has taken possession of Eva's body. She's lying on the cold concrete floor of this basement, her limbs contorted, her head in a pool of blood. Her eyes are closed as if in a slumber; they won't open no matter how firmly I grip her shoulders, no matter how loud I scream. Death is limp, heavy and ungainly. It's a whooshing in my head, like the roar of a waterfall. It's a room that starts turning, slowly at first, then faster and faster; it's a carousel and I can't see where to get off. It's a siren wailing in the distance, which against the roaring waterfall only creeps into my numbed consciousness as a muffled sound. It's a sudden commotion in the basement: people, voices, someone pulling me away from Eva. She was the one who made the emergency call before Meller caught her with the mobile and forced her back down here. Now she's dead. Dead. Slain by Meller when she tried to stop him attacking Steinhausen with the metal rod. Someone grabs my arm and asks if I'm all right, if I'm injured too. I can't reply, I'm breathing as if through a straw, I stare and pant until everything blurs. Death lays two delicate little butterflies on my eyelashes, which flutter until I finally give in and shut my lids. Then I'm away, swallowed by a kind, empty blackness, and I thank death for this at least.

Shock. (Ann, 8 years old)

When you have a shock its like when something is switched off for a bit like a mixer or some other machine. Nothing works anymore, you cant move and you cant think either. Maybe your trembling but you dont notice it. A shock is normally bad but sometimes it isnt. Because there are moments when you woud rather not feel anything. You just have to watch out the shock doesnt last too long or too many feelings get stuck inside you and you get blocked up or explode.

I'm sitting in a row of hard chairs with brown, washable vinyl covers, my head leaning against a white wall, gazing up at the cold light of the neon tubes. My nostrils are irritated by the acrid smell of disinfectant; I try my best to breathe deeply and calmly. Even though I'd rather scream. Grab one of these fricking washable chairs and smash it against the fricking white wall until it shatters and splinters, until paint and concrete crumble, raging until I collapse with exhaustion, back into another restorative blackness. And when I wake up again, none of this will have happened, everything will have merely been a bad dream. Breathe, breathe, breathe. Drawing my knees up on to the seat, I close my eyes. Bad idea; behind my closed lids is Eva's lifeless body, her head in a pool of blood. Stop it! I chide myself. She's alive, she is alive! Her heart is beating as it ought to and the doctors have said that this sort of coma is perfectly normal with a serious traumatic brain injury. She might wake up in the next few hours. They told me I should call someone and get them to pick me up. But I don't want to leave. I want Eva to sense I'm here. She can, can't she? I'm sure she can.

Steinhausen's being treated somewhere in this building too. I know nothing about his condition and whether he might have more injures than the ones I could superficially see in the basement. Nor do I know if the police have already questioned him about what happened, the circumstances surrounding events and, if so, how fruitful this was. I'm not under any illusion that the police will get more out of him than Meller, whose interrogation technique consisted of fists and a metal rod. No, Steinhausen will keep his mouth shut – especially now that he's safe. And there's nothing I can do about it. Even if I found out which ward and room he's in, he'd only have to press the patient bell and I'd be carted away before I'd uttered a word. And what should I say to him anyway? What could I threaten him with to make him talk? I've got nothing. My only chance is to beg the police to check Steinhausen out again without appearing like a demented Rainer Meller.

My mobile buzzes. In a better reality my father would have sent me a message now: *Just stay where you are. I'm on my way, my Beetle.* I've no idea why I check, even though I know it can't be from him. It's only the notification that my battery is almost empty. And something else that I missed earlier: an unread message from this morning. From Zoe of all people: *Nice of you to get in touch. I often wonder how you are. I'm fine. Do you remember . . .* Zoe, who was desperate to do a term abroad in Cornwall. A few days ago she was accepted. *It worked! PS, I miss you too.*

My fingers twitch over the keyboard. Zoe is going away – that's a painful thought. Although as far as I'm concerned, Zoe's already been far away for much longer.

'Ann!' The voice cuts cleanly down the length of the corridor. I leap up from my chair. Elke and Caspian Herbert come rushing towards me. What the hell happened? How the hell could it have happened? Elke, whose forceful grip on my arm I can feel all the way to my bones even through Dad's thick jacket. Her face, which has dropped in shock, her skin like a balloon emptied of air, and white, so white, almost as white as the walls here in the corridor of the neurological intensive care unit. In contrast to her eyes, which are huge, piercing and streaked with entire networks of red veins. Beside her stands the empty shell of Eva's father, Caspian. He doesn't blink, just stares at me with equally red eyes and a half-opened, speechless mouth.

'What did you drag our daughter into?' Elke says, shaking me; I don't resist. It doesn't matter that it was Rainer Meller wielding the metal rod, hitting Eva by accident. All that counts is that she was only in that basement because of me. 'Look me in the eye!' I can't. My gaze sticks to the lapel of her purple woollen coat, and the fact that she hasn't buttoned it up correctly is a further reminder of the enormity of the situation. Elke, who's always so perfect and who would never, ever step out of the house so sloppily. Unless she got a phone call from the hospital urging her to come at once because something bad had happened to her daughter.

Unable to bear it any longer, I wriggle free and run down the corridor to the lift. I hammer the button, wait impatiently for the ding and squeeze myself into the cabin before the door has fully opened, obstructing those who are trying to get out. They grumble and curse but I don't care; I simply have to get away from Eva's parents, I need to get out of here, I want to go home. But not even this will be granted to me, it seems; the taxi stand outside the hospital entrance is empty. Just like my phone battery. I wait a while for a cab to arrive, but the driver won't take me, saying someone else has booked him. 'Public holiday,' he explains curtly with a shrug. I've got no option but to go back into the hospital and ask if they can call me a taxi.

I join the queue of those waiting at reception. I'm nervous; I have to get back home before I completely lose it and break down howling.

'Stop fidgeting!' the woman in front of me hisses. It takes me a second or two to realise that she's not talking to me, but the little girl beside her who keeps tugging at the sleeves of her coat.

'Why can't we go to the playground, Mummy?'

'Oh, Amelie, it's all wet because of the snow. Anyway, we have to ask about Daddy first,' the woman explains, breathing a sigh of relief when the receptionist becomes free. My nose begins to run; everything is coming at once, liquefying. I never had a mother I could annoy. I only ever had my dad. I'm the girl with more than three hundred meaningless telephone numbers on my mobile. The girl who had her best friend back for a brief moment. Eva, who from the outset didn't want us to follow Meller on to the construction site. Eva, who even tried to dissuade me.

Putting my hand over my mouth, I start panting. I need a taxi as soon as possible. I'm pushing forwards, ignoring the blue tape stuck to the floor to safeguard confidentiality. Soon I'm so close to the mother–daughter team that the woman would be able to feel my breath on the back of her neck if she wasn't wearing a thick scarf. And then I hear it. 'My name is Steinhausen. I'd like to know which ward my husband's on.'

The ground opens up, the hole is deep and black. I plummet for a while, then the impact makes me realise what a Frau Steinhausen asking after her husband means. It means that Marcus Steinhausen was telling the truth in the basement earlier.

Please . . . home . . . my wife . . . daughter, I hear him in my mind, before I slapped him for these very words. *You're lying even now?*

I can't believe how readily I let Meller's delusions influence me. It didn't occur to me for even a second that Steinhausen, who'd always wanted his own family, might have actually acquired one in the meantime. And yet the assaults by Meller, both of them life-threatening, could easily have provided him with the long-awaited reason to finally cut ties with his mother and embark on a new life. Eva was right: I'm no better than the people who homed in on my father. Steinhausen is innocent. The lead I thought I had never actually existed.

Electricity shoots through my body and my legs blunder in the direction of the exit. I don't want a taxi anymore, I just want to get out of here, fast. I don't even mind walking, running until my body collapses.

'Amelie, wait!'

Steinhausen's daughter steps into the revolving door alongside me, then leaps out and makes for the playground that is to
the left. The girl's mother comes storming out behind her a few
seconds later. 'Not on the slide, Amelie! It's full of snow! If you're
wet, they won't let us see Daddy!'

I stop and watch the two of them. And then, without knowing
why, I follow them. Perhaps it's my bad conscience. Perhaps I do
after all want to be slightly different from those I despise for their
prejudice. Maybe I want to do something right, at least one thing
on this day that feels so totally wrong. 'Excuse me?'

The woman turns around. I put her in her mid-forties, about
as old as Michelle. A few grey strands stick out from her lush,
dark-brown hair, as if they'd gone astray. She looks friendly, but
very tired too. 'Yes?'

'I couldn't help overhearing that you're the wife of Herr
Steinhausen.'

'I'm Susanne Steinhausen, yes,' she says warily. I don't look
like a hospital employee coming to tell her she can see her husband now.

I point to the hospital behind me. 'My name is Ann. I was
there when it happened to your husband. At the construction
site, I mean . . .'

'What?' The woman's eyes grow large.

'It's thanks to my friend Eva that your husband . . .' I break
off when I see Frau Steinhausen's eyes well with tears. Like Elke
and Caspian, she is another of those people who've had to take
a call today that they'd rather not have received. 'Is he in a very
critical condition?'

'He's out of danger, but . . .' She shakes her head. 'Andreas and

I were going to get a divorce. Ever since I moved out in summer we've done nothing but argue. About money, about the house and especially about our youngest daughter.' She nods towards the little girl, who's sweeping snow from the swing. 'Had he died today, it would have meant that I'd had a really bad go at him the last time I ever saw him. And yet we used to love each other so much.'

I awkwardly put out my hand and pat her arm. 'Maybe this is a good day to make peace.' I smile – and then it hits me. 'Andreas?'

The wife looks confused.

'Your husband?'

'Andreas is my husband, yes.'

'Not Marcus? Marcus Steinhausen?'

'No, my husband is Andreas.' Now she's sounding impatient. 'Marcus is his brother.'

'His . . .' The machinery inside my head is finding it hard to get into gear; small, rusty wheels turn slowly, clattering like an old clock. Brothers who look so similar that Marcus could even show Michelle, who knew him well, a photo of Andreas with his family without her noticing the difference. Brothers so similar that Meller didn't doubt for a second he'd grabbed the right man from the school playground. Andreas Steinhausen, who was probably only there to pick up his little daughter Amelie. I imagine him not having a clue what's going on to begin with, then trying to persuade Meller he's made a big mistake. But Meller's so delirious that he's not listening. He keeps pummelling his fists into the face of the man he believes to be his stepdaughter's killer, until Andreas Steinhausen is barely able to speak anymore.

Once again I reach out for his wife's arm, not to comfort

her this time, but in my own self-interest, to keep me on my feet when the cogs inside my head finally creak into place. If Andreas Steinhausen is the patient in this hospital, then Marcus Steinhausen is still out there somewhere. Unscathed, at liberty and possibly guilty of ten murders.

Am I all right?

Am I feeling sick?

Do I need to sit down?

I'm not saying anything, I'm just swaying, reeling, gaping. Frau Steinhausen takes the initiative. She summons her daughter from the swing, links arms with me and takes me back inside, to the café, where she finds us a table by the window. Maybe she thinks the view of the snowy park will soothe me, or at least it can't do any harm.

'I'll be right back,' she says to both me and her daughter, who sits opposite me and is allowed to play with her mum's mobile until she comes back. I don't realise how overtly I'm staring at the child until she looks up and waves the screen in front of me with a smile. A masked cartoon girl in a ladybird outfit is swinging across the roofs in Paris.

'Do you want to watch? That's Marinette. She's a superhero, but nobody knows that because she's still at school.' I shake my head. As if offended by my ignorance, Amelie sticks out her tongue, gets up from her chair and immediately sits down again at the neighbouring table, her back turned. I gaze out of the window and think of Eva. Of how everything can change in a matter of seconds. And how absurd it is that the life you know and utter chaos are often separated by a mere breath.

'Here we are,' Frau Steinhausen says, placing a tray on the

table. Hot chocolate for her daughter, tea for her and a cola for me, to get my circulation going again. I'm so overwhelmed by her kindness that I almost start to cry. But I can't; I have to pull myself together. She's Marcus Steinhausen's sister-in-law and might be able to help me. I say the first thing that comes into my head: 'I think my father's in prison because of Marcus.' That's unfortunate and ill-considered of me, because of course now she's going to start asking questions. What's my father in prison for? What exactly is he accused of? What do I think Marcus did?

But there's nothing. No curiosity, no eyes wide in astonishment. Only: 'I'm not surprised.' She asks the girl to give her the mobile – 'Just for a bit,' as she assures the protesting child – and shows me photographs from their last family holiday on the Baltic. Andreas, her and two of their three daughters, the younger two. 'Look, Amelie, do you remember?' she asks the girl, but Amelie's sulking.

I can understand Frau Steinhausen. She can't wait to be let in to see her husband so she can tell him that the last six months aren't important. I'm envious of her for this, the chance to simply wipe the past half year from the table like a careless mess.

'Frau Steinhausen,' I say, to get her attention.

'Hmm?' She looks up. 'Oh yes, I'm sorry. Here, Amelie,' she says, giving her the mobile back.

'But that's not all,' I continue, earning a frown from her. 'I mean that my father's in prison because of Marcus. All that stuff only happened to your husband because somebody mistook him for Marcus.' Leaning into her, I lower my voice. 'You must've heard of the ribbon murders?'

She nods, perplexed.

'The stepfather of one of the victims is convinced that Marcus is the ribbon murderer.'

'And that's why he . . . Andreas . . . ?' Shocked, she slaps a hand over her mouth. 'Oh my God.'

'Could you tell me something about him? Please, Frau Steinhausen. Just like your husband, my father is the victim of a mix-up, and all of this is only because—'

'Of him?' Frau Steinhausen says, narrowing her eyes – a look of incredulity and why not? First the thing with her husband and now me, a complete stranger who's appeared out of the blue, accusing her brother-in-law of multiple murders. I can see her mind working away, wondering if all this is really happening. It's a feeling I know only too well.

'Frau Steinhausen, I know this might sound totally absurd and—'

She interrupts me with a heavy sigh. 'Or maybe not. You know . . .' She rubs her brow. 'When I think about it . . . oh God. Basically this man only ever caused trouble.' I give her a moment to collect herself. 'Andreas is just a year older than Marcus,' she says eventually. 'But as their father died when they were young, he was everything to Marcus: brother, father, a role model in every respect. People often think they're twins, although—'

'Look!' Amelie squeals. Her chair scrapes noisily across the tiled floor of the café when she leaps up. In a flash she's standing beside me, holding the mobile so close to my face that my vision goes blurry. 'That's Adrien. He's a superhero too, just like Marinette, but she doesn't realise even though they're best friends. Silly, isn't it?' She grins at me. 'Surely you'd notice that!'

'Amelie!' her mother says sternly. 'Leave the woman alone and sit back down in your chair.' We wait until Amelie obeys.

'Twins,' I say, reminding Susanne Steinhausen of what she was saying before we were interrupted.

She shakes her head. 'Utter nonsense. Yes, they do look similar, but that's mainly because Marcus always copied Andreas. Whatever haircut Andreas had, Marcus had his done the same way. Clothes, even some gestures and his laugh – Marcus seemed to imitate everything.'

'Wow, that's—'

'Creepy? Sure is. In the early days of my relationship with Andreas, I didn't take it so seriously, but increasingly it became a problem. It was like Marcus was studying him. Marcus was always there! Wherever we went, he wanted to be with us. If he knew we were going out to dinner, he'd suddenly appear at the restaurant and join us as if we'd arranged to meet there. Or at the cinema. It got especially bad after the birth of our first daughter. By then we had our own house, but he came to visit all the time and meddled in our life. Once I found him carrying the screaming baby on his arm, patting her back and saying something like, "It's okay, Daddy's here." *Daddy!* Can you imagine?' Yes, I can, because I've heard a similar story from Michelle, albeit not so extreme. 'It got to the point where enough was enough, as far as I was concerned. I realised that my husband, as the big brother, felt responsible for him. And that he had a bad conscience because Marcus looked after their mother on his own. But it couldn't go on like that. Eventually Andreas agreed to move, to Potsdam at least. That was far enough away to stop Marcus from turning up on the doorstep every day. As time went on, he did in fact come less often, but I expect that was because he'd found a girlfriend.'

'A girlfriend?' I almost knock my cola over in excitement.

'Yes. What was her name again?' Frau Steinhausen hesitates. 'Oh, it doesn't matter. I don't suppose they're still together anyway – I mean, it was ages ago.'

'Are you saying you haven't had any contact with Marcus for a long time?'

'Not for years, no. I do know he spent some time in rehabilitation. Then he put my mother-in-law in a care home and vanished. We couldn't even get in touch with him about the funeral because we didn't have an up-to-date phone number for him.' She clasps her cup with both hands and stares at her tea in silence for a few seconds. 'To be honest, it never occurred to us to look for him. We were glad to be rid of him.'

'But do you have an idea of where he might be? Even an inkling?'

When she looks up, her cold eyes pierce me. 'He's a rat. And rats always find holes to crawl into.'

I nod. Marcus Steinhausen, the rat. The monster. I thank his sister-in-law and say goodbye, but not without first giving her my telephone number, which she punches straight into her mobile. In case she thinks of anything else that might be of use to me. This happens far more quickly than expected – as I'm walking out of the café.

'Ann!' she calls out behind me. I turn around and wander back. 'It began with M. Melanie, Manuela . . .'

I shrug; I've no idea what she's getting at.

'The name of his girlfriend!' she explains. 'I remember now. It began with M.'

'M?' I gasp. No way. That can't be true. I ask to borrow Susanne Steinhausen's mobile, which forces her to engage in another little battle with Amelie, who's still watching her video. The child only relents with the promise of an ice cream. I start by going on the internet. Because my battery's empty I can't access my phone book, and I don't know Ludwig's number off by heart. The landline at his home address is unknown; he must have disconnected it seeing as he spends most of his time as a gentleman of independent means in Poland. But there is an entry under the name of his housekeeper, who still works sporadically for him when he's staying at his old place in Berlin, like now. Her husband answers, then passes me to her, who's known me for years – little Anni, how lovely to get a Christmas call from you. She asks how I am, but I don't have time for small talk, especially as I don't want to spend too long using someone else's phone. I ask her for Ludwig's mobile number which, somewhat surprised, she gives me. Finally I get through to Ludwig. Sounding puzzled, he asks me what number I'm calling from. I promise to explain it all later, but for now: 'I have to see you, right away. Outside police headquarters.'

'What?'

'I can't go on my own, I need your support. It's essential we speak to the inspector responsible for Dad's case.' When he doesn't respond, I add, 'There was an incident today at a construction site in Henningsdorf, Ludwig. Something bad.'

'What? What sort of incident? Are you all right?'

'Marcus Steinhausen's brother was seriously injured and my friend Eva . . .' My voice cracks; I clear my throat. 'I was there, Ludwig. I'm a witness and I have to make a statement. We'll meet at police HQ, okay?' I hang up. I finish by ordering a taxi, then I thank the patient Frau Steinhausen and hurry out of the building.

US

Sarah, Sarah, sweet little Sarah. So alone, so sad. You're shivering, you poor thing. Come with me, don't be afraid. We'll go and play in the woods. It's a fairy-tale game. You like fairy tales, don't you? Of course you do, all children love fairy tales. And, do you know what? You're the main character! Do you want to hear your story? Then listen carefully. Once upon a time, there was a little girl who was born with a heart of pure gold. Or at least that's what people said in the village where she lived. One day an evil dragon heard about this and decided he would steal the girl's heart. He wanted to destroy it because everything that was good and beautiful stirred his hatred. It reminded him that he himself was just a nasty old dragon. The girl had to flee. She ran as fast as she could to escape from the dragon . . . Go on, sweetheart, run! Run faster and don't turn around! Did you hear that? The cracking in the bushes? That's him! He's close on your heels! Come here, let's hide, right here behind this thick tree trunk. Shall I tell you a secret? Dragons don't always look like dragons. Not all of them are huge and black or dark green, with spines and scales and spouting fire from their huge mouths. Some are masters of disguise. They look like perfectly normal people, like men or women. They lead you astray and then to ruin. Some of them, with a bit of magic, can transform themselves so they don't just look human, they actually become human. Others can't do that as the evil inside them is too strong. They are lost souls. Are you afraid? No, no, don't be afraid. You're safe with me. I'll take you to a secret place, a magical place. It's a castle, and in the castle lives another girl with a golden heart, a princess. Would you like to meet her? Yes? I thought so. She wants to meet you too, she's been looking forward to it. We'll go and see her now, okay? But beforehand we have put out a few of the red ribbons I brought with me, look. What are they for? Oh, it wouldn't interest you, sweetheart. Let's just say it's a surprise for the dragon.

ANN

BERLIN, 26 DECEMBER 2017

'For God's sake, what kept you?' Ludwig's grey hair looks totally dishevelled; he must have been running his fingers through it while he was waiting outside police HQ in the drizzle, getting ever more nervous.

'I'm sorry, I'm really sorry! The taxi didn't come for ages.'

Now comes the roasting. I'm lucky; if it wasn't for his enormous heart, he'd be long gone by now. Especially after everything I've done. I know at once he's talking about the folder.

'I can explain.'

'What's there to explain, Anni? You asked me if you could have my documents and I said no. But instead of respecting that, you stole them from me. I realised yesterday evening that the folder was missing. You were lucky I resisted the urge to jump in my car and drive over to read you the riot act.'

'You could have called me.'

'Would you have answered if you'd seen it was my number?'

'No.'

'No,' he repeats, shaking his head in resignation.

'I'm sorry.'

'We're not done with this, my girl.' He points to the building in front of us. 'So, what are we doing here?'

I'm well aware that my statement is long and muddled. I'm like-wise aware that duty inspectors prefer listening to long, muddled statements on regular workdays rather than at the fag end of Boxing Day, where such things just mean overtime – time they'd rather be spending with their families. I don't hold it against Inspector Brandner that he makes me sense all of this as he looks at me across his desk. He's about the same age as Ludwig, with thinning hair, large bags under his eyes and frown lines that sug-gest he's often narrowed his eyes at all the things he's seen and heard during his many years in this job. Even when he doesn't, he still looks sceptical. If he didn't know Ludwig personally and have huge respect for him, I bet the inspector would have fobbed me off with a 'pop in another time' rather than allow me to sit here now. On the other hand, two officers were supposed to have questioned me at the hospital about the events at the construc-tion site, but I was in too much shock to be of any use. So they asked me to go to police HQ the moment I felt better.

Now I am feeling better and I'm here with the complete chro-nology of the day, ending with my conversation with Marcus Steinhausen's sister-in-law.

'Okay, Frau Lesniak, duly noted. Thanks.' That's all.

I look to Ludwig for help, who's sitting beside me like an embarrassed father before his badly behaved daughter's head-master. And the worst thing is that he's saying nothing.

'Marcus Steinhausen was obsessed first with his brother's family and then with the Mellers. He told his sister-in-law he'd got himself a girlfriend. She recalls that the name began with M. M for Michelle. Don't you understand? Marcus Steinhausen lied! Just as he lied to Michelle when he passed off his brother's family as his own.'

No reaction, neither from Ludwig nor Brandner.

'Okay,' I say, acknowledging defeat. 'I admit I've no idea how all of this fits together. But it's clear that it *does* fit together. And that Steinhausen is someone it's worth taking a closer look into. With his history and his obvious psychological issues, he fits the profile of the ribbon murderer far better than my father.'

The inspector raises his eyebrows in amazement. 'The profile?'

I nod keenly. 'Whatever Meller did and however wrong it was – I think he was correct. Marcus Steinhausen—'

Brandner turns to Ludwig. 'Did she just say something about "the profile"?'

And that was it. Brandner laughs as if he's just heard a brilliant joke. And I'm the punchline. A civilian who feels the calling to investigate. Hilarious. Then comes a lecture, delivered in a serious tone. My father is not in custody on some whim, and certainly not without reason. And Steinhausen was eliminated as a potential suspect years ago because he had alibis. Perhaps – an artificially sympathetic look – I should consider getting professional help to deal with my personal circumstances, which must be difficult. Not a police professional, but somebody familiar with the human psyche. A professional like Eva.

I don't say anything else; I just listen until Brandner has finished and says goodbye, not without the words, 'Get better soon' – of course not.

Shame. (Ann, 9 years old)

When your ashamed it feels like you shrink until your very small. But you wish you could be even smaller and even invisible for a bit. But unfortunately your not invisible, you can see this because everyone stares at you. And the staring burns you so badly that your face goes red and your ears get very hot. That's very embarassing.

We drive in Ludwig's car. He offers me his spare room for the night. We could go out to a restaurant first or order a takeaway if I don't feel like being out in public. I just want to go home. 'It's been a difficult day, Anni,' he tries. 'It's a difficult time for you overall at the—'

'Please, Ludwig, leave it.'

He shakes his head. 'I can't, my girl. Your father isn't here to look after you. But I am.'

'And that's why you left me high and dry in front of Inspector Brandner? I could have done with your support.'

'Anni, you've got to stop getting obsessed by all of this. You saw today what happened to your friend Eva. Isn't that enough? What more has to happen?'

'I don't want to talk about Eva.'

'But we have to.'

'No, what we really have to talk about is why, as our lawyer, you're wasting the opportunity to put the police on to a very promising lead! Surely you want the real killer to be caught, don't you?'

'Anni,' and this weary sigh – I can't listen to it anymore. Leaning my head against the window, I switch off. Now Ludwig's words are nothing but indistinct sounds, while the lights from the streetlamps and houses racing past are a blur in the darkness. It's like a slipstream dragging me with it, into a different setting where there are also lights, lights on a Christmas tree. It's only plastic but it's tradition. A fire is crackling; I hear soft music and a little girl's laughter. Christmas, Dad, like we used to celebrate it. As we might never be able to celebrate it again. Just as nothing might ever be the same as it once was. I don't know if I can cope with this possibility, Dad. I'm so terribly scared.

'Oh, my Beetle,' you would say now. 'Do you remember the story I once told you when you were a girl? The story about fear?'

Yes, but please tell me again. I'd love to have something I can believe in.

'All right, listen carefully . . . Once upon a time, there was a farmer who set off in his donkey cart for Constantinople. On the way he was stopped by a hunchbacked old woman who begged him to take her along. He let her climb aboard, but when she was sitting next to him on the box and he was able to see her face, he almost jumped in horror. "Who are you?" he asked. "I am cholera," the old woman replied. At once the farmer ordered her to get off his cart and make her own way. He was very frightened. But the old woman promised to spare him and only kill five people in Constantinople if he let her travel with him. As security she gave him a special dagger, the only weapon that could kill her. "We'll see each other again in two days," she said. "If I've broken my promise, you can kill me."

'Over the next couple of days, however, a total of 125 people died in Constantinople. And the farmer, who himself was fine, did indeed see the old woman again, and was going to thrust the dagger into her. "Don't do that," she said. "I kept my promise and only killed five people. It was fear that accounted for the other hundred and twenty."'

Have you ever been afraid, Daddy?

'Yes, my Beetle. That time you injured yourself with the sharp stone. I'll never forget how I felt—'

'Ann?' Ludwig says, interrupting my thoughts. 'Have you been listening to me?'

I say yes, to whatever.

'All right then, would you prefer Thai or Chinese?'

'What?'

'What food should I order? You can't have been listening to me.'

'Yes, yes, I was. It's just . . . I'm not really hungry.'

'Your appetite will come when the food does. And no more buts now, or I'll tell your father you nicked my folder.'

I shrug. Ludwig ought to know that it's hard to faze my father; he's had to put up with a lot from me. Ann and the cut wrist when she was six. Ann and her complicated puberty. Ann who does stupid things because she's unhappy in love. Ann who turns the car over. When did he ever lose it, Ludwig? When did he ever scream at me? My father, who was always controlled, his analytical gaze. He would ask me why I did what I'd done and what I was feeling when I did it. I'd describe my despair, my anger, my fear and he would understand me.

'Don't forget he's in prison now,' Ludwig says, as if he'd read my thoughts. 'You saw for yourself when you visited how much the circumstances have changed him. He's got enough problems at the moment, don't add to that list by becoming another one.'

I could object that I seem to be the only person making a serious attempt to solve his problems, but I hold my tongue. The last thing I want now is an argument; I don't have the energy for it, not after the day I've had.

When Ludwig parks the car, I see that the Harberts' house is as dark as ours; Elke and Caspian must still be at the hospital. Maybe I oughtn't be on my own tonight. I think of my father, of Eva, of Zoe and Jakob and everyone whose company I would far prefer to Ludwig's. But none of them are around. I sniff and persuade myself that an evening with Ludwig will at least give me the opportunity to convince him of my theory about Marcus Steinhausen.

'Thai,' I say, before reaching for the door handle to get out. 'Some kind of curry with coconut milk, but not too hot.'

'There we go,' Ludwig says, smiling. 'I'll hurry.'

I close the passenger door and watch the car until the darkness has swallowed its taillights. Then I turn to face our house and my eye catches one of the upstairs windows: my bedroom. I can't work it out at first, not in its entirety – only that something is different. The black shape doesn't belong there and my curtains shouldn't be moving.

I blink, confused. There's nothing up there anymore. No black figure, no movement of the curtains. Just another figment of my imagination, I reassure myself. Just my overloaded brain short-circuiting again. All the same I should take a look, make sure. There's no way I can let Ludwig come back to find the problem child still standing on the drive because she doesn't dare enter her own house.

I approach the house tentatively nonetheless.

'Do you remember the story of fear, my Beetle?' I hear my father say inside my head. 'The fear of fear gives rise to more suffering than the actual cause.'

Yes, Dad.

The silence is loud. It's the metallic scraping of the key in the lock. It's the sigh of the hinges as the door's pushed open, and the whimper of the handle. It's every single step that the heavy soles of my boots make on the tiled floor. It's the sliding sound of the carving knife I take out of the wooden block on the work surface. It's the clicking of my left knee when I climb the first step of the stairs and the groan of the wood on the second. It's another step and yet another, getting louder with each successive one taking me up the stairs, until they end on the landing.

I stop. Listen. My room is the second on the right. I can't hear anything. I'd just have to touch the wall next to me; that's where the light switch is. I don't do it; I don't turn the light on. Something is stopping me, a feeling. I edge forwards to my room. The door is open. That was me, I think, I left it open.

And yet . . . this feeling. It has bitten into my neck with sharp teeth.

My room is my room is my room. I can't make out any disruption to the system of forms and outlines accentuated in the dark by the streetlamps outside. I go over to the window.

There's nobody here. Nobody was here.

Get better soon, Inspector Brandner says in my mind. I shake my head in resignation about myself.

Outside a car is approaching. That can't be Ludwig already; it'll take him at least half an hour to return with our dinner. Pushing the curtains apart, I crane my neck. It's the Harberts' car turning into the drive next door. The outdoor lights come on; Elke and Caspian get out. I watch them go up to the house; it looks as if they're shuffling, weak and tired after the worst of all possible days. There's a clunk when Elke turns the key in the lock, and another clunk when she shuts the front door behind them.

The view from my bedroom window is ideal if you want to keep an eye on what's going on outside. If a car arrives. If someone comes home who could interrupt you. But my bedroom window is closed. So it couldn't have been Elke and Caspian who made the clunking noises.

I know exactly where they came from.

I heard them everyday when my father, lost in thought, would pace up and down on the old floorboards in his study. Carefully I slip my boots off. Then I creep back on to the landing, holding the knife in front of my stomach, tightly clutching the handle.

First my gaze falls on the console table at the end of the landing, the vase that has its fixed place in the middle of it. There's something comforting about symmetry, something dependable. I squint to make sure, though it's hard in the darkness, punctuated only dimly by the light from the streetlamp. But I'm sure of it: the vase is no longer exactly in the middle; it's a few centimetres off-centre to the right. I creep further down the landing. The study is still a few paces away on the left, but I can already see it: the door.

The only door in this house that – normally – is never open. Which I keep locked to preserve a sense of importance, hiding the key in the vase on the console.

My heartbeat goes wild, blood roars in my ears. I tense every muscle, an animal ready to pounce into the study in a single bound.

Then everything happens very fast. In the dark, crashing into a wall and being dragged off my feet. The room tipping and me losing my knife. The clank as it hits the floor. A moment later I slam into the wooden boards, a stifled cry. My opponent teeters and falls too, a hoarse panting. In panic, I feel the floor for my knife. My opponent hobbles out the door. Finding my weapon, I try to get up, but a pain in my right shoulder pushes me down. I fight against it, struggle to my feet, go after my foe. Their footsteps are already clattering on the stairs. I'm quicker; I know this staircase, having often taken it in the dark. My left hand shoots forwards, comes into contact with material and tugs at it; my opponent stumbles. I let go just in time, grabbing on to the banister before they can drag me with them down the last few stairs. A dull thud then suddenly it's silent again. Only two people breathing jerkily in the darkness, both numb with shock. Then, groaning. My knees trembling, I make my way down, my knife aimed at the noise. At the bottom of the stairs, I press the light switch and the groaning briefly stops. Standing as tall as I can, I look down at my foe, lying at my feet, doubled up with pain. A man. He's wearing dark clothes and a black balaclava that disguises his entire face apart from the wide-open blue eyes staring up at me, prompting something I can't put a finger on. I turn the knife in my hand to signal that he ought to stay precisely where he is and not try anything stupid. He blinks a few times rapidly in succession. Either he's understood my warning or he's merely adjusting his eyes to the surprising brightness of the hall light. My mind comes to life like a spluttering engine. Laid out in front of me is none other than Marcus Steinhausen. The man I've been trying to find. But who found me first. Slowly, very slowly, I kneel before him, still firmly clutching the knife with my right hand, while the left one reaches for the balaclava. I pull it off his head.

And freeze.

Now I know what it was about those blue eyes. I know them. I've seen them glisten when the man they belong to tells me in my lunch breaks how he crushes the old cardboard boxes at the recycling centre.

RECORDING 04

Berlin, 7 May 2021

- *(laughs)* Oh, you're afraid.
- No, I'm not.
- All right then, give me your hand. I want to show you exactly where I made the cut.
- No, I think you just want to test my reaction and unnerve me.
- Your mind seems to be elsewhere at the moment. Otherwise you'd make more of an effort. I'd have already explained your mistake to you.
- What mistake?
- No, you first. You're questioning my motivation, and I'm just as keen to know about your decision. You say you want to understand.
- Yes.
- Why? Do you feel affected personally?
- Look, like I already told you, I've met Larissa Meller's mother.
- Oh, but that's not all, is it? On the contrary, that's just a tiny bit

of it, maybe even just an excuse. I did some research into you before agreeing to our meeting.

– So what? I don't have any skeletons in my cupboard.

– We all have those.

– In your case there are ten of them, and not just proverbial ones. Talking of which, let's get back to Larissa. What did she trigger in you? Did she remind you of somebody? Why was she your first victim?

– Ah, yes, your mistake. You believe Larissa must have had a particular significance because she was the first one.

– Yes.

– No.

– No? She had no particular significance?

– Of course she did! They all did! I can remember every single name and every face. I know their family backgrounds, whether they had siblings or pets, and what their favourite subjects at school were. They were happy to tell me all of this quite openly because they sensed I was really interested. For the brief moment when our lives overlapped, there was nothing more important to me than each of those girls. The trust they felt outweighed the fear, the unease, their parents' warnings. I mean, that's what we drum into our children from an early age, isn't it? Never go with strangers. But are we adults any better? We go out, have one glass too many and all of a sudden end up in bed with someone who just happened to be in the same place at the same time.

– Is this part of your motivation? Is it about people's gullibility? Or were you trying to punish parents you didn't think had looked after their children well enough?

- No, those are merely findings. By the way, I've just remembered you had a few problems when you were younger.
- What are you getting at?
- So much for not having any skeletons in the cupboard. You were charged with criminal damage because you slashed your teacher's tyres. Twenty hours of community service and a counselling session with the juvenile court service, am I right?
- So? That was just a moment of stupidity. I was naïve and I was in with the wrong crowd.
- I think it might be quite similar.
- What are you talking about?
- Well, you mentioned needing strength to cut through skin. It might be similar to slashing a tyre. Although it has to be said that I've never slashed anyone's tyres. *(clicks his tongue several times)* That really is pointless and unnecessary.

ANN

BERLIN, 26 DECEMBER 2017

It's shortly after half past nine in the evening and I'm back in Brandner's office at police HQ. This time I seem to be arousing a different sort of pity in him, for in addition to the coffee I've been given, the inspector has also placed a tin in front of me. The writing on the lid spitefully wishes me a 'Happy Christmas'. I open the tin if only to be able to put the lid upside down.

'My wife baked them,' Brandner says, giving me a strained smile over his desk. Although I feel queasy, I poke around inside the tin and plump for a lebkuchen with chocolate icing. Ludwig's here too. Not long after I tore the balaclava from the intruder's face, he returned with our dinner. He was the one who called the police. Now he's sitting beside me, his arm across the back of my chair, which I take to be a sign of his protectiveness. He's got a bad conscience, just like Brandner, who's not sharing his wife's baked masterpieces without good reason. *Get better soon*, my arse. In addition to the red ribbon on our oleander and all my research, now I've been attacked too, and injured in the process. My right shoulder is bruised and there's a cut on my right brow. It's a really impressive-looking wound;

each time the men catch a glimpse of it, they're reminded to go easy on me.

'The thing with the files might be a problem,' Brandner says, waiting until I've finished eating. As if I hadn't picked out a lebkuchen but a sedative that takes a while to work. 'Who knew you had the folder?'

'Only my friend Eva, no one else.'

The inspector holds back his displeasure as best he can; the only thing he doesn't have under control is his twitching jaw.

'What are you thinking, Martin?' Ludwig asks him.

'Well, there are a number of possibilities as to who could benefit from such information. From that bunch of souvenir hunters who auction supposed crime scene material online, to relatives who think the investigation is proceeding too slowly. Then the press, of course, eager to boost sales figures with hitherto unpublished details. Or even—'

'The real murderer, trying to find out if you're on to him and how close you are,' I say, finishing his sentence.

Brandner just gives a curt, sullen nod, before turning to Ludwig once more. 'I don't have to tell you what I think of your having let her get hold of these documents.'

'No,' Ludwig replies. He neglects to mention how exactly the folder came to be in my possession.

'And are you sure that nothing else was stolen, Frau Lesniak? Neither from the study nor from the rest of the house? Just the files?'

I shrug, giving myself a sharp pain on my right side. *That's going to be a nice bruise*, said the doctor who had to make a note of my physical condition for the records.

'Not that I'm aware.'

Brandner mutters. 'The fact that the folder was the only thing stolen suggests the intruder had deliberately targeted it. But this doesn't fit your claim that nobody could have known about it.'

'Nobody apart from Eva Harbert,' Ludwig corrects him, looking at me.

'Absolutely no way! Who would Eva have told? And when? We were together the whole time until . . .' I blink wildly as the image of her lifeless body tries to form in my head again, her head in the pool of blood, her stiff, half-opened eyes. 'Absolutely no way,' I repeat shakily.

'It's all right,' Ludwig says, moving his hand from the chair to my back.

'I'm sorry, Frau Lesniak,' Brandner says, pointedly pushing the biscuit tin towards me. He must think I need another dose. 'I don't mean to upset you; I'm trying to protect you.'

Even though I don't fancy it, I take another one, this time a shortbread heart with a jam filling. Once again, Brandner waits until I've finished before asking the question that I must have already answered several times this evening. 'And are you really sure you didn't recognise the intruder?'

'Absolutely sure,' I say, nodding. 'I hadn't turned any lights on, so it was pitch-black in the house when I tore the balaclava off his face. Then he knocked me over and disappeared through the terrace door.'

You would approve, Dad.

Maybe you'd even be a bit proud of me. I'm following the great philosophers: Machiavelli, Bentham, Kant. I've checked the end and the means. The end is not exclusively selfish, but morally right and important for the common good as well: the longer you're in prison, the longer the real killer remains free, able to claim the lives of more innocent victims. The end is to expand the police's narrow view, the means is the break-in. They have to investigate and thus explore every possibility, including that Steinhausen might be behind it. I know it wasn't him, but the police have no option but to take a closer look at Steinhausen. They have to check out everyone who might have had a reason for breaking into our house now that I've started asking questions. I'm still sure they'll hit on Steinhausen one way or another, but until I've got clear, definitive proof of his guilt, outwardly I need to be careful. They mustn't think that, like Meller, I've developed an obsession about this man. They need to take me seriously when the time comes.

The end justifies the means.

It's okay that I lied, slightly twisting the circumstances of the attack in my favour. It's okay, that doesn't make me a bad person, does it, Dad?

'Don't worry, Anni,' Ludwig says in your place. I'm beside him in the passenger seat, sitting slightly crooked from the pain in my shoulder. I'm nervous to boot, but not because – as he probably thinks – I'm traumatised by the attack. 'I'm going to take better care of you from now on.'

'I'm fine, Ludwig,' I protest for the umpteenth time, starting to sound annoyed. Which is counterproductive because he mustn't become suspicious. I'm Anni, who was standing in the doorway when he came back with dinner. Anni, as if paralysed, and holding a black balaclava. Anni, who could only stammer when she told him about the intruder she'd surprised in the study. It had been a man, that much was certain. But she couldn't see him properly in the dark. He'd wrestled her to the floor then escaped via the terrace. Ludwig immediately sat her in his car where she could feel safe while he went into the house, switched on the lights and inspected everything before calling the police.

'Really I am,' Anni insists, giving him a conciliatory smile. 'After all, nothing bad happened. I just want to go home and get into my bed.'

'You want to do what?' Ludwig looks aghast. 'No way. You're going to stay at my place tonight.'

'Honestly, there's no need. I—'

'Really? What happens if the intruder comes back?'

'After that turnout? The police spent two hours searching the house, garden and garage, securing evidence. If I were the intruder, I'd get out of the city as quick as I could.'

'There's still the question of how he got into the house in the first place.'

I lower my eyes guiltily, just like earlier when giving my statement to Inspector Brandner. 'The terrace door. I must have left it open again, there's no other explanation I can think of.'

Ludwig sighs. 'I realise you've been out of sorts recently, Anni. And I can understand it too, but—'

'I really should be more careful, especially now I'm living in the house on my own,' I say, finishing his sentence with the words Eva said to me yesterday. A yesterday that seems an eternity ago. 'I know, Ludwig.'

'Apart from that, the meaning of the red ribbon on your oleander needs looking into again. That might have been him too.'

'Do you think he's been watching me for a while?'

Ludwig just growls quietly, the reaction of the man who only yesterday was still downplaying this and stopping me from notifying the police. *Someone was in your garden and tied a red ribbon to the oleander. Nothing else actually happened*, a shrug of the shoulders. All the same, I don't protest anymore when he takes the wrong turn. I'm desperate to go back home, but Ludwig's arguments are better and he has a more credible scenario. We say nothing more until he turns into his drive.

'Here we are,' he says, reaching behind for the bag with the two styrofoam boxes from the Thai restaurant.

We get out. Before us is his swanky villa, a house whose art nouveau opulence spits a big fat 'ner, ner, ner, ner, ner' in the face of every guest. This is home to someone who's made it, who doesn't know what to do with his money. Ludwig could have sold the place after entering retirement – which he's spending in the forests of his Polish homeland – and simply stayed in a hotel on his sporadic visits to Berlin. But he doesn't do this because he doesn't have to. He can afford to keep a house he no longer lives in, like an outsized trophy, a memorial to his life's work.

'The world will look a very different place after you've had a good night's sleep,' he says, punching a code into the number pad beside the front door. People like Ludwig aren't surprised by intruders in their studies because nobody can get past the alarm system. In the hallway I put my rucksack down and take my boots off. I'd really love to go straight to bed, but I know Ludwig. He will want to be sure that I really am all right. Moreover, he won't be able to sleep himself until he's soothed his conscience with a little paternal care towards me. But he must – he must fall asleep if he's not going to notice me stealing out of his house in the middle of the night. I've thought it over very carefully. I'll ruffle the bedclothes a bit in the spare room, then wait for a while before doing a runner. And tomorrow, when he realises I'm not there and calls me, I'll simply tell him I got up early and didn't want to wake him. I've got everything under control, Dad. I'm not going to let myself be helplessly churned up by the chaos any longer; that's enough now.

I go into the kitchen, fetch two cups from the cupboard and then tap my way through the functions of the coffee machine, which is complicated if you've never used it before. But I have, on numerous occasions. I know which drawer I'll find a packet of cigarettes in. Ludwig, who hasn't smoked in ages apart from the odd cigar on special occasions, keeps one there for emergencies. For emergencies like me. I also know that there's an ashtray hidden next to the cleaning things in the cupboard under the sink, and where to find the matches. I know I have to open the window, not because of Ludwig but Frau Cluth, the housekeeper, who gave me his mobile number earlier. She'll moan – she always has – if you're careless enough to fill the room with smoke. I know all this because I've been a regular visitor here. As a little girl I used to sit at this kitchen table with a cup of hot chocolate and a roll that Frau Cluth had buttered for me. I climbed on the leather armchairs in the library or built a camp in the loft while Ludwig and my father were deep in conversation.

'Are you smoking again?' Ludwig asks, entering the kitchen and putting the bag with our dinner on the work surface. He's got changed and is now wearing a cardigan with a shawl collar rather than his jacket. I sit at the table puffing smoke rings into the air. Zoe showed me how to do it after we'd been out dancing one night, which ended on the balcony of the student halls of residence where she was living. Slightly puff your cheeks, keep the smoke in, form an 'O' with your lips, then carefully push your tongue forwards. As simple as that and yet for the life of me I couldn't do it. Now that I can, Zoe is living alone in our flat and getting ready for her term abroad – Cornwall, without me.

'Off and on,' I say to Ludwig. 'But please don't tell Dad. You know, my asthma and all that.'

He mutters something and fetches a cigar. We drink our coffee and smoke. The food remains untouched in its bag.

'I know you're as unconvinced by my Steinhausen theory as Brandner and the rest of the force. But I also know I'm right. I can't say for sure where this feeling comes from, only that it's uncannily strong.'

'You're unmistakably your father's daughter.' Ludwig laughs. 'For him, feelings have always been more important than facts too. It's a miracle he turned into such a successful academic.'

I shake my head. 'That's not completely right. Feelings lead to deeds and deeds lead to facts, he always says. He regards them as the basis of everything. And he's right about that, isn't he? I don't think there's any question he's asked me more often in my life than: *What were you feeling?* He would never be fobbed off, he always wanted to know precisely. When I was a little girl, I even had to write short compositions about my feelings and give them to him so he could see I really had engaged with them.' I laugh too, but only briefly. 'As far as I'm concerned, it makes it even worse that someone like him – someone who's always been so genuinely interested in others – is now locked away in a tiny, cold cell. And nobody's asking what *he* is feeling.'

'He could save himself a lot of bother if he started talking, Anni. You're behaving as if nobody wants to listen to him. But that's not the case. On the contrary.'

'You don't understand him.' I stub out my cigarette with brisk, ungainly movements. 'None of you understand him. He's a highly sensitive man. These charges have broken him.'

Leaning back, Ludwig crosses his arms.

Whereas I lean forwards over the table. 'Marcus Steinhausen, Ludwig. The police are going to investigate him over the break-in. And you have to make sure their enquiry is thorough.'

'You need sleep, my child.'

'It's not a question of whether he's got an alibi for this evening. It's whether he's the ribbon murderer.'

Ludwig gets up and leaves the kitchen without a word of explanation. I check my watch – just before midnight. Barely four hours since I caught the intruder in our house. Ludwig's right: I really need to go to bed.

No sooner am I on my feet than he comes back with two glasses containing a brown liquid. A single malt, I bet. From the globe bar in his library. As a child I was fascinated watching Ludwig flip back the northern half of the globe to take out one of the valuable bottles inside. He sets the glasses on the table, swapping them for the coffee cups. I sit down again without protest. A sip can't hurt, not today – today warrants a huge gulp.

'There's something not right about the case as set out by the investigation team,' I say, putting my glass on the table. I must have taken a larger sip than I'd thought – it doesn't matter; I can hold my drink. 'They're missing something.'

'Something that you're going to find.' His words surprise me as much as the smile that accompanies them. Until now, Ludwig has given me the impression that although he's taking the break-in seriously, he's not so convinced by my theories about Marcus Steinhausen. I nod all the same. Which feels strange. As if the weight of my head had increased; it's as heavy as a stone I'm trying to balance on the thin, feeble spindle that used to be my neck.

'The motive,' I say, attempting to sound unfazed. 'I've asked you about this before, but you didn't give me an answer and I couldn't find anything in the documents either. What reason would my father have had to kill ten little girls?'

Ludwig raises his glass to me once more and I join him in a sip, in the hope the alcohol will loosen his tongue.

'Well?'

'You've read the files. Which means you know the girls' wrists were slit. The left one, as in your case.' He leans towards me. 'Although they can't say for sure, the forensics team believe the killer used a knife with a very blunt blade. Do you have any idea how much strength is needed to slit the wrist of someone with a blunt knife?'

'But that's exactly my point, Ludwig! Nobody did it to me! There was no madman with a knife. It was me, myself!'

'The left wrist, Anni,' he insists. 'Do you seriously believe in such coincidences?'

'A few weeks after I started working at Big Murphy's, I found out that my colleague was the mother of the first victim. So, yes, Ludwig! I do believe in coincidences! Unbelievable coincidences!'

'Oh, my child,' Ludwig says, his outline faintly blurring.

I blink a few times until my vision is sharp again. 'And that's still no reason,' I say, sticking to my guns. This time I'm not going to give in.

Ludwig points his chin at my glass. I drink up – why not? 'As an anthropologist, your father's a scientist, Anni. And as a philosopher, he's a thinker striving for answers to the fundamental questions in life.'

I want to object but my tongue is stuck to the roof of my mouth. Ludwig puts his hand on mine. 'Death is also part of life.'

His face dissolves, everything dissolves. It's as if everything before me is a painting which someone has poured water over. Colours run, flowing into one another, everything fluid. There's something wrong with me; my weighty head slumps on to my chest. Once again I try to say something, but it feels as if my lips have been stitched together.

'Anni,' I hear Ludwig's muffled voice. 'You've got into something that isn't good for you.'

Summoning all my strength, I manage to lift my head, which rolls around on my neck uncontrollably.

'But trust me.' All of a sudden his voice is by my ear, very close; it's a whisper and a warm breath. When did he get up from his chair and wander around the table? 'Everything's going to be all right.'

Do you remember?

Six years ago, when Eva disappeared from the city overnight.

I'd already been suffering heartache for a long time. Eva and Nico felt like my asthma – a chronic illness that was unpleasant but which I'd learned to live with. I'd realised, at least, that I couldn't lock Eva away, not like when we were fourteen and I wanted her to miss her drama club audition. I'd simply shoved her into a toilet cubicle and barricaded the door from the outside with the caretaker's broom. I didn't want her to get the part of Luise in Schiller's *Kabale und Liebe*. We'd read the play in our German lessons and I knew that there would be a Ferdinand she would have to fall in love with. Three years later this Ferdinand was called Nico and I was powerless. I had to tolerate their relationship if I wanted to avoid losing Eva completely. But that was precisely what happened just a year later, right after our school-leaving party. Eva and Nico went away together and didn't come back. With every day that passed, my heart broke anew and I began to wonder why I hadn't already collapsed and died of a cardiac arrest. I was so exhausted by grief and yet couldn't find rest. All I wanted to do was to sleep – not die, for God's sake! – just enjoy a long, restorative sleep. And when I woke up, my body and mind would be refreshed, my appetite would have returned and I'd see that although a world without Eva was different, it was still nice and worth living.

They were your pills, Dad. You kept having phases where you were so consumed by work that you couldn't switch your mind off at night. I took too many, a silly accident. It felt as if I were lying outstretched in a swamp. With every breath, my body grew heavier and I sank slightly deeper. My heartbeat slackened, getting slower and slower, which seemed wrong in view of the gathering panic I felt. I sensed I was going under and was absolutely terrified. I just managed to call out to you and point sluggishly to the tube on my bedside table.

'Am I going to die now, Dad?' I also managed to say.

'Don't worry, my silly Beetle,' you said, putting a hand on my head. 'You'd have to swallow a kilo of these pills to be in danger. You're just going to have a deep, long sleep.'

Then I sank into the swamp.

I'm getting a similar feeling now in Ludwig's kitchen. My body unbelievably heavy, my heartbeat like deep, lengthy sighs. I slump on my chair into a thick, grey fog. I'm just about aware of Ludwig grabbing me under the arms and also feel the pain in my right shoulder. Am I going to die now, Ludwig? I want to ask, but that's too many words, too much effort. All I manage is a pitiful, meek, 'Why?'

US

Drink, Sarah, drink up. This is a magic drink. It will help you have a wonderful dream. And when you wake up, I'll take you to see the princess. She has to rest too, just like you, because it's late and it's been an exciting day. I'm going to go out again, I have to. They've started looking for you. The police are here already with their men and dogs, their searchlights and even a helicopter. They're playing blind man's bluff – cold, cold, very cold, I want to shout out. But I don't, of course, because their ignorance is handy for us. We don't want to take any risks, we mustn't. That's why I'm going to join them, the police and the people from the village. I'm going to be part of the search; that way I'll be up to date and find out when it's getting dicey for us. It's an old trick – be there, but invisible, like a ghost or a shadow in the night. Now, sleep well, my sweetheart, settle down. When I'm back, I'll lie down beside you. I'll be very close, hold you tightly and stroke your lovely soft hair. You'll feel it, even in your sleep; you'll feel safe and protected, just like you deserve. The princess is always asking me to lie beside her too, just her and me, with the rest of the world far away. And of course I'm happy to do it, I do everything for her. That's what you really want too, isn't it, sweetheart? Someone who does everything for you. You'd like to be a princess too, wouldn't you?

ANN

BERLIN, 27 DECEMBER 2017

I wake with a start in panic, my heartbeat and breathing at maximum speed. I'm in bed in Ludwig's spare room. The digital alarm clock on the bedside table says that I've slept for a good ten hours; it's almost noon. My thoughts are black, even briefly entertaining the possibility that Ludwig might have interfered with me. I push the duvet back. He's only taken off the jumper over my T-shirt; other than that I'm fully clothed. Despite this, I feel naked because I was at his mercy. He decided to sedate me with sleeping pills or something similar; he had power over me. And even if he only did it out of concern for me, it makes no difference. I swing my legs over the edge of the mattress. My body combats these snappy movements with a dizziness, but I won't give in. It's been more than sixteen hours since I apprehended the intruder. I have to get home. Putting on my jumper, which is on the chair beside the bed, I grab my rucksack and make for the door. For a moment it occurs to me that Ludwig might have locked me in, but I'm wrong, thank God. I hurry down the stairs, almost stumbling.

'Morning, sleepy head!' Ludwig calls out as I pass the kitchen. He gets up from a lavishly laid breakfast table. Without responding, I hasten down the corridor to the coatrack to fetch my jacket and boots.

'Anni? Is everything okay?' Now he's standing there, looking at me in astonishment, as I yank my jacket off the hook and make heavy weather putting it on with my injured shoulder.

'Nothing's okay. You should be ashamed of yourself!'

'What are you talking about?' He takes another step towards me and tries to help me with the jacket. I turn away. 'Anni, I really don't know what—'

'Really? Are you going to try to deny it? You gave me a sleeping pill!'

'I . . . what?'

I don't reply. He knows exactly what he did. But I don't want to discuss it anymore; I don't have the time or the inclination. I've got to get home, right now. Ludwig thwarted my plan of slipping back home during the night. Now half a day has gone and the worst-case scenario is nagging at my mind.

'Anni . . .' His tone changes: a sanctimonious purr. 'I'm worried about you.'

'Oh really? Just like you're worried about Dad?'

'What's that supposed to mean?'

'It means you're being astonishingly passive seeing as Marcus Steinhausen is a serious lead. A lead that might help exonerate your client.' I flop down on to the floor inelegantly to put on my boots. 'Shouldn't you already be in Inspector Brandner's office, making sure he interrogates Steinhausen again?'

'I'm just trying to protect you, child.'

'From Steinhausen? You've got a funny way of—'

'From yourself, Ann.'

Those words are like a slap to the face. I look at him as if numbed. 'Fuck you!' That's the last thing he hears me say before I leave his house.

I run as if my life depended on it.

My shoulder hurts from the jarring as I pound the streets, and my eyebrow throbs. I don't find a taxi until I get to Richard-Wagner-Platz. Judging by the driver's glances in his rear-view mirror, he's suspicious of me. I could have been boozing all night; at the very least I look like trouble with my scruffy black hair and the plaster on my face. And I don't stop panting.

'Let me know if you want me to stop for a bit, won't you?' He must be worrying about me vomiting all over his upholstery.

'It's okay, I'm fine. I'm just in a real hurry.' It is winter, after all; even during the day the temperature is below freezing, to say nothing of the nights. A feeling tightens around my chest. What if I've made a huge mistake?

'Are you really okay?' The driver again.

'Couldn't you drive faster?'

'I'm doing fifty as it is.'

And I'm doing my head in. I slide my hands beneath my thighs; my whole body is shaking. Behind my closed eyelids is Eva, and alongside her, the realisation of how everything can change in a few seconds. A conclusion I'd reached a while ago. I can't help burp – a mouthful of sour fermented whisky from last night. My plan was different. I just wanted to drink a tiny sip with Ludwig, to soothe his conscience, then steal away secretly. I'd have got home in time. What now?

Where we live is a 30 kph zone; I'm going up the wall. I beg the driver to let me out here, two streets away from our house. I don't even hear the price he mentions; I just shove a twenty in his hand, leap out of the cab and start running again.

Please, I didn't mean . . .

I'm throbbing with pain and tension, exploding with speculation. What if . . . ?

I run faster, already feeling for the unfamiliar key. The jeep is on the corner of a street, around two hundred metres from our house. Now, in the snow and sunshine, its redness is crying out for attention, whereas I didn't notice it yesterday evening, when Ludwig and I drove past it after our visit to Brandner.

Please . . .

I'm still running when I point the key at the vehicle to open the central locking.

I yank open the hatch to the boot.

He flinches, blinks. He's still alive.

I smile and say, 'Hello, Jakob. Now we can chat in peace.'

Recap:

On Thursday, 9 November 2017, around 9 p.m., an unnamed suspect was arrested at home in the connection with the ribbon murders, a series of killings stretching back a number of years. This message arrived at exactly 21.24 in the editorial office, where the journalist Jakob Wesseling was doing overtime writing another article. Like an animal advancing on its prey before the rest of the pack, he immediately seized on the topic, not without sensing the possibility of being promoted to deputy chief editor. Although the police were still keeping the identity of the suspect under wraps, Jakob knew exactly who he had to call at HQ to get hold of the name. A name he couldn't publish immediately – in part to protect his source – but which gave him a huge research advantage over his rivals. And Jakob did his research. This was going to be massive. A reportage, a glimpse behind the scenes, shedding light on the depths of the souls of those involved, a special spread or even an entire special issue, and he, as a much sought-after expert, would be invited on to TV talk shows and podcasts as soon as the anonymity of the suspect was lifted. Who was Professor Walter Lesniak? How could a killer raise a child? Why hadn't his daughter been aware of anything? Or did she know about it, maybe? What secrets was she hiding?

Jakob, for whom it was a doddle to find out Lesniak's address. Whose daughter now lived a very secluded life there. Jakob began watching her. Whenever anyone rang the doorbell, she would send them away, and she herself only rarely left the house, at most to go shopping. Moreover, in the first couple of weeks after her father's arrest she was still blonde. He felt it would be pointless to intercept her and solicit an interview. And there was no use him ringing her doorbell if friends and acquaintances were being turned away on the spot. But then one morning she left the house with black hair. The new colour seemed to have changed her; whereas she'd been stooped before, now he fancied she was walking more upright. He followed her to a fast-food outlet called Big Murphy's, where she was having a job interview that day, and got the idea of making friends with her.

From all the interviews he conducted as a journalist, he'd developed a keen sense for people. She was someone you had to be patient with. Someone who was lonely. So he made up a role for

ANATOMY OF A KILLER

himself: the uncomplicated, carefree and cheerful Jakob from the recycling centre. A guy who didn't look as if he'd saddle her with any additional burdens. Who you could just go for a beer with and listen to music. A friend who made it easy to open up, a confidant.

On Christmas Eve he managed it.

They drank, they danced, she talked.

Jakob, who at the end of that evening laid a plastered Ann on the sofa. Covered her and sat beside her for a moment, sweeping strands of her hair from her face. To make sure she really had fallen asleep. Jakob, who made use of an opportunity his rivals could only dream of: snooping around Professor Walter Lesniak's house undisturbed. He switched off the light and, using the torch on his mobile, roamed every room. He inspected the contents of the cutlery drawer in the kitchen as well as the book spines on the sitting-room shelves. When he was finished on the ground floor he went upstairs. Now he knew which aftershave Lesniak used ('Fahrenheit' by Dior) and that Ann didn't wear tangas (but briefs, with a preference for pink and light grey). But he was most interested in the room at the end of the landing, which surely couldn't be locked for no reason. Jakob felt the door frame, but didn't find a key on top. Looking around, he saw the console table in front of the window and opened the drawers. In the left-hand one the Lesniaks kept their candles; in the right, a random selection of small things that didn't appear to have found a place elsewhere: spare buttons, sellotape, a roll of parcel string, a few CDs. On the shelf beneath the desk were books – shamelessly commercial literature, too unworthy for the shelves in the sitting room. But no key. Jakob had no idea why he now reached for the vase. Coincidence, instinct, or just one final, not particularly serious attempt to convince himself that he had really searched everything in this house? And so he got hold of the key. But at that very moment, he heard noises coming from downstairs. A sigh, a few words babbled in sleep – or was she merely dozing? His eyes darted to the window above the console table. It hadn't occurred to him that he hadn't used his mobile-phone torch for a while; it was already light outside. He'd have to come back another time to find out what was behind the locked door. He briefly toyed with the idea of hanging on to the key, but felt it was too risky. What if Ann noticed it was missing? Someone who had good reason to lock a room would also be minded to keep an eye on the key. So he returned it to the vase and went back downstairs. He checked on Ann, who was no longer breathing so deeply and slowly. By the time she woke up – which couldn't be long now – he had to work out how to get into the house unnoticed next time. When Ann stirred, Jakob darted into the hallway. He thought of those films in which door locks were opened with credit cards. But Jakob wasn't a cunning Hollywood burglar; he wasn't capable of that sort of thing. He was, however, a cunning journalist, and as such he had a professional eye for details. Hanging beside the coat hooks was a bunch of keys, including the one for the Audi. Because the car belonged to Walter Lesniak, Jakob could assume the bunch of keys was his too. Each of the five keys had a plastic tag. The red one said 'Uni office', the blue one 'Uni Library', the green one 'Garage' and the yellow one what he'd been looking for: 'Home'. Jakob fiddled the key off the small metal ring and slipped it into his trouser pocket. Then he made some coffee. For Ann who was going to wake up soon . . .

'... For Ann who he fucked over big time.' I'm leaning against the work surface, my hands crossed, shaking my head in disbelief. Jakob is sitting at the table. He looks pale, wrecked by what must have been the longest night of his life. The woollen blanket I've fetched him from the sitting room is over his shoulders like a coat. He's warming his hands on a mug of tea. In spite of everything, he doesn't appear in the least ashamed; while he was talking, he even managed to look me overtly in the eye.

'As if what you did was any different.'

'What?'

'The way you tricked your colleagues at Big Murphy's.'

'Oh, I see, and for that you think I deserved this charade.'

'I'd be very happy to discuss whether I deserved to be locked in my boot for half a day,' he says, slamming the palms of his hands on the table and getting up. 'I could have died, Ann!'

'Sit. Down.' On the work surface are a knife and my mobile, both within reach. One glance at them is enough, along with the fact that, after last night, he's no longer able to size me up. I could be Ann who acted on impulse, or Ann who doesn't care about anything anymore. I might call the police and report him as the intruder from last night, or thrust my knife into his chest. I could even do both, and justify the one thing as self-defence against the other. So he does what I ask and drops back on to his chair.

'Fine. What now?'

I clench my jaws. I don't want him to know how I feel. That I can hardly believe how we got into this situation. Him lying there, yesterday evening, at the bottom of our stairs. Me kneeling over him, expecting to discover Marcus Steinhausen's face beneath the balaclava. Instead it was Jakob, my friend. We'd danced together to Lou Reed. We'd circled like aeroplanes in a blue summer sky. Jakob the traitor. He scratched the record and broke my wings.

Disappointment. (Ann, 9 years old)
Disappointment feels like having water poured in your face. First your sad and you want to cry because you never thought someone could be so mean. And then your angry at yourself because you were so stupid to trust that person. That's why your to blame for your disappointment too and next time you should be more clever.

Yesterday evening.

I waved the knife about as I frisked Jakob's body. 'Who are you?' I said, shouting and howling. He just lay there, dazed after falling down the stairs, dazed after the shock of having been unmasked. In the inside pocket of his coat, I found a wallet as well as his car keys, and inside that his press ID. Fury paralysed my wits, leaving nothing but bitter hatred and the thought that Ludwig might be back with our food soon and so I didn't have much time. I tugged at Jakob's body until I'd forced him to his feet. He made an attempt to resist, but I was the one with the knife. I wasn't going to let him go. The garage, I thought. Or – even better – our car, to stop him drawing attention to himself by shouting and banging. Then I had another idea: I could use the break-in to steer the investigation back towards Steinhausen. Although then the police would go searching our house for clues and would definitely examine the garage as well.

'Where did you park?' I asked. Jakob, who in his state probably thought I just wanted to get rid of him as quickly as possible, told me. We took a detour via the garage, where I knew there was a roll of thick masking tape left over from when I helped Dad redecorate the sitting room a few months ago . . .

'You must realise you can't keep me detained here for ever,' Jakob says now, in the kitchen, rubbing his mouth. The masking tape I used to gag him has left visible red marks. 'Yesterday evening, after I'd fallen down the stairs, I was easy prey. I was completely out of it and you had a knife.'

'That hasn't changed,' I say, nodding to the knife beside me.

He shakes his head. 'You're not like that, Ann. I simply don't believe it.'

'By all means stand up and go to the door if you want to find out.'

'Let's both agree that this whole thing has got out of hand. We've both made mistakes.'

'Nice try.'

'I need to see a doctor, Ann!' Now he wrings his hands and forces a pained expression on to his face. 'I fell down the stairs and lay in a car boot for twelve hours in freezing temperatures. I've got hypothermia and I might have damaged a vertebra. For fuck's sake, Ann, honestly, why are you doing this?'

Without answering, I take hold of the knife and move towards him. Jakob leaps up from his chair and lurches backwards. Smiling, I withdraw to my initial position and put the knife back down beside me. 'You seem fine to me.'

Jakob growls; his reflexes have given him away. 'All right, what do you want?'

'Like I said, I want to talk.' With my chin I motion for him to sit down again. 'What were you looking for in my father's study? For proof the police have overlooked?'

'I dunno, perhaps. It seemed strange, at least, that the room was locked. And then I found the documents.'

The documents. Ludwig's folder, which I claimed the burglar had stolen. In fact, I'd actually hidden it in my rucksack before Ludwig returned and now it's lying on the kitchen table in front of Jakob, its cover closed.

'You're on thin ice, you know that, Ann?'

I nod feebly. He's right. This isn't me. The crack running through my life since my father's death seems to end in a crater that's getting wider and wider, swallowing up ever larger pieces of my old world. And maybe me as well. I hid the folder because I thought it would be good if the burglar had taken something linked to the case. Besides, it can't hurt to keep hold of the information about the case. Merely the thoughts my mind has been entertaining – they're so callous, so calculating. I had no problem forcing Jakob into his car boot, switching off all the lights in the house and then waiting as the distraught victim for Ludwig.

The end justifies the means, I tell myself. I'm not a bad person, just determined.

'You're not a hostage, Jakob. You can leave whenever you like.' I pointedly take the knife and return it to the block on the work surface. 'Go back to your paper, sit in front of your computer and write an article about your miserable night in the boot of your car. Or . . .' I smile.

'Or what?'

'You help me and end up writing the article of your life about one of the greatest miscarriages of justice this country has ever seen.'

*

It's the *or*, of course. Someone who's gone as far as Jakob has doesn't shuffle off without reaching the end. I remember what he said to me on Christmas Day: *Seek out a trustworthy journalist and give them an exclusive interview with your version of what happened.* From day one, *he* wanted to be that journalist. And when he broached the subject of my supposed daughter after my attack on the newspaper dispenser, this was just an attempt to break my shell. He already knew I didn't have children; he'd been watching me, studying me for weeks by then.

I don't trust him one bit, Dad. But I trust his ego. He'll do anything and everything for his story. And I've got support again.

Jakob's now in one of your jumpers. He's used your shower gel and shampoo. I don't like it, but I didn't want him to go home just for a hot shower. We can't waste any more time. He's read through all the documents in Ludwig's folder and he listened attentively as I told him about the past couple of days. He believes me, or at least he doesn't think it out of the question that Steinhausen, given his backstory, could be the real ribbon murderer.

'The guy's got to be somewhere,' was the last thing he said before unlocking my laptop to comb the internet. Sitting opposite him, I've drawn up a timeline of the murders in the hope of stumbling across a pattern.

> June 2003 – Larissa, 10
> January 2004 – Jana, 8
> June 2005 – Kati, 9
> 2006 – Nothing
> September 2007 – Olivia, 7

March 2008 – Laetitia, 10
2009 – Nothing
2010 – Nothing
April 2011 – Hayet, 9
2012 – Nothing
October 2013 – Jenny, 6
December 2014 – Saskia, 8
2015 – Nothing
July 2016 – Alina, 9
November 2017 – Sophie, 7

'One killing per year, albeit at different times, and then there are the years of inactivity: 2006, 2009, 2010, 2012 and 2015,' I summarise, sighing. 'That isn't a pattern. It could—' I'm interrupted by the ringing of my mobile, which is charging beside the empty fruit bowl on the work surface. I get up to check: it's Ludwig. Either he wants to appeal to my conscience or apologise. I reject the call.

'If you ask me, one murder per year is enough of a pattern,' Jakob says, when he sees I'm not going to take the call. 'As for those years when he takes a break, you're right. Either he didn't kill anyone because he couldn't, or he was abroad. Or there's a third possibility: the bodies simply haven't been found. When exactly was Steinhausen in rehab?'

I check the papers. 'September to October 2003, and then again from June to October 2005.'

'So he could . . .'

'Yes, he could. What have you found?'

'I've got . . .' Jakob starts to turn the laptop to face me, then stops. 'I've got a confession to make.'

'Okay?'

'Maybe it wasn't Steinhausen who tied the red ribbon to your olive tree.'

'Who, then?'

'Maybe there's a journalist out there who thought a little psychological pressure might help you open up.' He lowers his eyes, probably in expectation of my next outburst – screaming, scolding, swishing the knife. But I don't even shrug; I'm not surprised.

'Say something, Ann.'

'It's an oleander, you idiot.'

'That's not what I mean.'

'I realise that,' I say, shaking my head. 'It doesn't change anything.'

'With regards to Steinhausen or between us?'

'Steinhausen. I didn't get why he would threaten me and risk blowing his cover.'

'And between us?'

'*Maybe*,' I say harshly, 'you know by now that I'm able to defend myself, and so in the future you'll spare yourself the bother of trying to provoke me.' I nod at the laptop. 'Show me what you've found.'

A website. From Spain. *Servicio de artesano*, a tradesman working near Málaga. My heart leaps when Jakob points to a M. Steinhausen on the homepage. I'm already breathing with excitement, but Jakob beats me to it: 'Not so fast. This site hasn't been updated in over three years and it's impossible to say for certain that this is our Steinhausen.'

'But Steinhausen used to work as a site manager . . .'

'Which doesn't automatically make him a tradesman.'

'Surely we can find that out?'

My mobile rings once more. Again it's Ludwig and again I'm about to reject the call. But . . . if I do, he might decide to jump into his car and drive over here.

'Excuse me for a sec,' I say to Jakob, then answer the phone. 'Hello, Ludwig.'

'Anni.' As so often, it sounds like a sigh, only less resigned and more exhausted. Our row seems to have really affected him.

'Let's talk about it another time, Ludwig, okay? It doesn't suit—'

'No, listen to me,' he interrupts assertively. 'I've spent at least half an hour wondering whether ringing you is the right thing to do. But I thought I had to, to prove you have no reason to doubt me. Anni, it's like this . . .'

Ludwig waffles on and on – I can't take any more, not a single word.

It's only when he asks me if I've understood that I manage a 'yes', a lie. I've heard his words, but when it comes to their meaning my mind has abandoned me.

Six minutes, fourteen seconds, I see on the screen when we hang up. That's how long the call lasted. Jakob is standing beside me, stroking my arm. I didn't notice him get up from the table.

'Ann? What's wrong?' Now I can feel his hand on my cheek.

I shake my head. Sometimes it only takes a second to change an entire life. That's how it was with Dad's arrest and also with Eva in the basement of the building site. But sometimes it takes a moment longer. Six minutes and fourteen seconds, to be precise.

I look at Jakob. 'Steinhausen isn't in Spain. But I know where we can find him.'

'What?'

I nod. What Ludwig just told me is both horrific and a miracle: *Anni, it's like this. There seems to be a new case. In Schergel, in the Bavarian Forest.*

US

Sarah, sweetheart, wake up, wake up. I know you feel a bit woozy, but that's not bad. It's the magic working, you see? We're now going to eat together: you, me and the princess. Yes, that's right, the princess. Finally, it's time for you to meet her. But first we need to take you to the loo. You have to do a wee, Sarah, be a good girl and do a wee so we don't have another accident. That wouldn't be very nice, would it? I often wet myself when I was your age, you know. I was so scared when my mummy shouted at me that I lost control over my body. I'm not saying she was a bad person, she just had weak nerves and wasn't able to come to terms with her own anger. But all that's in the past and unimportant now. Oh, look at your hair! It's all dishevelled. Let me comb it for you, sweetie, okay? And then we'll go into the kitchen. Your legs are still too feeble, I'd better carry you, come here. By the way, I've made a sausage casserole. Do you like that? I hope so. I want you to be very happy here. This is your place, sit down, Sarah, go on, sit down. Oh no, don't topple off the chair, sweetheart! Lean back. It might be best if I fed you. Open your mouth like a good girl – yes, that's right, that's good. The way you're looking at her . . . I can understand. She's gorgeous, isn't she? What about you, princess? Are you still angry that I slept beside

Sarah last night? I just wanted her to feel comfortable, seeing as how everything here is still unfamiliar to her. Surely you understand that? Of course you do. Isn't this marvellous, the three of us? I could get used to this. The two of you are such lovely girls, such lovely, beautiful, well-behaved girls ... Now, now, Sarah, careful! Chew slowly and swallow – it's no wonder you're sick if you bolt it down. We'll have to clean you up and then I think you should have another lie-down. I can read both of you a story if you like. What's your favourite story, Sarah? *Sleeping Beauty*? That's perfect.

ANN

BERLIN – SCHERGEL, 27 DECEMBER 2017

'A seven-year-old girl, Sarah, from Schergel, a village in the Bavarian Forest with just under a thousand inhabitants. Yesterday she and her mum went for a festive lunch with friends who also live in the village. Her mum sent her home early. It wasn't far, just a few streets in a place where it's impossible to disappear unnoticed. But when the mother got home in the afternoon to find Sarah not there, that's exactly what seemed to have happened: Sarah had gone and nobody had seen her. By the evening, friends and neighbours had gathered to search the village and surrounding area. There was no sign of Sarah, but they did find red ribbons in a wood.'

'Red ribbons, but no body?' Jakob narrows his eye in puzzlement. 'Where did the ribbons lead to?'

'Nowhere, according to my father's lawyer. They were just put at random in the wood.'

'That doesn't make sense.'

'No, maybe it does,' I say, then relay the rest of what Ludwig said, about the two possibilities the police in Schergel are considering. 'Either the abductor still has Sarah in his power – but for some reason he thought it important to let the police know he's active again and that they've arrested the wrong man – or the alternative is that it's a copycat crime, or just a bad joke in poor taste. If so, the question still remains: where is Sarah? She's not going to have run away and put out the red ribbons herself.'

'What are you going to do now?'

'I think you can guess that, can't you?'

'Good,' Jakob says, nodding decisively. 'I'm in.'

His jeep is parked in our drive, the boot facing the garage. I moved it myself this lunchtime from around the corner. I didn't want a neighbour to see Jakob climb out of the boot, let alone risk a scene in the street. My concerns about that were greater than my inherent anxiety about getting behind the wheel of a car, and it was only a few metres down the road. Now Jakob suggests we take turns driving to Schergel and that I go first, giving him the opportunity to do some more research, but also to establish contact with the police and try to find out more details.

'I haven't driven since I had a car accident two years ago,' I say, smiling helplessly.

'It's high time you did then.' He takes from me the bag I packed in a hurry, puts it in the boot, and then goes around to the passenger side as if the matter were decided. Not wanting to show any weakness, I get in and start the engine, while Jakob programmes the satnav. Schergel seems to be so small that only its main street is listed.

'Five hours, twenty minutes,' he says, doing the calculations. 'We won't be there before eight, half eight.' Particularly as we have to go past his flat first so he can pack a few things and pick up his laptop.

I shrug my shoulders, and the pain immediately flares up in the right one again.

'Everything all right?'

'It's okay,' I say, then ask him to find a news station on the radio. 'We have to take the gamble that we're going to get there too late. But until we hear that Sarah's been found, there's still the possibility the killer is keeping her captive. And so long as that's the case, it's also likely that he's in the vicinity of Schergel. He wouldn't have any reason to take her elsewhere. With the Berlin killings, he always stayed in the surrounding area.'

'That's not certain. He might change his pattern. I mean, hasn't he done that already? There's already been a victim this year: the little girl found in the Königswald. This would be the first time he's killed twice in a calendar year. And he's chosen a different region.'

'But it's also the first time that someone else is in prison, robbing him of the dubious fame of being the ribbon murderer.'

Jakob sighs.

'What?'

'Or is this really a copycat crime?'

I shake my head. 'Call me crazy, but I know we're on the right track. I can just sense it.'

'Red light!'

I brake just in time. We're jerked forwards abruptly, before being thrown back into our seats. My heart misses a beat – the memory. That appalling Saturday night two years ago: Zoe and I at a party in Spreenhagen. We had an argument and I drove home without her, furious and exhausted – but most of all, I shouldn't have been behind the wheel because I'd drunk too much. A shortcut I thought was a good idea at the time. A road through the woods that was so narrow and bendy it required a degree of concentration that a few bottles of beer had sluiced from my head. And then, as if in a bad film, the deer suddenly there in the middle of the road. Wrenching the wheel to the side, I found myself racing down a slope. Time lost its dimension, stretching, extending, then I heard the deafening crack. The crack of branches, of metal and finally of my jaw. The airbag activated too late. The driver's door had jammed into a tree, but I managed to crawl over to the passenger side and call my father on my mobile. I remember blood running from my mouth down my wrist as I spoke, trying to convey where I was. He came. The ambulance came too. I lay on a stretcher, my father holding my trembling hand. 'How do you feel?' he said, and I gave a pained smile with my bloody mouth. He could see how I was; he could imagine it too. In hospital they put splints and screws in my jaw and for the next few weeks all I could eat was soup and yoghurt.

'Ann?'

'Yes?'

'It's green.'

'Sorry.'

Jakob mumbles something.

'What?'

'I'm just thinking . . . You said the red ribbons were placed at random in the wood. Which means there's no way of working out the beginning and end of the trail?'

'So far as I know, yes. Why?'

195

He says nothing. It's only when I tap his thigh that he reacts. 'Just because Sarah's body isn't lying there for all to see doesn't mean she isn't there at all.' He pauses. 'Maybe they should try digging.'

'Maybe,' I repeat, snorting in frustration. 'This is exactly what gets me so down, you know? Everything is just *maybe, perhaps, possibly, conceivably* – all fricking speculation. My entire life is uncertain. There's nothing genuine, nothing real left, nothing I can rely on.'

'You can rely on me.'

I snort again, in amusement this time. 'Two liars heading off to find out the truth. Sounds like the beginning of a rather stupid joke.'

'Or the beginning of a first-rate reportage.' He puts out his hand. 'I live over there on the left. You can park right outside. I won't be long.'

The beginning of a first-rate reportage. I'm glad he's reminded me who I'm dealing with. We're not friends, we never were. We're of use to each other, no more, no less. And it's like a game, an exchange. I tell him about my childhood, which feels like a summer's day, about a little girl sitting on her father's shoulders with her arms outstretched. In return I make Jakob call the hospital and claim to be a journalist reporting on the incident at the construction site, so they'll give him information about Eva's condition. They certainly wouldn't say anything to me; I'm not related to Eva and those who are – Elke and Caspian – want me to go to hell.

'Unchanged but stable' is what Jakob eventually finds out. 'The doctor treating her says there haven't been any complications so far, which is a good sign.'

I thank him by talking about my puberty. Me as a difficult teenager always getting into trouble, and my wonderful father, a human instruction manual on how to bring up children. Someone who was always controlled and dependable. Never, not once, did he scream at me, shout, or even use harsh language, let alone slap my cheeky teen face – or any other part of my body, for that matter. And they reckon someone like that could have slit the wrists of ten little girls? Jakob records with the dictation app on his mobile, while scribbling in a notebook on his lap.

Then it's his turn again. This time he calls his contact at the police – Inspector Brandner's secretary, as he reveals to me. A young woman he sometimes meets for a drink out of work – nothing serious, but incredibly useful. I refrain from passing comment. I don't care about Jakob's private life and his morality; I just want to know what she said. It's sobering but unsurprising. 'Finding Sarah is the top priority. The local police are being assisted by search teams from nearby towns. So far, however, there are no new leads and . . .' He breaks off.

'Go on, I can pretty much guess already.'

'Although they're not ruling anything out, they're moving further towards the idea that this is a copycat crime. I'm sorry, Ann.' He does actually manage to sound concerned. 'They're saying it's the most probable—'

'"Everything that is merely probable is probably false,"' I interrupt him, smiling when he looks baffled. 'A quote by René Descartes. He wasn't just a philosopher, but a mathematician and scientist too. For him, doubting everything was the basis of all knowledge.'

'You mean I know that I know nothing?'

I shake my head. 'Wrong guy. That was Socrates. Who, by the way, actually said: "I know that I don't know." Your version comes from a mistake in translation. Socrates never claimed he knew nothing. Instead he questioned what it meant to know.'

'Jesus!' Jakob laughs. 'Maybe you ought to have studied philosophy rather than German.'

'I did to begin with, for four semesters. But the world becomes unpleasant when you only ask questions rather than simply living life. It's enough to have one person in the family doing it.'

'What about your mother?'

'Didn't you find out in your research? She died of cancer when I was six.'

'I'm sorry.'

'That's okay.'

'My mother's dead too. She died last year, following a stroke. I really miss her.'

I sigh. 'I miss mine too, even though I hardly have any memories of her. But I think that's quite normal. I mean, our parents determine a large chunk of our identity, don't they?'

'So if – and this is purely hypothetical, so don't flip out and lock me in the boot again – your father was convicted beyond all doubt of being the ribbon murderer—'

'I wouldn't only lose my father, but my identity too.'

Jakob scribbles something; I appear to have given him a quotation for his article. 'I understand,' he says, but he doesn't, he can't. For him these are just words, whereas for me my entire existence depends on it. Who would I be – what would remain of me? – if everything I've been up till now turned out to be a lie?

Security. (Ann, 9 years old)

Security means you don't have to worry even if something bad happens. Like when you lie awake in bed at night and there is thunder and lightening outside, but you know nothing is going to happen because Daddy has made sure that we have a lightening conducter. Without this the lightening could hit our house and then my room might burn down and I might die. But I don't believe that is going to happen. Because of the lightening conducter and because Mummy is already dead. People can't keep dying in the same family otherwise there would be nobody left.

Although Jakob took over the driving when it started getting dark, we haven't sped up. We keep having to stop so he can take a pee. He suspects he got a touch of hypothermia during the night but he's refraining from any reproachful looks. We get to Schergel just after half past nine. The village sits between the mountains, as if encircled, a deep hole that's very difficult to climb out of once you've fallen in. We follow the only road that snakes past houses set far apart from each other. Barely any streetlamps, an oppressive darkness that baffles me. I'd expected light, all sorts of light. Light in the houses, light from the searchlights, flashing blue lights. But there's not the slightest indication that a child has disappeared from here, presumably kidnapped by a dangerous serial killer.

'Are we really in the right place?'

Jakob just grins. Of course this is the right place – it's what the sign said, and what the satnav says too.

We keep driving down the road until we come to more houses, arranged around a circle, the centre of which is marked by a long, scrawny maypole without a crown. The heart of the village. Parked here are half a dozen patrol cars and police minibuses. But where the hell is the activity? People swinging their torches in all directions, search dogs excitedly tugging on their leads, desperate calls for Sarah?

Nothing of the sort. Only a village that looks as if the night-time bell had already been rung.

'What now?' I ask. Jakob points at the large building on the other side of the circle: an inn. At least there appears to be some sort of life, bathed in a yellow light, behind its leaded windows. Shapes of people moving through the room.

'I come from a village like this originally,' he says, parking the jeep outside a small grocery opposite. 'Life is very different from in the city. Usually there's great cohesion amongst the people, which has its advantages. On the other hand, it gives rise to a sort of hostility to anything that comes from outside.'

'You mean they might not welcome the police here?'

'No, not that. It's just they might not help with the search to the extent that you would expect, because they see the disap-pearance of a child here as a stain on the village. It doesn't fit with the way they perceive themselves, it dents their pride. After all, it's precisely what differentiates them from a big city like Berlin: being sheltered, safe, people looking out for each other.' Switching off the ignition, he turns to me. 'Somewhere there's always an Auntie Erna leaning out of the kitchen window, playing village sheriff.'

'Wow, it's great to know you don't have any prejudices.' I take my mobile from the rucksack and see I've missed several calls en route. Two from Big Murphy's, another from Michelle, who's also sent me a message. I ought to have been back at work today, on the late shift starting at four. *None of the others know anything. I've told them you're sick. Take a few days off and have a think about whether you want to continue doing the job. Michelle.* Then Ludwig, who tried calling about an hour ago, no doubt to find out my whereabouts. He's no idea we've come to Schergel; he'd give me hell if he knew.

'Is everything okay, Ann?'

'Yes.' I quickly slip the mobile back in my bag. 'I'm just amazed at you, I really am. I mean, as a journalist you should always be neutral and impartial, shouldn't you?'

'As I said: I grew up in a village like this.'

We get out. Jakob locks the car and we make for the inn. 'And I also want you to be mentally prepared for this. The moment we go in, it's going to be like one of those old cowboy films. Two strangers enter the saloon, conversation stops and everyone eyes us up and down suspiciously . . .'

We're only a few steps from the door when it opens suddenly. Police officers come pouring out and head for their vehicles.

'You see? They're not keen on interlopers here. We'd better watch our step or we won't get any information out of them.'

I roll my eyes and go ahead. 'That doesn't mean they've been shown the door. Maybe they just went in for something to eat and now they're finished.'

The inn is called 'Zum alten Brock'. It's furnished in rustic oak, the air is thick and the tiles sticky. It smells of spilled beer, sweat and gravy. My attention is drawn at once to the silver serving platters, at least five on each table. Some still have a few sand-wiches, others are empty save for the odd crumb and the parsley garnish. A fat old man with a shiny bald head peels away from a group of people in civilian clothes, some of whom are holding beer tankards.

'Welcome, welcome!' he says, his arms wide open, and all eyes now focus on us. 'Police, psychological support, press?'

'No, no,' Jakob stammers beside me. 'Just, er ... passing through.'

The man looks visibly disappointed. 'You can have a room but the kitchen's closed,' he says, turning away. I think of Eva, who immediately sensed who we had to pretend to be so that Rainer Meller would talk to us.

'Press! From Berlin!' I call out, then say more quietly to Jakob, 'Come on, show him your press pass.'

The man's name is Brock. Together with his wife, who he introduces to us, he's the owner of this place, which has been in his family for three generations. One of the Schergel old guard, a village elder, chairman of the local council and treasurer of the heritage association – he comes up with all sorts of labels to make us aware just whose serving platters are on those tables. We also get two tankards of beer on the house and a promise of the best accommodation. Because we're journalists – finally, some journalists! – and what's more, we're from Berlin. Although the regional paper was here today too, all the guy did was take a few photographs of the police search. Which makes Brock's face turn red with indignation.

'They're only interested when there's a dead body,' he complains, and he's probably right. So long as Sarah's still missing, there's hope, and hope doesn't sell papers. 'They don't even think it *was* the ribbon murderer who took the little girl, because he's meant to be in prison in Berlin. But who put all those red ribbons in the woods, then?'

To signal my agreement, I lift my tankard and take a sip of beer. The group that was standing in the middle of the room when we came in has now gathered around the table where Brock has placed us. It's the best table, normally reserved for the council. Jakob sits next to me, on the corner bench covered in coarse woven fabric, looking stiff and bewildered. *Things happen differently here*, he just whispered to me. And he wasn't talking about canapés.

'What are the police up to?' I ask Brock, in reference to the men we just saw leaving the pub. 'Have they clocked off for the day?'

'No, no, they just needed a little break for refreshment. In fact, they're expanding the search area tonight. The village community was out there too, all day long, looking for the little one. The police wanted to discourage us, worried that we might destroy potential evidence. But they were banging their heads against a brick wall there.' He turns to the group around us. 'Sarah will come back home!' General agreement, clinking of tankards. 'She's Kerstin's daughter, you know. Kerstin Seiler, who runs the butcher's here, a good woman. She's all on her own with the child and does her work too.' He shakes his head. 'She doesn't deserve this, does Kerstin.'

'Who does?' I say quietly, thinking of Michelle, whose entire family died along with Larissa.

'I'm sure the police have questioned all of you already,' Jakob chimes in. He finally seems to have stirred from his numbness. 'But did you notice anything in the days before Sarah's abduction? Any unfamiliar faces in the village?'

'Well,' Brock says, rubbing his chin. 'Helping with the search yesterday and today there was all manner of outsiders. But in the days beforehand . . .' He shrugs. 'I mean, it was Christmas, wasn't it? Not much happening here. Even though it's a wonderful place to spend your Christmas holiday. The woods, the mountains, the old fortress ruins. We've spent years trying to raise our tourist profile. I've got a few holiday houses of my own on the upper common, if you fancy taking a look.' Again the clinking of tankards, no doubt toasting the magnificent local landscape.

'It's really shit that there's no photo of Steinhausen on the internet,' I whisper to Jakob, but no sooner have I said this than something occurs to me: brothers whose resemblance has deceived many people. I take out my mobile with trembling fingers and do an image search for Andreas Steinhausen. Apart from the blond hair and freckles, he has scarcely anything in common with the man on the chair with a swollen eye and fat lip who I saw in the basement of the construction site. Nonetheless I recognise him at once. The architecture practice he owns has a website with photographs of all the members of staff. I hold out my screen to Brock and the others. 'Recognise this man?'

'Hard to say; maybe, maybe not. Is that him? Is that the guy who's taken our Sarah?'

'Yes,' I say.

'No,' Jakob says. 'But he is someone we'd like to speak to. Talking of which, do you think it would be possible to have a word with Sarah's mother?'

Brock gets up at once. 'Come with me.'

In a second. First Jakob and I have to get something clear, just between us two. We do it outside in a whisper. Am I out of my mind, setting the village mob on to Steinhausen? 'Just imagine if he really did turn up here and they recognised him from the photo you showed them. He'd be lynched, Ann! And if later people are asking, *How could that have happened?*, the spotlight will fall on those two journalists from Berlin, who were so reckless with their information.'

'Are you worried about your reputation, or do you really sympathise with that bloke? Steinhausen is a murderer, Jakob!'

Jakob grabs my arm and I immediately feel a stabbing pain in my injured shoulder. 'No, right at the moment your father is the murderer and Steinhausen is just a lead. Can you get that into your head?'

I jerk my arm to free myself from his grip, which causes more pain, but most of all I feel anger. At Jakob, who's right. I mustn't make any mistakes now. Steinhausen could be close by. What if he got wind of the fact that he's no longer a phantom? That the village mob is openly looking for a blond man with freckles? He would disappear, perhaps for good. And he'd take Sarah with him or dispose of her.

'I understand,' I growl.

'Good. Then let's talk to the mother.'

A mother like Michelle. I picture her lying on the rug in her sitting room, writhing with anxiety, her chest open; and us, the supposed journalists, lusting after sensation, leaning over her, rummaging in her pain, disembowelling her. The worst thing is that Jakob seems to think nothing of it. He strides buoyantly as we follow Brock to the butcher's, which is opposite the inn, with only the round marketplace in between. Jakob, who's concerned about the safety of a killer, but who has no scruples when it comes to the victims. I feel sick.

A few minutes later we're sitting in the large, cold kitchen of

Seiler, the butcher's. It's inhospitable here, the floor and walls all covered in tiles. Like a repurposed slaughter room, I think, all the more so when I spot a drain the size of a beer mat beside my foot. Only the units along with the cooker and fridge, and the chunky wooden dining table suggest that this is a kitchen. Sarah's mother, Kerstin Seiler, is a petite woman, more like an overgrown little girl. It's strange to think that she slaughters animals and processes them into the joints and cuts that will later be on display in her shop. Her face is young and pale; her dark ponytail looks as if it had been tied a few days ago and not touched since. She's sitting limply on a chair, the focal point of a tragedy, slightly apart from the table where Jakob and I have sat. A man with gelled hair and a severe side parting is standing just to the right of her, his hand protectively on her shoulder. He's barely taller than me, in stark contrast to his beefy upper body with its pumped biceps that he puts on show in his stained, white sleeveless T-shirt, despite the temperature. This is Schmitti, from Schmitti's Garage, Brock told us. Kerstin Seiler's fiancé, a good bloke – he can fix everything that goes wrong in Schergel, from a car to a toaster. To Kerstin's left is a friend, an attractive blonde woman who strokes her knee and passes her fresh tissues at irregular intervals. Everything about her face is so delicate, perfect and symmetrical – it reminds me of Zoe. I would often stare at Zoe, simply fascinated by the interplay of her features. When the woman catches me gazing at her, I look away. Brock is leaning against the edge of the table. He's really selling us to Kerstin Seiler: Jakob and me, two important journalists who are going to bring the search for Sarah to the attention of the media nationwide. Frau Seiler doesn't seem to hear a word he's saying;

she just sobs. Schmitti, on the other hand, gives us suspicious looks vicariously. Me with my baggy turquoise knitted hat over my unwashed, jet-black dyed hair, and the plaster above my eyebrow as if I'd just been in a street fight; and Jakob, who's still wearing my father's jumper, its old-fashioned diamond pattern making him look like a penniless student.

'What good's it going to do Sarah being in the national newspapers?' he snarls at Brock. 'What's important is that the police are here looking for her. And that's exactly what's happening. So how would it help us?'

'Come on, Schmitti, it means Schergel will be on everyone's radar! We'd get more people volunteering to join the search. And if the kidnapper tries to flee with her, he won't get very far, because everyone will recognise Sarah as the missing girl.'

Schmitti growls again. '*Schergel will be on everyone's radar* . . . Is that your new ploy to attract tourists, Peter? Or nutters who get a kick out of visiting crime scenes? I mean, those people have to stay somewhere and eat too, don't they?'

Brock takes a step forwards, as does Schmitti, who plants himself in front of Kerstin like a barricade.

'How dare you accuse me of trying to profit from the disappearance of an innocent little girl!'

'No, Peter, how dare you—'

'Wait!' I say, getting to my feet. 'We won't publish anything you're not happy with. We only want to help.' I look at Jakob, who ought to be backing me up, but he's just sitting there, arms crossed like a passive spectator.

'We had a row,' a voice says softly from behind Schmitti's back. Kerstin Seiler, who's now commanding everyone's attention.

'Kerstin, you don't have to—' her fiancé says, but she shakes her head.

'We were invited for lunch with friends. I sent Sarah home early because she was playing up. She was so loud and hyper, she kept interrupting every conversation – she was being impossible. I grabbed her by the arm, dragged her into the hall and told her she was being a right nuisance.' Kerstin sobs loudly. 'It was all my fault that she was out there on her own. If I'd been with her . . .'

'You mustn't write any of that!' Schmitti hisses. 'Nobody must find that out, least of all the police.'

I look at him, puzzled.

'That there was an argument!' he explains. 'The police won't take the thing seriously anymore because they'll think Sarah simply ran away. They might even stop their search.'

'I don't think there's any danger of that. I mean, they found the red ribbons, just . . .' I break off, ashamed.

'Just like the ribbon murderer always left,' Kerstin Seiler's friend says, finishing my sentence, dabbing her eyes with a tissue.

'I'm sorry,' I say softly, but it's too late. The air is thick and heavy with unspoken speculation and fears. It's Schmitti who brings an end to the unpleasant situation.

'Right then. Here's the plan. You're going to leave now, all of you. It's late and Kerstin really needs some peace and quiet. You' – he points at Brock – 'are going to keep your nose out of it from now on. The two of you' – Jakob and me – 'can make yourselves useful by joining the search tomorrow. We're going to the upper common. The more we are, the better. And Nathalie' – that's the friend's name – 'I'm going to take you home now. Your little one will be wondering where her mummy's got to.'

'But Kerstin can't be on her—' the woman tries to protest.

'I'll stay the night with her,' Schmitti says. 'And then we'll all meet back here tomorrow morning, seven o'clock.' He gives Jakob and me a look of defiance. 'Woe betide anyone who's not punctual.'

US

Can you hear that, my girl? The shouting. It's echoing up from the valley. It's the red ribbons in the woods making them sound shriller, louder, more panicky. Was it too early to put out the ribbons? Maybe. But they're all part of it, just like the missing shoe in the *Cinderella* story or the poisoned apple in *Snow White*. Look, Sarah! Come here, I'll lift you up so you can look out of the window. The men from the search unit have been having a break, but they're getting going again now. It's said that the first twenty-four hours after someone goes missing are the most important – you've been missing considerably longer than that. What's more, it's supposed to get down to minus ten or more tonight again; they must be really worried. The dancing lights of the torches in the woods, the shouts, all the commotion – and just for you, my sweetie, just for you. What would they give to get you back unharmed, hmm? What do you think? Their lives, they'd answer if they were asked. That's what they've all said, in the paper, on telly, all the parents who've ever spoken publicly about it. *I'd swap my life for my daughter's.* That sort of thing's easy to say when it's not an option. I mean, they've never been offered a deal like that: *You've got the choice. Your child's going to die unless you sacrifice yourself.* That's not what this is about. That was never part of this story. Still, saying something like that sounds good. Words society expects to hear in such a situation. But what I want to know is, how many of these people really meant it? If they were given the offer to swap places with their children, how many would take it up? Let me tell you, sweetie: none of them. But your mummy, she might be very close right now. She's at rock bottom, broken, chastened. You know what that means, don't you? It means it's time, Sarah. The last act, then the end.

ANN

SCHERGEL, 28 DECEMBER 2017

A restless night, a peculiar dream. Me, sitting motionless on the bed in room 113. It's a simple room: a bed, above it Christ on his cross as a reminder, a wardrobe with a double door and a narrow desk. The only slight nods to luxury are a small television set, a kettle, a basket with a selection of teas, sugar sachets and capsules of condensed milk, and a cup. I'm still fully dressed in my coat, hat and boots. Beside the bed is my bag, with tracksuit bottoms and the fresh sweatshirt I could wear to sleep in after a nice shower. Jakob has the room next door. I'm grateful for the wall between us, for some distance. I'm exhausted and confused. As if I were trapped in one of those psychedelic spirals that open and close again and seem to be permanently rearranging themselves, while I desperately look for a fixed point to focus on. But the spiral twists and turns, overloading my brain. Why Schergel, this tiny, anonymous village in the Bavarian Forest? What has driven Steinhausen here?

I dream that I get up from the bed, in a trance, being controlled remotely. I leave my room, cross the landing to the stairs, and then creep downstairs. I turn the key in the back door and step out into the night. I dream I'm running. There's no particular goal; I tell myself to be guided by my instinct. Down the main street, past houses where only the odd light is on. A few insomniacs who likewise feel it's wrong to happily go to bed while Sarah's outside somewhere, in the cold, in danger, terrified for her life. Maybe she's no longer alive. Maybe she's lying undiscovered in the woods, her face blue and the blood from the deep wound on her wrist already frozen. Something is driving me, I dream, driving me on. The distance between houses increases, the broad road becomes narrow and uneven beneath the blanket of snow. There's no longer any light to help guide me; it's a darkness I've never experienced in the city. I take my mobile out of my coat pocket and turn on the torch, but it has a tiny radius. I spin around, first in one direction, then the other. I'm wheezing as I breathe, hemmed in by the blackness closing in on me. *The fear of fear gives rise to more suffering than the actual cause* . . . I don't believe myself. I try to shout for help but the cold constricts my throat. My chest contracts. My spray, is all I can think. My asthma spray, which is in my rucksack, which in turn is on the desk of room 113. I dream I fall to my knees; now I'm on all fours in the snow, not knowing what to do next. They say you don't die in your dreams; you always wake up in time. So I roll on to my side, curl up and wait. Soon I'll wake up, I must wake up soon . . .

My mobile rings. A sound that bores into my head like a nasty little hand drill. I sit bolt upright in bed. Orientation. Room 113 and sunshine slanting dazzlingly through the window. My heart racing, my mouth gasping in panic for oxygen, as if I'd just been holding my breath for minutes. Jakob sitting on the edge of the bed. His outstretched hand stroking my cheek.

'Hey, nice and calm now,' he says gently, then turns away and remarks, 'She's really hot.'

I recoil in sheer panic. What's Jakob doing in my room? How did he get in here? What's happened?

'We should at least take her temperature,' a woman says, and a moment later Frau Brock, the landlady, comes into view. She sits on the other side of the bed and hands me a thermometer. 'Here, put this under your armpit. And then drink your tea.'

A cup is thrust into my hand and sympathetic smiles come from both sides of the bed.

'You gave us quite a fright.'

I can barely get a sound out, but Jakob seems to understand me. 'Just after three o'clock this morning, Kerstin Seiler's fiancé, Schmitti, found you on the lane from the village to the woods. You were completely frozen and torpid.'

'He called my husband and tried to keep you warm until Peter arrived with the car to bring you back here,' Frau Brock adds.

I shake my head in bewilderment. I recall my dream, ending with me curled up in the snow, and nothing else. There's no Schmitti finding me, and no Brock heaving me into his car. There's nobody carrying me up the stairs to room 113, taking off my wet clothes and putting me to bed in my underwear.

'What were you doing?' Jakob asks, but I just shake my head again. Looking for Sarah? For Steinhausen? I don't know; I wasn't even aware I'd left the inn.

The thermometer beeps.

'Your temperature's just a bit high, no cause for concern,' Frau

Brock says, smiling again. I still feel totally spaced out, and the sun is so blinding that tears come to my eyes. Seven o'clock sharp, I remember. That's when we were going to meet at the butcher's. To search for Sarah on the upper common. It would have still been dark then.

'What's the time?'

'Just after nine,' Jakob says.

'What about the search?'

'A few have set off already,' Frau Brock says, getting up off the bed. 'Your colleague and I wanted to make sure you were okay before heading out ourselves.'

'What? No!' Flinging the duvet aside, I leap up on to my wobbly legs. 'I'm coming too! You've got to wait for me! I'll get dressed in a jiffy.'

'Oh, Ann . . .' Jakob thinks I'm stubborn.

Yes, yes, I am, I always have been.

He also thinks I ought to take it easy.

Thanks, but no need. That was strange, last night, I realise. But let's not get it out of proportion. It must have been my nerves, a little blackout; this sort of thing can happen after all I've been through recently. End of discussion, I hop into the bathroom, Jakob stays in my room.

Meanwhile Frau Brock has gone downstairs to make a breakfast I can take with me. I don't want anything to eat and I've told her that, but she says I've got to get something in my tummy, even if it's just a dry roll.

'You haven't told anyone about my dad, have you?' I ask Jakob through the closed bathroom door. It's horrible, this bathroom. Cramped and windowless, with ventilation that sounds like a broken hair dryer. There's a yellowish light and it smells mouldy. I try to breathe through my mouth as much as possible.

'As an explanation for your crazy little nocturnal outing, you mean? Of course not. I told them that we've spent the past few weeks researching a complicated story and you haven't had much sleep. Talking of which . . . are you getting enough at the moment? Studies suggest that even after twenty-four hours without sleep, the human brain finds it more difficult to process information. Occasionally people develop symptoms similar to those displayed by schizophrenia patients, who are bad at distinguishing important things from unimportant ones, or unable to do so altogether.'

My reflection rolls its eyes and mutters, 'He knows that, but he can't distinguish an oleander from an olive.'

'Ready,' I call as I step out of the bathroom shortly afterwards. Jakob's standing beside the desk where my mobile is. I see him pull his hand away – caught in the act.

'You've had three or four calls this morning. Maybe you ought to see who's been trying to ring.'

I do. It's Ludwig who's called and who also sent me a message: *Where are you?*

Very soon, I promise him in my head. Then I put the mobile in my rucksack and grab my coat.

'How come Schmitti found me? Have you got any idea?'

Jakob looks at me. 'Hmm?'

'Well, you were all wondering what I was doing on the lane in the middle of the night. What about Schmitti? Why was he there?'

'He said Kerstin Seiler had remembered something. Apparently there's an old haystack where Sarah plays sometimes. When Schmitti went to take a look, he practically stumbled across you.

'He was on his own?'

'Just like you.'

'Yes, but I . . . I wasn't quite myself.'

Jakob grins. 'Who is?'

When we enter the dining room, we interrupt Brock and his wife in conversation. In the middle of the table they're sitting at is a thermos. Beside it a camera and two fist-sized objects wrapped in foil. I guess they're my rolls.

'Okay, let's go,' Brock says, standing up.

'Just a moment,' I say, because I hear my phone ringing again in the rucksack. I know it's Ludwig before I take the mobile out and glance at the screen. I nip outside because I don't want the others to hear my conversation. It's absolutely freezing out here. The sun has gone in again, leaving an ugly winter greyness. A few people are out in groups and Sarah's name echoes from some-where in the distance.

I take the call. 'Hello, Ludwig.'

He says he's tried to reach me half a dozen times already. Now he's standing outside our house but nobody's answering the door. Where the hell am I?

'I've come to Schergel.'

You've got to be joking, he says. Have I lost my mind com-pletely? And an astonishing array of expletives for an educated man in his prime.

'I had to do it, Ludwig. I know he's here.'

'Who? Steinhausen? For Christ's sake, Anni, stop meddling and let the police get on with their work!' He screams so loudly that it grates in the earpiece of my mobile. It's so unpleasant that my patience is wearing thin. I don't want to be patronised anymore.

'Oh, so I should copy you, should I? Just sit around doing bugger all?'

'I can't believe the—'

'You're right. I am being impertinent. I mean, you do everything for your clients, don't you? Your commitment even stretches to slipping me sleeping pills.'

'How can you think that of me? I didn't give you anything, do you hear? I'd never . . .'

Whatever he's saying goes in one ear and out the other when my attention fixes on what's happening on the other side of the marketplace. A crowd is gathering outside the butcher's. People are streaming as if in rays towards a centre, a single point. I almost drop my mobile when I realise what this point actually is: it's Sarah.

Throwing open the door to the pub, I scream, 'Sarah! Sarah's back!' I see Jakob and the others leap up from the table, hear the clatter of the chairs. We dash across the marketplace to the butcher's, right into a wall of people. There could be thirty, or even fifty. Brock's massive frame clears a way through for us to the front, where it's almost reverentially quiet compared to the back. Schmitti is lifting Sarah into his arms. He's taken his coat off and wrapped her in it like a cocoon. She's got a face like a doll, with large round eyes and a heart-shaped mouth. But she looks blank, just staring into nothingness. Beside her is Kerstin Seiler, pale and stiff, her face as expressionless as her daughter's. A puzzling sight, but I expect she's still in shock. Her friend, the petite blonde, is there too, offering Kerstin a tissue she clearly doesn't need. I wince when Brock's elbow digs into my side as he thrusts his hands up to take a photo of the miracle. My eyes meet Jakob's. He appears to find it as hard to believe as I do. As everyone does. Sarah is back, she's alive. She got away from Steinhausen.

US

You found the way back – respect, little Sarah. It's a long way, and in this cold weather too. That shows willpower and remarkable determination. Your reappearance caused a huge commotion; of course it did. They're practically pouncing on you, they're all gawping. You're a sensation. The girl who escaped from the ribbon murderer. That Schmitti is showing you off like a trophy; your mother is so vulgar.

It went wrong, all so wrong.

The wrong ending.

If I could do what I want to do, I'd push them aside and grab you, here and now. I'd snatch you from Schmitti's arms and run away with you. But then it would be over for good; I realise that. They'd arrest me. So I've got no choice but to observe the situation from my cover.

You won't tell them anything, will you, Sarah? Surely you're not going to expose me? No, you won't; you're well aware of the consequences, you know what's at stake.

Calm, calm, stay calm, I tell myself. It's just gone wrong. But that doesn't mean it's over. And isn't that the lovely thing about a story? It's flexible, it can change with every new word. And who else has the power over the characters and the narrative, if it isn't the person who created them?

ANN

SCHERGEL, 28 DECEMBER 2017

Another hospital corridor, again the typical sterile smell. I think of Eva and how she was admitted to hospital only two days ago. Two days that have felt like an eternity, as have the past few weeks – a yawning gap between me and my earlier life. The time before Dad's arrest, I think. A time I can scarcely comprehend now, and only remember as if it were a film where the main character looked like me. In my new reality, for the past two and a half hours Jakob and I have been hanging around the coffee machine in the waiting area of the children's ward. From here we can see the closed door of the room where Sarah is. Her mother is with her, as well as two police officers and a psychologist, who are carrying out a preliminary interview. We know this from Brock, Schmitti and Kerstin Seiler's blonde friend, who were also in Sarah's room, but have been sent out for the questioning. Schmitti's standing with us, the blonde woman has excused herself to ring her mother, and Brock has one ear pinned to the door, which I find both appalling and practical. For we can be confident that everything he overhears will be relayed to us without delay.

'Physically she's fine, apart from a few bruises,' Schmitti says, giving us the essence of the doctor's diagnosis. He's a changed man, so much friendlier and more open than yesterday evening at the butcher's. 'But they've found traces of an unknown substance in her urine and so now they're giving her a blood test too. And she's not speaking. Not a word. Must be the shock.'

I nod, If she's lucky, it's only shock, I think, recalling the conversation I had with Eva a couple of days ago. About the gaps in the chronology of the killings. Eva thought there might be victims who'd escaped Steinhausen's clutches, but felt too ashamed to tell anyone. They'd kept it to themselves to this day, years of silence which might last for ever. Disgruntled, I take a sip from the paper cup Jakob got me from the machine. This is my third coffee and I'm only drinking it to have something to do.

'Doesn't the girl have a father?' Jakob asks, nodding in the direction of Sarah's room.

'Pff,' Schmitti responds. He's also holding a cup of coffee. 'A total loser. He's the one who originally comes from Schergel, not Kerstin. The butcher's belonged to his uncle, who died ages ago. Kerstin only moved here because of Sarah's dad; they had the child and ran the butcher's together. Although basically she did all the work. He spent most of his time popping over the border to the Czech Republic to have his way with whores. Then one day he never came back. Since then, Kerstin's had nobody apart from us – a blessing and a curse.' Pointing at Brock, he laughs. 'No, seriously, it's what makes our village so special. We'll take in anyone who's willing to integrate into the community. And Kerstin isn't the only single mum in the village. There's Nathalie too.' He points over his shoulder. Nathalie – that's right, that's her name. Kerstin's blonde friend who reminds me so wonderfully and yet painfully of Zoe. I spent the whole morning racking my brains, but her name eluded me. 'She moved here from Wuppertal, literally fled from her violent ex, poor thing. Up until a few weeks ago, she kept herself totally shut off from everyone, but in the meantime she's been working in the butcher's with Kerstin. And at the kindergarten, two of the teachers are a gay couple. They're from Munich and they wanted to escape the consumer society with their own little house and a few chickens.'

Two more things that remind me of Zoe: Wuppertal, where she comes from, and the dream of making a fresh start, somewhere completely different. Where the sky is blue and there are no vapour trails. A little cottage with colourful shutters and a garden she would allow to become elegantly overgrown, preferably in Cornwall. A feeling washes over me, a scene from the past: Zoe's head in my lap, my finger tracing the contours of her face. 'What will become of me when you're dancing barefoot in your magical English garden?' I ask.

She laughs. 'Either you can stay here in Berlin, devoured by longing, or you can come with me . . .'

I hastily take a sip of my coffee, as if it were a medicine for forgetting. Eva was right: *Memories are only lovely when there's hope.*

'Goodness gracious!' comes the exclamation of surprise from Brock, attracting all of our attention. The door to Sarah's room has opened right by his nose, and no sooner have the two officers and the psychologist come out than he slips in. Schmitti too hands me his half-drunk coffee and hurries into Sarah's room.

Jakob clears his throat. 'Now you can watch a professional at work,' he announces, intercepting the officers and psychologist. He tells them he's from the press and asks for information. But

223

they give him the brush-off. Ongoing investigation. 'Be patient until we make an official statement, Mr Newshound,' one of the officers says before the group head for the lifts. Pointing his index finger in my direction, Jakob says, 'You dare,' but I don't feel like passing comment. Because although I'm relieved that Sarah has come back home unharmed, I find it unsettling too. What does it mean that Steinhausen's victim slipped from his clutches? Is he going to disappear? Will he simply snatch another girl or will he try to approach Sarah again? She is, after all, a witness who could describe and identify him. I look around: the corridor is empty, nobody here apart from us. All the same, I'd feel more comfortable if the police posted someone outside Sarah's room, like you see sometimes in films. 'She must be safe here?' I ask Jakob. He sighs.

'We don't even know what really happened, Ann. But I don't think you need worry about—'

'Where is everybody?' Nathalie interrupts him, having come back from her phone call.

Jakob points at Sarah's room. 'Maybe we ought to go in too,' he says as we watch her head for the door. 'It doesn't seem to bother Sarah's mother that people are piling in. The poor child.'

'Maybe she's just glad not to have to go through this on her own.'

He laughs. 'You'd make a terrible journalist. Far too sentimental.'

'It's what my father taught me,' I say. It's a fleeting pain, like pulling off a plaster, but there's no denying it's there. 'Everything that happens in the world, every single action and every consequence, is based on an emotion.'

'I always thought scientists were only interested in facts.' Jakob reaches for Schmitti's coffee, which I'm still holding, takes a sip and pulls a face.

'Folks!' So abruptly that both of us jump. Brock comes out of Sarah's room and hastens excitedly towards us. 'I've got something for you!'

'New information?'

He waves the camera in his hand. 'Schmitti and Nathalie didn't think I should, but – well!'

'Go on, tell us!'

'It'll cost you fifty euros,' he says, and after Jakob and I nod in unison, he shows us a photo on the screen. Sarah in her hospital bed. He made her close her eyes specially for the photo. All he says is, 'I thought this would be good for your article,' and winks. But what he means is: the girl – white face, pale lips, but most of all the way she's lying there, eyes closed and hands crossed above the covers – looks dead.

I have a brain fade: 'How can you be so fricking callous?'

'Ann!' Jakob says, trying to keep me in check.

And Brock, in indignation: 'Look, I'll happily go and sell my information to another paper!'

'No, no, Herr Brock,' Jakob insists. 'She didn't mean it like that.'

Oh yes, she did. But she realises that new information is more important than her personal opinion. So she apologises, gritting her teeth. Brock accepts the apology, along with the fifty euros from her purse. For that we make him delete the photograph under our supervision and get him to promise he won't take any more of Sarah in her hospital bed.

'She told the police officers she was with a princess in a castle,' he now starts up, theatrically planting his bloated body on one of the chairs in the waiting area. 'Hiding from the evil dragon.'

'Which princess?' Jakob asks.

'What sort of castle?' I ask.

Brock can't answer either question; apparently Sarah didn't say any more. Fifty euros for a smattering of words, and even these don't make any sense. I sigh. 'Is there a castle nearby she might have meant?'

Brock says no, not a castle, but there are some old fortress ruins. 'Maybe we should take a look around there,' Jakob says.

'Or,' I ponder, 'she's talking about something completely different. When we were children, my friend Eva and I had other names for the places where we used to play. There was a raised hide we used to call the tower, and an old gravel pit was our sea.'

Jakob looks at me as if I'm not all there; he must have been a very unimaginative child.

'I mean, she's hardly likely to have been with a real princess either,' I add. 'And so far as I know, dragons don't exist.' My gaze catches Kerstin Seiler, who right now is coming out of her daughter's room with Schmitti and Nathalie. I stride purposefully towards them. 'Excuse me, Frau Seiler, just a quick question. Can you think of where Sarah was talking about when she spoke of a castle? Or who the princess and dragon might be?'

'Piss off!' she snarls, scurrying away, followed by Schmitti. I turn to Nathalie, helplessly.

'You do know the doctors found bruises on Sarah?' she says sotto voce.

I try to square this with Kerstin's angry reaction. *A deranged paedophile*, comes to mind. These were the words Eva used when we were wondering what motive might be driving the ribbon murderer.

'But her abductor didn't . . .' I slap my hand over my mouth.

Nathalie shakes her head. 'No, no, it's not that. It's the fact that the bruises are older,' she says, giving me an emphatic look. 'Sarah didn't get them from the kidnapper.'

RECORDING 05

Berlin, 7 May 2021

- Are you saying that criminal damage is a pointless act, whereas murder isn't?
- If you put it that way, yes. Why else did you slash your teacher's tyres?
- Like I said, I was in with the wrong crowd. I think I just wanted to be cool. There were no higher motives.
- You see?
- *(sighs)* Okay, I took the bait. Well?
- Well, what?
- Your *higher motives*.
- Oh God, that tone.
- What were you expecting?
- Expecting? Nothing. More like wishing. I wish for impartiality, more for your sake than mine. Because you say you want to understand, and I actually believe you do. But how can you understand when your preformed opinion is in the way? You regard me as a psychopath, don't you?
- I, er . . . I don't know . . .
- Go ahead and say it, don't be shy. You wouldn't be the only one. In your eyes, what makes someone a psychopath?
- Well, to the best of my knowledge, psychopaths are people who

have no feelings about their crimes, neither empathy, nor regret, nor guilt.
- There is an official checklist for diagnosing psychopathy, did you know that? It's called PCL-R, and it contains twenty points, a lack of empathy or guilt being just two of these. Others include a low threshold of boredom, a tendency to infidelity, criminal activity when young, impulsiveness, or a parasitic lifestyle where they exploit other people for money or favours. It's hard to believe that such a weighty diagnosis should be based on these commonplace attributes, isn't it?
- To be honest, I'm not really sure what you're getting at.
- I'm trying to point out that I'm probably just as much or as little a psychopath as you are, and that understanding psychopathy becomes difficult once you start specifying such rigid patterns of thought.
- With respect, the fact that you committed the worst crime a person is capable of – and did it over and over again, ten times – isn't a pattern of thought, but a fact. And this is something you know yourself, everybody does, there's no need for discussion. According to the Bible, murder is a sin and according to the law, it's a serious crime. But precisely because of this, I'm even keener to understand what made you cross that line. What did Larissa trigger in you to turn you into a killer?
- Oh yes, that's right. You wanted to know why she was the first, and my response was that you were mistaken.
- Really?
- Think back. It'll come to you.
- Once again, that's not how this works. I'm not here to play

games with you, but to talk about the murders. About Larissa
and all the other girls.

– Laura, Miriam, Jana, Kati, Olivia, Laetitia, Hayet, Jenny, Saskia,
Alina, Sophie. You see, I wasn't lying. I still remember all their
names, and for each of these there's a face in my head. Take
little Laura. Blonde, big blue eyes, pink T-shirt with a horse on
it. She was sitting on the kerb, in roller skates and with a fresh
cut to her knee, but she wasn't crying. It was in Hellersdorf,
very close to where Larissa lived too, and I just happened to be
passing in the car. I stopped and asked if I could help her. She
thanked me, but refused.

– Clearly you didn't accept that.

– No, I persuaded her to get into my car by telling her I knew a
place where all the little girls learned to roller skate. Did you
roller skate as a child too?

– In-liners, yes. In-liners, roller skates, bike, skateboard, I pretty
much tried them all, and I expect I fell over endlessly.

– You can't remember exactly?

– No, I . . . I mean you forget a lot from your childhood.

– Or you distort it afterwards.

– Yes, that's possible. The more time that passes, the further your
childhood recedes into the background, apart from the really
formative experiences.

– Oh, I think you're wrong there. Those formative experiences are
like stories – you keep telling them over and over again until one
day their content is completely different. What's yours?

– My what?

– The most formative experience of your childhood?

ANN

SCHERGEL, 28 DECEMBER 2017

We're back at the inn from the hospital, having a briefing at the table that's normally reserved for the council. In front of us are two huge plates with dumplings, beans, roast pork and a sea of dark brown gravy, on the top of which a thin brown skin has formed. I eat even though I'm not hungry; it's pure common sense. All I've had in the past few days are the two biscuits baked by Inspector Brandner's wife and half a ham roll, left over from the police officers' supper at the pub last night. I remember the two plates that are still in my father's study. The dinner that Elke made for Eva and me: goose leg with red cabbage. When I get home again, the smell of that rotten food will have stunk out the entire room.

Jakob takes huge mouthfuls, like he did in the lunch breaks at Big Murphy's where he managed to devour the largest burgers in what felt like seconds. 'Dustbin,' I teased him, and we laughed. I really liked him, my friend Jakob from the recycling centre, with his bobbing dark locks of hair and the childish exuberance in his eyes.

'What's up?' he asks, chewing. I shake my head.

Brock offered to take us up to the ruins after lunch. Apparently they're beyond one of the adjacent areas of woodland, near a gorge. About half an hour by car, then a few minutes' walk. I don't want to go, because I don't think Sarah meant the ruins when she talked about a castle. Nor do I believe we'll find Steinhausen huddled there amongst the derelict walls.

'Think about it, Jakob. You only spent one night in these temperatures in the boot of your car and now you always need the loo. But Sarah doesn't have the slightest sign of hypothermia, even though she's supposed to have spent two whole days and nights out in the woods. That's practically impossible, do you see? She must have been kept inside, somewhere protected and warmish, at least.'

'It's all a question of having the right gear. There are thermal sleeping bags, thermal mats, and he could have made a fire too.' Jakob quickly shovels a mouthful of beans down him. 'And the ruins of an old fortress are similar to a castle, aren't they? I really don't understand why you want to pass up on this opportunity.'

'The opportunity to see the ruins? We're not fricking tourists, for God's sake!' I slam my cutlery down on to the side of my plate; it clatters unpleasantly. Leaning over to Jakob, I lower my voice. Brock, who's drying beer glasses behind the bar, doesn't have to hear everything. I'm surprised he didn't stay at the hospital with Kerstin and Sarah, like Schmitti and Nathalie. He seems to find it more important to keep an eye on the work of the journalists who've come from Berlin. Or to spread a new rumour. Sarah with her bruises, and particularly whether her own mother might have had something to do with them. 'You heard Brock. It takes half an hour to get to the ruins by car, and then there's a walk on top

231

of that. Do you seriously believe a seven-year-old girl could have managed that on her own? She'd never have found her way back to the village. No way.' I shake my head energetically. Once, when we were ten, Eva got lost in a section of the Grunewald, not far from where we lived. We'd often played there; it was where our tower was – the old raised hide. And although we knew the way off by heart, she spent hours wandering about until my father eventually found her.

'She must have been really close to here. In the village.'

'You mean the village that the police spent two days turning upside down? Is this where her abductor is supposed to be hiding, undetected by Sherlock Brock and all the others?' His laughter turns into a sigh. 'Ann, if you're being honest with yourself, you'll have realised by now that it must have been a copycat crime. Maybe just some stupid teenager playing a sick joke with the red ribbons to put the wind up the community here. And when the police turned up with this huge posse, he got cold feet and let Sarah go.' Unfazed, he cuts a piece of meat. 'Could this be the very reason why Sarah's not talking? She knows her abductor and doesn't want him to get into trouble.'

I'm flummoxed. And aghast. Jakob's theory makes sense. But I know it's wrong, I know, I just do. I begin to tremble for a different reason. Jakob's sitting here, happily eating his fill of the daily special. I realise he doesn't care what story he gets in the end. The key thing is that it's different from what his rivals write about the ribbon murders. And whatever happens, it will be because nobody else has exclusive access to the daughter of the chief suspect. As far as he's concerned, I'm a job; he's never left any doubt about that. And yet it hurts again.

'Ann? Is everything all right?' Something in my expression makes Jakob put his cutlery down now too. Maybe I've turned pale or done the opposite: come out in nervous red blotches.

'I need some fresh air.'

Jakob makes to get up.

'No, you continue eating.' I stop him. 'I just need a few minutes to myself.'

'What about the ruins?'

'I'll think about it,' I say, grabbing my rucksack, leaving the table and, a few seconds later, the dining area.

I really want a cigarette now. And maybe something sweet too. The small grocer's, which Jakob's jeep is still parked in front of, is open. The cashier adjusts the slightly wonky name badge on her apron and greets me effusively. I am, after all, an important journalist, as she will already have learned. Wandering down the aisles I spy a familiar face: Nathalie. She's filling a shopping trolley with tins of food, and at her feet is a basket filled with sliced bread, cat food, margarine and all manner of other stuff.

'You're back from the hospital,' I say stupidly, pointing at her shopping. 'Looks like you're feeding an entire company.'

'Yes,' she says, sweeping a hair behind her ear, almost looking embarrassed. 'I don't like shopping so I always get as many supplies as I can in one go.' She pushes the trolley, which under the weight of its load is as obstinate as an old dog. I bend down to pick up her basket to take it to the cash desk. She lets me go first as I'm only getting a packet of cigarettes and a bar of chocolate.

When the cashier has scanned all her items, I help Nathalie pack away the tins, and in my thoughts I'm briefly back with Zoe on our weekly Saturday shop. We're only buying trash food to put in small bowls for our film night. It will go straight on our hips. So what? We'll make up for it tomorrow with smoothies for breakfast. I sniff. Berlin is Schergel and Nathalie is Zoe, and the cashier asks if there's any news about Sarah.

'She's doing well in the circumstances,' Nathalie says.

The cashier looks slightly disappointed – no new gossip.

'Is it true, then?' she probes. She means the thing about the bruises, the vague suspicion that now hangs over Kerstin.

I can see Nathalie struggling to keep her cool, but then it all comes out. 'Everyone makes mistakes. Big ones too sometimes. But everyone also deserves a second chance. It's only if they don't . . .' She breaks off. Whether she wanted to or not, she's confirmed the rumour. When it appears she realises this too, she gasps in horror. The cashier gives a mortified smile.

'Come on, we ought to go,' I say softly, and so we leave the shop, Nathalie pulling her trolley, and me with the laden basket.

'Where's your car?' I ask, but she doesn't have one. 'Okay,' I say in astonishment. 'Is it far to where you live?'

'It's fine,' she replies evasively, reaching for the basket. The sliced bread and a tin of cat food topple into the snow.

'Oh dear! How about I go with you for a bit? I wanted a walk anyway to clear my head.' Without waiting for an answer, I slip my rucksack off my shoulders and stuff the bread and cat food in it.

'A bit, all right then.' Nathalie's smile reminds me of Dad's when I last saw him in prison. It looks slightly fake, as if her face had almost forgotten how to do it. And that's the impression she gives overall: shy, and strangely lost when not with Schmitti and Kerstin. She says she's living in one of Brock's holiday houses on the upper common with her mother and daughter. 'It's quite far. You really don't have to come the whole way.'

'That's all right.' I try not to let show how much of an effort it is to heave her basket. I can only carry it in my left hand as otherwise my right shoulder whinges. 'Schmitti told me you're working with Kerstin at the butcher's.'

'Oh, I just help out here and there in the background. Vacuum-packing meat, cleaning. Can you imagine what the place looks like after an animal has been slaughtered? The blood sprays all over the room, right up to the ceiling. You have to hose the tiles down.'

I glance at Nathalie. Her boots look high quality and her coat is from an expensive brand. They must be from a time when she couldn't have even dreamed she'd one day be cleaning in a butcher's for pocket money.

'It's just everywhere. Look here!' She stops abruptly and points at a stain on her jeans. It's only small but clearly visible.

'Does it come out?'

'With bleach, yes.' She sighs. 'I tell myself every day that I'm doing it for my daughter.'

I nod. Nathalie is my chance. She's a friend of Kerstin's and through her job spends a lot of time with the family. 'Sarah talked of a castle. Have you got any idea what place she might have meant?'

She shakes her head then starts walking again. I follow her. For a while we don't talk; she looks lost in thought. Maybe she's still thinking about her outburst in front of the cashier, or wondering what people are now thinking of her. For if Kerstin Seiler really did beat her daughter, she and Schmitti ought to have noticed something and acted correspondingly. I'd love to tell her I know how something like this feels. Only then I wouldn't be a respectable journalist anymore, but Ann, the daughter of the alleged ribbon murderer. I bet I'd scare them off, her and the entire village, and my hunt for Marcus Steinhausen would be over.

The path climbs; it's difficult but beautiful. A winter panorama that could be from the front of a postcard. Before us is nothing but a white expanse that pushes its way into the woods in the distance like a tongue. In the middle of all this, surrounded by a few solitary trees, a small house.

'That's where you live?'

'Yes,' Nathalie says with a smile. 'Idyllic, isn't it?'

'Absolutely, but . . .' I turn around to estimate the distance from the village, 'a little bit isolated too, no?'

'I don't have a choice,' she says, letting go of the trolley and resting her hands on her knees as if taking a short break. 'You must have heard of the circumstances in which we ended up in Schergel?' Still bent over, she gives me a searching look. 'Don't be shy. I've been living here almost two months and I know only too well about how the village gossip works.'

'Well, I've heard you had problems with your ex-husband.' I put the basket down to relieve my aching arm.

Nathalie stands up straight again; her face looks sad and serious. 'That's not the extent of it. It's more . . . we're hiding from him.' She points to the little house in the distance. 'My daughter would love to go to kindergarten, but she's not ready yet. She jumps with fright at the slightest noise and is still having nightmares.'

'I didn't know that. I'm sorry.'

She nods. 'Yes. We cut ourselves off completely in the first few weeks, but people in the village are curious. They're only trying to help, but, well . . . At any rate, I realised you're never really alone anywhere in the world, and I had to put my cards on the table. After all, if everyone knows the score, it helps keep us safe.' She laughs. 'Brock rolled up his sleeves and said, "If your ex turns up here, we'll give him a good hiding."' She takes the handle of the trolley and gets going again. I follow her, deep in thought. Nathalie is like me, only she works in a butcher's rather than a burger joint, an attempt to preserve at least a vestige of normality and avoid going crazy under the burden of one's life history.

We approach the house. Half of it is cladded with horizontal planks and there's a balcony beneath the pointed roof that must have a breathtaking view over the valley.

'Where do you come from originally?'

'Wiesbaden. And you're from Berlin, aren't you?' By way of explanation, she adds, 'Village radio.'

'Oh, I see. Berlin, exactly.'

'Do you know the weekly market in Nestorstrasse?' As if at the push of a button, the hint of a smile gives way to a serious expression. 'And I suppose that's also the reason why you're here, isn't it? Because the other ten girls all came from Berlin?'

'That's right, yes. My colleague and I are writing about the case.'

We stop outside the house. It's small, but on three floors and divided into two apartments. The bottom one is empty, according to Nathalie. To keep it that way, she's renting it as well, she tells me. Because the house is on a slope, the front door to the upper, larger apartment, where Nathalie lives with her family, is accessed via steps on the left-hand side. Plenty of steps that are going to require plenty of effort again. 'Just put the basket down here, I'll take it inside in a minute,' Nathalie says, as if she's read my thoughts, heaving the trolley up the first few steps.

'I'm not going to abandon you with just a few metres to go,' I reply with a laugh. Only now do I notice that all the shutters are closed. 'When you're working at the butcher's or go shopping, does your mum look after your daughter?'

'Yes, she's almost eighty and physically not very fit anymore. So she doesn't venture outside on her own these days. But she gets on brilliantly with Lenia. I don't know what I'd do without her.' Nathalie opens the front door and calls out, 'I'm back!' I don't catch the response because I'm still a few steps behind. She manoeuvres the trolley into the entrance, then comes back to me to take the basket. 'Thanks so much. Will you find your way back to the village, or should we have dropped a few crumbs on the way?'

'Keep going straight, I know.'

'Thanks again.'

'No problem, my pleasure . . .' I stop short when out of the blue Nathalie hugs me. Maybe she's sensed how similar we are. For a few seconds I'm worried my eyes will fill with tears, but the moment passes, as does the impulse to tell her who I really am. She lets go of me and says, 'Right, then' – my cue to leave. She waves at me from the top of the steps; I keep turning back to see if she's still standing there. So gorgeous to look at in spite of all her pain. Then she suddenly goes into the house and I shake my head, amused by myself. Oh, Ann . . .

Bond. (Ann, 10 years old)

A bond is a magical feeling and that's why it's a bit unbelievable too. You never have to think too hard about what your saying because you know the other person will understand you anyway. Your like twins even if your not related and nobody can separate us even though Eva sometimes says girls should love boys. But it's not what you should do, it's about finding someone you feel like a twin with.

My head is empty, yet at the same time swimming with a thousand thoughts, none of which can be fished out in isolation. With every metre, every step I get closer to the centre of the village, I become more ponderous, angry, disillusioned, until I finally reach the inn and am utterly livid. We don't have a new lead, just a child who won't say anything, and otherwise, no idea. Jakob is still sitting at the same table, although now he's got his laptop in front of him rather than a plate. When he sees me he leaps to his feet.

'Where've you been? I've been looking for you.'

'Why?' I gesture to him to sit back down and plump myself on the chair opposite, the same one I sat on for lunch – a shitty metaphor: everything's the same, nothing has changed, and no doubt we'll be sitting here like this tomorrow, and the day after that, because we're stuck, bloody well stuck again unless a miracle occurs and Sarah opens her mouth. 'Were you worried the copycat might have got me?'

'What copycat?' Frau Brock asks, coming over to our table with a cup of coffee for Jakob. 'Would you like one too?'

I shake my head. *The village radio* comes to mind, the expression Nathalie used. But it's a chance. 'Tell me, Frau Brock: Sarah's disappearance and the red ribbons in the woods . . .'

'Yes?' In a flash she's sitting beside us. Jakob nudges his laptop to one side to make way for Frau Brock's crossed arms on the table.

'You're all very observant here in Schergel. What are people saying? Who could have done something like that and why?'

She leans across the table conspiratorially. 'My husband says it's the real ribbon murderer. It's definitely him.'

I look around. Brock's nowhere to be seen, not a good sign considering that he's been shadowing us ever since we arrived in Schergel.

'That's why a meeting's been called for this evening,' his wife continues excitedly. 'We want to discuss the precautions we should take, and make a plan of how we can help the police clear this up.'

'The invitation to this meeting has even gone out nationally,' Jakob remarks sarcastically. 'That's why I was looking for you.' He turns his laptop so I can see the screen. It's the online edition of one of Germany's best-known dailies, even bigger than the one he works for. A photograph. Sarah, her face pixellated, in Schmitti's arms, beside Kerstin and Nathalie. None of the adults' faces are pixellated and they're easily recognisable. That was this morning in front of the butcher's. Sarah, who'd suddenly reappeared, the miracle; and Brock capturing the moment with his camera.

My hands shoot across the table and pull the laptop closer. The headline of the article accompanying the photograph reads: *Have they got the wrong man?* Beside it, a small photo of my father, doctored to make him unrecognisable. The screen turns blurry, I can't make out whole sentences, only scraps of text. A little girl, abducted in the style of the notorious ribbon murderer. An idyllic village in great danger. The police, who undertook a large-scale search but did little else, either to help the terrified inhabitants or to solve the case. But, most strikingly, a quote from the village publican and chairman of the local council, Peter Brock: 'We're looking specifically for a man with short blond hair and freckles.'

I look Jakob square in the eye. 'This is a disaster,' I say, unable to manage any more. A few days ago I'd have been happy if the reporting had been in my father's favour, but now the timing couldn't be less helpful. My head throws up images, the worst-case scenario: people from everywhere flooding to Schergel because they're inquisitive, and eager to take part in the murder hunt as if it were some kind of tourist event. Other journalists, now that the first major article on Schergel has appeared, wanting to get a piece of the story as quickly as possible and arriving in their droves too. But, most importantly, Steinhausen, who, if he's still in the area after Sarah's escape, is now going to do a runner.

'Hopefully Kerstin will have had a good rest by this evening,' Frau Brock says, her voice mingling with my thoughts. 'As the mother of the victim, her presence would help people realise how serious the situation is.'

Jakob and I first look at each other, then at Frau Brock.

'God knows we'd all be deeply shocked if the rumours turn out to be true,' she adds. 'But she should have the chance to explain herself, shouldn't she? I mean, Sarah might have got those bruises while playing.'

Jakob is the first to twig. 'Are you saying Kerstin Seiler's back home?'

'Yes, why?'

'She's not with Sarah in the hospital anymore?'

'No, she left early this afternoon. She wanted a hot bath and a nap.'

Jakob flips shut his laptop and both of us spring to our feet in sync. We don't need to discuss our plan; both of us realise we have to see Kerstin at once. Maybe we can make her understand how important it is to decipher Sarah's words without her feeling under attack again. It's worth a try – maybe we'll get lucky and find Steinhausen in his hideaway before he disappears.

We leave the inn at a canter; I stop when we're halfway across the marketplace.

'What's up?'

'Sarah,' I say, grabbing Jakob's sleeve. 'Right now she's alone in the hospital.'

'No chance, I bet Schmitti or Nathalie are there while her mum—'

'Takes a nice hot bath?' What an absurd thought; I shake my head. 'No, Nathalie definitely isn't there. I just met her out shopping.'

Jakob gestures to me to go on. 'Somebody will be there for sure. And the police will have posted someone outside her room.'

'Hopefully.'

'For sure.'

As the butcher's is a residential house too, we start by ringing at the front door – in vain. So we decide to try through the shop. The lights are off even though it's already getting dark outside, and we can't detect any movement inside. On a whim, Jakob tries the handle; the shop is indeed open. A bell above the door announces our entry.

'Hello?' Jakob calls out. 'Frau Seiler?'

Our footsteps squeak on the tiles and the drinks fridge buzzes monotonously. A blueish light illuminates the empty counter, the only, inadequate source of light in the room.

'Can you smell that?' I whisper. A strange, unpleasantly sweet aroma.

'That's what freshly slaughtered meat smells like,' Jakob whispers back. 'It hangs around. I know it because my grandad was a butcher too. His house smelled like this even years after he'd retired and closed the shop.'

We come to the corridor behind the counter, separated off by a plastic curtain.

'Frau Seiler!' Jakob calls out again. When there's still no answer, he raises his eyebrows at me. I point my chin at the curtain, but he's hesitant.

'What if she's in the bath?'

'If she is, she's hardly likely to have left the shop open, is she?' Jakob shrugs.

'Let's call it investigative journalism,' I say, pushing ahead.

A cold, dark corridor, tiled like everything here. I think of Nathalie, who told me how she had to hose down the tiles after an animal had been slaughtered.

'Frau Seiler? Are you here?' There are two rooms on either side of the corridor; straight ahead are the stairs to the living quarters. 'It's us: Ann and Jakob from the newspaper!'

Who – cowed by the darkness, the smell and the fact that everything in this house is washable – advance very slowly until they finally come to an open door on the right-hand side. It's a cold store with a flickering light, dim but satisfactory enough to see. I thrust my hand blindly behind me, for Jakob, for support.

Someone makes a sound, probably me too. Someone shouts, 'Shit!' probably Jakob, who now pushes me to the side and rushes into the room. Towards the body lying on the floor. In all that blood on the washable tiles.

RECORDING 06
Berlin, 7 May 2021

- I'm assuming your silence means you don't want to share your childhood experiences with me. Ah well, listen in and I'll begin. My childhood. With your love of cliché, you'll feel vindicated now, but in truth I did have a strict upbringing. I wasn't beaten and nor were there any other unjust punishments. But it was all about discipline, obeying the rules and being able to show what we'd achieved. My brother, in particular, always felt he had to prove himself. We competed with each other from an early age and soon we went beyond the usual benchmarks, such as school grades or good behaviour, which your parents would praise you for. I vividly remember the time I was sitting in a tree in our garden, boasting how high I'd climbed. In response, my brother climbed over the rose trellis and on to our garage roof. Then he took a run up and jumped down. But he landed badly, breaking his left ankle. I won't forget the noise, nor his screams. I'd never heard him make such a sound before, never heard anyone do it, in fact.
- Did you like the sound? The girls must have screamed too.
- Some did, yes. Most, however, were shocked into silence. Do you have siblings?
- No, I'm an only child.
- Would you have liked some?

- No, basically . . . It was okay as it was. I always had lots of
  friends.
- So did I, believe it or not. And yet I never felt as if I belonged.
- Because you felt different?
- Sort of, yes. There were things I began thinking of at an early
  age. Things that kept me awake some nights.
- Certain . . . fantasies?
- No. No, not fantasies, that sounds so . . . no, that sounds all
  wrong. Just like the word 'excited' you used earlier. Surely you
  know I never touched any of the girls inappropriately.
- You just killed them.
- But I didn't deprive them of their dignity. On the contrary, I gave
  them meaning. And they gave meaning to me.
- A meaning that was otherwise missing from your life.
- Yes, that's exactly right. Tell me, have you read the files on the
  murder cases?
- Of course, several times. Why do you ask?
- I'll let you mull this over until the next time we meet.
- What, no, hold on! Are you going to send me home? Now?
- What was your favourite subject at school?
- My er . . . German. German and PE, I'd say.
- I see.
- I see? What now?
- Now go home and have a think.

245

ANN

SCHERGEL, 28 DECEMBER 2017

It's as if I've been catapulted back in time, back to the basement where Eva is lying like that, on a cold floor, in her own blood. How sure I was she must be dead, but she was alive, thank God, she was alive. It must be exactly the same now. A horrendous sight, a shock that momentarily clamps the blood vessels in my body and brings everything to a standstill. But it looks worse than it is. Kerstin Seiler isn't dead. She's lying there, blood everywhere, as if her body were floating on a lake, blood on her clothes and smeared all over her stiff face. The meat hook in the side of her neck. Jakob kneeling over her, checking for a pulse, while I remain in the doorway, just trying to stay on my feet. There's no reason to collapse now because he's just about to look at me and say she's alive.

But she needs help, of course, she needs immediate help. Frantically I feel for my mobile and call an ambulance. Now Jakob does look at me and just shakes his head. I don't know what that's supposed to mean; I yell down the phone – Schergel, butcher's, a woman with a serious neck wound, 'Please come quick!'

Jakob gets up. From the knees downwards his trousers are red, just like his hands that have been touching the body.

Me: 'They're on their way.' Him: 'It's too late.' I refuse to believe it; I *can't* believe it. Because this is just like it was with Eva. I want to check myself, I want to go over to Kerstin, lay her head in my lap and tell her everything's going to be fine, the ambulance is on its way. Jakob doesn't let me; he holds me firmly with his bloody hands until I calm down. Then he takes me out of the cold store, back to the dark, chilly corridor, back through the shop, back outside. We leave red footprints behind. The tiles will have to be hosed down.

Disbelief. (Ann, 10 years old)
Disbelief feels like when you walk across a frozen lake and then you suddenly break the ice and it's like your paralised with shock and cold, even your brain. You can't understand what's happening and that's why you forget you have to move and hurry away from the crack or you'll end up under the ice and drown. That's why disbelief is a very dangerous feeling, you must'nt stand there in disbelief too long or you'll die.

I open the curtains in room 113. People have gathered outside the butcher's, bringing candles. I strain to see if Nathalie's there. I've been thinking of her a lot over the past few hours. Kerstin's death will hit her hard – a painful blow to the stomach, a cruel fist in her face. I know this as if I knew her, and I sort of do in a funny way. I felt it when she hugged me.

I have to realise it's dark outside; the faces are merely small dots blurred by the candlelight in the blackness. The mortuary van has driven off and there are just two police cars left. The crime scene has been secured, Jakob and I have been questioned and our personal details taken. How did we end up finding Kerstin Seiler, what did we want from her? The truth: Jakob is a journalist writing about the ribbon murderer, and I'm the daughter of the chief suspect. Frowns, incomprehension. A story and a background that defy cursory explanation. So we've got to come back to the police station in Bad Kötzting tomorrow morning to fill in the gaps. I feel like Bill Murray in *Groundhog Day*: police, hospital, bodies covered in blood. I'm stuck in a fricking time loop, a nightmare. And why? My father's still in prison; I haven't achieved anything. On the contrary, all I'm doing is causing chaos.

Jakob's face appears in the reflection of the windowpane. Standing right behind me, he puts his hand on my shoulder. I still see the blood on it, even though he's had a thorough wash. Both of us took a shower, first Jakob, then me. As if what we've just been through could be rinsed down the drain along with the blood. The police have taken our clothes in a plastic bag. Jakob's coat and his blood-smeared trousers for forensic examination. To confirm that all the blood got on him when he was checking Kerstin for a pulse, rather than when he killed her. My – *Dad's* – jacket has gone too because Jakob touched it with his bloody hands. I'm already missing it; I feel as if I've lost more than just an item of clothing.

I turn around, straight into Jakob's embrace. Jakob, who holds me tight, my cheek against his chest, and his heart beating comfortingly. He strokes my hair. There are no words. I think of Sarah. Imagine the police psychologist trying to make her understand what's happened. They told us that her hospital room is being guarded around the clock. For it may have been Sarah's abductor who killed Kerstin. But why? Nothing makes sense anymore; only one thing is clearer than ever: Sarah needs to talk. She has to say what happened from the moment when, on her way home alone on Boxing Day, she met her kidnapper. What he looked like. Where he took her. How she was able to escape from him. A loud sobbing reclaims me from my tangled thoughts. It's me, crying and sobbing so uncontrollably that my whole body is shaking. Jakob continues to hold me, stoically, firmly, solidly.

'I just want to wake up.'

'I know,' he says. Then he lifts my chin and kisses me. It's the situation, the deep despair, two people clutching each other because there's nothing else. It feels good somehow, and yet . . . I pull away, turn away.

'Have I done something wrong?'

I shake my head. Think back. How we used to sit in the Big Murphy's car park during my lunch break, separated by the coy distance of two people who'd really like to arrange a proper date. But they don't; the woman has her reasons.

'There is someone,' I tell him, then sniff and wipe the tears from my eyes. 'That's to say, there was someone until recently. I'm not quite over it yet.'

'Okay, I understand. Sorry.'

'Me too.'

'Did it fall apart because of the thing with your dad?'

'Yes.'

I drop on to the bed; Jakob sits beside me.

'Then he's a fool, Ann, he really is. Whatever your father might or might not have done, it's got nothing to do with you. You're a good person. Most of the time, at least.'

'Locking you in the boot – I imagine you still hold that against me.'

'You've no idea. I've had to pee at least a dozen times today already.'

I lean my head against his shoulder. 'What are we going to do now?'

'What should we do? There's no point going to pay Sarah a visit at the hospital. First, they wouldn't let us in, and second – even if they did – there's no way she'd talk to two strangers. I think we've no choice but to leave it all to the police and hope they can clear the bloody thing up.' He puts an arm around me and kisses me on my head. 'We ought to go home.'

'Home,' I repeat. The mere thought of it makes me tense up. Back to Berlin where my father's in prison, Eva's in hospital and Ludwig's waiting to lecture me. Where there's nothing but ruins, debris and pain. 'Shit, it can't be *that* difficult, Jakob!' I lift my head and look at him. 'Logic! Logic's the way to solve this. Think! Why would Marcus Steinhausen kill Kerstin? What would he gain by it?'

'You still believe it then.'

'What?'

'That Steinhausen's behind all of this.'

'When you said today that Sarah might be keeping her mouth shut because she knows her kidnapper, I had a moment or two of doubt. But now . . .' I get up from the bed and pace up and down the room. 'No copycat who merely wanted to put the wind up the village would commit murder, would they? That must be going too far! That could only be someone who's utterly ruthless. Who's used to killing.' I stop right in front of Jakob. 'Out of all the dreadful things that have happened over the last few days, do you know what the worst one is for me?'

His response is to raise his eyebrows. I pull up my left sleeve and hold out my wrist. 'The moment when Eva and I found out *how* he killed the girls.'

Jakob takes my hand and examines the scar. 'What happened?'

'About nine months after Mum died I had an accident on my bike. A stone dug into my wrist and cut it.' As I gently turn my wrist in Jakob's grip, the scar shimmers in the light. 'It's a piece of information the police don't know about. It would fit far too neatly with the clues they've already got.'

'So you did have doubts about your father.'

'I don't know if I'd call it doubts. But it's the only thing I still can't explain. Why does he kill the girls in this way? On the other hand, maybe you start drawing parallels like mad if you're searching for meaning. Maybe you come across connections that don't really exist. Things your mind bolts together by itself because it's desperate to understand. But now,' I say, carefully taking my hand out of his, 'I'm more certain than ever. Kerstin's murder is the proof.'

'Of your father's innocence?' Jakob rubs his brow. 'I mean, you're right. Someone who just wanted to give the village a fright, then got such cold feet when the police turned up that he let Sarah go, wouldn't be capable of committing such a gruesome murder the very next day. I mean, he really . . .' He shakes his head as he breaks off. I crouch down and put my hands on his knees.

'We can't go home, Jakob, please! Think about it. He could have done a runner when Sarah escaped. Or at least hidden and kept quiet. But he didn't. On the contrary, by killing her mother, he's literally shouting in our faces: *I'm still here, you fools!* He's making fun of us.'

'I don't know,' Jakob says, sighing. 'What are you suggesting?'

'We mustn't let ourselves get led astray! You could call Brandner's secretary and find out if Sarah's said anything yet. And then I think we ought to talk to Schmitti and Nathalie again. Even if they don't know what Sarah meant by the castle, dragon and princess, they can tell us whose Sarah's friends are. Children don't share everything with adults, but they might with their best friend.'

'Sure, I don't mind,' Jakob says, fishing his mobile from his trouser pocket. 'Let's see if we strike lucky, it's already gone eight o'clock.'

I stand up and move to the window.

In spite of the cold, the people are bravely keeping up their vigil outside the butcher's. Is it fear? The fear of being next? Curiosity? The feeling of not wanting to be idle, of needing to do something even if it's only hanging around outside?

Behind me I hear Jakob asking about Sarah, before grumbling several times. 'Okay, I understand,' he says, then enquires about the general state of the investigation.

Meanwhile I watch some of the people outside head for the inn. Brock's meeting, I recall. *We want to discuss the precautions we should take, and make a plan of how we can help the police clear this up,* his wife told us this afternoon. And: *As the mother of the victim, her presence would help people realise how serious the situation is.*

Now Kerstin is dead. Did she really leave her traumatised child on her own in the hospital just hours after she'd escaped from her abductor? Could her own state of mind at that moment really have been more important than her daughter, who she thought she'd lost for ever? I don't want to think that Kerstin would still be alive if she'd stayed with Sarah – but that's what runs through my mind. I turn to Jakob, who's just said goodbye and is taking his phone from his ear. He opens his mouth to start speaking but I'm quicker.

'What if the killer wasn't after Kerstin at all? What if he just found out that she was back from the hospital and so assumed that she had Sarah with her? I mean, it wouldn't occur to anybody that a loving mother would abandon her child in a situation like that. He wanted Sarah! He wanted to take her back! And when she wasn't there, he lost it. Think about it: the meat hook. He didn't take it along as a murder weapon, he grabbed it on impulse at the butcher's, a knee-jerk reaction when he realised his original plan wouldn't work.'

'It's possible,' Jakob agrees, pointing to his mobile. 'The girl still hasn't spoken since her mention of the castle. Not even when she was told her mother had died . . .' He shakes his head. 'She's now on sedatives and tomorrow she'll be transferred to the children's psychiatric department. They've also located her father, who's on his way. By the way . . . I suppose you know that a few months after his second period in rehab, Steinhausen spent quite a while as an inpatient in a psychotherapy clinic?'

'What? When?'

He nods. 'From February to November 2006. A specialist clinic in the Allgäu.'

I grab my rucksack, which is on the floor beside the desk, and open it in such haste that the bag of sliced bread and tin of cat food fall by my feet. Nathalie's things I'd packed in there and must have forgotten to give back to her. Leaving them where they are, I pull out Ludwig's folder and the notes we've made about the murders, including the timeline.

'You said 2006?' My eyes dart from the piece of paper in my hand to Jakob.

'Yes. After the second attack by Larissa's stepfather, he suffered post-traumatic stress disorder, nightmares, paranoia, the whole works.'

'In 2006?' I ask again, just to be sure. *Whoever killed those girls must have a few gaps in his CV*, is what I told Eva three days ago. And a gap, a complete year that passed without a girl dying, is precisely what happened in 2006. I put the sheet of paper under Jakob's nose. 'So? Believe me now?'

The air in the dining room is stale: too many bodies crammed together. Sweat and bad breath, the windows already fogged up. Jakob and I are standing at the back, by the door that connects the dining room with the stairs to the guest rooms. I can't make out if people from outside or other journalists have turned up. But I do see Nathalie, standing on the opposite side of the room by the exit. The way her eyes keep darting around like a timid animal makes her seem nervous. Brock looks unusually tall behind his bar. Jakob, who's got a better view, says he's standing on an upturned beer crate. When Brock rings the bell, the angry murmur subsides. First: Kerstin Seiler, one of their own, whose life has been gruesomely cut short. Then: Schmitti, who'll now be choosing a coffin rather than an engagement ring.

'The man responsible for this is known as the "ribbon murderer". For more than a decade, he's terrorised Berlin and now it seems it's our turn. But, ladies and gentlemen, we're not going to accept that. We're not going to lock up our children. We're not going to barricade ourselves away for fear that he might break into our houses as he did into Kerstin's. We're not going to let ourselves be slaughtered like defenceless livestock.' The mob starts baying its agreement; Brock can only bring the meeting under control by ringing his bell again. 'From this evening, a village guard will begin their duty. We will conduct patrols both day and night. To assist the police, we will also set up an office where observations and suspicions relating to Sarah's abduction and Kerstin's murder can be recorded. Totally discreet, of course.'

'If he hasn't already done so, Steinhausen's going to pack his things and clear off now,' Jakob whispers into my ear.

'Or he'll have the time of his life running rings around this pompous crowd,' I reply.

'Pompous?' He shakes his head. 'Highly dangerous, if you ask me. They're going to get completely manic about it now. How long is it going to be, do you think, before they lose control of the whole thing and start tearing each other apart if they can't find the guilty party?'

'You're right. Steinhausen's hardly going to turn himself in.'

'Shhh,' the woman beside us says, pointing to the bar. She's urging us to listen to Brock, who's just begun reading out a list of names for the patrols. I crane my neck towards the exit. Nathalie's still here, but seems on the verge of leaving.

'Be back in a sec,' I say to Jakob, and head for the door behind me. As well as leading to the stairs, the corridor also goes to the rear exit that I took last night during my blackout. I have to hurry because although I've avoided the scrum in the dining area, I still have to make my way around the building.

'Nathalie!'

Walking quickly, she's already halfway across the marketplace.

'Please wait!'

She has no intention of that and instead keeps going, even faster now, it seems. I speed up too, breaking into a run until I finally catch up with her behind the butcher's.

'What do you want?' The hostility in her voice takes me by surprise.

'I just wanted ... er ... I'm really sorry about Kerstin.'

Leaning her head back, Nathalie gazes up at the black sky. I gently put my hand on her sleeve.

'A couple of days ago, I almost lost a friend too. Her name's Eva. I've known her since we were children. She was seriously injured and is now in a coma. The doctors say she's stable and making a textbook recovery. But I still don't dare ring the hospital because I'm terrified they'll tell me her condition has got worse.'

Nathalie looks at me, her eyes astonishingly alert and large in an otherwise very weary face. 'Is it true?' Although her tone is different now, milder, the question is still puzzling. I shrug, at a loss. 'I mean, I know it's not true you're a journalist,' she clarifies. 'Someone found out what you told the police officers who questioned you after ... er ...' She tails off. I nod as a sign that she doesn't have to spell it out. 'Anyway, they say you're the daughter of the man they arrested in Berlin.'

My heart stops momentarily; I'm mystified. Nobody has spoken to me about this, not even Brock. And yet, in whatever way, it must surely come like a bombshell that I'm the daughter of the chief suspect.

'Don't lose sleep over it, everybody has their own lies. And Brock's bound to talk to you about it,' Nathalie says, as if she's read my mind. 'He thinks your father's innocent and he's wondering how he can use you to get the media's attention for his campaign here. I've got to go now.' Her last words are harsher again, just like the way she shakes my hand from her arm and moves away. Stomping off purposefully. I don't want to let her go.

'I'm sorry about that too!' I hurry to keep pace with her. 'I didn't want to lie to anyone. But you can't imagine what it's like. I'm trying to prove my father's innocence, but till now I've been completely on my own. Apart from my friend Eva, and Jakob – who really is a journalist, by the way – nobody's been prepared to listen to me.'

Nathalie stops. Something's weird. As if from nowhere, the night has descended on to her face, souring her features and paralysing her expression.

'Nathalie?'

'It's not your fault, Ann. But what he did is unforgivable.'

'What do you mean?'

'Ann!' Jakob's voice cuts across the marketplace. I whip around, first to him, then back to Nathalie, who's running away.

'Nathalie!' I cry, setting off after her.

'Ann!' Jakob again. 'Stop! It's important! They know who he is!'

Marcus Steinhausen – it strikes me like lightning. I stop so abruptly that I almost slip, and Nathalie vanishes into the darkness.

US

Nathalie, Nathalie, Nathalie.

Keep running, you won't get away.

Run like Sarah ran away from the dragon. Defend yourself like her mother tried to defend herself. Throwing her hands up, ducking desperately – still the heavy metal hook sank into her neck. The blood spurting everywhere and her gurgling like a blocked drain. She collapsed to her knees, forced into humiliation at least for the final moments. Too late, you miserable, worthless creature.

Run, Nathalie. Save yourself.

It won't be long before everyone knows.

What then? A final battle? Fine by me. I will protect my little princess by all means necessary. We've become good at hiding, expert. And nobody will destroy what we have created.

Spring, my angel, think of spring.

When the meadows turn green and are dotted with daisies, ground elder and red clover. We'll dance in the sunshine, squint at the light. You are my courage, my comfort, my life. I'm ready for anything.

ANN

SCHERGEL, 28 DECEMBER 2017

I'm sitting huddled by the shower in room 113. Although there are two doors between me and the insistent knocking, it still sounds deafening, like menacing fists striking wood which is about to succumb. I feel like howling. And anyhow, Brock doesn't have to break down the door; he could simply use his master key.

Please, stop! Stop knocking, leave me in peace!

'It seems like he's not going to go away,' Jakob says from the other side of the bathroom door, his voice muffled. It sounds like a question, as if he's asking my permission to sort the matter out.

'I don't care what you do,' I call out. 'I just want him to stop!' I need peace and quiet, for God's sake. I have to concentrate. In my head there's something I can't get at, as if it's covered, buried under this fricking racket. All I know is that it's got something to do with Nathalie.

It was already too late to turn around and follow her after Jakob had pointed out my misapprehension. *They know who he is.*

I thought he meant Marcus Steinhausen.

No, Ann, your father! They know he's in custody in Berlin as the chief suspect. Brock just announced the fact: an innocent man is in prison for

259

the crimes of the real ribbon murderer, who's now wreaking terror here. The most heinous crime in German history, a huge scandal.

We slipped back into the pub via the rear entrance to avoid the crush in the dining room. *They want to know everything and they see you as the greatest support in their hunt for the ribbon murderer.*

The knocking has stopped and a murmur has taken its place. Jakob trying to get rid of Brock. I only catch snippets of their conversation. Brock is insisting on talking to me, especially as we wormed our way into his village under false pretences.

'Please, Herr Brock, let it wait till tomorrow, okay? It's all very unsettling for her.' And I need a good sleep first, he adds. Just like Kerstin Seiler, I think. Kerstin, who also wanted some sleep and is now dead. I start shaking. I'm a total mess and I need to sort myself out.

Nathalie. It's all to do with Nathalie. My encounter with her, the things she said. *It's not your fault, Ann. But what he did is unforgivable.*

Did that sound like she knows my father? Like she thinks he's the killer? That's impossible; she lives here in Schergel with a mother who's verging on eighty and a daughter of kindergarten age. Although they only moved here a few weeks ago . . .

'Ann?' Jakob through the closed bathroom door. 'He's gone but he wants to talk to you in the morning. He's in a bit of a huff that we kept the truth from him.'

'Okay, thanks.'

'Are you going to come out now?'

'Just give me a moment.'

'I'll make us some tea if you—'

'Jakob, please!' I yell at the door, which I'm immediately sorry for. But I do need my peace, not only from Brock and his knocking, but from everyone, including Jakob. Peace to order my thoughts. To understand. 'Just give me a few more minutes, okay?' I say again, this time more softly. Jakob responds with silence. I hear his footsteps moving away, then the mattress springs faintly creaking: Jakob must have settled down on my bed. I breathe a sigh of relief.

Okay, Nathalie.

She originally comes from Wuppertal, Schmitti said. She, on the other hand, told me she moved here to Schergel from Wiesbaden. Two cities beginning with W; Schmitti might have got them mixed up. But how does she know the Nestorstrasse weekly market in Berlin?

And I suppose that's also the reason why you're here, isn't it? she says in my memory of our conversation this afternoon. *Because the other eleven girls all came from Berlin?*

Eleven!

Leaping to my feet, I tear open the bathroom door. Jakob's slouched on my bed, busy on his phone. It slips from his hand when I hurl his name across the room. 'Just imagine this, all right?'

'All – all right.'

'Your daughter is kidnapped by the ribbon murderer, but, like Sarah, manages to escape . . .'

Eva's theory now hammering inside my head: victims who didn't go to the police.

Jakob sits upright. 'And?'

'What would you do?'

'What do you mean, what would I do? I'd go to the police, of course. And no doubt my child would need therapy too.'

I wave my arms around wildly, an expansive gesture. 'Look at the upheaval! Interrogation by the police, which Sarah finds so intimidating that she's not saying a word! Probing questions from a psychologist! Medicines and child psychiatry!'

Jakob gives me a searching look.

'Do you know the weekly market in Nestorstrasse?' I ask him, but all I get is the same expression. 'It's in Wilmersdorf, Jakob! And it's tiny. Even you don't know it, though you live close by!'

'I really don't understand what you're—'

I throw my hands up and grab my head. I wish Jakob could look inside here, simply penetrate the few millimetres of skull with his gaze and access my mental world. But of course he can't, so I need to explain what's going on inside my mind, and I've got to be patient, focused, organised. I take a deep breath. Compose myself. A new approach, as calm as possible. 'Do you know what you could also do with your traumatised daughter to spare her all this upheaval? You could put her in the car and drive a few hundred kilometres away. You could find a safe place and shut yourself away to finally give your child some peace and quiet. It would have to be secluded, this place, but not too remote in case you need help. You tell the people around you that you've fled from your ex-partner so they don't wonder why you're behaving slightly oddly. That way you stop them being too nosy, while also securing their support. Just like she said: *everybody has their own lies.*'

'What? Who said—'

'Nathalie! That's what she told me earlier: *everybody has their own lies.*'

'Is this about Nathalie?'

I nod wildly. 'And do you know what else she said, albeit this afternoon when I helped her with her shopping?'

'You helped—?'

'She talked of *eleven* girls who'd fallen victim to the ribbon murderer. *Eleven!* Not ten! And before you say anything, no, she can't have included Sarah. Her exact words were: *Because the other eleven girls all came from Berlin.*'

Jakob gets up off the bed, muttering, and wanders over to the window. Although I'm finding it hard to keep quiet, I leave him to ponder his thoughts for a moment. I realise this is quite a lot for him to take in: a brand-new theory, a bizarre scenario. 'It doesn't sound completely off the wall,' he says eventually, turning back to me. 'But I think it's more likely that Nathalie – like everyone else – has simply read the papers and seen the news. And someone not directly involved wouldn't know for sure whether there were ten or eleven victims.'

'All right, then, what about Nestorstrasse? How would she know that if she comes from Wuppertal? Or Wiesbaden? Or from wherever else – maybe even Berlin?'

'Don't tell me you've never visited another city as a tourist. How about relatives living elsewhere?' He comes closer and places his hands on my shoulders. 'You've got to understand—'

'No, you've got to understand, Jakob! We were wondering how Steinhausen hit on Schergel. What he's doing here. It's because of Nathalie! She's the reason! He's playing games with her! He wants her to know he's here and that's why he kidnapped her friend's daughter and killed Kerstin. He wants to torture her, present her with a window on her own future. As if to tell her that she won't even be able to save her child from him.'

Now Jakob bursts out laughing. 'We're talking about the woman who earlier on walked through a dark village all on her own. Would you do that if you felt there was a crazed killer after you and your daughter?'

'She was completely on edge, Jakob! She literally hotfooted it out of the meeting! She knows! She knows her family's in danger! But it seems like she's going to confront the killer on her own!' Within seconds, I've taken a second sweatshirt from my bag, in an attempt to make up for the jacket that the police confiscated. Jakob just gawps. 'For goodness' sake, Ann!'

That sceptical look he's giving me. There's concern in his face; he's become genuinely friendly towards me, or at least has got used to me and my ways. But of course there's the other side to him, the journalist, who in this situation can spot something fantastic to milk. If the protagonist is right, she's a heroine who might end up saving a number of lives. But what would he have to write if she's wrong? That she got carried away and became obsessed with her quest to prove her father's innocence?

'Don't worry, I haven't forgotten why you came with me to Schergel,' I say. 'I just want you to realise that I've begun to properly trust you.' As if to prove it, I hold out my left arm with the scar on my wrist. 'Only five people know about this: my dad, Eva, my friend Zoe, Ludwig – and you.'

'I trust you too,' Jakob says, nodding, although he doesn't look me in the eye.

'Let's go then. You can always decide later whether you came as a friend or journalist. And to be quite honest, Jakob, I'd rather read an article about an overly cautious madwoman who got it wrong than someone who failed to act at the right moment.'

He nods again, decisively this time, and straight at me.

We leave the inn quietly and again by the back entrance. Judging by the noise coming from the dining room, the meeting is still in full flow. Out the front is a group of smokers; we go the long way round like thieves in the night. Taking the car might attract attention so we walk. Jakob asks me what I'm expecting. I say I just want to talk to Nathalie. I want to know what's up. That's all. We're not in some film where we turn up in the nick of time, as the killer is launching the big finale. And yet it's a strange feeling walking along the dark village street – a cold feeling on the back of the neck that we're being watched or followed.

'We haven't even got a weapon,' Jakob comments, making a sound that was probably meant to be a laugh, but which got caught somewhere in his throat. 'I mean, when I think of everything you said . . . the idea that Steinhausen's playing games with Nathalie. If all of that is really true . . .' Another sound, with a slight quiver in its tone. And he's right. How can I be so convinced and yet so careless? What if we really do come across Steinhausen? I shake my head – just at myself. It's true, Ann. You've gone mad, you've totally lost it. The thing with Dad, the thing with Eva and then Nathalie, whose pretty face has got you in all of a fluster. You're distraught, bewildered and lonely.

'Is this the right way?' Jakob does a 360-degree turn as he walks. We've left the village behind and now the path to the upper common rises before us. At least I hope it's that. I think of Nathalie and how she asked if she ought to have dropped a few crumbs of bread for me. *Keep going straight*, I replied.

'Keep going straight,' I now tell Jakob. And I'm right.

A veil of mist has gathered below the house, which in the

moonlight looks like thick, white smoke. The snow reflects it too; it's the only light to guide us. Inside the house itself, all is dark, or at least that's how it looks, for, just like this afternoon, the shutters are closed.

'Looks abandoned,' Jakob whispers as we approach from the side in a wide arc.

'They've got to be there,' I answer. 'Nathalie doesn't have a car. They wouldn't be able to get away from here so quickly.'

'Maybe they're already asleep.'

'Maybe.'

We extend our arc around the front of the house to make for a stand of trees, which means wading laboriously through knee-high snow, as hard as concrete. It breaks and crunches far too loudly in this eerie silence. Here we stay hidden for a while; we call it 'observation', though it's more likely uncertainty as to what to do next.

'Okay, Jakob,' I say, when I notice that his eyes are on me rather than the house. 'This is what we'll do: you wait here and I'll wander over.' I wave my mobile. 'Put your phone on silent. I'll call you and stay on the line while I talk to her. That way you'll hear everything and can intervene if necessary.'

He shakes his head. 'No way. We'll go together. What if Steinhausen really—?'

'Let's assume that everything's fine and I've only come to see Nathalie for a chat. I don't want to frighten the poor woman.'

'You're not so sure anymore, are you?'

'To be honest, I don't feel like I know anything anymore.'

I trudge off towards the house through the crunching snow, metre by metre. My heart seems to be ahead of me, its tempo has left me far behind. I get to the simple black steps, which the cold of the night has covered with a layer of ice, and I move slowly, carefully, but, most of all, quietly. As if I were doing something illicit. As if I shouldn't be here.

Now I'm outside the front door. In the moonlight I can make out the bell. It's still possible for me to turn around and go.

'Decisions, my Beetle,' I hear my father say with a smile. The sound of his voice in my head soothes me at once. '"Our reason can tell us what we should avoid doing. But our heart can tell us what we have to do."'

Who said that? Blaise Pascal?

'Joseph Joubert, my love. And now . . .'

I nod at thin air and press the bell.

Nothing. I try again and listen. Has the bell been disconnected? Perhaps – I mean, that's exactly what I did at home. I knock, tentatively at first, then slightly louder. 'Nathalie?' I try to call out, but it's no more than a hoarse whisper. I look at my mobile; I'm still on the line to Jakob. 'I don't think the bell's working,' I say in a hushed voice.

'Come back, then, forget it,' says Jakob, my voice of reason.

But my heart sends me around the house. Logs for the stove are piled up against the wall. Instinctively I look up. No smoke drifting from the chimney. I continue to tiptoe, passing a corner. To my left is another wall of firewood and on the other side, a strip of land beneath the thick layer of snow which could be a garden. I try peeking through the slats of one of the shutters, but see nothing, only darkness. Then a noise. I freeze. Listen. A faint clatter. It's not coming from inside, but my ears tell me it's very close, behind the next corner of the house. I go on. As quietly and cautiously as I possibly can, always one foot in front of the other. A tawny owl shrieks. And then there's another noise. A clicking, like someone using a lighter. In my ears I now hear the rushing of blood, like a waterfall, that masks everything else. 'Do it!' my heart screams. And I obey. I take the final, decisive step around the corner.

First I see the tiny red light, on the ground to my left. Then the black shape of a person getting up from a sitting position as if in slow motion. I hear the hissing voice asking who's there. My mouth opens, but I merely croak. Then the figure reaches for something. A long handle; something metallic scrapes across the icy ground. I see the flash of the steel blade of an axe. I want to run away but it's too late.

RECORDING 07
Berlin, 10 May 2021

- So, I'm back.
- Of course you are . . . *(coughs)* I'm sorry. Did you make use of the weekend to think about our last meeting?
- Yes, I did. I listened to the recordings as well. We were talking about the girl with the roller skates.
- Do you remember her name?
- Yes, Laura. Her name was Laura. You lured her into your car under the pretence that you were going to show her a good place for skating. What happened then?
- I took her to the Kuhlake in Spandau. Do you know the area? Really pretty. There was a hut there, so overgrown that it looked as if the walls were made of ivy and brambles. As if

nature herself had made the hut sprout there and someone had recently nailed a few wooden slats to it. I told Laura that the hut was on the way to the roller-skating place, and she believed me. She even put her hand in mine as we walked. If we'd bumped into anyone, they'd have thought it was a father going for a walk with his little daughter. That did actually happen a few times. Someone seeing me with one of the girls, I mean.

– And nobody ever got suspicious?

– Well, I don't look like a dangerous person. Even you remarked on that at the beginning. You said you'd imagined me differently. And that's why you feel guilty.

– What? Why should I feel guilty?

– Because you're another of those people who failed to notice anything. But console yourself with the fact that nobody did, really, nobody at all. You feel guilty most of all, however, because you can't find me repulsive, no matter how hard you try. My crimes, maybe. But as a person you find me fascinating, you like being here, you enjoy our conversations. And you think that's wrong. After all, I'm a criminal, a serial killer, shattering your ideal image of the world. Let me remind you that the world cannot be controlled and it has a number of cracks that can't be patched up. You're not only wondering how I came to kill the girls, but more importantly, what it must be like to act outside of all norms. Am I right?

– I haven't thought about that.

– Yes, you have. You've done nothing else since you first met me three days ago.

– No, I've been dwelling on something different.

– Such as?

- The nature of our conversations, the constant feeling that you're playing with me, making me dance like a silly monkey.
- Dance, oh, dancing. Maybe I ought to have danced more often in my life. People who dance usually look so relaxed, as if they're in a different sphere. I've always enjoyed watching people dance, and have even tried it myself, just as I've tried out lots of things that I thought might make me happy. But, because I couldn't find my way into this sphere, I soon gave up dancing.
- But killing, did that make you happy?
- Not the killing. The death. The death made me feel alive. Like with an organ transplant, when a heart is removed from a dying person and put into another person's body so they can go on living.
- But nobody kills the heart donors; they die of their own accord.
- Oh, heavens, you're nitpicking again. Now, just imagine that only one of us can survive this meeting. Is it going to be you or me? According to your morality, you'd rather die than kill me. Is that the case? Really? Are you absolutely sure?

ANN

SCHERGEL, 28 DECEMBER 2017

'You?' a reedy voice says.

My rigid body twitches and I open my eyes wide. Still alive, breathing, heart pounding. Only now do I let out a scream; it's a delayed shock. The figure comes towards me, the axe thuds on the frozen ground and I'm blinded by the bright light of a torch.

'Are you out of your mind? What are you doing here? I thought . . .'

'Ann!' cries another voice in the distance. Jakob, who must have been alarmed by my scream. 'What's happening, Ann?'

Bit by bit I come to my senses. Nathalie. It's just Nathalie. In a towelling dressing gown, black, blue or grey – some dark colour I can't make out in this light. And just thick woolly socks on her feet. As if she's unaffected by this biting cold, as if she has no feeling. Her hair is tied in a messy bun. A few stray strands stick to her forehead. 'I . . . I just, er wanted . . . to talk to you,' I stammer, distracted by the effort of trying to take in my surroundings. The place I just saw Nathalie squatting as a black figure. A dark patch on the ground. A square, set with fist-sized

271

stones and, in the middle, also formed of stones: a heart. And finally the red light. A lantern with a cemetery candle in it. A grave . . .

Do you remember . . . ?

Mum, who's now lying under the black earth. White lilies, red candles. I'm six years old. I'm not crying; my feelings are as dead as my mother.

It was me who discovered her like that: her eyeballs rolled upwards and her mouth wide open as if about to scream. I'd just been chattering away on the carpet beside her bed, her little Cinderella who sorted out her pills. She'd just been laughing at something I'd said. Then it suddenly fell silent. I got up to check. Her eyes, her mouth and the way her hand had tensed around the side rail of her bed.

I'm stiff and utterly numb, a person who's still breathing but who is no longer really alive. My father tries to explain death to me, but even he, with his profound understanding of the world, has reached his limits.

– Why are the candles red, Daddy?

– Those aren't normal candles. Those are soul lights, my Beetle. They're showing Mummy's soul the way to the other side.

– Mummy doesn't need to be shown the way anymore, Daddy. She's dead.

– Only her body is dead. Her soul lives on.

– Why can't we see it then?

– That's not possible. A soul is invisible.

– So how do we know there is a soul?

– The world is more than our eyes can see. And even if we think

we see something clearly, sometimes we're wrong because
we're interpreting rather than truly understanding.

– Huh? What does that mean?

– It means that understanding is painful, Ann. Maybe the most
painful thing of all. Let me tell you a story. It comes from a
very wise man called Plato . . .

'Our kitten,' Nathalie says, interrupting my memories and
pointing at the grave. 'It had epilepsy and died after an attack.
My daughter simply won't stop crying. We loved that little thing
so much.'

Now I remember the packet of cat food in my rucksack.
Nathalie only bought it this afternoon. Which means she's lost
her friend and her pet within a day of each other.

'I'm sorry.'

'I thought there ought to be a definite place for Lenia to come.
It's good for the grieving process, as I'm sure you know.' She
bends down to the lantern with the grave candle and pushes it
more firmly into the ground. 'It's just a little candle and yet it
lights up the night. Quite comforting, don't you think?'

I nod. 'Lenia . . . Is that your daughter's name?'

'Ann!' Jakob again. Only now do I notice that my mobile is on
the ground. I must have dropped it in shock.

'What's going on?' Nathalie asks, pointing her torch at it.

I pick the phone up, say, 'Everything's okay, Jakob,' then end
the call. 'You must think it's weird that I should be creeping
around your house at this hour. But I was worried about you.' I
look past her at the terrace door, which is open. She could invite
me in, where there's light and somewhere to sit. Instead she

switches off the torch, clamps it under her arm and bends down for the axe. I instinctively take a step backwards.

'The frozen ground,' she says, nodding at the cat's grave. 'And stubborn tree roots too. You were lucky I recognised you in time.'

'I rang the bell,' I say in my defence. 'Besides, you could have put a light on.'

Leaning the axe against the wall of the house, she pulls the belt on her dressing gown tighter, the torch still clamped under her arm. The cold seems to be getting to her after all. 'No, I couldn't, I'm afraid. Something's up with the electrics. Nothing's been working since this afternoon, no light, no cooker, nothing. I need to let Brock know, though I don't suppose I'm high on his list of priorities at the moment. Come in.'

I follow her through the terrace door into the sitting room. It's bitterly cold, even in here, and it smells a bit musty, like my bathroom at the inn. Maybe there's mould on the walls. To the left, beneath the shuttered windows, I can see the outline of a sofa with a coffee table in front of it and an old-fashioned standard lamp beside it. To the right, some narrow stairs lead up.

'I was going to wait with the grave till tomorrow morning because of the light,' Nathalie says, moving to the table and placing the torch on it. Once again the click of a lighter. This time she lights the candles on the table – half a dozen stumps, burned to different heights, on the bare wood with nothing beneath them. 'But Lenia was crying so much and wouldn't calm down. She got to the point where she almost collapsed with exhaustion.' She bends down, takes off her woolly socks, rolls them up together and thoughtlessly drops them on the floor. At the sight of her bare feet on the cold tiles, I wrap my arms around my chest. The two sweatshirts I'm wearing, one on top of the other, are no substitute for Dad's jacket.

'You get used to some things,' Nathalie says, as if she could read my mind. 'But not others.'

I just nod, still overwhelmed by the situation. Not to mention the cold, the musty smell and the flickering shadows cast by the candlelight.

'Do sit down. Would you like some tea? My mother and the little one are both asleep so we should try to keep the noise down.'

I shake my head. I mustn't forget why I've actually come here. 'Does the name Marcus Steinhausen mean anything to you?'

A brief silence, shadows dancing on her face. 'No, who's he?'

'Are you sure?'

No answer, just the dancing shadows.

'How do you know the weekly market in Nestorstrasse if you lived in Wuppertal before moving to Schergel?'

'The . . . ? Oh yes, that. I've got friends in Berlin. They took me there once when I was on a visit. Is that why you've come all the way up here? To interrogate me? What's this about?'

She's about to turn away but I grab the sleeve of her dressing gown. 'You're afraid, Nathalie. I can sense it. You know who I am. Now tell me who you are!'

'Please, not so loud.'

'I can help you!'

Jerking out of my grip, she looks over at the stairs. 'You'll wake the entire house up.' A diversionary tactic I'm not going to fall for.

'Wiesbaden,' I say.

'What?'

'Schmitti told me you come from Wuppertal. Whereas this afternoon you told me yourself you come from Wiesbaden.'

She shakes her head. 'Wuppertal! I said Wuppertal. You must have misheard. And now I'd like to know what this is all about.'

'I'm just trying to make sense of our conversation earlier. Make sense of *you*. As well as the whole situation here in Schergel. Sarah's disappearance and Kerstin's murder. You talked of eleven girls the ribbon murderer abducted in Berlin. How did you get that number?'

Nathalie thumps her chest as if trying to calm her heartbeat. But she doesn't answer me, she says nothing.

'Please, Nathalie.' My eyes well with tears. 'Does this violent ex-husband of yours really exist? Or is it what I'm thinking? Was your little daughter one of the victims too? Only that, like Sarah, she managed to escape her kidnapper?'

'My ex-husband . . .' she repeats, her voice cracking.

'Did he really hurt you? Or Lenia? Or are we actually talking about someone quite different?'

Nathalie sways; I grab her arm again, to support her this time.

'Are you feeling unwell? Do you want to sit down?'

She shakes her head, very slowly, as if mechanically. 'In November. It happened in November.'

'What happened in November?'

'He . . .' She falters.

'Speak, Nathalie! I want to help you!'

'Nobody can help us.'

'Yes, I can! I'll do everything possible, I promise. Now, please just talk to me.'

Nathalie looks at me for a long moment. I open my mouth to

implore her again – the truth, please, I beg you! – but it doesn't work; I'm silent as if under a strange spell. Her gaze works it way deeper and deeper, first into me, then through me. 'He kidnapped Lenia from a playground and took her to a hut in the Königswald,' she begins, in a voice that sounds monotonous, almost trance-like. 'When he took his eye off her briefly, she saw her chance and ran off. She'd made her way through the woods for more than a kilometre when she came across some walkers. She told them she was lost. Luckily she knew our address by heart.'

My stomach churns and I don't feel steady on my feet. I'm not mad; I've been right the whole time.

Nathalie closes her eyes. 'When the two walkers brought her home, I knew at once that something dreadful must have hap-pened,' she continues as if everything were playing out again behind her closed lids, now, at this very moment. 'Can you see her breaking down in my arms, Ann? Her tiny body shuddering and quaking? Can you hear her crying so terribly? There, there, my darling, it's okay. Your mummy's here. What happened? Tell me, Lenia, speak to me! She is speaking. Oh God . . .' Nathalie, her eyes still closed, is now swaying so badly that I'm finding it hard to keep hold of her. I push her forwards to the sofa; I want her to sit down. 'It must have been the ribbon murderer. That's how he works, that's his pattern. He kidnaps little girls and takes them away to kill them. What has he done to my baby? And what . . .' She sobs intensely. 'What are we going to do now? What if he means to snatch her back? If he looks for her and finds her? Can we trust the police to protect us from him? Those same people who've been trying to catch him for fourteen years but failing time and again? We have to go away, my angel, far, far away. Don't worry, okay? Your mummy will make sure you're safe.'

I flop down wearily beside Nathalie, take her hand and hold it tightly. She opens her eyes and is back here with me now, back in her sitting room.

'So then you left Berlin?'

Nathalie nods. 'I decided to rent a car and leave our one outside our block so nobody would notice we'd gone. That would give us a head start . . .'

'Your mother was the only one you told.'

'Yes. I packed everything that would fit in the boot and we just drove off, heading south. It was pure coincidence that we came to Schergel, but I thought at once that this would be the perfect place. Remote, insignificant, just the tiniest of dots on the map. We would be safe here. At the entrance to the village was a sign about renting rooms and holiday homes – ask at the inn. Right away I thought Brock was a money-grubbing show-off, but that also had its advantages. He likes cash as he can slip it past the tax authorities. When I put a few notes on the counter he didn't even insist on seeing my ID, let alone make me sign any sort of agreement or other form. Two hundred and thirty euros a week for both apartments, which is basically the entire holiday home. That would be tricky once my savings were used up, but what kind of a problem is that compared to . . .'

'It's okay.'

'No, Ann, it's not okay. It's hell.' Now she in turn squeezes my hand so firmly that I can feel my knuckles. 'I had to lie to them all, all those people who were so kind to me, the entire village. But people notice if you shut yourself away altogether, and you end up achieving the exact opposite of what you'd intended. So you integrate a bit, to stop drawing unnecessary attention to yourself. To avoid questions and suspicion.'

'That's why you invented the story about your violent ex-husband.'

She shrugs. 'They all took pity on us and Kerstin even offered me the job at the butcher's. We needed the money, and now I was always able to find out what people were gossiping about in the village. In case—'

'He came back,' I say, finishing her sentence. 'Nathalie . . .' I wonder how to put this and why I'm finding it so difficult, because basically both of us know: it's happened. The man she wanted to protect her family from has tracked her down.

'I'm really sorry,' Nathalie says, beating me to it. Something I can't understand. 'It's not your fault.'

'My . . . ?'

Freeing her hand from my grip, she strokes my cheek instead. 'Since his arrest, they've only shown his picture in the papers and on the telly with a black bar over the eyes. But Lenia is sure. The nose, the mouth, the grey hair. She recognised him. It was him, Ann. It was your father.'

For a moment I'm falling, but the moment is short and I land on my feet. Because I've been doing a lot of falling recently, because it's something you learn. But most of all because I don't believe what she's saying. It's not true. Is it? Dear God, please don't let it be true. 'Let me speak to Lenia!'

'No way! You haven't got the slightest idea what we've been through! Because of your father, Ann!' Nathalie leaps up from the sofa, as do I.

Lenia must be mistaken. Of course she's deeply traumatised. Just like Sarah, who's silent, Nathalie's daughter is processing her trauma by pinning it on my father. As the alleged ribbon murderer, he's been in the press so often, always that same photograph with the black bar over his eyes. It's the perfect projection screen, isn't it? Isn't it?

'Please, Nathalie! You've got to understand that I have to be absolutely certain! This is about someone's life!'

'Yes, my daughter's! I want you to go now, at once!' She hurries into the hallway, wrenches the key and throws open the door. 'Get out of here!'

'Nathalie . . .'

'I've told you to go!' She's got a glass in her hand; I don't know where that's come from. But it doesn't matter, nothing matters now.

It was him, Ann. It was your father.

No. Nonononono. 'So who kidnapped Sarah? And killed Kerstin? Nathalie!'

With a firm shove, she pushes me out of the house and closes the door.

Despair. (Ann, 11 years old)

Despair is a bad feeling. It's like sitting on a small raft without a mast, sail or paddle, and just drifting on the sea in the middle of the night. Everything's dark and you can't see the shore and you don't have any hope, because there's no wind and so there are no waves either. All you can do is wait to see what happens, and maybe pray. But God doesn't always hear you.

I stagger down the outdoor steps as if I'd been badly injured. My mind is wrapped in swathes of apathy. I can see Jakob rushing towards me, but it doesn't feel real, more like a scene from a film.

'What happened?' he asks, though his voice barely reaches me. I want to return to the world behind my closed eyelids, want it to be intact again. I want to be five again, happy and unsuspecting. But most of all I want my asthma spray.

'Ann?!' Jakob again. He manoeuvres my body down the remaining steps as if it were a bulky piece of furniture. I wonder how he could have got here so quickly, but then I reckon he must have made his way to the house when I ended our conversation.

'It's all right,' I croak when we're at the bottom.

But Jakob doesn't believe me; he can hear the whistling in my breathing, the rattling in my chest, and it sounds really horrible, critical. 'Oh God! Sit down!'

Not wanting to, I drag myself onwards, desperate to get away from this house, away from Nathalie and Lenia and the mother and the dead cat, further and further, down the hill. Jakob is frantically prancing about beside me. I wheeze, flounder and eventually my knees give way in the middle of the path, as if someone had kicked me from behind. Jakob kneels beside me, cradling my head in his hands.

'Asthma,' I whimper.

'What? Shit!' Letting go of my head, he reaches in his trouser pocket for his mobile.

'No!' I punch the air: my protest against his intention to call for an ambulance. 'Really, I'll be better again in a sec.'

He hesitantly slips the mobile back in his pocket while I breathe against the constrictive feeling in my chest, in on one, out on two, again and again. And indeed it does get better.

'What happened in there?' Jakob says, pointing back to where Nathalie's house is a mere outline, black against the moonlight.

I shake my head and put out a hand so he can help me up. 'The air. I think the house is full of mould.' Jakob pulls me to my feet. 'It must have been too much for my asthma.'

'That's all? I heard shouting.'

'I got a fright. She was sitting behind the house in the pitch-black, digging a grave for their dead cat.'

'At this time?'

'Parents do that sort of thing,' I say, shedding a tear. 'Once my father drove three hours from Berlin to the Baltic in the middle of the night just after we'd got back from holiday. I'd left my diary at the hotel and almost had a breakdown.'

Jakob wrings his hands impatiently. Right now he's not interested in the diary of my fourteen-year-old self. But what happened inside Nathalie's house.

Decisions, my Beetle . . .

The head. The heart.

I shrug. 'I'm sorry about tonight. It was a total non-starter. The name Marcus Steinhausen seemed to ring no bells at all. And she knows the weekly market in Nestorstrasse from a visit to friends in Berlin.' Sluggishly I get moving again, back towards the village. My jeans are soaked and sticking to my legs. I'm walking as if I were made of wood.

Jakob catches up with me. 'So we're no further than we were before. The only difference being that her mouldy house almost killed you. What now?'

'No idea. I'm just completely shattered.'

*

There are two parts to me. One is numb, the other hurting. I stare at the ceiling, doubling up inside. Jakob's lying next to me, snoring softly. Every time I move, I find myself sticking to him in some way. He's not wearing a T-shirt and he's sweating. I don't want to feel his bare, warm skin, but the bed is too narrow to get away from him. It was his idea to spend the night in the same room. In view of the situation, it's safer, he said, and I expect he also wanted to be there to support me, sensing I was a bit of a mess. Maybe he was hoping for more too. So I told him that the fool I'm still hung up on goes by the name of Zoe. He found that exciting, which is still the best reaction you can expect from many people to a woman loving another woman. Normally this gets me worked up. But *normally* no longer exists; it's an adverb from a forgotten time.

Now everything is just surreal. Supposedly my father is the ribbon murderer; it's actually him, in all seriousness, unquestionably, it really, really, really is him. Nathalie said this to my face without leaving the slightest room for doubt. *Lenia is sure. The nose, the mouth, the grey hair. She recognised him. It was him, Ann. It was your father.*

Oughtn't I to hate him now? Be livid? Feel as if my entire existence had been betrayed? Instead I feel more like I've got a hangover. A state that's unpleasant but only temporary. And yet I know that Nathalie wouldn't have had any reason to lie to me. On the other hand, I still have my doubts as to whether a profoundly traumatised child can be taken seriously as a witness. The only positive side to this is that Nathalie hasn't gone to the police with Lenia. She hasn't made an official statement that might incriminate my father, and, in my estimation, she won't for the time being. She just wants some peace for her daughter. My head is buzzing; I need some peace and quiet too. Finding a position in which I can feel as little as possible of Jakob's body despite the lack of space, I try to get some sleep. In my dream my father is chasing Larissa Meller through the woods. I'm there too, helping him.

RECORDING 08
Berlin, 10 May 2021

- This discussion has nothing to do with your crimes, so I'm not going to get caught up in it. We were talking about Laura, the girl with the roller skates. You took her to the Kuhlake in Spandau. What happened then?
- You appear to be in a hurry.
- No, but you're starting to wear my patience thin. I'm here to discuss the girls, the cases.
- Yes, of course, do forgive me. So, Laura. Oh, she was really charming. And clearly she hadn't got out of Hellersdorf often. Nature fascinated her – the glittering water, the aromatic grass, a carpet of thousands of wood anemones – 'like in a fairy tale,' she said. And her excitement when we got to the hut! How enviable children are! That genuineness, that enthusiasm for little things. I asked her if she would do me a favour – stick out her left hand and close her eyes.
- And then?
- I did it. I grabbed her wrist and made the first cut.
- How did she react?
- Well, she didn't scream at first. She just opened her eyes and

stared at me. But right after that, she tore herself free with a strength and determination you couldn't imagine in a child, and then she ran off.

- Are you saying she escaped? The girl survived?
- (*chuckles*) Last time I asked you what your favourite subjects at school were, do you remember?
- You're doing it again.
- What?
- Dangling a carrot in front of my nose, only to pull it away again.
- Do you want to know what my favourite subjects were?
- No, I want to talk about Laura.
- Art and religious studies.
- (*sighs*) I see. Typical subjects you can bluff your way through.
- More like subjects that allow plenty of scope for discussion.
- Whatever. We were talking about Laura.
- No, we were talking about our favourite subjects. Yours were German and PE, I recall. I'm extremely attentive and observant, which has stood me in good stead throughout my life. For example, I know a great deal about you now.
- What's that supposed to mean?
- Laura, Miriam, Larissa, Jana, Kati, Olivia, Laetitia, Hayet, Jenny, Saskia, Alina and Sophie.
- Laura, Miriam, Larissa . . . (*pants*) There were more! There weren't ten, but . . .
- (*slow handclap*) Twelve.
- So Laura didn't survive.
- No, not her.
- *Not her?* But that means someone else did?

ANN

When I wake up, it's not quite yet light. My right eyelid is stuck and there's a stain on the pillow. Blood? I sit bolt upright and make a sound that wakes Jakob. He reaches past me to the bedside table and switches on the light. Then he stares at me and leaps out of bed. Soon afterwards I hear the rushing of water in the bathroom, then he comes back with a handful of damp, scrunched-up loo paper. It burns when he puts it on my face. Now I understand; it is actually blood on the pillow. And I also understand what's happened: the stitches have unravelled and my eyebrow has opened up again. My sleep was very restive, which is no surprise given that I was chasing my father through the woods. I've been brought back down to reality with a bump. Yesterday, Kerstin Seiler's murder, my visit to Nathalie, the end of the world. I knock Jakob's hand away from my face; I can't take being touched.

'Going for a shower,' I say, getting out of bed and gathering up my clothes that I put on the radiator to dry. Yesterday Jakob asked me what we were going to do now. All that's certain is that we have to go to the police station in Bad Kötzting this morning to

286

give our statements about finding Kerstin's body. And that Jakob promised Brock a conversation with me.

On the way to the bathroom, my attention is caught by the bedroom door. There's a water glass on the handle. 'Jakob?'

'Oh, that.' He wanders past me into the bathroom, and again I hear the sound of running water, briefly this time. 'Just a security measure. I mean, there's a killer running around in the village.'

Fascinated, I go to inspect the construction close up while Jakob comes back from the bathroom. I hardly notice that he's filled the kettle. 'If someone presses the handle from outside . . .'

'The glass falls off and smashes on the floor.'

'An ingenious alarm system.'

I know someone else with an alarm system like that. Nathalie, who suddenly had a glass in her hand when she threw me out of her house yesterday. I didn't see where it had come from – perhaps because she'd just taken it off the handle? There's a click behind me and then the sound of water heating in the kettle.

I spin around. 'What are you doing?'

'Why not? I mean, breakfast doesn't begin until half past seven. Or have you been rationing them?' Laughing, Jakob dangles a tea bag over his cup. 'If you insist, I'll give you one from my room later.'

Do sit down. Would you like some tea?

'You need electricity to make tea.'

'Yes,' he says, laughing again. 'Or fire. But I reckon we've got enough problems in this village already without setting light to the place. Especially now that everyone knows who you are. Brock is going to fall on you like I will his breakfast buffet. God, I'm absolutely famished . . .'

His words fade beneath Nathalie's voice in my mind. Yesterday evening: *Something's up with the electrics. Nothing's been working since this afternoon, no light, no cooker, nothing.* And yet she offered to make me a cup of tea just a moment later.

'Ann?'

'What?'

'Would you like one too?'

Without responding, I rush into the bathroom with my pile of clothes. No time for tea, no time for explanations.

When I come back out, the television is on. A children's programme. Jakob's back in bed, the remote control on his bare tummy. He's fallen asleep, an empty teacup on the bedside table. For a moment I stand there, looking at him, unsure whether to wake him and ask him to come with me. Then I realise I've already made my decision – yesterday, when I only told him about half of my conversation with Nathalie. Just like I kept to myself what occurred to me about the glass on the door handle, and the kettle.

I don't have a choice.

I silently put on my boots, grab my rucksack and leave the room. It's quiet in the pub – the breakfast preparations don't seem to be underway yet – and it's tranquil outside too, on the marketplace. I imagine Brock and his wife lying in bed, the whole village still asleep, exhausted from the previous day and all the beer that was drunk during the meeting.

I have to be sure, I *have* to be. So I make my way yet again up to Nathalie's house on the upper common. I walk briskly; my shadow, leading its own life beneath the light of the streetlamps, is making me feel uncomfortable. I look back over my shoulder several times, and several times I hear crunching footsteps in the snow that aren't there. But Jakob's right: a killer's still running around this village. He might be lying in wait for me behind the corner of the next house or the next tree, and nobody would see anything happen. So much for the village guard that Brock said would be up and running yesterday evening, doing round-the-clock patrols. I quicken my pace. Something is more important than danger. The minutest of possibilities, the last straw.

The shutters closed even during the day.

No electric light that might draw attention to the fact that this house is being lived in.

The glass over the handle as an improvised alarm system.

Nathalie's lightning reaction as she grabbed the axe. As if she were on permanent alert and prepared for everything.

But most of all, this: why hasn't she gone back to Berlin if she's so sure that the man she believes to be her daughter's abductor has been locked up in prison for almost seven weeks?

And who's she afraid of?

The answer: Kerstin Seiler's killer, of course. But why should she be his next target? Her house is outside the village; nobody unfamiliar in this area would find it. So the killer must know her.

I shake my head; I just don't get it. There's only one thing I know: Nathalie's lying. For some reason she's still lying. And I've got to find out why. Apart from this, they can tell me as often as they like that my dad's the ribbon murderer, but I'll never be well and truly convinced of his guilt while words are still words and, like the evidence, don't constitute clear proof. I stop and rummage in my rucksack amongst Nathalie's things – the bread and now redundant cat food – for the packet of cigarettes I bought at the shop yesterday. Then for my lighter, but fruitlessly. I check my trouser pockets. For a moment I think I've got it, but it must still be in the jacket that the police took away for forensic examination. I take something else out instead: my old talisman that I found in the wooden box in Dad's study. The stone that dug into my wrist almost twenty years ago. Which Dad saved after the bike accident and gave me later as a reminder of the terrible experience I'd survived. On the sharp side, some brown discolouration is still visible. My blood. This stone that seems to be a sign, an encouragement to follow my feelings. A minor miracle just when I need it.

A few minutes later, the incline to the upper common appears before me. The holiday house is already in view, a dead, black outline, as if it had been slotted into an equally black bay of trees. And right there . . . maybe it only occurs to me because I've just been thinking about smoking. A tiny, luminous red dot, the glow of a cigarette. Am I mistaken? I blink. It glows again, the little red dot in the gloom. Then something moves – *someone!* – from the cover of the trees and makes straight for Nathalie's house. I instinctively squat and narrow my eyes, concentrating as hard as possible. Now I see it, I see it perfectly. A tall figure, not Nathalie this time. A man, creeping past the downstairs apartment. He stops, looks around. Gets moving again, approaches the steps. My brain is in overdrive: Steinhausen. He's here.

I start running the rest of the way up the slope. Nathalie, Lenia and the grandmother. Unsuspecting, maybe still asleep in their beds. When the glass slides off the door handle and smashes on the floor, it'll be too late. He'll already be inside the house. I speed up, remember the mobile in my rucksack, and ponder: call the police or Jakob? It would take too much time. Time that Nathalie and her family don't have. I reach the house, the steps. Then I think of the axe that Nathalie used yesterday evening to hack out the tree roots from the hole for the cat's grave. She leaned it next to the terrace door. A weapon. I don't mean to hurt anyone, just keep them at bay. But to get to the axe, I'd have to go past the front door and along three sides of the house.

The front door – relief. It hasn't been touched. He wasn't so far ahead of me that he could have cracked the lock, gone into the house and closed the door again from the inside. Besides, I didn't hear the breaking of glass. I put my ear to the wood and listen. Nothing. Has he got in some other way? Through the terrace door, perhaps? Or has he only come to nose around, have a recce? Did he spot me and bolt?

I creep my way around, one wall after another, until I get to the terrace. The lantern on the cat's grave. *It's just a little candle and yet it lights up the night.* The axe. It's gone. Did Nathalie put it somewhere else after I left? Or is it in the wrong hands? I look around nervously. The terrace door – also shut, with closed shutters. I peek through the slats. There's flickering light in the sitting room, candles like yesterday evening. Have they been burning all night? A shadow flits past; I flinch. It could just be Nathalie. Or the killer. I want to undo the catch that keeps the shutters fastened on the inside. So I try to slide my hand through the gap, but it doesn't fit.

My stone, my talisman! It's flat, triangular, and large enough that I can hold it by the wide end and push the narrow tip under the catch until it flips to the other side with a clack. I open the shutters and get another shock. Through the window I see

Nathalie wander over to the coffee table and pick up one of the candles. She looks like a ghost, she's spaced out. Surely she must have noticed the shutters being opened only a metre and a half away from her? I knock on the window.

Nothing, she doesn't react. Just stands there holding the candle, staring into the flame. I knock again. Now. Now her eyes see me and she tentatively comes closer; in the gloom of dawn she probably doesn't recognise me immediately. I gesticulate wildly and mouth her name. I don't want to be loud; someone apart from me is prowling around out here.

She opens the door, visibly surprised. 'Ann? What are you doing here, after—'

'After our argument yesterday evening? Let's just forget that, okay?' I push my way into the room and immediately lock the door behind me. 'There's someone here, Nathalie! I saw a man creeping around the house. Just now.'

'What? Who would . . . ?' She falters, her face suddenly vacant. 'Are we in danger?'

'I'm afraid we are. You lied to me, didn't you?' I slip the rucksack off my shoulder and drop it to the floor, prompted by the crazy thought that I might be about to get into a fight, and will need to be as agile as possible – no unnecessary encumbrance on my back.

Nathalie looks away.

'It's okay.' I reach for the candle, which has started shaking alarmingly in her hand, put it back on the table and pick up instead the torch that is there too. 'None of that matters now. We'll call the police and barricade ourselves in here till they come. It would be best if we took one of the upstairs rooms. Where's your family?'

Nathalie points behind her. 'We're just having breakfast. Ann . . .' She grabs my arm. Her grip is so desperate, so tight that I feel it in my bones. 'I'm scared.'

'I know. Me too. But we'll get through this, okay?'

Nathalie lets go of my arm. I switch on the torch.

'We should keep the overhead light off. We mustn't serve ourselves up to him on a platter. If he wants to get us, he's going to have to work for it.'

Nathalie looks horrified.

'I'm sorry,' I quickly add. 'That was inappropriate.'

I hurry across the sitting room. It's not hard to find the way to the kitchen; the house is small and the ground floor is probably only half the size of the apartment I shared with Zoe. The beam from the torch jerks haphazardly, staccato impressions, one per heartbeat. The furnishings, like those in the sitting room, aren't much cop in here either – the veneer is already peeling away from the nut-brown kitchen units. A fridge with a children's drawing stuck to it with magnets, together with signature: Lenia. A sink with days' worth of dirty dishes piled in it. A bin, its lid gaping open like a mouth stuffed with food. Empty tins of preserved food like the ones Nathalie bought masses of at the grocer's yesterday. The breakfast table laid with two plates, two cups, two sets of cutlery. A carton of milk, a pot of tea or coffee, crispbread, butter, jam. I've no time to think or embark on lengthy explanations. 'Come on!' I call to the old woman and little girl. 'We've got to . . .'

I falter.

Both of them ought to be staring at me now. Me, a strange woman in their house, a shock this early in the morning. The moment when everything falls apart, weeks of playing hide-and-seek, of uncertainty and permanent tension, but also the slight hope that they might have come through it all, and finally the great misapprehension. They ought to be beside themselves, terrified, confused, shocked. They ought to be *something*. But they're not.

The kitchen's empty.

I wave the torch about in disbelief. Finding a light switch, I push it. It's as I'd suspected: Nathalie lied about the electricity. The kitchen is bright, but remains empty.

'It happened in November,' I hear a voice behind me. Dropping the torch, I whip around and look directly at Nathalie. 'He kidnapped Lenia from a playground and took her to a hut in the Königswald.'

I nod as if on autopilot. That's precisely what she said yesterday, even using the same words. 'But where . . . ?' I ask, my throat constricted. Because there could still be a rational explanation for why there's nobody at this table, no Lenia, no grandmother. A different explanation from the one that's brewing in my head, like a storm suddenly filling a clear sky with darkness.

Nathalie says nothing.

I pant. Now I understand. The storm is raging. 'She . . . she didn't make it, did she? She couldn't escape because the ribbon murderer killed her just like the other girls in Berlin.'

Her face twitches with incomprehension. She staggers past me to one of the chairs, where she places a hand on the backrest. As if someone were sitting there.

'Don't worry, my little princess,' she says with a soft voice, her eyes staring into the void. 'Nobody's ever going to part us again.' Then, directed at me, 'Not even her.'

RECORDING 09

Berlin, 10 May 2021

- Wrong. I'm sorry. They all died. Beginning with Laura and ending with Sophie.
- That means Larissa wasn't the first.
- No, that was Laura, in summer 2001. One year later, in autumn 2002, came Miriam, and only then Larissa.
- That's what you meant when you said I was mistaken. My mistake was to think Larissa was the first victim. Correct?
- Correct.
- But they never connected Laura and Miriam to you.
- No, but they couldn't because those two girls were never found. As far as Laura is concerned . . . that was my first time, even though the idea had been fermenting in me for quite a while. But the impulse to actually do it came spontaneously when I saw her sitting by the road.
- You say it was spontaneous, but you had the weapon on you.
- I'd been carrying it around with me for some time. Like I say, the idea had been fermenting in me, and I'd often imagined doing it. So when I came across Laura, everything just slotted together.
- What did you do with her body?
- What would you have done with it?
- I've never thought about that and nor do I wish to.
- I heard about someone who once sawed up a body and then drove across the country, breaking into various farms and placing the parts in pigsties. Pigs are omnivores, you see, and

because dead flesh just smells of carrion rather than humans, they'll happily eat it.

– Why are you telling me this?

– Because I'd like to know your opinion on it.

– What do you expect me to say? It's disgusting!

– I see.

– What do you mean by 'I see'? Please don't tell me you're that man! You didn't feed Laura to pigs, did you?

– What do you take me for? That sort of thing would never have crossed my mind. First, I put Laura in the boot of my car, then I drove home. Although I'd imagined killing, just like you it had never occurred to me what I'd do with a dead body. I had to spend some time thinking it through. That night I drove back to the Kuhlake with Laura in the boot, and a shovel, to bury her. The following year, when I killed Miriam, I had the shovel with me.

– Where did you take Miriam?

– To the Blumenthaler Wald. Very close to where Saskia later died.

– Does this mean that the parents of Laura and Miriam still don't know what happened to their daughters?

– You're right, they don't. I suspect the girls are still officially classified as missing. It was only when it came to the third girl, Larissa, that I decided it would be better not to bury her. I'd allow the parents to do that.

– You got a bad conscience?

– No, it was more theoretical. I knew it was wrong to bury them and deprive the parents of the opportunity. The parents ought to find them and make a grave for them.

– (laughs) With respect, it sounds strange to hear the word

'wrong' coming from your mouth. And this distinction you make: you thought it was right to kill the girls, but wrong to bury them?

- I didn't say I thought it was right. 'Necessary' would be more accurate.
- Was it like a compulsion, then?
- I'd call it an urge.
- Where did this urge come from? What did Laura trigger in you to turn you into a killer, unable to stop murdering?
- Well, clearly, I have stopped.
- Yes, but not voluntarily. It was only your arrest that put an end to your crimes for good.
- My arrest. (*laughs*) In dubio pro reo, don't you think? Absolutely crucial was what happened in Schergel. Even I hadn't expected this turn of events.

ANN

SCHERGEL, 29 DECEMBER 2017

I want to get out of this kitchen, away from Nathalie; I'm finding her creepy. *Don't worry, my little princess,* she reassured the empty chair. *Nobody's ever going to part us again.* Stumbling backwards into something, I squeal in shock. I turn around; it's just the fridge. I stare at the drawing stuck to it. On the left is a small figure wearing a sprawling dress and a crown. A monster is making its way into the picture from the right. It's dark green with spiky-looking scales and fire shooting from its huge, open mouth between sharp teeth. It occupies the entire length of the piece of paper; it must be three or four times as big as the girl with the crown. The princess and the dragon, just like Sarah said.

But there's someone else: a third figure in the middle. A being in a long dress, perhaps an angel or a good fairy. With yellow hair – blonde, like Nathalie's. In her outstretched hand, she's holding a sword or a knife, something with a blade at least, the tip of which she's pressing against the dragon's neck.

Reeling, I turn back to Nathalie, who's still in exactly the same position: standing, her hand on the back of the chair, looking at me.

'Sarah?' is all I say at first, because, no, that can't be true. That's completely crazy. 'Is that the reason she's not making a statement? Because she knows you and doesn't want you to get into trouble?' Nathalie doesn't react. 'By castle, she meant your house, didn't she? Sarah was here the whole time, which was why there were no signs of hypothermia . . .' I look at her in silent supplication. Interrupt me. Tell me I'm wrong. Ask me if I've taken leave of my senses. Say something, anything.

Nothing.

'But why? Why would you kidnap that little girl? I mean, Kerstin was your friend . . .' I pause. Kerstin Seiler, who's now dead, murdered. Lenia's old drawing on the fridge, which suddenly seems like a prophecy. The fairy holding the blade to the dragon's neck. And Kerstin, who later had a meat hook rammed into her neck. No! No, no, no, no!

'What have you done?' I bellow, throwing myself at her. Grabbing her, shaking her. She allows me to do it, as if her body were just a shell and the rest of her somewhere completely different. 'Talk to me!'

She cocks her head. Reaches for my wrists in slow motion, tightening her fingers around them. I shake myself free.

'Children,' she begins quietly, 'are the greatest gift, Ann. Kerstin didn't understand that.'

I gasp. Is this a confession?

She smiles. 'Lenia was desperate for a friend. I knew at once she'd get on well with Sarah. And Kerstin would have the opportunity to rethink her role as a mother. Killing two birds with one stone.'

I cautiously take a step backwards. It *is* a confession. Only now

I'm no longer sure I want to hear it. Nathalie, who I was so taken by because she reminded me of a feeling. Of Zoe, of love. Please don't let her be a bad person.

'Kerstin didn't treat Sarah well,' she says, clutching the left side of her chest; maybe her heart is as painful as mine. 'The little one was for ever in her way; Kerstin always made her feel she was interrupting. The butcher's was important, Schmitti was important. But what about Sarah? It was dreadful, Ann. When I came to work, she wouldn't leave my side. She sucked up the attention I paid to her like a sponge. Although she never said so, I soon suspected that Kerstin was beating her. And?' She raises her eyebrows at me. 'I was right! Or how else do you think she got those bruises they found on her body in hospital?'

I don't reply; I can't.

'I thought Kerstin needed to have her eyes opened,' Nathalie continues, in a voice I'd fall for in other circumstances, so warm and soft. 'To have an experience like the one I'd had. Because, do you know what, Ann? When your child disappears and you fear for their life, it makes you humble, really humble. You pray to God, offering him one deal after another. And if, like me, you're lucky, he listens to you and grants you a miracle.'

I look to the empty chair, but don't dare say anything.

'That's exactly what Kerstin was forced to go through,' Nathalie continues. Her tone has changed; now she sounds cold. 'I wanted her to be devoured by worry, I wanted it to turn her into a new person. And I thought it had worked, I really did! She cried her eyes out when Sarah disappeared, she almost died with worry. But then she got her daughter back and everything went wrong! Think back to the moment outside the butcher's. Kerstin was like a stone – she didn't even pick her little girl up, let alone shed a tear out of relief or gratitude. I suppose you could make allowances for the shock. But what was all that later? In the hospital? She let Brock photograph Sarah like an exhibition piece and exploit the poor girl's misery. She left her child alone and drove home to have a rest. Have a rest, Ann! Is that the sign of a good mother? Is that someone who's reformed and making the most of their second chance?'

I shake my head, but not in response to her question. I'm thinking of yesterday. How I bumped into Nathalie in the grocer's and then accompanied her home. The fleck of blood on her trousers – now I know where that's from. She was wearing a black, knee-length winter coat. Who knows what she looked like under that? How much blood was there on her? I feel terrible. Guilty. Because I wandered beside her like a loving puppy, hauling her shopping up the hill while Kerstin lay dying in the cold store of the butcher's. Why didn't I realise anything? She might be still alive if she'd got help earlier.

'She wasn't a good person, Ann,' Nathalie says insistently.

'So that gave you the right to kill her, did it? Was it up to you to pass judgement on Kerstin for leaving her daughter alone? What is wrong with you? The girl was here while you sat with her mother late into the night, hypocritically comforting her. It was more important to you to delight in the mother's suffering than to look after Sarah.'

'Do you think Sarah was unhappy here? On the contrary, Ann! She didn't want to leave! She enjoyed having a proper mother around, telling her stories, cooking for her, giving her baths and cuddling her! And of course I made sure she'd be fine when I wasn't home. During those periods she'd be out for the count like Sleeping Beauty.'

'You couldn't know that for sure! She could have woken up and got scared in this strange, dark house.'

'She wouldn't've woken up.'

'You . . .' *They've found traces of an unknown substance in her urine*, I think, recalling what Schmitti said in the hospital. 'You drugged her?'

'Who do you think I am? Benzodiazepine isn't a drug! I took it myself for a while.' She gives a twisted smile. 'Besides, *Sleeping Beauty* is Sarah's favourite fairy tale.'

I can't believe it. 'You still think you're a heroine, don't you? You should have contacted the child welfare office. They would have helped Sarah. But no. Instead you traumatised the girl for the rest of her—'

'The child welfare office?' She laughs. 'They wouldn't have done anything because Sarah would never have betrayed her mother. And Kerstin – they'd have been taken in by Kerstin, she was able to wrap everyone around her little finger.'

Just like you, I think wearily. 'You're no heroine, Nathalie. You're no better than the man who took Lenia away from you.'

I see her shoulders tense and hear her strained breathing through gritted teeth – someone trying to get a grip on themselves. My eyes dart around, trying to gauge the distance between Nathalie and the cutlery drawers. In one of those there will be a knife.

'There's someone outside, Nathalie,' I say urgently. 'Someone who clearly has a reason to creep around your house at dawn.' For a moment I think of Schmitti, who could have found out what Nathalie did to his fiancée. Then I remember that Schmitti is barely taller than me, unlike the figure I saw. Steinhausen! is my next thought. But that wouldn't make sense after Nathalie's confession. Would it? 'Whoever he is, he might be really angry with you. Let's call the police. For your protection.'

'The police? Those losers who spent fourteen years standing back and watching the psychopath you call your father kill little girls?'

I'm seized by something bright and gleaming: rage. At a mentally ill killer who takes the liberty of judging others, and at myself because I happily let myself be deluded by her.

'My Lenia was lucky, but what about the others who your father—'

'Lenia didn't identify anyone, Nathalie,' I growl. 'Neither my father nor anyone else. And do you know why?' I take a step towards her, then kick the chair as hard as I can. 'Because nobody's sitting here, you deranged woman!'

The chair crashes to the floor and Nathalie exhales audibly. Taking advantage of her shock, I rush out of the kitchen into the sitting room, where I grab my rucksack. I need to get out of here. I tug the handle of the terrace door but I'm not fast enough.

'You're not going to call the police!' Then comes a blow to my back which momentarily leaves me unable to breathe. Losing my balance, I fall, and am just able to put my hands out before my jaw goes crashing on to the tiles. Now Nathalie's on top of me, her knees clamping my sides, her weight pressing my chest against the floor, and her fists pounding me. I thrust my elbow backwards, hitting her in the stomach, then I hear her clatter into the terrace door. The glass quivers noisily. Crawling forwards, I seize one of the straps of my rucksack. I then crawl in the opposite direction, to the hallway and front door. All of a sudden, her hand takes hold of my leg. I kick, once, twice, hard and harder; a whimpering sound tells me I must have hit her. I'm free. I get to my feet, my chest wheezing. Nathalie is lying bent double on the floor. She gives me a beseeching look; I just shake my head. It's over, and at the same time it's not. I've just solved a murder. And yet my father's still going to be in prison.

I'm sorry, Dad. I'm so, so sorry.

I stagger to the front door and turn the key in the lock. The glass slides off the handle and smashes. I can't hear anything; it all happens silently, or at least the sounds don't reach my ears. I blink hard. Blood is obstructing my vision. My eyebrow must have opened up again. I'm not in a good way, and not merely because of that. My body feels like one big bruise; my circulation is careening.

I can't do any more. Forgive me, Dad.

I stumble down the steps outside; I need to get away as fast as possible in case Nathalie comes after me. I need to find a safe place and notify the police from there. I need to breathe, in on one, out on two. The stand of trees where I hid with Jakob yesterday. Here I'll be protected but have a good view of the house. I duck behind a thick trunk, then rummage in my rucksack. The bread and cat food land in the snow. I wipe my eyes – tears and blood. My mobile. I press the first two numbers, and am about to tap the third when from behind a hand rests on my shoulder. Nathalie, is my first thought, but I'm wrong. It's a man's hand. I turn to look and just manage to pant 'Steinhausen' before passing out and toppling into the snow.

US

What are we going to do now, princess? What on earth will we do now? Help me, tell me what to do. Ann is so mistaken, but she doesn't realise it. She thinks she knows what happened – she thinks she knows everything! – and that's exactly what she'll tell the police. A catastrophe. Because once we're on the police's radar, it won't be long before *he* comes. What if Ann's right and he's already here? Is everything we've undertaken to be in vain? That would be my fault, my darling, my own bloody fault, I know. I never should have got myself mixed up in it. I shouldn't have taken Sarah or told Kerstin my opinion. How could I forget myself so badly and ruin everything? What do you think, princess? Should I look at your picture, the picture on the fridge? The way you drew me, so full of confidence in my abilities. Me, your eternal protector, with my sword at the dragon's neck. My oath that nobody will ever succeed in parting us.

One last battle, of course. My word still stands, it stands for ever. You know that, my darling. But you've got to help me. Mummy feels a bit weak, Mummy needs you. Will you do that, yes? Will you help Mummy? Will you help me look for a knife?

ANN

SCHERGEL, 29 DECEMBER 2017

When I come round, I'm sitting in the snow, my back against a tree trunk. My body is stiff from the cold, my head is heavy, and my thoughts are like porridge. Before me, the maltreated face from the basement of the construction site, overlapped a second later by the portrait photo from the architectural practice's website. Steinhausen, Steinhausen, Steinhausen. I start to scream. Two hands grab my head roughly. One holds it tight, the other clamps my mouth. I stare at him, the man kneeling before me. Pale skin, bags under the eyes, deeply etched lines on his forehead, dark stubble, hollow cheeks.

That's not Steinhausen.

It's a total stranger.

'Okay?' the man asks, slightly relaxing his grip. I nod as an understanding that he can take his hand away from my mouth. He does.

'Who are you?'

'That's not important,' he says, shaking his head. He looks nervous; his eyes flick between me and Nathalie's house. 'You were just in there with her. I watched you. What happened?'

I freeze. This isn't Steinhausen, it's the man I saw creeping around the house. I smell stale smoke and think of the tiny glowing dot in the distance. It's him, I'm absolutely certain of it. And there's something menacing about him.

'I don't know what you're talking about.'

Again he grabs my face, his hand squashing my cheeks together. But he's shaking, everything about him is shaking, even his voice. 'I'm talking about her! About Nathalie!'

I shake my head; I'm no traitor. Not even after everything she's done.

The man lets go of me. He gets to his feet and paces up and down while rubbing his brow, then his neck, clearly thinking things through. I tentatively stand up. To his left I can see a branch, a long, thick piece of wood in the middle of the snow. I just have to reach it.

'What do you want from her?' I ask to distract him, while I edge towards the branch.

He stops and looks at me. 'Are you a friend?'

'Sort of.'

In a flash he leaps towards me and grabs my upper arm. 'Then help her by helping me. I'm Steffen Fester, her ex-husband.'

'Steffen Fester,' I repeat, drawing out the words. And yet I couldn't care less about his name. All I'm thinking about is what till now I've believed was an excuse to disguise Nathalie's real reason for fleeing Berlin: that her ex-husband behaved violently towards her.

'I've been looking for her for weeks . . .'

'Let me go – now!' I hiss. The fact that he does tells me he's uncertain. Or unpredictable. I take a large step to the side, a step

further towards the thick branch I've nominated to defend me –
but without taking my eye off Fester. He's very tall, with broad,
angular shoulders, and his emaciated face exudes an alarming
harshness.

'Where's my mobile?' I ask. I remember trying to call the police
before passing out.

'Oh yes. You dropped it in the snow.' He reaches nervously into
his coat pocket and holds out the phone and a cloth handkerchief.
'For your face.'

I take both, dab my eyebrow and say, 'I'm going to call the
police now, okay? Because whatever's going on between you and
Nathalie, it would be better for all concerned if it were sorted
out under supervision.'

'No, no, no!' Again he comes at me, but this time I'm quicker.
Two large, quick steps and I'm facing him with the branch.

'You're not going anywhere near me or Nathalie, understood?'

He makes a placatory gesture, as if I had a real weapon in my
hands rather than just an improvised bit of wood. That's fine by
me; I jab the wood in his direction to make him keep his distance.
Fester stumbles but recovers.

'You don't understand. If you call the police, she'll kill herself, definitely. And then I'll never find out where she took our
daughter.'

'Lenia?'

He nods. 'She ran off with her.'

'Don't try to muck me around. I know Lenia's dead.'

Fester grits his teeth. 'I'm talking about her remains.'

'Her . . . ?'

'Not now, please . . .' Later, he says. He'll give me a detailed explanation later. 'We need to go to Nathalie right now before she gets any silly ideas!'

Not with me. I don't trust him and I make a few provisos, or I'll call the police. Fester agrees sulkily, but insists we head for the house without any further delay. I have trouble keeping up with him. He runs, he pants, he tries giving me the story in a nutshell. The grave had already been dug and Lenia's body laid out for the burial. But then, the night before the funeral, there was a break-in at the funeral director's and the body was stolen. Fester immediately suspected his ex-wife was responsible. He felt justified when he went to the family home he'd left to Nathalie after their separation and found it deserted. He also discovered she'd hired a car, as well as the fact that this car had been returned in Munich a few days later. He assumed that she was either there or somewhere nearby. Only later did it occur to him that Nathalie might have hidden Lenia first, before giving the car back and then simply taking the bus, the train or hitchhiking to her new bolthole, which might not be that close to Munich after all. In the end he was led to Schergel by an online newspaper article about a little girl who had returned home safe and sound after a suspected abduction. He'd recognised Nathalie in the accompanying photograph. I nod, realising that he's talking about the picture Brock took outside the butcher's yesterday morning.

'I've read all there is to read about the ribbon murderer,' he says. 'If only because after Lenia's death, Nathalie seemed to be obsessed with the man.'

'Does this mean you've been searching for her for weeks on your own?' I ask, still suspicious. 'Why didn't you put the police on to it?'

He did, of course, he says. But nothing much came of it. Nathalie was a grown woman, they told him, who could go where she liked when she liked. Especially as the substantial sum of money she'd withdrawn from her bank beforehand suggested that Nathalie had *wanted* to go – it was her free decision rather than a case of coercion or even abduction. And as far as Lenia was concerned ... He stops abruptly. We're at the house. 'No leads so far in your case of the missing body, they said.' He lowers his gaze. 'You might find this hard to believe, but ... once upon a time I really loved Nathalie.'

'You don't want her to go to prison.'

He nods. 'She doesn't belong there. She needs help.'

He climbs the steps; I follow him. 'Herr Fester?'

'Yes?'

'The girl you read about in the online article. It was Nathalie who kidnapped her.'

He stops again, as if he'd been struck by lightning.

'And there's more. She also—'

'She needs help,' he reiterates, more emphatically this time, and climbs the rest of the steps to the front door.

He wants me to try, to knock, call her name.

'I don't know how she's going to react to seeing me,' is his reasoning.

I shake my head. 'She was landing punches on me only a few minutes ago. I doubt I'll do any better.'

'Please, we've got to give it a try.'

I hesitate. His story sounds convincing, and yet ... 'What are you planning to do to her?'

Rather than answer me, he now jiggles the handle, gently at

310

first, then more forcefully. 'Nathalie!' his voice thunders. 'Open the bloody door!'

My stomach tightens; there's a vague hunch rumbling inside. Something bad's about to happen. I feel for the stone in my trouser pocket, for support, for protection. Fester lets go of the door and dashes around the house. 'What the . . . ?' he cries in horror when he discovers the grave behind the terrace.

'That's her cat,' I explain, upon which he puts a hand in front of his mouth.

'Oh no. Our Milly? She took her from Berlin too. And she—'

I just nod.

Fester hammers against the shutters in front of the terrace door, which Nathalie must have closed again after I ran out of the house.

'Wait . . .' I tighten the grip around the stone in my hand, in the knowledge that it's the very tool Fester could use right now. 'She's not going to end up in prison. People will realise she's sick. Please, let's call the police.'

'I want my daughter back,' he says. He picks up a large and – judging by the way he's breathing – heavy piece of wood, which he slams against the shutters until they break open. I jump with fright when he also uses it to smash the glass. But tears come to my eyes too. I don't know why. I've seen the monster inside Nathalie. I've seen it in Kerstin Seiler's lifeless body, in the wound in her neck, in the sea of blood. I've experienced it myself, earlier when she came rushing at me. And yet I fear for her.

'Herr Fester, wouldn't it be better if we called the police?' We climb through the frame of the terrace door, one at a time. The candles are now out. Fester turns around like a spinning top, then rushes to the windows above the sofa to open the shutters.

'Didn't you smell that when you were here?'

'Yes . . . I . . . I did,' I stammer. 'That's the mould—'

'That's Lenia!'

He hastens towards the kitchen, whereas I run up the stairs to the top floor. Straight ahead is the bathroom; its door is open. On either side of it are two other rooms.

'She's not here!' Fester shouts from downstairs.

No, I think. Because she's here. Nathalie. In the room to the left of the stairs. A bedroom. She's sitting in a thin white nightie on the floor beside an unmade bed. Her legs outstretched, a teddy in her lap. The smell . . . I wish I could still believe it was just mould. Half a dozen grave candles are lined up by the closed shutters. The room flickers black and red.

Those are soul lights, my Beetle.

'Ann.' She smiles as if in a trance. 'You're back. You didn't leave us all alone.' How weak she looks, how vulnerable. A gorgeous, broken work of art. A monster. Right beside her is a knife. Not one with a long blade, more like a vegetable knife, and yet it's a knife, an unpredictable weapon.

'Have you found Nathalie?' Footsteps clatter on the stairs. Without thinking about it, I throw myself against the door and lock us in.

'Your ex-husband is here. He says you took Lenia, Lenia's—'

'What the . . . ?' The handle is wrenched several times. Then Fester pounds his fists against the door.

'But you already know this, Ann,' Nathalie replies. 'I had to get Lenia to safety.'

I approach her slowly, focusing on the knife. One slight movement, not much more than a twitch, and it would be in her hand.
'Can I sit down next to you?' I carefully squat down and try to
discreetly nudge the knife away with my foot.

'Open up!' followed by a thud against the door that's so hard the
frame shakes. I wince, whereas Nathalie looks alarmingly calm.

'Have you taken something?' The Sleeping Beauty pills.

'Nathalie!' That's Fester, now forcing his whole weight against
the door.

'He's not going to go away,' I say. 'He wants to know where
Lenia is.'

'She's hidden herself away. She hates it when people argue.'

I instinctively tilt my head so I can take a glimpse beneath the
bed. But I don't see anything.

Nathalie closes her eyes and smiles. 'Don't worry, my little princess. Ann has come back to help us. Everything's going to be all
right.' I swallow with difficulty and understand. Nathalie too has
a world behind her closed eyes. Only her world isn't content with
a space in her imagination. Did she perhaps use Sarah's abduction to enact her version of how Lenia's story should have turned
out? She must have been disappointed by the finale, though, the
moment when Sarah returned unscathed and her mother failed
to react as Nathalie had envisioned. How she herself would have
reacted had Lenia actually managed to escape.

'Do you remember what happened to your daughter, Nathalie?'

She opens her eyes and her smile widens. Then she nods at
the knife by the tip of my boot.

'Today could be the day you bring the real ribbon murderer to
justice. Do you realise that, Ann?'

313

'No, no, Nathalie,' I say, pointing to the door. 'The man out there is your ex-husband, not the . . .' I stop. She's just smiling, smiling on and on.

'It's our story, Ann. Our truth.'

'But . . .' I shake my head in confusion. 'You said yourself that you think my father's—'

At that moment the hinges crack and the door gives way. Fester rushes at Nathalie and yanks her up by the arm. 'Where's my daughter?'

'Ann!' Nathalie whimpers. Grabbing the knife, I get up too.

'Where is she?' Fester is livid. His concern for his ex-wife seems to have been obliterated. Instead he's now flinging her around like a playful dog might an old rag doll. 'Tell me where she is!'

'You left us,' Nathalie howls at him. 'You have no right to see your daughter anymore.' This seems to hit Fester as unerringly as a bullet in the stomach. Letting go of her, he teeters backwards.

'Nathalie, please, you've got to—'

'He made his decision, Ann. Since last year he's been in love with a secretary. He packed his things and just upped sticks.'

'My new relationship has got nothing to do with any of this. I still looked after Lenia,' Fester says. Pain flickers in his face. 'I picked her up for the weekend every fortnight.'

'Every fortnight, yes. Then you bought her toys, took her to the zoo or went for an ice cream. You call that looking after?' She moves over to him, swaying. Again I wonder if she's taken anything – sleeping pills, Benzowhatevers, the stuff she gave Sarah – and perhaps too much of it. 'Having a child is so sacred, a gift. You showed you weren't worthy of it.'

Fester's jaw twitches; he seems to be chewing words, undecided whether to utter or swallow them.

'Two birds with one stone, Ann,' Nathalie says. 'He never deserved to be a father.' She now looks at me – not my face, but the knife in my hand. 'Not even before the kidnapping, when he was still with us. Two years ago, for example. In 2015, Steffen. Do you remember what happened?'

Fester opens and closes his mouth.

Nathalie laughs idly. 'Lenia fell and knocked out her front teeth. And who looked after her? Who comforted her, fed her? It wasn't you, it was me! You just went to work as usual and left everything to me. Or earlier, in 2012, only a few weeks after she was born. The bad fever fits. Who sat at her bedside day and night? Who cooled her little body and held her hand? Me, Steffen, only ever me!'

I purse my lips, thinking of my father who was so different from Steffen Fester. Like Nathalie, he sat by my bed, held my hand and fed me. And he was always there for me. In 2015, after my car accident. In 2012, during my existential crisis, which ended up with me changing subjects. He even took leave from the university to travel across France with me, so I could clear my head . . .

'I was always there when Lenia needed me. There was nothing more important in my life. I was her good fairy. The one who fought against the dragon, against sickness, fear and all the bad things.'

'Don't do this, Nathalie,' Fester begs. 'Don't paint me like that, it's unfair. You know I did my best over all the years to make both of you happy.'

I feel giddy; the knife is trembling in my hand. I want them to stop, both of them.

'You made sure we had a certain standard of living, Steffen, that's all. But we never needed a big house or extravagant holidays. We just needed each other and you're not going to take that away from us. Lenia and I—'

I can't take this any longer; I don't want to hear any more. 'Lenia is dead, Nathalie!' I shout. 'You've got to stop lying to yourself!'

'No, Ann! No, she isn't!' she exclaims, making an uncoordinated gesture. 'This is precisely what I've been trying to get through to you the whole time! It's *our* story, we're writing it ourselves! It's dynamic and can change with every word. We alone have the power over the characters and what happens. Look at him—'

'Nathalie, what are you talking about?' Fester comes towards her, but Nathalie is unfazed and remains facing me.

'*He* could be the ribbon murderer! Let's say he's just admitted it to us! He's kidnapped and killed little girls for so many years. Because he's a sick bastard by nature. Just look what he did to me, Ann! When I became suspicious of Steffen and fled Berlin because I was afraid of him, he came looking for me and finally tracked me down here. Look! Just look what he's capable of!'

Then everything happens very fast.

She rushes at me. Grabs my right wrist and thrusts it towards her. The knife is now stuck in Nathalie's stomach. I want to scream, pull the knife out, do something – but no, I'm totally paralysed. Fester steps in, tries to grab the knife. Now Nathalie forces my hand in his direction. He screams and falls to the floor. I hear myself screaming too, I scream and scream; I'm never going to stop. Everything stretches out, I now see it all in slow motion.

Nathalie, bent over, struggling to the bed, collapsing on it. Fester, his hand pressed to the left side of his chest, falling to his knees. 'Tell me where she is!' he beseeches.

But Nathalie closes her eyes and smiles. 'And they all lived . . .'

US

... happily ever after.

Right, my angel, that's it, time to go to sleep. That really was a long story tonight ... What? What are you saying? That it wasn't a proper ending and you want to hear what happened afterwards? What my little angel wants, my little angel gets. So listen carefully. Mummy was lying injured on the bed. The dragon was dead. Our friend Ann called an ambulance and the police. She told the officers what had happened and especially about the confession she'd just heard. Before the dragon died, you see, he admitted that he'd killed lots of little girls, crimes which Ann's father was innocently in prison for. For a long time Mummy had suspected that something wasn't right about the man we'd thought of as your daddy. That in reality he was just a dragon in a clever disguise. That's also why we had to leave Berlin. But then the dragon tracked us down and of course he was really angry. He killed Kerstin because I'd confided in her. He was worried, you see, that Kerstin might get the police involved, and he had to do everything he could to prevent this. He even tried to kill Ann, but I managed to stop him just in time. Now he's dead and we don't have to be frightened ever again. He won't hunt us anymore, and we can look forward to a future we've more than deserved after all the hardships we've suffered. Spring, my angel, spring is on its way. You and I, we'll dance hand in hand across the meadow, amongst daisies, ground elder and red clover. We'll puff up our cheeks and send dandelion clocks on their way. Free, we're free. Don't worry that they're taking us to hospital first. It's quite normal and unfortunately we have to go because I'm hurt. Can you see? There's blood coming out of my tummy and my lovely white nightie is soaked red. It looks worse than it really is, but of course the doctors have to patch it up. Apart from the physical injuries, they're going to want to give us psychological treatment too, my darling. But you don't have to worry about this either, as it's also perfectly normal after what we've been through. They'll say that we're suffering severe trauma brought on by our stressful flight from your father, the dragon, the child-killer who's caused so much misery. But we stopped him, my darling, we put an end to his terrible deeds. You and I and our dear friend Ann. Even the papers are writing about us, you know? They're saying I'm a heroine. It's flattering but no, no, really not. I'm not a heroine. I'm just a mother who would defeat any dragon out of love for her child. We did it, we got through it. Because we will get through everything so long as we're together. You and I, princess, for ever and ever and ever . . .

That really is the end now, okay. We badly need some sleep as it's been an exhausting day. I love you, princess. Goodnight . . .

ANN

SCHERGEL, 29 DECEMBER 2017

Nathalie has lost a lot of blood; the ambulance has already departed. Police cars are parked beneath the property. Although the blue lights are flashing silently, light is still light and it's doing what light does: attracting the moths. The first villagers, the nosy ones, those after a bit of a thrill. Brock is bound to be here soon with his camera, and Jakob, too, I hope. A few police officers ensure the locals are kept at an adequate distance from the house. I'm sitting on the frozen steps by the front door. How long have I been here? I don't know. It's light now; the sky is blue and there's even some sunshine. As if nature didn't know what's appropriate on a day like this. Everything ought to be grey and murky, as if the sky had slipped and were hanging menacingly over my head, about to collapse at any moment. At least I can rely on the iciness. It's eating its way through my jeans, my kidneys are aching, and I bet I'm going to catch the most severe cold of my life after today. I don't care; there are worse things in life. A woman who chooses to get stabbed by a knife and, on top of this, injures her ex-husband. Steffen Fester's lucky he was wearing a thick coat. Although the wound between his ribs is more than a scratch, the treatment he got from the emergency doctor means he can stay here while the police search the house. I take the stone from my trouser pocket. A reminder of what I've come through in my life.

'Here you are.' Steffen Fester comes up from behind and stands next to me. He takes off his coat, puts it around my shoulders and groans as he sits down. There's a huge bloodstain on his beige cardigan.

'You ought to be in hospital,' I say.

Fester glances at the stain. 'What's that compared to the nightmare of these last few weeks?'

I just nod, twiddling the stone in my hand, deep in thought.

'She never was . . .' Fester shakes his head. 'You know, she was a perfectly normal woman, never unstable in any way. She even got through Lenia's illness with such courage and optimism. Although she was aware of the risks, she always said they were just statistics, and they mostly concerned men who died before they reached the age of 56.'

'Lenia was ill? I'm sorry, I didn't know.'

For a few seconds, Fester's face is expressionless, then he makes a noise signalling astonishment.

'But that's what this was all about.'

'What do you mean?'

'Well . . .' Fester looks at me as if I've lost my marbles. 'Lenia had epilepsy. Although she took medication regularly, she still had the occasional seizure. Two years ago, in 2015, she had a serious fit in which she fell, knocking out her front teeth. After that, they adjusted her medication and things went really well. I couldn't imagine that . . .' He shakes his head again. 'I didn't

321

leave Nathalie because of Lenia's illness, you've got to believe me. We just drifted apart. She and Lenia stayed on in our old house. Anyway . . .' He looks down at his hands. 'It was a Saturday morning on one of the weekends I was going to have Lenia. I turned up early and Nathalie was still in her nightie when she opened the door to me. She said Lenia was still asleep and that we'd wake her up together.' I hear him swallow. 'We found her lying on her tummy with her head in the pillow. She'd bitten her tongue, making it bleed, and wet herself. She must have had a serious fit in her sleep, probably leading to breathing problems. But because she didn't wake up, she didn't realise she wasn't getting any air. It was too late.'

I realise my own breathing is fitful, my chest constricting. 'But I thought the ribbon murderer . . .'

'It happened in early November,' Fester says. 'At the time when the latest case in the series of ribbon murders was all over the media. The girl . . . I think her name was Sophie. She was abducted from a playground and dragged off to the Königswald.'

I nod weakly. According to Nathalie, that was exactly what had happened to Lenia. *He kidnapped Lenia from a playground and took her to a hut in the Königswald.*

'Nathalie became completely obsessed with the story,' Fester continues. 'I think she blamed herself for Lenia's death, as if she ought to have noticed there was something wrong with her. But she slept soundly while our daughter died in the next-door room. You must have seen the picture on the fridge?'

'Yes.'

'Lenia saw her illness as a wicked dragon and her mother as her protector. Nathalie believed she'd failed at the crucial moment.

And because she couldn't get over this, she projected the guilt on to someone else. A sort of defence mechanism. She even told the people at the funeral director's that Lenia had been a victim of the ribbon murderer.'

'But at the time she still realised Lenia was dead?'

Fester nods. 'At that point, yes. But when the grave was dug and Lenia was laid out for the burial, her mind finally went to pieces. She snatched the body and then . . .'

'She invented her own story,' I say, finishing Fester's sentence.

'One step after another into madness,' he says, putting his hands in front of his face and beginning to sob.

I stroke his back. 'What about Nathalie's mother? Nathalie said she didn't just come here with Lenia, but with her mother in tow as well.'

'Nathalie's mum is in a care home in Berlin,' Fester sobs into his hands. 'They didn't get on.'

I try putting myself in Nathalie's shoes; I think aloud.

'Nathalie knew that people would have become suspicious if she'd worked at the butcher's and left her little daughter at home alone. So she invented a babysitter as well.' The tears come to my eyes too. 'I'm so sorry about all of this. My suspicions ought to have been raised earlier.'

He looks up and gives a faint shrug. 'How could they have been? We see what people make us believe.'

'No, that's not the problem. It's that we accept it far too easily.' I immediately think of the bloodstain on Nathalie's trousers. I'll always wonder whether Kerstin Seiler's life could have been saved. Whether I could have saved her, but failed at the crucial moment too. I also think of all those weeks that Nathalie lived here amongst people who regard themselves as a community. They were all curious and yet nobody was really interested. And I'm no exception in this regard. I was focused only on Steinhausen and proving my theory that he's the real ribbon murderer. In the end was I just thinking of myself too?

'Look who we've got here,' we hear a female voice say behind us. We turn around. A policewoman has just come out of the front door, holding a black kitten. 'This sweet little thing was hiding under the bed the whole time.'

'Milly!' Fester calls out, getting up in visible pain.

It comes to me in a flash. 'I know where you'll find Lenia!'

Do you remember . . . ?
- Beside Mummy's grave.
- Let me tell you a story. It's by a very wise man called Plato. He was a philosopher—
- Like you?
- Yes, but he was far more important. He did what I try to do: find answers, for himself and other people, to the fundamental questions in life. For, as I've said, nothing in this world is clear and simple. Just because we don't see something, it doesn't mean it doesn't exist, and vice versa. And even if we can agree on the existence of something, we still interpret it in different ways—
- Tell the story now.
- I see the little madam is impatient. Okay then. We humans are sitting in a dark cave. We're tied up so that we can look in one direction only – at a wall where we see shadows. We think the shadows are real; we don't know any different, after

all. And yet, in truth, these shadows are the outlines of what's happening behind us, cast by the light from the cave entrance. But we don't know this, because the way we've been tied up means we can't turn around. Only if we're able to free ourselves can we go to the light and see the things as they really are. But here's the crux: quite apart from the fact that our shackles are tight and unbreakable, we've got used to them. Just like our eyes have got used to the darkness inside the cave and would hurt really badly when they were first exposed to the light. Basically we've got used to what we consider to be our reality, and it would be painful for us on so many levels to have to admit that we were wrong. That our reality doesn't – in reality – exist and never has existed ... Oh dear, look at that face you're making. Maybe you're still a bit too little for this story.

– I understood it, Daddy. You have to be brave about the real things.

– Not bad, my Beetle. But most importantly, we always have to think very carefully about things. Our senses – sight, hearing, smell, taste and touch – can deceive us. With those alone, we'll never fully understand the world. We have to think. And feel ...

Feel ... I wish I didn't, Dad. It's too much. Too much pain, grief and despair. I don't know what to do with it all. I'm still sitting on the steps, running the point of my stone along the scar – only very gently, without any pressure. The stone that taught me how to feel in the first place. Something that right now seems like a curse. On the other side of the house, behind the terrace, they're excavating the grave where Nathalie claimed to have buried Milly. I hear the cutting of the spade, which is loud in the frozen ground, and finally Fester howling like a wounded animal. I know he's suffering, suffering immensely, but now that he's found Lenia, he'll be able to find peace too. Unlike me. My story doesn't have an ending; there's only one thing I've managed to establish for sure: the feelings I've allowed to guide me over the last few days, the instinct I've been following blindly, have deceived me. Steinhausen was never here. Although I know I've helped someone achieve certainty, what about me? And you, Dad?

Realisation. (Ann, 24 years old)

Sometimes it hits you like a lightning bolt, suddenly and powerfully, as if at the flick of a switch, a flash of light in the dark night. An awareness, like a revelation, to which even your body immediately reacts, with shock, panic, a racing heart and sickness. But the biggest, the most important realisations sometimes come very quietly, very superficially and softly, like a gas you've been breathing in for quite a while before you suffocate from it. And yet it was all there from the very beginning . . .

Last summer. The evening after a perfect day, our tiny balcony, bare feet, a bottle of wine. The view over the city, the prospect of our future. A little cottage with colourful shutters and a garden she would allow to become elegantly overgrown.

'Either you can stay here in Berlin, devoured by longing, or you can come with me,' Zoe said, having already hatched a plan. She would apply for a semester abroad in Cornwall, a first step towards her dream. 'The only thing is, it's difficult to get one. The selection process can take up to a year.' In the end, it only took half a year . . .

Because I loved her. Because Cornwall was so important to her and she was so excited: 'Here, this is for you.'

'What is it?' she asked, puzzled.

Something so important to me that it would never have ended up in a mishmash of meaningless things.

'That's the stone I cut my wrist on when I was a child. My father kept it and gave it to me later. It's still got my blood on it.'

Zoe, eyeing me critically.

'It's thanks to this stone that I'm able to love you,' I explained.

'It's more than just a stone then.'

'Yes. It'll bring you luck for Cornwall and remind you what you mean to me.'

It fulfilled its purpose. Only three days ago she messaged me, saying she'd been accepted to go to Cornwall. *It worked!* How did I not pick up on that? How could I forget that I'd given her the stone? I ought to have realised when I was tidying up Dad's study and found the wooden box. Or, if not then, when Zoe messaged me. I stare down the steps to the hole that the stone has made in the snow.

Two stones. Blood on both. But only one is mine, the one I gave to Zoe. I feel giddy, like when Nathalie and Steffen Fester were arguing earlier on. *Two years ago, for example. In 2015, Steffen. Do you remember what happened? Lenia fell and knocked out her front teeth. And who looked after her? Who comforted her, fed her?*

In 2015, my car accident, my father nursing me back to health. In 2012, my existential crisis, our trip through France. In 2010,

Eva and Nico disappearing from Berlin, and me in despair every day. In 2009, Eva falling in love with Nico, breaking my heart. In 2006, I'm thirteen and an adolescent nightmare.

I was always there when Lenia needed me. There was nothing more important in my life.

2015. 2012. 2010. 2009. 2006. You were always there when I needed you. Because there was nothing more important in your life.

Shaking, I get to my feet and go down the steps to where the stone landed in the snow. I just stand there, gazing at it.

Although they can't say for sure, the forensics team believe the killer used a knife with a very blunt blade, Ludwig says again inside my head.

Or it wasn't a knife at all, I answer him silently.

Decisions, my Beetle . . .

BERLIN, 21 FEBRUARY 2018

Dear Dad,

As Ludwig is keeping you updated, you'll know I was in Schergel and what happened to me there. All the same, I'd like to explain my decision to you, and find myself – as you're bound to recognise – quoting Kant: 'Act only according to that maxim whereby you can, at the same time, will that it should become a universal law.' I couldn't just make the stone disappear; it had to be examined. Because ten murders are not a scratched moped. And even if I can't undo what's happened, it's still my duty to provide clarity to the victims' families. Michelle, who for years has merely been trying to make it from one day to the next. Rainer Meller, who was effectively driven crazy by his theories about Larissa's death. Saskia E.'s father, who's been appearing in public as an attempt at therapy. And all the other parents and relatives who till now have had to deal with uncertainty as well as their loss. I know myself how bad that is, albeit in a very different way. So, yes, I did it for me too. To give me certainty. I gave the police the stone in Schergel, explaining my theory and requesting they pass it on to the appropriate authority for examination. The results came in the second week of January: they'd found traces of DNA that could clearly be attributed to the dead girls. I can't say it surprised me, after I'd worked out that no murders had taken place in those years when I'd been a demanding, needy daughter. I still harboured hope until the end. So much so that, after my telephone conversation with Inspector Brandner, who told me about the result of the DNA analysis, I immediately called Jakob to ask him to drive me to the hospital. Systems overload, a nervous breakdown. I spent two weeks as an inpatient, and was prescribed medication and counselling. In theory, I realise I'm not responsible for your crimes, but I can't get over the fact that surely I ought to have noticed something. Or that if I'd made even more trouble over the course of my life, fewer girls would probably have died. There's no medication for that, nor the right words.

So you really are the ribbon murderer, Dad.

You killed ten girls and destroyed the lives of their loved ones.

You're 'Professor Death'.

And I'm your daughter. Ludwig says I shouldn't be fixated on my belief that our parents determine the largest part of our identity. According to him, my identity is only who I – me, myself! – decide to be. I'm sure you know that I'm staying with him at the moment. He didn't have to persuade me; I asked him. For one thing, now that the trial has started, our name has leaked out and journalists from all over the place are besieging our house. But also I don't want to be alone. I'm clinging to the illusion of a family, even if Ludwig is only my godfather. But he's there. As is Jakob, who hasn't yet finished his reportage. He says he feels that nothing he puts to paper can even begin to capture the enormity of this story, and I say, 'I know.' 'You're not to blame, Ann,' he adds, as well as a few other cute words that might reach my ears, but not my heart or soul.

And so I beg you, Dad, please talk. Finally make a confession. The trial begins tomorrow and the evidence, particularly the stone, will lead to your conviction. You're guilty, there's no doubt about this, and remaining silent won't do you any favours, not for you. But you'd help the girls' relatives to understand. And not just them, but me too. This is me we're talking about, your little Beetle. Help me, Dad, please. I'm not going to come to the trial, but I promise to visit as soon as you've made your confession.

Ann

BERLIN, 02 MARCH 2018

Dad,

I still think of that moment when, sitting outside Nathalie's house, it dawned on me that Zoe had my stone, whereas I'd been carrying a totally different one around for days. Recalling what Ludwig had said about the weapon. They were so set on their theory of it being a knife that when the house was searched, nobody gave the slightest thought to the brown-grey stone amongst all the other stuff in the wooden box in your desk. Things like this happen; after all, even the most dedicated police officers are human beings, who, like in Plato's allegory, sit in a cave and stare at shadows.

I've done nothing different for twenty-four years either.

And I liked our cave, Dad. The shadows that were my reality. My shackles that I didn't find tight and unbreakable, but more like a support. Our cave was my home and part of me will always miss it. I'll miss you.

You were a good father.

And a great thinker. As an academic, you wanted to find answers to the questions of life and, as Ludwig said, death is also part of life. But there came a point when theories were no longer enough, were they? You wanted to carry out practical studies and, what was worse, you did carry them out, at the expense of the lives of ten little girls, at the expense of entire families.

I can't believe that the world is still turning. That the sun rises and sets, that I'm breathing and am alive. It all seems so strange and wrong.

At least Eva is feeling better. I visit her almost every day. Two weeks ago she woke up after almost two months in a coma, and has been making fantastic progress since. She can already eat on her own again. And talk. And so I now know the real reason why she came back to Berlin after all these years. She speaks of a feeling, something indefinite that's been nagging her for many years and which may have influenced many of her life decisions – for example, the decision to leave Berlin, or to become a psychologist. Back in May 2003, when we were ten and Eva got lost in the Grunewald for no apparent reason. She says she doesn't have a concrete memory of that day; it's like a black hole in her consciousness, as if she'd blocked it out. All she knows is that you were the one who found her. But sometimes she dreams that you took her there in the first place, claiming that I was waiting there for you.

Was Eva to be your first victim?

She came back to Berlin after hearing about your arrest, with the aim of finding this out. She didn't say anything to me when she realised how convinced I was of your innocence – she is, after all, a psychologist, which in itself means she's very circumspect – and anyway, she wasn't sure herself. We don't want to accuse you of anything, but there's no denying she had red hair as a child, just like Larissa Meller, who you abducted shortly afterwards in June 2003.

And there's something else I'm wondering. Did it ever cross your mind to kill me? Is it possible the girls were merely substitutes? In the darkest moments, I think it might have been better. My life for that of so many others.

Oh, Dad – for Christ's sake, Dad!

Help me understand it all. It's not going to change anything; the sentence is fixed – life imprisonment. And for my part, I'm sticking to my guns: I won't visit you until you're ready to talk.

Ann

BERLIN, 13 MAY 2018

I was at Ludwig's yesterday evening. You remember I stayed with him for a while. I imagine he would have gone back to Poland a while ago, but he's still here – out of concern for me, I think. We drank whisky, a bit like that evening which ended with me thinking he'd slipped a sleeping pill in my drink. Now I know of course that he'd have never done anything like that. I'd been drinking on an empty stomach; I was tired, run-down and paranoid, which was more than enough for a breakdown that evening. I just didn't want to see it. Like Nathalie, I put together my own puzzle, twisting pieces and simply forcing in corners that didn't fit. I made connections where there weren't any, turned coincidences into evidence and simply rewrote the story. Until the end blew up in my face.

Ludwig knows how to cheer me up, but I can see from his face how much he's suffering too. He's lost his best friend; we share the pain, the self-reproach, the doubts. And yet he represented you as your lawyer to the very end. I asked him why he didn't stop acting for you. He replied that he needed his brain to engage with what had happened so he could process it. He recommends I do the same and says I should visit you. But my condition still holds, Dad: I won't come until you break your silence.

Anyway, yesterday we raised a glass to his birthday as well as to hope. Although, to be honest, having met Nathalie, I'm no longer so certain that hope is exclusively a good thing. I mean, look at me. I got utterly carried away because of a hope. I expect that's why strangely I also felt such a connection to Nathalie. Subconsciously I recognised myself in her. Her stomach wound has healed without complication, by the way, and the treatment she's getting in an excellent psychiatric institution seems to be helping her too. I imagine that's where she'll stay, because there's no way the court will send her to a normal prison for having killed Kerstin Seiler, kidnapped Sarah and injured her ex-husband. An assessor has concluded that she wasn't of sound mind. As it turns out, she'd been living for weeks in the house with Lenia's body. She bathed and dressed her, read to her, played with her; they even had meals together. Sarah must have 'met' Lenia too. Ludwig, who's keeping me in the loop about her case, says the public prosecutor will argue that Nathalie was sufficiently compos mentis to let Sarah go free on the day they were going to search the upper common, i.e., where Nathalie lived. This was when she buried Lenia's body too.

'You can only lose if you try to find sense in madness,' Ludwig said with a shrug. Then we looked at each other in horror, well aware that this isn't just true of Nathalie, but you too.

Please, Dad, don't let me go on begging.

Give me an explanation, finally.

Ann

BERLIN, 17 JUNE 2018

I don't understand why you're torturing me like this. Isn't it bad enough that I've got to spend the rest of my life bearing the stigma of being the ribbon murderer's daughter? Don't you owe me this, for God's sake?

By staying silent, you're ruining everything that ever made you a good father.

BERLIN, 26 JUNE 2018

This is our last chance, Dad. Next week I'm leaving for Cornwall. I'm going to move in with Zoe.
   Please!

BERLIN, 2 JULY 2018

If I'm not worth an explanation, then it's no longer worth me thinking of you as my father.
   Farewell.

RECORDING 10
Berlin, 10 May 2021

- Do you have children?
- No, I don't. I'm still young and so I've got plenty of time left for that. But also, hmm . . . when I work on certain topics like your case, I sometimes think it would be better not to bring any children into this world. Although I haven't experienced it myself, I think that loving a child must be the most intense emotion there is. But this love can break you too. Saskia E.'s mother committed suicide, did you know that?
- No.
- Yes, she did. A few months after your trial, it was. She just couldn't get any closure, which must be partly down to the fact

334

that you've never spoken about your crimes. The question of why still hangs over everything like a shadow.

- But the public prosecutor came up with a reasonable answer, don't you think?
- That you wanted to study death?
- Precisely.
- But why exactly in that way? Why at the expense of the lives of those innocent children? I've done my homework and found out that there are already plenty of studies on the topic, but those were carried out by interviewing people who'd had near-death experiences. Nobody had to suffer for these interviews.
- That may well be true, but the findings are based on the statements of adults. I'm convinced that the adult mind, through age and life experiences alone, tends to put things in a self-constructed context that is far more subjective. By contrast, what could be more authentic than the mind and soul of a child? Who would give you a more honest answer? Those girls were still young enough to be genuine, and old enough to articulate themselves in an intelligible way. I questioned them as the blood was running out of them. I asked what they were feeling, what they were seeing, as their circulation gradually became weaker and their eyelids began to flutter. It was fascinating. They were freezing, they were scared, their breathing was panicky. But then, the longer it went on, the calmer and clearer they became. They told me about nice experiences they'd had with their parents, or about their pets. Some of them saw a light. It was uplifting, especially as they took their last breaths.
- What specifically did you find out?
- Love. I think that summarises what I discovered. They thought

of lovely things, their families and animals. They made sure their final moments weren't dark and panicky, but full of love and light.

– With respect, that's a pretty sick interpretation. It sounds as if you did good work. But you didn't. You killed twelve innocent children and caused immeasurable pain to their families.

– In the end, that's nothing more than an interpretation too. I wish I could show you my notes, although it has to be pointed out that the number of girls was far too small to constitute a meaningful study.

– Where are they, these notes?

– I burned them, I'm afraid. Rather rash of me.

– When?

– The evening I was arrested, just before the police turned up. I had a hunch that I might be in trouble after I'd bumped into that acquaintance in the Königswald. Particularly as I'd already been questioned about the murders in relation to a lecture I'd given . . . Are you all right? You look so pale again.

– No matter how hard I try, I simply can't understand. Especially as you're a father yourself.

– Yes, that's right, I am a father. That was always the best thing about me. *She* was the best thing about me. And what's more, she was the one who gave me the red ribbon idea.

– She?

– Oh, please, Herr Wesseling! Didn't I tell you last time that I did some research into you beforehand? I know your personal connection to the cases isn't that you met Larissa Meller's mother, but that you're a friend of my daughter's. That's also why, out of all the requests for interviews I've had over the years,

yours is the only one I've consented to. Or did you think it was
down to your reputation as a journalist? Don't delude yourself,
there are plenty in your profession more talented than you.

– *(clears throat)* Anyway, are you saying it was Ann who put you
on to the idea of the red ribbons?

– Uh-huh. The first Christmas after my wife's death, I gave her
a trampoline. The box was too big for wrapping paper so I just
tied a red ribbon around it. Ann put it around her head like
a hairband – to make herself pretty, as she said. Then she
lay in the box as if it were a coffin. Those images imprinted
themselves on my mind. A lost girl who wanted to be found.
And, later, other lost girls who also had to be found.

– You do realise the damage you've done to your daughter too?

– 'Pain and suffering are always inevitable for a large intelligence
and a deep heart,' Dostoevsky said.

– She wrote you letters!

– I read them.

– You ought to have talked to her.

– To say what? She wasn't at the stage where she could
understand.

– Nobody, Herr Lesniak, will ever understand.

– *(chuckles)* It's possible.

– All the same, I'd be interested to know why, after all these
years, you're now ready to talk.

– Oh, Jakob . . . May I call you Jakob? The reason is her: Ann.
You're friends with her. And I'm ill, as you may have been told.

– Yes.

– Well, I'm ill and she's stubborn. She made it very clear to me
that she won't visit until I break my silence. But now she has to.

You are going to play her these recordings, aren't you?

– If she wants to hear them.

– She will. And if not, then persuade her to, please.

– But everything you've said to me you could have told her to her face.

– Yes, but this way we'll have more time to discuss things that only concern us. And she'll be prepared; I won't take her by surprise or shock her. It's important she has a clear head when she visits me. (*clears throat*) Ann, if you're listening to this, come with a clear head and with the memory of everything you've overcome in your life so far. And as for you, Jakob, have a good think about whether you really do want to write a book about experiences you've never had yourself. You won't end up with anything better than probabilities, and 'everything that is merely probable . . .'

– '. . . is probably false.' René Descartes, I believe.

– Well, well. Not bad, my boy.

338

ANN

BERLIN, 19 MAY 2021

Life finds a way through. It uses the tiniest cracks to burst forth, even in the most adverse conditions, like a seedling through asphalt. A laugh that pinches at first, because it's been so long since you used those muscles; a laugh that sounds soft, subdued and perhaps faintly artificial. And then one day you laugh properly again, a loud, booming laugh of such intensity that it makes your tummy hurt. Then happiness forces itself on you; it doesn't ask about guilt, or right and wrong – happiness is blind and deaf, and that's a good thing.

Almost three and a half years have passed.

I'm twenty-eight now.

Zoe and I made up because, well, people are people, because they make mistakes; they're overwhelmed or anxious, or just sometimes plain stupid. Maybe because Zoe was lonely in Cornwall too, and the thing about loneliness is it makes you romanticise things, it softens you, it stirs regret and longing, and in the end there's a message written on impulse that determines your future: *I wish you were here*. Six months later we married on the beach in St Ives and, half a year after that, thanks to a sperm donor, Zoe was pregnant with our son Noah. We never spoke about why it was her rather than me who carried the baby. There are unwritten rules when you live with the daughter of a killer, and one of these is avoiding the subject of genetics. I know myself that I'm being silly about this, but a leopard can't change its spots.

Cornwall was lovely, even though we didn't get that cottage with colourful shutters and a wild garden. We did, however, have a nice apartment on the Penryn River. Despite this, we decided to move back to Berlin, given that we would soon have a baby and could do with the support of Zoe's parents. And there was a house too: the one I grew up in. Zoe had her reservations at first, but I was able to convince her that, in the end, a house is just a house – just a few walls and a roof, a man-made construct. It's also got a beautiful garden and is big enough for each of us to have our own retreat. Mine is the study. Sometimes I stand there by the window, gazing out at Noah, who's now one and a half, playing on the trampoline under Zoe's supervision. It's a new trampoline; mine was completely rusty so we got rid of it. Zoe works half-days as a translator in the cultural department of the Berlin senate; I stay at home with Noah. I haven't finished my German studies, but what's ironic is that all my father's academic publications will probably enable me to enjoy a comfortable life for many years.

Life is beautiful.

But it's no fairy tale.

There are good moments, full of blind, deaf happiness. And there are the others. Those that are as dazzling as strobe lights and as loud as piercing screams.

Zoe and I are arguing more often. She calls me difficult and I call her unsympathetic. This happens when two people in love collide like two stars. Either they fuse together or break apart and dissipate in clouds of gas. I don't know how our relationship is going to pan out, only that it's lost a little of its lustre. Zoe's never experienced anything that's rattled the depths of her soul and destroyed her entire world. Her worst memory is her grandmother's funeral a few years ago. The grandmother who was eighty-five and died in her sleep, in peace and after a life of fulfilment. Zoe says she still can't believe that her nana isn't here anymore. I know I can't hold this against her, but I do it unconsciously. I permanently make her feel that she's naïve and doesn't have a clue about real life. She hates me for this; I hate myself for it too.

The truth is, it's never over. No matter what people say – Ludwig, Jakob, any therapist. It gets better but it's never properly all right again. Sometimes I go into the garage, sit in the car and scream, just like that. And each time that 'Perfect Day' plays, I begin to cry. Because this song always brings back the summer when I was seven and sat on my father's shoulders with my arms outstretched. As if, thanks to him, I could fly. And then, towards the end of the song, when Lou Reed sings, with that strange monotony in his voice, about reaping what you sow, my grief is replaced by fear, a paralysing, ice-cold fear. If my father's a monster, then who am I? What am I capable of? Is evil passed down the generations or is it a choice? Coincidence? A devious game of chance in which a higher power deals the cards on a whim? Or more like a cold that some people catch, while others, those with a more robust immune system, are spared? I don't know; I don't even know why I choose to put the song on again and again when basically all it does is torment me.

341

It's so fricking complicated.

Only in Noah's presence does everything crumble away. For him I don't have a past or any inner demons. For him I'm just his mummy. He's not expecting any explanations, apologies; he's just content with a few biscuits, my time and my love. Jakob is his godfather and one of the few people who doesn't ask questions if I suddenly fall silent. He never finished his article about my father. But he has been working on a book for ages. I've got nothing against it, because there's always someone writing a book about those sorts of crimes and people like my father. I'd rather have Jakob doing it than a stranger. Especially as he was always clear that the book he's writing would also have to look at my father's side of the story. He calls it 'journalistic duty of care', but both of us know it's about money too. My father's never talked about his crimes, not even to me. A testimony would be a sensation. That's why Jakob isn't the only one who's kept requesting interviews over the years. My father turned them all down.

Until the beginning of this month. He's allowed Jakob to talk to him over a number of sessions. I've listened to the recordings of these and tried to form a judgement. Do I hear a psychopath, with his endless provocative digressions, making fun of Jakob by circumventing questions and throwing them back in Jakob's face? Or is this, by contrast, a man desperately stalling for time because he's suffering from having nobody to talk to and play his intellectual games with? I haven't reached a conclusion – the man on the recordings is a stranger to me; all I recognise is his voice. The police have heard the whole thing too and now they have to check if my father committed any other murders. For if what he says in Jakob's interview is true, he didn't start killing in 2003, but back in 2001, two years after my mother's death. Two more dead children, two more destroyed families, more guilt and pain for everyone. For my part, I don't know how much more I can take. Despite this – or maybe because of it – today I'm granting him his wish that I visit him. After more than three years, since my visit at Christmas 2017, before Schergel, before the truth. I would have come long ago if he'd ever made a confession.

On the other hand, he never before asked me for a visit or even answered the letters I wrote to him.

So today's the day.

Ludwig organised the meeting and has come from Poland especially. We often visit him there. Zoe stopped going a while back, but Noah loves the woods and the wild nature. He's over the moon when a deer appears in Ludwig's garden, or he sees a wild boar burrowing. Ludwig says he'll make a hunter out of him when he's old enough.

We're driving in his car, and haven't said a word since we got in. The sun is bright, shining off the buildings that race past, and the sky is blue. Summer's almost here.

We turn into the prison car park.

'Ready?' Ludwig asks.

I give him an honest answer: 'No.'

Once inside, I hand over my bag, Ludwig his mobile, wallet and car keys. We're allowed to keep our watches on and we're only scanned by a detector rather than being searched by hand. Ludwig's name prevents any of those unpleasantries – he's a personal guest of the prison governor. Handy for us, but not without its risks. Nobody would have noticed if either of us had something in our coat pockets that the metal detector didn't pick up.

We're taken to a special visitors' room where we wait outside the door until the governor comes. Handshakes all around and Ludwig jokingly enquiring after the man's handicap. I giggle. It feels like Ludwig's played them all at tennis or golf.

Then the governor explains how this is going to work. 'As we discussed, we'll refrain from posting an officer in the room. But he'll wait right outside the door. Just in—'

'Nothing's going to happen,' I say. 'He is still my father, after all.'

'Of course.' The governor nods keenly. 'You have half an hour. If you wish to leave earlier, just knock. The officer will let you out.'

I thank him. Then I turn to Ludwig. 'For days I've been thinking about what to say. I've even been practising in front of the mirror.'

Ludwig gives me a hug. 'You'll be fine,' he says, adding that he'll wait for me in the governor's office.

The room isn't any different from the one I met my father in three and a half years ago. The same pale walls, the soft buzzing of the neon lights on the ceiling, the sparse furnishings consisting of a table and two chairs. And yet everything is different. Back then, my father was my father, the person I loved most in the world, who I trusted unfailingly, who I believed to be innocent. Today he's a convicted killer. And I'm stigmatised.

When we got married, I took Zoe's surname, which means I'm now Ann Brambach. I'm just a random woman amongst three and a half million people in Berlin. It's been a long time since the media were interested in me; my face was only in the papers a few times in 2018, around the time of the trial. So it's completely absurd for me to sometimes think that people are staring at me.

344

And even more absurd that, in spite of everything, I should occasionally find myself envying Nathalie. Seen from the outside, she's anything but enviable. She's imprisoned in a psychiatric institution, up to her eyeballs with medication. But internally, it's possible she's doing better than I am. Because she took a clear decision: to inhabit her own story, the world behind her closed eyelids. She's happy there.

I take a seat. My left arm is trembling; I feel sick. Briefly, I fancy I can hear footsteps out in the corridor. Heavy, sluggish footsteps, redolent of evil. I've often imagined what my father might look like now, drained by the last few years, illness and himself. Jakob has already warned me that he must have got very thin.

The door opens; I leap up as if conditioned.

He's dragging his feet, but walking upright.

He must have lost five kilos at least. Ten, maybe.

His hair is almost white. Cut short with a precise parting. He's got a beard, which I've never seen on him before. It suits him, allows him to look respectable, like the captain of a large boat.

However . . . the way he's moving, his emaciated physique, his thin face that looks grey.

'My Beetle,' he says. It's like a death blow, a command for my tears.

'I'll be outside if you need me,' says the prison officer who brought him in.

'Thanks,' my father replies politely. He makes a gesture which I take to be an invitation to sit. He does the same.

I hastily wipe my eyes and clear my throat. 'Here we are then.'

He nods. 'Indeed. How do you feel?'

I swallow with difficulty; the back of my chair is hard and

digging into me. All the same I try to sit up. My pride, my defiance, my disappointment. For three and a half years, my father has refused to give me an explanation; all my life he's been deceiving me. If I'm unable to hate him, at the very least I want to make him feel this. He's still the man who carried me on his shoulders. And he looks so ill. Colon cancer, his death sentence. It might be quick, or he could waste away.

'I haven't come to talk about me.'

A smile twitches on one side of his mouth. 'You must have heard the recordings your friend Jakob Wesseling did. So now you know everything.'

'I know what happened, yes. And yet, I still don't understand. On the contrary, it comes across as so banal, despite the barbarity of it all. You wanted to study death, and to do this, you committed murder. What a cliché.'

'Death is neither banal nor a cliché, Ann. It's humanity's last great unanswered question. Think of your mother. Did you never want to know what she saw or felt at the end, after her face was stuck in a scream?'

I shake my head. 'She was in pain, Dad. That's all. She wanted to scream in pain, but she didn't have the strength to.'

'That's what you're guessing, Ann. But you don't know.'

'What about you? Do you know now? Do you? You've destroyed dozens of lives to find out this answer. What good does it do, Dad? All of us are going to die one way or another. And for this reason alone, it makes no difference if it's heaven, hell or just the big black void waiting for us at the end, because there's nothing we can do to change it. We're born to live and then, at some point, to die. That's nature.'

'No, Ann, that's blind acceptance. And man is definitely not created for that. We search for meaning in our existence, an intended purpose. Look at yourself – you're the best example of this. You listened to Wesseling's recordings and yet you still came today. Because for you, it's not enough to know what happened when, where and how. You can't be done with this until you see some meaning in the whole thing.'

'Once again, Dad. This isn't about me.'

'But of course it is, Ann! It's only ever been about you, my Beetle.'

I breathe as if I'm ragged. How often have I wondered whether he was just looking for a sort of substitute in those girls because he really wanted to kill me?

He still has no trouble reading me. 'It never even crossed my mind to hurt you. I didn't even manage it with Eva. And do you know why?'

I shake my head.

'Because I knew how much she meant to you. You, Ann, were my life. My greatest gift and my greatest insight. Only through you was I able to feel. Because, you know . . .' He looks at his hands. They've become old, just like him. His pale skin is dotted with brown spots; blue veins protrude conspicuously. 'I'm ill.'

'They've told me.'

He looks up. 'I don't mean the cancer. All my life I've suffered from a completely different condition. It's not a recognised illness – at least not for people who merely invent terms for the condition, but never have to live with it – alexithymia. I suffer from alexithymia.'

'Ale . . . what?'

'Alexithymia.'

I shake my head in bewilderment.

'Alexithymia means you feel little or nothing at all. You don't have any idea what it's like to be frustrated. All your life you wonder: is grief painful? What does rage feel like? Or love? I don't know, Ann. I've never really been overcome by an emotion. My heart has never raced, nor has my throat ever felt constricted. What is envy? What is hatred? For other people, emotions are like bulldozers; for me, they're more like . . .' He looks up as if the correct description were stuck to the ceiling. 'A breath of wind,' he says finally, looking me in the eye again. 'A breeze that gently wafts past almost without my noticing.'

'You . . . ?' I pause while my thoughts begin racing, uncontrolled, back in time. Memories like spotlights. Eva getting an earful and being grounded because of a bad grade, whereas my father just shrugged. All the shit I got up to aged fourteen. Joints, beer, skipping school and slitting mats in the gym. Locking Eva in the girls' loo. It's true: he never shouted at me. Never sent me to my room. When I scratched Nico's moped and Dad covered for me. When I had the accident in 2015 through my own fault: too much beer. He didn't just pay the fine, he also got Ludwig to see to it that I didn't lose my licence. No dressing-down, no shouting. Just these words: 'Don't do it again, my Beetle. I still need you.' My dad, the eternal stoic, fazed by nothing. And his arrest – of course. All those things I attributed his clueless behaviour to: shock, tiredness, pride, defiance. Can it really have just been *nothing*? Nothing at all, merely emptiness?

'But . . . what about Mum? You loved her, didn't you? Or me . . .

What about me? You did everything for me. You always looked after me.'

'That's my problem, Ann. I know I love you. And that you belong to me. But . . .'

'You don't feel it? How can that be true, Dad?' I shake my head for this very reason: it can't be true. 'I distinctly remember how worried you were about me when I closed up after Mum died . . .' When I didn't feel anything, my head adds. Just like you.

He nods. 'Alexithymia can be hereditary, but it can also be brought on by serious trauma. Which means I could see you had two risk factors.'

'That's why you dragged me off to the child psychologist,' I conclude. 'And that's why I always had to explain my feelings in great detail and even write them down. You didn't want me to become like you, did you?'

'No, I didn't. It may sound paradoxical, but people like me – and by the way, there are far more of us than you could possibly imagine – are not completely cold. They're often very aware of being different from other people. And they suffer from this. They suffer when they come across someone who is wildly happy, and all they can do is imitate this person, simulate a laugh like an actor. They practise interpersonal rituals until they're as comfortable with them as a tailored suit. But they never feel complete.' He cocks his head. His eyes are clear and cutting sharply right into my thoughts. 'How is someone to understand the world if they cannot feel it?'

'"The Allegory of the Cave,"' I say, it having just come into my head. 'I remember exactly what you told me: *Our senses – sight, hearing, smell, taste and touch – can deceive us. With those alone, we'll never fully understand the world. We have to think. And feel.* But that was precisely what—'

'I wasn't capable of, ever.' His laugh ends in a coughing fit. The sounds pain me. 'My immune system isn't the best these days,' he explains with a shrug. 'Well, now you know. Professor Walter Lesniak, the great, internationally renowned philosopher and anthropologist. He wants to answer all the questions about life and the world, but he'll never succeed because he's lacking the vital piece.'

I breathe to calm my heart down and counter the misplaced empathy. 'You say that lots of people suffer from this thing. How many?'

'According to studies, around fourteen per cent.'

'What, and all of these go off and start killing people?'

'No, but not all of them have seen the light either.'

'The light?'

'It's hard to go back into the cave, my Beetle, when you've been outside and seen the light.'

'What bloody light?'

'In my case, you were the light, Ann.'

'Me?'

'Your bicycle accident, do you remember? Your bleeding? The deep hole in your wrist that functioned like an outlet for all the pent-up, suppressed feelings inside you.' He pulls his hands apart. 'And it was like a miracle, for in that moment, I felt something too, Ann! For the first time in my life, it was more than just a breath of wind, an insignificant breeze. I felt your pain, your distress, your fascination. I felt anxiety, the fear of losing you. The determination to protect you from anything bad. For a few seconds, it was all there, so real, so great and overpowering, rather than just dry theory. It was genuine! But also over far too quickly.'

'So you didn't start killing two years after Mum's death, but one year after my bike accident.' I slap a hand over my mouth. I was the trigger. 'The first girl, Laura, who didn't cry despite her cut knee. She reminded you of me and the bike accident.'

'I'd have done anything to experience that again.'

'And you did.'

'Yes, I did.'

'You re-enacted it time and again. You didn't just want to study death, but yourself. And that's what you meant when you told Jakob in the interview that the girls had given you a meaning. They allowed you to feel something. You're sick, Dad! In many respects.'

My comment doesn't affect him; he just smiles. 'Do you remember the conclusion of the allegory, Ann? The person who manages to get out returns to the cave to tell the other prisoners what he's discovered. But they just ridicule him and, worse than that, they're so attached to their view of the world – to their shadows – that they want to seize and kill him. That's what happened to Socrates, Plato's teacher. The Athenians sentenced him to death for what he said. He was to poison himself by drinking hemlock. Socrates didn't resist, he said, "Cheers!" and drank up.' Dad leans across the table. 'What do you feel now? Disgust? Sympathy? What, Ann?'

I shake my head. 'What about the stone? You gave the one from my accident to me and I passed it on to Zoe.'

'I happened to find a similar one when I was out walking. Ought that not to have been a sign?'

'You used it to kill.'

'Yes, I did. What are you feeling, Ann? Tell me.'

'Forget it. I'd feel like a dealer giving a junkie a shot.'

'No, no, no, my Beetle.' He reaches for my hand. 'None of this is your fault. You were my emotion. Like a prosthesis for a maimed body. You were my light, my everything.'

'And doesn't that very fact make me complicit?'

'That's a fascinating thought. Is it possible that I was a better father to you because I gave myself an outburst of emotion once a year?'

I pull my hand out from under his. 'You're not being serious?'

'I don't know, my Beetle. But what I do know for certain is that you made me a better person, a more complete person.' I suddenly think of 'Perfect Day', the second verse where Lou Reed tells the person being addressed that because of him – or her – he was able to completely forget himself and persuade himself he was someone different.

'Don't go thinking your crimes haven't had an effect on my life. Zoe and I are on the verge of separating.'

'Really? Why?'

'Why? Because she hasn't been through what I have. And for this reason, she can't understand. She's stuck in her little, cosy world, whereas I . . .' I stop when I see something flash in his face: my worry, a feeling that nourishes him. 'What am I saying? We're going to get a grip on our problems. And whatever happens, I'll have my little Noah. He's—'

'Your light,' my father says, completing my sentence for me. He looks around for the camera that's above the door in the corner. Then he holds out the palm of his hand towards me and says, smiling, 'Cheers, my Beetle!'

Love. (Ann, 28 years old)

Love leaves us with no choice. We don't go searching for it; it's love itself that seeks and finds us. It nestles deep inside us as the essence of our existence. Everything we feel derives from love. Hope, belief, confidence, determination. But hate too, as well as fear, anger and all the negative emotions that sometimes turn us into beasts. In the end, they too come from love that has been disappointed or violated. Love is the most delicate but at the same time strongest thing in us humans. And it's always present. Sometimes large, colourful, loud and shiny like the colours of summer. Sometimes barely perceptible, a mere waft and a whisper. Just a small red light, but one that's still visible, even in the deepest, darkest night. And even when there is nothing remaining of us, love is our last prayer. Our last breath.

My father died on the evening of 19 May 2021, just a few hours after my visit. He was found lifeless in his cell after slitting his left wrist; assistance came too late. How he got hold of the stone that was astonishingly similar to the one he'd killed the girls with years earlier is unknown. It's suspected that he found it during his yard exercise one day and smuggled it back into his cell. In an official statement released to the media, it said his health had rapidly deteriorated because of his bowel cancer, ultimately leading to his death.

I know better, everything.

But most of all, I know he did it for me, so I could draw a line under all that had happened and finally find peace. That alone shows he must have been capable of feeling something. I hope he was aware of this before he died.

I'm avoiding as far as I can the question of whether I've forgiven him. What he did can't be forgiven, but now I've understood it to a certain extent. I'd never say that out loud, for fear that people might confuse what I mean by 'understand' with 'relativise' or 'justify'. It's not like that at all, of course; I know perfectly well what's right and wrong, otherwise I'd never have voluntarily given the stone to the police in Schergel for examination. But at least I can, to some degree, understand what drove him. Just like Nathalie, he kept striving to get to a certain point, and this point simply wouldn't let him go. What for Nathalie was the day when, in her fantasy, Lenia escaped from the ribbon murderer, was for my father the day when he first felt something in his life. The day of my bicycle accident. And just like Nathalie, he wasn't content with imagining it in his mind; he allowed it to become reality. The fact is, there were two sides to Walter Lesniak the man: one of these was a brutal killer; the other, my father, perhaps the best I could have had. And yes, I do now distinguish between the two. But I keep this to myself as well, for fear of being judged by others.

Thanks to the interview with Jakob, two previously unsolved murders from 2001 and 2002 – seven-year-old Laura and nine-year-old Miriam – were later proven to have been committed by him. Their families now have certainty.

Jakob's still working on his book. He says he wants to give it time to make best possible sense of the story. In the course of his research, he recently discovered that Marcus Steinhausen emigrated to Spain in 2010. He met a woman there, started a family and worked as a tradesman. In 2014, Marcus Steinhausen died in a car accident.

Eva has fully recovered from her injuries. She still works as a psychologist at the psychological counselling centre for victims of crime and their relatives at Frankfurt University Hospital. She and Nico are back together and plan to get married this summer.

Michelle Meller has remarried too. In 2018, her ex-husband Rainer Meller stood trial for false imprisonment and two charges of grievous bodily harm. He was found guilty and is currently serving a ten-year sentence.

Sarah Seiler is living with her father in Čachrov in the Czech Republic. She's eleven years old now and at secondary school. Once a week she still sees her therapist, though she's doing really well, which must be in part down to her father who, having been a washout in the early years of her life, is trying extremely hard to finally be the father his daughter needs.

Steffen Fester has a healthy little girl with his second wife. He says he can see lots of Lenia in her.

Lenia is buried in a cemetery in Schöneberg.

Nathalie is still in a secure psychiatric unit near Berlin. Once a month she's allowed visitors under supervision. She looks good and talks enthusiastically about her release, which in her world seems to be just around the corner.

Zoe moved out. Noah and I are still living in the house in Charlottenburg. Every evening we light a candle, place it on the windowsill in the study and look at the flickering shadows on the wall. Noah always sees something different: dinosaurs or monster trucks or a castle in a storm. Whereas I see a man carrying a little girl on his shoulders. Always. And then it's summer, I'm seven years old and Lou Reed is singing about a perfect day.

AFTERWORD AND ACKNOWLEDGEMENTS

Although I've written about a specific phenomenon in this novel, I make no claim to understand the reality of living with such a condition. What must it be like when love is just the breath of a breeze and every tear no more than a meaningless physical reaction? To be honest, I don't know. I can only assume that those affected are burdened by a life in which many things are complicated and, often, just one feeling is clear: the feeling of being different, maybe even 'wrong'. Despite this, those affected do their best to integrate and – unlike in this novel – are, of course, not necessarily a danger to society. I hope I've succeeded in describing a character who is clearly an individual case; it's essential that my readers realise this. Because what's at issue here is respect. Life is a lottery – we can't choose where, when and as whom we're born, nor the conditions in which we begin our lives. We don't even have complete control over what we do with our lives, apart from one thing: every day we can decide afresh how we treat each other.

I'm someone who's incredibly profligate with their emotions, and being so emotional gets me into hot water sometimes, because it makes me vulnerable and leaves me exposed. Nonetheless, I think that all of us ought to be grateful for the power of our feelings, realise that the positive ones are as important for our personal development as the negative ones, and let ourselves get carried away by them more often – no matter what others think, whether we make fools of ourselves or make ourselves vulnerable. For our feelings determine a large chunk of our identity, and each emotion has a right to exist, in a world where not everyone has the ability to feel anything at all, and in a world that is often cold enough. So let's be loud and feisty, let's laugh and love and cry and shout. It's more than okay; it's right and it's important.

As I write these lines, I find myself becoming overwhelmed by emotion once more. By gratitude for this life that I'm able to lead and in which I can invent stories for you. By gratitude for the people standing by me on this adventure that I still find absolutely incredible. Here I'd like to thank three special women: Caterina Schäfer, my agent; my editor Bianca Dombrowa; and you, Mum. You three were my most important supports as *Perfect Day* came to fruition. You put up with me, comforted me, motivated me, nourished me with your clever ideas and kept reminding me why I embarked on becoming a storyteller, and that I can and must continue to go my own way.

Thanks too to all the committed people at dtv who understand what writing means to me, and who frequently (have to) let me take my own path, especially Barbara Laugwitz, Andrea Seiber and Gudrun Marx.

I'm indebted to my foreign publishers and translators, thanks to whom my stories can now be read in so many countries – particularly Stefanie Bierwerth, Jamie Bulloch and Christine Kopprasch, who've helped me overcome another personal hurdle over the past year: establishing direct contact with my foreign readers despite my linguistic shortcomings. What at first was accompanied by a pounding heart and sweaty palms has now become so enriching (as well as great fun) – and that's all down to you.

I'd also like to give special and long overdue thanks to Astrid Eckert, as well as to my family, friends and of course you the readers, bloggers, booksellers and event organisers. Thanks for reading my stories and telling others about them.

Finally to you, Lou Reed, up there in heaven. Thanks for that song. Say hi to "kleine Miep" from me.

From my heart,

Romy

REDISCOVERING PRAYER

Rediscovering Prayer

Pierre Guilbert

New City

First published in France 1981
as *La Prière Retrouvée*

© 1981 Nouvelle Cité, Paris.

First published in English 1983
by
New City

© 2012 this English translation New City

Graphics and cover design by Hildebrando Moguiê

British Cataloguing in Publication Data:
A catalogue reference for this book is available from the
British Library

ISNB 978-1-905039-15-9

Typeset in Great Britain by
New City, London
www.newcity.co.uk

Printed in Malta
By Gutenberg Press

Contents

FOREWORD

This book has no other ambition than to pass on an experience. It does not matter in the least that it is my experience. The only thing that matters is that it is an experience, that is to say, not a reflection or a thesis, not an exposition or a treatise, but the telling of a story, a road that has actually been travelled.

What reassures me is that it is the work of Another, with the advances, the stages, the retracing of steps, the irreversible discoveries, with the joys and the difficulties, the lights and the nights, in a word, all that goes to make up a story, in this case, the part of my story told by this book. As for myself, I have done nothing but receive. It is indeed the work of Another that I am preparing to pass on to you.

But no one receives anything for themselves, to make them wealthy, for their own satisfaction. What you think you are keeping as a treasure, decays in your hand and rots. Even the gifts of God are not immune from this.

No one receives anything except in order to give. Not so much to give the things that have been received, as to give the life which they have brought to birth and which they nourish day by day. It is your life that you must give, for 'He who seeks to save his life loses it' (Mt. 10, 39) and life too decays when you keep it for yourself: it becomes like a cancerous growth and begets death.

There is another reason why, through this book, I wish to give a little of the life I have received. For a long time, in many and various ways, I sought prayer. I sought it in books and I did not find it. Far be it from me to speak ill of books; many were very good and I learnt many good and useful things from them about prayer. But I did not learn to pray from them.

You can know everything, with your head, about prayer, and yet not know how to pray. No treatise has ever afforded anyone entry into that life of prayer to which you are aspiring. You will not find it in this book either. You will only find it, or rather, in due course, you will only receive it, in your own heart, in the course of an experience that is all your own. My wish is that this book may help you, to some small extent, humbly, poorly, to enter into it. Because it is a bit of the life that I received that I shall give you, in order that in you too, by the work of Another, it may bear fruit.

For a moment I was tempted to sign this book with a pseudonym, in order to preserve the gratuity of God's gifts, because God's gifts do not give one the right to boast or to take the credit oneself. 'I' am only the one who receives, who receives everything from that Other who is Father, Son and Spirit, that Other who desires to fill you in your turn, for 'everything comes from him, everything is through him and for him' (Rom. 11, 36).

So, be sure to give back to God what belongs to him: everything. And forget my name, except to pray for me.

I

Prayer: how much are you ready to pay for it?

1. A tiny, insignificant 'yes'

I was no longer praying, or hardly at all. The time which I did still devote to prayer, at rare intervals or in circumstances which made it an obligation for me, seemed long, interminable. I was bored stiff, head and heart were empty; I looked for the moment to be 'delivered', longed for the moment of my 'deliverance'.

I always had something else to do, something more urgent, more important, more useful. There was scarcely any time left for prayer and I was a past master at finding or creating things to do or reasons for doing nothing. Year after year the rot sets in and immobilises you. You are bound hand and foot, or rather, I would say, faced with a mountain to be shifted. How can you do that when you have lost all your flexibility and, to tell the truth, all true hope, perhaps even all really serious desire. A few listless efforts (for you're not much bothered about succeeding then), some abortive attempts which make you say: 'You see, there is nothing one can do.' A retreat from time to time (thanks be to God, some links still remain) and occasionally a spurt, quickly exhausted, for retreat resolutions do not last long once life is resumed, with the habits that are only too firmly rooted.

At times I was conscious of a certain regret. Formerly I

had prayed, had had a taste for prayer. I had even increased the time I devoted to it. I had lived through experiences of consolation and peace. I had even, for a moment, considered the contemplative life. And then it had all melted away like a summer haze. I was left with some nostalgia, as it were, the memory of a (small) Paradise Lost.

But there were no angels with flaming swords (Gen. 3, 24) barring the entry to it for me. It had simply become choked up with undergrowth, like those old paths overgrown with brambles. And if I had not lost the memory of it, access to it appeared to be closed to me. I had let the brambles hide the path. A certain nostalgia, then, but ineffective and, in any case, insufficient to 'shift the mountain'. I was well aware that more fresh starts would be needed. But did I really want it?

If it had been brought to me on a dish, like the head of St John the Baptist to Salome (she had at least paid for it with her dancing!), I would have accepted it without any doubt. But probably it would not have lasted. The desire in my heart was not as yet sufficiently awake, the countless disappointments and setbacks which followed almost every endeavour were too painful. And then you tell yourself that in the end one can live very well without prayer. True, it is nothing to be proud of, but if appearances are preserved, one is able to put up with one's brief shame quite well. Inevitably, my spiritual life continued to deteriorate. Already whole sectors of it had caved in. Thanks be to God, that secret nostalgia which dogged me, goaded me to action at times, and at other times caused a moment of panic: 'All the same I must... This sort of thing can't go on indefinitely!' Blessed nostalgia, which prevented me from resigning myself wholly to the situation, to this practical absence of prayer.

'This sort of thing can't go on.' That is what the Jesuit Father whom I continued to see once or twice a year said to me one day. Those words rang like an alarm for me. I was dimly aware of the fact, but I was reluctant to face up to it, for that would have obliged me, at least, to take the necessary steps. In the last resort, it is clear to me today, I was afraid of having to be truly converted. I had gradually settled down into a *modus vivendi*, a sort of compromise with mediocrity, nothing very dreadful, but nothing, either, to be proud of.

Then the good father went on: 'Would you be prepared to make a ten-day retreat?' Ten days! I, who never lasted out a four-day retreat and who was already seeking to escape on the evening of the third day, alleging a mass of urgent business – ten days – an eternity! Happily the person who was to lead these spiritual exercises was the right man for the job. I knew him to be excellent and had already appreciated him on other occasions. Doubtless I would have declined those ten days if it had been anyone else.

The fact remains that, God alone knows by what grace, something in me had moved. Another desire had made itself felt. 'Very well, I'll do it!' I replied. Prudently, faced with so quick a compliance, the good father booked me in for the retreat at once. It was still a few months off and I felt much foreboding. Meanwhile, nothing in my life changed. It would be quite soon enough to worry about that if the retreat shook something in me. But the desire for it remained alive and I think that it was true.

When the day came, I felt that I was ready for anything. My forebodings had melted away. Even the prospect of

13

having to be converted was pleasant. I was cheerful, full of hope. Something was going to happen. Life was going to be new. Ten days: I should have time to make a bit of a beginning then and there. And, for that matter, quite a bit had been done already. It had happened of its own accord, without any effort on my part. Yes, I mean that: without any effort on my part. I had still done nothing, but I was no longer the same. The gloom which had haunted me for years, and a certain weariness with everything, was giving way to a bit of a smile, though still tentative and hesitant. But it was a smile: God's first smile.

At the time I didn't notice anything. I am quite optimistic by nature and new experiences have always brought me satisfaction. It is only now that I have realised that it was God's smile. More and more the smile which I received seemed to me quite out of proportion with what I had agreed to do. I had simply offered a small 'yes', the 'yes' of the man who says to himself, and is told by others, 'this sort of thing can't go on.' It was a tiny, insignificant 'yes', a 'yes' which had not yet entailed any change in my life; a 'yes' which had not been endorsed by any effort.

But this 'yes' that was so slight a matter, this tiny and insignificant 'yes', was enough for something in my heart to rock, like when one finds oneself suddenly relieved of a weight without having moved a finger. That much I had received, and I was not even aware of it. With a small 'yes', a 'yes' that you say to God, you release, unknown to you, and set in motion that whole power of God's love, the whole of his generosity, which is never satisfied with what it has done for you and is already giving back to you, hundredfold, what you have scarcely begun to give.

2. You don't know where the shock will come from

It was then a September evening – retreats always start in the evening. In that way, the next morning when you wake up, you find yourself already on the other bank of this new world on which you wish to land. The night will already have taken some steps for you, almost instead of you.

So then it was the evening, this first evening when one is still tempted to say to oneself: 'The serious stuff only begins tomorrow.' I was aware of a small joy, a sort of secret innocence which reconciles you with yourself. I seem even to remember that a smile hovered around my lips, as when a cloud is edged with light to indicate that the sun is returning.

On that first evening there were no great mystical flights, just a brief introduction to persons and things. You can never foresee where the shock will come from. In fact, it came to me that evening from the timetable. A timetable is a nuisance, and mysticism cares nothing for it. Yes, but there you are. This timetable (at such a time, this; at such other time, that), presented with perfect ingenuity (with a perfectly calculated ingenuity, at least I presume so), this timetable left enormous gaps, large voids of 'free time'. And then I heard the retreat director, with that simplicity which is more terrifying than a blow from a club, say: 'For the rest... (this 'rest', dear friends, which by itself took up two thirds of the day!) for the rest, it is enough that each of you makes sure of four hours a day of personal prayer.'

Four hours a day of personal prayer! All at once my smile became fixed, my brow furrowed and a storm broke out in my head. Four hours of personal prayer a day! Four hours! He really said four hours! No doubt about it. It really is four hours, and four hours each day, so, in ten days, forty hours of personal prayer! I was dizzy, I tell you.

Never yet, never, do you understand, had it happened to me, not even once in my life, to devote four hours in one day to personal prayer. It really was a question of personal prayer, not liturgical prayer, for example. In the past, during Holy Weeks at the Major Seminary, adding everything together, sung offices, meditation, rosary, etc., it might have come to four hours, but not four hours of personal prayer. During my ordination retreats there had been long intervals on a walk of recollection and peace. But at the most there was one good hour of personal prayer, and often spread over several periods. The same applied to the most 'fervent' retreats that I had made since then. I freely admit that I found it, then, quite hard going, that solid hour of personal prayer. But four hours!

I was simply stunned. Often in such circumstances people say: 'I couldn't believe my ears.' But now I did believe them. And what they recorded resounded in all directions within me, like an interminable echo thrown back by the walls to fill the valleys to their outmost depths. Four hours a day! Four hours a day! I was not even tempted to make light of it by saying to myself that I would fill those hours with my own plans! Why did this temptation not come to me? I don't know, but it didn't. Today, going back over the experience I lived through, I believe that the small 'yes', so tiny and insignificant, which I had said some months earlier, was giving birth to a new child, and was bearing fruit once more. God does not tire of making fertile even the most barren land.

Nevertheless I can still hear myself muttering: 'Four

hours a day! I could never manage that! I am absolutely incapable of it! I no longer know how to pray!' But at the same time I felt the desire for it well up from the depths of my being and I knew that I was going to try.

Do you catch a glimpse of the inner contradiction here? Everything in me cries out: 'Impossible.' The depths within me answer: 'Try!' It is one and the same person who utters the two opposing words. But they do not both come from the same source.

On the side of the 'impossible' there stands the whole of a human experience, the experience of quite a few years (perhaps a good twenty years!), an experience immunised again and again by shattered illusions and abortive attempts. Ordinarily I could not hope to break the circle of all that.

On the other side, that of the 'depths', as I said, a dawn was breaking, very timid and hesitant, on a night which all at once grows less black: the night of disappointed hopes, the night of the 'impossible'. Have you noticed that it is always from the deepest, the most distant parts, that the dawn begins to break? It does not shine out on high, it comes up from below, from underneath the horizon. The point from which it shines is never here, near you, it is down there, as far away as you can imagine, at the edge, beyond the horizon.

But have you yet seen any darkness resisting the dawn which is breaking? Have you yet seen a night which gets the better of the dawn? It may take time, perhaps, but the dawn will always give birth to daybreak and daybreak to broad daylight.

That is why, although humanly speaking all the evidence pointed to the sheer impossibility of the undertaking (in fact it is impossible, humanly speaking), I knew that I was going to try. Something in me, at that very moment, had decided to try. It was not only a star in my night, for a star does not vanquish the night. No, it was definitely the dawn which was proclaiming this hope that the night was beginning to die.

But you will never be able to command the dawn and find it obeying you and breaking in your life, in your night. It always comes at its own time, which does not depend on you. You receive it from Another. I was receiving it from that Other who is master of the impossible. His hour had struck.

As for me, I had still done nothing. I was there, the spectator, at once attentive and surprised, of a story which was my own and which was unfolding beneath my eyes, while a part of myself was gradually acquiescing. So it is that the conversion of the heart has its point of departure in the conversion of desire. Other desires arise in your heart, of which your old habits knew nothing. You begin – but it does not come from yourself and is not the outcome of an effort – to desire what you used to dread and to feel scruples about what you used to wish for. How that may be possible I do not know. But so it is. And it is a great wonder.

3. The slope of desire

Did I pray that first evening? Did I make progress? I no longer know. To tell the truth, I don't think so. In any case, the next morning there I was, faced with that yawning gulf of free time and that prospect of four hours. It is always risky to stand on the edge of an abyss. A certain anxiety oppresses your chest and would impel you into the void, into flight, even if you feel the wish to disregard anguish. Nothing is won at the outset.

That first day I succeeded in praying only for three hours. It was something that happened rather than something I did. But it was quite a lot for a first step. I had nibbled at those three hours, bit by bit, filling up a scrap of the abyss here and there, escaping to take a breather or to put myself at ease in a book, returning to the chapel for a moment, striding through the grounds, sunlit and with their trees resplendent in the tints of autumn, drawn by the intimacy of an oratory.

What was that prayer, made up of bits and pieces, in those poor three hours of my first day? To be sure, it was nothing to be proud of. No mystical transport. Often the time weighed heavily, dragged, and my capacity was decidedly short. What had I 'said' to the Lord? So little, things so awkward and so hesitant, incapable of retaining my attention. But never had I thought I could keep it up for three hours.

Every habit begins with the first attempt. The die was cast, the hardest part was accomplished, the circle of the impossible broken and lying there beneath my eyes, the yawning gulf was becoming a slight gap.

Already on the second day it was filled: I had prayed for four hours. Yet it was not a victory. It was fragile, infinitely so, dangerously so. I wager that it would have been enough for me to put on a triumphant air for everything to crumble, for me to find myself again like the man lost in the desert when the mirage vanishes from his eyes and the oasis from his thirst. What I mean is this: a small joy was bringing me light, a sober and fragile joy, incredulous, as it were, not believing my own eyes. But, thanks be to God, it was a humble joy. For what had I done? What share in that could I claim as my own contribution? Once again I had said a tiny and insignificant 'yes' to that desire which had arisen in me and which Another had sown there. When a desire haunts you so, you are not a hero for consenting to it! The consent which you give, your small 'yes', so poor, puts you on a slope and all you have to do is to follow it. When a desire is infused into your heart, there is no slope for you to climb: it is enough for you to go down it, to follow its gradient, to make its inclination your own. And to the extent that you follow its slope, your speed accelerates and you count for nothing in it: you have no effort to make. It is the slope which carries you on and draws you so that you are towed by desire.

There is nothing very exalting in this experience. I repeat, what strikes me is the impression of fragility with which it leaves you. Rather like a charm which an inconsiderate movement or an external intervention would be likely to break. Or, if you prefer, as if you were hanging by a thread a little too weak for your weight: then you avoid any brusque movement, you make yourself light, as light as you can, you become 'airborne', for in truth, 'you are only hanging by a thread'. That is your share in the experience, your tiny little part: not to break the thread, not to shatter the charm; fear, but without anguish. Rather, a slight apprehension which impels you to be more careful. And that apprehension is only the reverse of the desire which leads you on and carries you along and lightens you so that the thread will not break, reinforced as it is by the whole tension of your desire...

But the desire does not come from you: you receive it, it is given to you. Hanging by your thread, you feel it grow in you, without you (for your part, all you have to do is to consent to it). The intoxication of the slope down which desire impels you, supports you and thus you traverse unforeseen distances. You hardly notice it: you are carried on the wings of the wind.

That was the way things went. And gradually prayer came back and stayed with me, like an old acquaintance whom one finds to be just the same after years have gone by, as fresh, as young, as if we had parted only the evening before. Simple and joyful rediscoveries, without ceremony, with that wink of complicity which indicates that the links are not broken or that they have been reforged. Humble gratitude also for this new gift which has been given you and which no reproach comes to mar.

Even the slight feeling of sadness which accompanies the memory of your infidelity, or better, the very tranquil regret which stays with you, does not trouble this inner joy. And this regret and this sadness are not emphasised more than they should be, but sufficiently for you to appreciate an astonishing gratuity and to prevent you from imagining that all this is normal and to be expected. No: you receive, you do not deserve anything.

Did I in fact have any grounds for pride? What was there that I could have been proud of, without at once being convicted of an illusion or a lie, without the thread by which I was so miraculously hanging, breaking at once? It is true that on the second day and every day that followed I had devoted the four hours to prayer that we were asked for. But what of that? When desire carries you along, what merit is there for you in abandoning yourself to it? God was putting this desire into me and all I had to do was to welcome it. You know how joy follows the fulfilment of your desire. That means that it happens of its own accord. All that is needed for continuance is a few ounces of logic. And logic was asking me not to steal bits and pieces from the time of prayer but to refuse to do anything else during that time. Yes, essentially not to do anything else, not to accept any other occupation, if possible not even any other preoccupation (you know how quickly preoccupations become obsessions). That is the only way in which one must be steadfast. In a word, that was my only effort: not to do anything else.

As for the rest, what goes on during those four hours, what you can do, what you can experience, that is to say, live, does not depend (almost) any longer on you. In any case, it is not your concern. Your part is simply that of the driver whose driving steers to right or to left: you straighten out whenever necessary and resume your route. You are there to pray; you come back to it every time something draws you away from it. But beware of twisting the wheel too violently, for you risk ending up on the verge. For prayer also straightens out, but with flexibility. Smile inwardly at your distractions: it is quite normal that your time of prayer should be strewn with them, like stars in a clear summer sky. Return to your prayer with that smile at yourself and, in particular, do not let yourself make a fresh distraction out of your distractions. However long they last, however frequent they may be, distractions have no importance. Only one thing counts: that you keep to the time of prayer, four hours.

For in fact what in prayer is prayer is not done by you,

but by the Spirit of God in you, who in order to succeed only needs the time which you offer him. Then avoid stifling him by trying to 'act' in his place. Let him pray in you and only be the place where the Spirit, at this moment, is praying to the Father...

4. Resolutions

When a retreat is over, you go back home with a new resolution in your suitcase. And often that is what it remains, for you rarely manage to put it into practice. Remember that book or that trinket which had enticed you and which you rediscover some years later, useless junk, and quite new.

There is a lot I could say about resolutions. Like so many other people I have taken them in large numbers, but I have kept very few of them. There are presumptuous resolutions, in the style of: 'I take the firm resolution never to offend Thee again.' Those are the resolutions which one takes for the sake of having taken them rather than in order to keep them. Have you yet seen anyone, even a saint, who is no longer a sinner because he has taken such a resolution? They are insidious alibis, which justify you forgetting them immediately (since they are impossible to keep) and which encourage you in your good conscience.

There are generous resolutions. Seized by a certain enthusiasm, you do not mince matters. You have glimpsed some facets of the ideal which one part of you dreams of pursuing and you say to yourself: 'That is what I must do! That is generous: for a certain length of time you repeat: "I must!"' But it is in vain that you strain your energies, beat your brow and clench your fist, it all collapses very quickly as soon as your enthusiasm cools.

There are evasive resolutions, those where one says: 'I ought to!' Your heart wills and does not will. And deep within yourself you know already that you don't want it very much because you are somewhat afraid of it. It would have to come to you ready-cooked, like the quails in the desert. And I am not sure that scarcely is the quail in your mouth than you start protesting that it tires you and prevents you from attending to some very important business that is awaiting you. Because you had sown your resolutions (almost on purpose) in that stony ground in which you knew very well they could not take root.

There are distracted resolutions. They are taken with only a small part of yourself, the lightest part and the most superficial. They hardly engage your attention or your memory. Some of them are so distracted that you have forgotten them within the very hour, even just a minute later. How can you expect them to last?

There are resolutions which are non-resolutions, which have been perhaps in part extorted from you and which you know in advance that you will not keep. They are false resolutions which enable you to get rid of an interlocutor who is too insistent or too curious.

And then there are the serious resolutions, which, apparently, have all that they need to succeed: they are simple and precise, they take the realities of life into account, they express a positive will on your part: you even want them to succeed.

Have you seen how, on the surface of a lake, the ripples created by the fall of a stone fade away? It is the same with resolutions. Such at least is my experience, without exception. One manages to console oneself in a facile manner by telling yourself that after all, if they are kept for some days or for some weeks, there is always that much gained. I am not so sure about that.

For you risk ending up with reconciling yourself to it and coming to an agreement with your resolutions: you know in advance that you are taking them in fact for a week or for a month (mine have rarely lasted as long as that!). And this tacit surrender brands your spiritual life with barrenness. Repeated failure turns into scepticism for you and you end up by convincing yourself that you cannot change. One cannot avoid making ruts in ground that is too soft and over which one is going to and fro unceasingly.

It is in this way that tepidness becomes installed in a life. By dint of failing you tire yourself out and there is a danger that desire itself will abandon you. The stage is set now for you to start purring in your mediocrity and it may even be that you are content with it. You comfort yourself to some extent in that your mediocrity is 'honest', and you get to your feet again with that saying on your lips that is so convenient (and is responsible for so many desertions): 'After all, God in his goodness does not ask for all that much!' I know all about this because ten days earlier I was at that point. And how can you be sure of getting out of it? Really there is no reason why you should get out of it. You have entered, without noticing it, into a vicious circle. Your resolutions will not now be able to break it.

The angel of the church at Laodicea can then challenge you and repeat to you, to you personally: 'I know your works: you are neither cold nor hot. Would that you were either cold or hot! But because you are tepid and neither cold nor hot, I am going to vomit you out of my mouth' (Apoc. 3, 15-16). That is not something one likes to be told.

I was, then, well and truly on my guard against resolutions, whether great or small. In those hours of clear vision I hardly had any illusions left. And for good measure, right into the middle of the retreat there fell the statement, able to shatter the most tenacious illusions and setting in motion within me currents which I leave it to you to imagine: 'It is in six months' time that you will judge the value of the retreat.' True as one may know that to be, it leaves one shaken.

The last of my securities, almost my hope, crumbled away. Once again a precipice yawned beneath my feet. Was the patch of blue sky glimpsed in that rediscovered prayer going to cloud over again soon, grow dark and disappear, and was I going to settle back into the old ruts, when my resolutions had melted away as usual? Would this retreat be one more step in vain? As you see, I was not altogether overflowing with optimism...

Yet there remained that inner desire which had possessed me for several days, and also that experience that the vicious circle had, for a moment, been broken. At all costs I had to avoid it closing up again.

There are inspirations you receive just like that, all at once, and you are astonished at not having thought of them sooner, so simple and obvious do they appear...

In the course of one of those periods of prayer which were given to me, I heard myself formulating this line of reasoning. I don't mean that I formulated it myself: I didn't make it up, I received it. 'I cannot rely on my faithfulness, for experience has shown me that I am not faithful.' Archimedes said: 'Give me a fulcrum and I will lift the world.' That is indeed the nub of the matter. As fulcrum for these resolutions that never came to anything I only had the illusion of my faithfulness or of my desire for faithfulness. In other words, as fulcrum I only had emptiness and nothingness. How could I hope to 'lift' my life? So, I did not make any resolutions, deliberately. But things never stop where you think they will.

5. A toll-free motorway

I knew then that I was not faithful, and that I could not count on my faithfulness. But I knew also that God, for his part, is faithful. I had just experienced it through all that had happened since my first small 'yes'. God, who is faithful, had come himself to meet me. He had smoothed out my paths. This text from Isaiah came to my mind:

> There is a voice that cries:
> Prepare a road for the Lord through the wilderness,
> clear a highway across the desert for our God.
> Every valley shall be lifted up,
> every mountain and hill brought down;
> rugged places shall be made smooth
> and mountain ranges become a plain.
>   (Is. 40, 3-4)

Strange isn't it? Previously I had thought I ought to prepare a road, myself, for God to come into in my life –

an undertaking in which I was failing at every turn. Now I realised that everything was working in reverse, the Lord himself was preparing the road in me, clearing the paths, levelling the mountains and hills, filling up ravines and valleys. And what is more, he himself was inviting me and driving me along that highway which he had made in me, for me, like a toll-free motorway. I did not even feel the fatigue of the road. I was being 'carried in his arms' and 'for fear that my foot might strike against a stone' (Ps. 91, 12), all the obstacles were disappearing before me, in order to avoid my stumbling. I was being 'drawn with bonds of love' (Hos. 11, 4), with that delicacy and at the same time that prudence which marks dangerous stretches of road with beacons, avoids risky occasions and banishes temptations that would be too strong.

I experienced then a new joy, a happiness, as it were, at feeling myself in harmony, reconciled with myself. It was something quite indefinable, but, after moments of anguish or tension, confidence returned, a tranquil confidence, a sort of calm serenity. I had said to the Lord: 'Since I am not faithful I entrust myself to your faithfulness.' And I was feeling that this secret agreement had been ratified by God. It was being repeated to me at every instant by the interior peace in which God was strengthening me and which I was receiving from him as a marvellous gift.

And yet, at that time, I was burdened with depressing after-effects which were keeping vast wastes of sadness in store for me, dismal stretches of boredom to which I could see no end. An evening of solitude was a heavy trial for me. I dreaded that emptiness which seemed infinite and I took refuge in agitation: I 'did something', anything, to divert my

28

thoughts. At the end of those ten days the sadness was swept away, the void was filled, the boredom was forgotten. Even that painful weariness which had dogged my days and made me heavy-hearted, had disappeared, vanished. I was on top form, without a powder, a pill or a tablet. All I needed was a concentrate of prayer and trust in God's faithfulness.

I noticed it only much later, when my Jesuit Father put the oblique question to me: 'And your health?' Well, there it was! I had not yet become aware of it, this 'top form' that had returned by itself. You have received from God an unexpected and prodigious gift, you reap the full benefit of it, you experience a deep joy at it, but you do not even recognise it for what it is. Someone else has to help you put your finger on it. In other words, a brief passage from the Gospel had become applicable to my life without the slightest warning: 'Seek first the kingdom and the justice of God and all the rest will be given to you in addition' (Mt. 6, 33). I had sought prayer and in addition I was receiving health. No, I exaggerate: I had not so much 'sought' prayer, I had agreed to receive it and it had been given to me, with, in addition, something I was not expecting. I declare that this very simple fact quite overwhelmed me. It is also in this way that you discover how faithful God is. As for me, I had felt a flood of tenderness and astonished gratitude rising in my heart. God is faithful, to that point. Then why fear, what is there to worry about, for the future, if things turn out like this?

I returned home, cheerful, buoyant. I had been rejuvenated, if I may say so. I was feeding on my daily bread of prayer. Not that it was a matter of four hours a day of course: not many people have the leisure or can afford to create the leisure for that in daily life. No, but one hour a day, then, as occupations mounted up, half an hour.

But that much was maintained. I was well aware that it was being maintained in me, almost without me. I was keeping my taste for prayer. This experience was leaving its traces, that desire which continued to carry me along, recalling me, as if by instinct, to the daily appointment. I didn't find it at all troublesome; the effort called for was not great; it followed the direction of my desire.

At the same time, I knew how fragile it was. But I was not unduly worried, because my fulcrum was solid and kept coming back to mind: God was faithful. I recognised it with joy in all those little things which a new awareness enables you to discern. For instance, today I didn't think I would be able to find any time, and there it was, given to me, unexpectedly. And there was always that impression of a toll-free motorway, on which your cruising speed can be maintained without any great effort, by its own impetus: all you have to do is stick to the road, without using the brakes, without sudden acceleration, the steering-wheel turning smoothly. And the beauty of the countryside comes to break the monotony, renews your attention and arouses interest and joy.

Beyond all expectation, God was being faithful, with that delicacy and that freedom, which are his hallmark. Don't imagine for a moment, however, that every day I experienced sublime transports or mystical favours, far from it. On the contrary, very often I had to hold out during the allotted time in the midst of distractions and with that desire for something else which takes hold of you at times…

For the essential, God's fidelity upheld and reassured

my own. The part which fell to me, my 'effort', consisted simply in holding out, in not running away. But so many 'additions' which I discovered as the road twisted and turned, brought me encouragement, spurred me on, inspired me with fresh desire for prayer. Through the desire which had been given me I was receiving prayer. I was opening my hand and finding it full. My heart was filled to overflowing. I was offering a little of my time and it was gaining stability. A presence was making itself felt in my life and gradually changing it, first arousing desire, in order then to win consent. And the rest came in addition. Do not look for the reason: there is only one secret, one explanation for all that: it is that God is faithful, faithful in truth. And everything follows from that, flowing as if from a spring.

6. A false start

You will want to know what happened at the end of the six months. I was off to a good start. Everything seemed to be going smoothly. The auspices were good. Well, in spite of everything, before the six months were out, everything had collapsed once more. The reason was simple: about the beginning of Lent I found myself with some extra work. It was demanding, urgent work, which took up all my time. And I said to myself: 'Too bad! But I no longer have the time for it. The half hour which I was devoting to prayer now has to be sacrificed for work. Later on we shall see what happens.' It was true that I didn't have a minute to spare, I had so much work to do. This extra workload lasted for the whole of Lent.

But when Easter came round, with a little more leisure, I did not return to daily prayer. The charm had been broken. To tell the truth, I didn't let everything slide. I did not return to the previous situation in which prayer had been absent. I still had the chance for prayer from time to time and I took it willingly. The desire was still alive in me, but the enthusiasm for it was no longer strong enough, the slope was losing its gradient gradually, and my old laziness and inertia were once again hampering any revival.

Then things start to deteriorate rapidly. It is like watching an old house falling apart. It begins with a tile that breaks or falls off. The hole grows, the woodwork rots and falls in. And in no time at all the rain comes in, loosens the stones, frost expands the joints and cracks them and one fine day the whole wall collapses. 'And how great is its ruin' (Mt. 7, 27).

What had happened? Had my fine theories on God's faithfulness been illusory? Was it too good to be true, or at least to last? A poor consolation, after the hope I had glimpsed, to have persevered less than six months. Was it impossible to succeed? I am going to tell you what happened. I see it more clearly today and I understand better the trap in which I let myself be caught.

God's faithfulness is unshakeable. You will never exhaust or weary it. But you still have to take hold of his faithfulness and cling to it, and continue to trust in it, exclusively. Now the temptation, subtle, hidden, deceitful, consists in gradually regaining confidence in yourself, resuming control of your life, putting yourself at the helm. Thus you pass, imperceptibly, from one faithfulness to another: from the faithfulness of God, who is faithful, to your own faithfulness, and you are not faithful.

It is not surprising then that everything breaks down. God has not let you go, his faithfulness has not failed you; it is you who have let him go, who have failed him, because you exchanged the fulcrum of God's faithfulness which had succeeded in lifting your weight, for the fallacious fulcrum of your self-confidence. The line of reasoning, perhaps unconsciously to some extent, proceeds with an imperturbable logic, beginning with that little side-turning towards yourself from which all the rest takes its origin. And so I was landed with a load of important extra work. If I had clung to God's faithfulness I would have said: 'I do not know how I am going to manage it. But for you, Lord, it is no great difficulty: you will know quite well how to deal with it.' But I didn't say that, I said the opposite. Reviving some secret complicity already at work in me (I had already, for example, reduced my prayer time to a half-hour, deciding that that was quite enough) I decided: 'I have too much work. I can no longer pray, for lack of time.' What could God's faithfulness do then? I was no longer counting on it: I was steering my ship, planning my projects, doing my accounts and my calculations, by myself. Humanly speaking they were right, irrefutable. We all know that there are only twenty-four hours in a day, and that some of them must be devoted to food and sleep.

It was all perfectly logical, but it was that logic which kills and devastates, leaving behind it only ruins and death. However, the desire for prayer, thanks be to God, never left me. For the moment it was not enough to make me begin again. But I was waiting for a favourable opportunity. That was all I asked for, incapable of anticipating the grace which I was hoping for from a fresh retreat. Besides, my choice

33

was simple: I chose a rather longer retreat in which I was sure of being able to devote four hours again each day to prayer.

I looked forward to this retreat eagerly and I no longer experienced the slight apprehension of the previous year. I entered into it as a ship arrives in harbour: the anxieties and the difficulties of the crossing are over, the permanent risks of damage and the fear of shipwreck. But don't imagine that this boat, happily moored to the quay, had had me as the pilot who had guided it in the storms and had held it on its course against winds and high seas. No, I felt I was a passenger, incapable of any of the work, incapable of putting my hand to anything, just able to be taken as a passenger. I had been led to this harbour in which the desire for prayer was to be renewed, rebuilding in me what had crumbled during the months in which prayer had been too infrequent.

Once again assiduous prayer, of which I received the grace as on the first occasion, shook things up, putting my life back on the rails. Once again that change of focus was brought about in me, that restoration in which it is God who takes you back, rebuilds you, gives you fresh life. Once again I was having the experience of receiving everything from him, of being saved yet again.

Carried along by a very strong current of fraternal charity, by the quality of the prayer from your brothers and sisters, and above all by the Spirit of God who gives form to our prayer because 'we do not know how to pray as we should' (Rom. 8, 26), you find that you are praying more than four hours a day. That seems quite natural to you and is done without effort. Since, after all, in those eight days, you have nothing else to do, why not answer that call which is made to you in the depths of your being? That is the part which falls to you: some small 'yeses', joyful and easy, after which all the rest comes to you in addition.

That year it lasted a bit better and a bit longer. But I still didn't succeed in 'doing the trick'. Even before the holidays, once again I had given up. The holidays are rarely, at least in my experience, a time for spiritual renewal. At most, perhaps, they can maintain the cruising speed attained previously. But the state of mind which they foster hardly lends itself to a fresh beginning. I hardly prayed at all during those holidays.

I had to make a fresh beginning, start the car up again. The third retreat devoted to prayer enabled me finally to keep it up for the whole of the year. Or rather I received the ability to keep it up for the whole of the year and to be drawn down the slope by desire day by day.

7. Nothing like experience

Three retreats in a little more than two years is the price I had to pay to repatriate prayer to my life. To be more precise, I exaggerate when I say that it is I who paid the price. As you will have seen throughout my account, I did very little myself. Everything was given to me, including, and first of all, the desire to return to prayer. You may recall the miniscule 'yes', tiny and insignificant, which set everything in motion.

If you have opened this book it is probably because you too feel a certain call to prayer and because your own efforts have hitherto met with little success, or because you value prayer without being able to find time for it. Forgive my presumption in giving you some advice. It is, rather, a reflection on the experience which I had and which I want to share with you.

Don't imagine that you are going to succeed in prayer without paying the price. But you will have understood what I mean – or rather what the Lord means – by 'paying the price for it'. You too will have to utter some small 'yeses', tiny and insignificant; that is your part, as it was mine. But take care, it is there that everything can either start or dry up.

It matters little, it seems to me, whether you have had or not had a period in your life in which prayer was familiar to you. If that was the case, you begin with a slight advantage, for you already know some outskirts of the country to be explored and you have tasted something of the joy of it now and then. If not, you will discover it gradually, marvelling.

Convince yourself of one thing to begin with. If you have the desire to pray it is because God has put it into your heart. You have not found it all by yourself. It is he first of all who desires prayer for you. At the very outset this conviction sets you on firm ground: as for yourself, you may always be fluctuating, hesitating, turning back, putting it off. But God will never cease desiring prayer for you. Every step that you take you will find him ready to give you all that is necessary in order that you may achieve it, and in the first place the strengthening of your desire.

Then you must accept the fact that it requires time. There are times when I have difficulty in getting to sleep at night and stay awake for hours. I had asked the doctor for something mild that would help me to get to sleep on those nights of insomnia. He said: 'I'm going to give you something, but it would be better to take it regularly for a certain period in order to restore the natural function of sleep.' He was right. Intermittent dosing is decidedly less efficacious. A more sustained treatment gives better results.

I believe that this therapy can also be applied to 'restoring the function of prayer'. Treatment is called for. As for me, as you have seen, I took this treatment by means of the retreats which enabled me to rediscover prayer. How will it be with you? Don't be fooled into thinking that you will be able to succeed with 'a bit now and then', a few minutes gleaned from time to time. Follow the doctor's advice: undertake a treatment for your prayer which will be sufficient to 'restore its function' and give it back all its (supernatural) effects

To my mind that is the price you have to pay. Get yourself organised, set your life in order, cut out what needs to be cut out in order to take the time for a prayer treatment. Understand what I mean by 'taking the time'. It won't fall into your lap ready made.

Is it difficult? Certainly. Do obstacles mount up? What if they do? Does it seem impossible? I wouldn't be very surprised if it did. Do your responsibilities prevent you? Obviously. Does your desire diminish on closer examination? I am familiar with that reaction. Are you afraid? That is quite normal. Many things will cross your path and threaten to derail your decision. Don't worry: it would be surprising if it were otherwise. Be stubborn and hold fast humbly.

Then there are two things you have to do, which are well within your reach. The first consists in letting the desire for prayer grow in you until it becomes a passionate longing. Do not be afraid: it is the Lord who makes it grow in you. As for you, 'bustling about will not enable you to add one inch to the height' of your desire (cf. Mt. 6, 27). You have simply to say 'yes' to the rising desire in you. And for desire to rise, all you need do is ask and you will receive it: God is faithful and he will give it to you.

The second thing is to trust in God to smooth out your difficulties. If God wills it for you – and you must believe that he does – he will prepare the road for you, as he did for me. The path will probably be different from what you imagined: that is a good sign, for 'my thoughts are not your thoughts, and my ways are not your ways, says the Lord' (Is. 55, 8). Just be alert (to seize the opportunities) and available. Don't worry about the objections which will assail you at once. They will be many and at times pressing. Do not let yourself be pressed. Remain firm in the confidence that has been given you, without wishing to know anything else, without letting doubt take over. Here lies the war you have to wage, there and nowhere else. Above all never let yourself believe that you are going to succeed by dint of will power or cleverness: you will inevitably be laid low again.

You have entrusted your boat to Another: you have put him at the helm and given him your faith. If you take the rudder back you will not avoid the reefs or the shoals in which you will be stranded. Remember: it is when I took things back into my own hands that everything collapsed for me. Perhaps you will not avoid every mistake, and now and then you will take things back. When all is said and done, it isn't too serious: you will start again, from the beginning, in confidence. And you will keep your patience. It is what you have received that will last in your life, not what you have done by yourself. Such a confidence calls for a bit of humility.

The busybody is convinced that everything succeeds because of his own efforts. Often you will be the busybody and you will become aware of that fact only with difficulty: you will start thinking that you have progressed by your own strength or your own will power. Then you will come tumbling down very quickly. Pick yourself up and, with a sense of humour, smile at your vanity. But above all, do not take yourself seriously, still less fret at yourself. Fretting is the child of pride. No, simply smile at yourself and start again.

When St John Vianney happened to commit some small infidelity, he used to say to the Lord, with that very healthy humour of his: 'There you are, Lord, I have just played one of my tricks on you!' It is a good formula. I recommend it to you. It puts quite a few things in their proper place and avoids making them bigger than they really are.

Believe me, falls and setbacks are the best school of humility. They gradually teach you the truth about yourself (you are, I am, poor, weak and sinful) and distrust your own strength, 'this broken reed which pierces your hand when you lean on it' (Is. 36, 6). You will tell me that you know that you are weak. But there is nothing like experiencing the fact. Then gradually you will learn to rely only on the Lord, because 'it is in weakness that his power finds its opportunity' (2 Cor. 12, 9). And you will receive from that all that you need. You will receive 'all you hope for', as St Thérèse of Lisieux says. 'Buon voyage.'

II

Find the way to your heart again

Find the way to your heart again

The path sank into the wood, welcoming, intimate, shady. Generations of men had hollowed out its track with their steps. And, through having been trodden down, the vegetation was no longer growing. I am fond of these little paths. I was walking along it at my ease, one amongst the countless people who had walked there. Through the foliage the sun's rays chequered everything with shadow and light. The branches seemed to part of their own accord in order to open a passage for you and came together again over you, a protective arbour, a living hole which accompanies and guides you. The way is marked out: it will lead you where you intended to go. You have only to follow it.

And so I was walking. Curiously, the other paths, which crossed this one or branched off from it, had a different aspect. Their character was not the same. It was becoming almost impossible to go wrong. I was going deep into the forest. Soon a branch struck my face, then a creeper or a bramble wrapped itself round my ankle... another branch. From step to step the vegetation was gaining the upper hand, reconquering the ground that had been trodden down, the path was narrowing again, my beautiful path. I had to capitulate: branches, ferns, creepers, brambles interposed, blocking the intruder's passage. The path was becoming lost, eaten up by the vegetation. It needed clearing again with scythe or secateurs, at times with an axe.

Only the regular steps of walkers maintain a path, keep it open. Once it has vanished, assimilated to the life around it, hard work is needed to open it up again. And it will disappear just as quickly if it is not constantly trodden down. This path was the 'way to my heart'. It is closed up very quickly, discouraging my efforts. Wider, more welcoming, more comfortable, highways offered themselves to my spirit, to my steps, to my distraction. The way to my heart was overgrown, obliterated. I had forgotten its course. I had to clear it again. Thanks be to God, each step forward resurrected memories that had been buried, evoked that presence towards which I was walking. Beyond my forgetfulness, remembrance of the way was coming back to me.

There was a time in the past, a long time ago, when this way had been open. I would be afraid, recalling the memories of the first journey, of mingling old and new. So I will content myself with relating how the forgotten path was remade for me. In your life, is this 'way to your heart' to be recognised – to be rediscovered in the depths of oblivion – or to be discovered for the first time? Perhaps you have never ventured on it yet, or scarcely at all: too little in any case to recognise it. Do not worry: whether it be discovery or recognition, the process is the same and you will 'recognise' it in proportion to your discoveries. All you need is a little time: the signs that mark it are slight and uncertain. In order to mark this way and to prevent it becoming obliterated again, you will have to take it often, so that your steps may be impressed on it and get the better of the vegetation which will do its best to obliterate it. There are a lot of things to be said, and they ought to be said at the same time; an impossible synthesis. We will advance humbly, freeing each step in its turn, branch by branch, creeper by creeper, bramble by bramble.

Come. Come with me on the 'way to your heart', while I tell you about mine.

1. Listen to the silence

Here we are, at the spot.
With which bramble shall we begin? Or which branch?
Let us leave brambles and branches alone.
Let us sit down for a moment.
Listen.
Listen to the silence.
Breathe the silence, in and out.
Plunge into the silence.
Welcome and enjoy the silence.

In this corner of the forest the noises of life and of the world come to you muted and from a distance. They do not break the silence, they give it its weight. Neither the wind in the branches nor the singing of the birds break the silence. They live in it and enable it to be tasted.

Taste the silence.

The 'way to your heart is frightened by the noises of humans, it hides itself from their chattering.

Today, in the silence of the forests, people make their way with music in their ears. Not to listen, but for the sake of creating a certain mood, for the noise, like a drug, to exorcise silence. For at times silence makes people afraid and oppresses them. Silence leaves you alone with yourself: a difficult company. I know something of that. Before the experience I have told you about, a background of music or of talk accompanied my life. I didn't listen to it, or very little. But it had become automatic. Like the cigarette of the inveterate smoker, who no longer knows that he is lighting it. I furnished the silence, with noise, no matter what; with classical music or the radio. A noise which reassured, a sort of presence, facing me or at my side.

In order to rediscover the way to my heart I had to conquer silence again, turn my radio off. I had taken it to that first retreat (subsequently I didn't even put it in my luggage). But it was only for the news. Besides I was not often in my room. I liked to walk slowly through the grounds, amidst the trees and the birdsong, or to sit on a bench in the fresh air, beneath the autumn sun. A natural cure, one of silence. Many hours of that rediscovered prayer were spent thus.

We were then in silence all the day, during meals as during free time. A beneficent silence, which envelops you and gradually pacifies you, unravels your knots for you, sets you free. Oh! that silence of long retreats!

Sometimes it is very trying during the first few days, when the habit is not formed. Your tongue itches: it would be so comforting, so reassuring, so beneficial to give yourself up for a moment to a spiritual colloquy: just another way of flying from silence. Fortunate are you when the brother or the sister to whom you speak puts his finger on his or her lips with a bright smile. Swallow the words you have prepared, your useless chatter (which probably seemed to you then imperative, irreplaceable, vital!) and rejoice in that silence, that gift of silence which your brother or your sister has renewed for you. Stay with your silence.

The silence of those grounds was a precious help to me. That sort of return to nature was beneficial to the city-dweller that I am. It contributed to re-educating the taste for silence in me. It is there that the way to my heart began to reopen for me. Then the silence around you begins to seem like a haven of peace. Whereas you used to fly from it, now you begin to seek it out. You feel that you are coming back to life, as if noise had gradually suffocated you and silence, like a prolonged deep breath, is renewing you and purifying you.

Yet it happens that on certain days, especially on certain evenings, silence is a burden. I remember winter evenings on a mountain. The snow muted still further the slight noises in the distance. The silence really could be heard, like a very particular invitation to the expectant ear. It took on an unwonted density and weight, as the fir branch laden with snow no longer responds to the call of the breeze until it has shaken off the coating which paralyses it. Every word then seems indiscreet, almost a profanation, as when out of curiosity one raises a heavy curtain which parts and then falls back again. It loses all resonance and is soon muted in the silence which takes things and people back into itself.

An oppressive silence at times, in which there rises a touch of anguish, to the rhythm of your heart beats. Smile at this anguish: it is a reminder of a solitude which a short while before you could not bear. Smile, for this silence is heavy, if you welcome it, with a presence which gradually reveals itself to you and comes to stay with you, on condition that your heart is at peace. If, on the contrary, you feel that agitation is winning you in this silence, that it is too much for you, do not persist: straining oneself does not serve any useful purpose. Go and speak for a moment with someone whom you are not likely to inconvenience. Do not disturb the silence of a brother or sister: there is someone at your disposal for that. And then, as soon as you are calm again, at peace, come back to silence.

Just as your lungs hanker after pure air, your heart desires this silence. Let that desire grow in you, let it impose itself on you as a necessity. Cultivate it: it is given to you, a condition for the meeting, an obligatory prelude to prayer, and you feel that it is increasing in you.

2. Create silence

External noise, a sort of false pretence that had become familiar, had turned me away from the way to my heart. I had had to find that silence of things and of people again. But in fact exterior silence is not enough. It is only a first step. True silence is interior and achieving it is difficult in other respects too.

Scattered to the four winds of fantasy and meaninglessness, the imagination develops the habit of flying off at the first call, at the least solicitation. It wanders in vagabond fashion at every excuse and without any excuse, in trains of fantasy that at times are strange and unforeseen.

When I need to call upon it, my imagination reveals itself

poor, rather barren, desperately slow. But at the moment of prayer it takes its revenge, with an unsuspected fecundity. A film in quick motion, like those old newsreels which are resurrected today, pictures of a world in a feverish hurry, insatiable, distraught, a caricature. I think about everything, no matter what. Questions arise, problems demand a solution, curiosity strays hither and thither, finding its pasture in everything and in nothing, maintaining an ill-defined movement, jumping from one thing to another and in general having a fine time, taking its flight, whirling and fluttering, from the important to the urgent, from the essential to the basic.

I was quickly discouraged. What use was there in persisting when imagination is so unbridled and when one gets nowhere? It is called 'the madcap imagination'. But do not be taken in. It is no madcap. It is only caught in the trap, encouraged by your betrayals, strengthened by your meaninglessness. It accentuates the slope of your capitulations. In this sense it confronts you with quite an accurate picture of yourself: that of dispersion, of superficiality. It is not your imagination which is straying, being distracted and making the job hard for you. No, it is your very being which is running off and dissipating itself, and your imagination follows in its footsteps, along a facile road which does not lead anywhere. You will only master your imagination if you begin by putting your whole being in order again, begin truly to 'exist' again.

At one time I liked to bathe my prayer in nature, amidst trees and birds. That, as I realise now, established me in a pleasant euphoria, tranquil and scented with pastoral symphonies. But under the cover of prayer I was tasting, first and foremost, the pleasures of the countryside. Doubtless nature was revealing somewhat of its Creator's face. But trees, branches and flowers were speaking to me in the first place of odd shapes, evoking pictures of anything and everything, while the birds were drawing my eyes by their flight or their unsuspected presence, and soothing my ears by their singing. What was left of prayer? 'When you pray, go into a room by yourself, shut the door, and pray to your Father who is there in the secret place' (Mt. 6, 6). The 'room by yourself' possesses some virtues. It is discreet, certainly, and hidden and does not lend itself to the small conceits which flatter our vanity. Only the Father is there, in the secret place, with you. He is the only one to know.

This 'room' is not a choice food either for the imagination. Bare, somewhat dark, it fosters recollection and favours interior silence. Its disposition soon becomes familiar to you and one is less distracted there than elsewhere.

For my part I have taken the course of arranging a 'prayer corner' for myself. It is bare and functional. A crucifix or a picture which speaks to you is enough, to catch your eyes when they wander. It is almost always there that I pray, at least for the daily period of prayer which is offered me. Gradually the place itself introduces you to prayer and takes on a soul. As soon as you retire to it, a tranquillisation, as it were, is effected in you, a certain interior silence, which can shorten the preliminaries.

The 'room by yourself' sets you on the way to your heart when you go into it, for it is that interior part of yourself where the presence of the Father meets you, more intimate to you than your own heart. There God and you live in the silence which prepares for meetings.

Are you thereby guaranteed against distractions, against that kaleidoscope of thoughts and of preoccupations which at times invades you? The 'room by yourself' favours interior silence. It does not suffice to ensure it. To tell the truth, interior silence always remains fragile. Let a preoccupation that is at all urgent, let a care appear in the clear sky of your recollection, and straight away you begin to wander off: you construct plans, you look for solutions, you prepare a defence, you argue. What makes up your daily life invades you, not as food for but as an obstacle to your prayer. It is the familiar array of 'distractions in prayer'. Don't fret about it any more than is necessary. For if you do worry about it you are only adding one more care and you are compromising recollection and silence a little further.

With calm and gentleness, come back to your prayer. Without any reproach just say: 'Forgive me, Lord, I was off again!' That is all. That is enough. Come back. Come back once, twice, ten times, a hundred times, as often as is necessary. And do not let yourself be discouraged. Do not say: 'I shall never get there!' It is true that you will never get there. But no one, and especially not your Father who is there, in your own heart, in the secret place, is upbraiding you on that account, nor even asking you not to be distracted. Come back. That is enough. Nothing more is needed. Nothing more is to be hoped for. There is your faithfulness, coming back every time that you wander off in your thoughts. Like a silly but faithful dog which always comes back to its master's feet and moves him to tenderness by his look. Do not grow weary of coming back. Your Father will not grow weary of welcoming you back. He knows of what stuff you are made, he will not be surprised. He likes your persistence, in coming back to him. He alone possesses faithfulness without default: as for you, like every human person, you only possess the faithfulness of your fresh beginnings. Be faithful in that way.

I wager that then, one time or another, your Father who is in the secret place, will make you the gift of a moment of interior silence. Then, peaceful and concentrated, but never straining, you will experience that joy of feeling yourself entirely recollected, pulled together, unified in a single purpose, in a single thought, in a single attention, which nothing or almost nothing comes to disturb. And if a moment of distraction assails you, it remains on the surface and does not reach the depths of your heart. Almost anything is enough for you to come back to that one thing necessary, to that better part which is being offered to you.

Do not think however that thereby you are established now in a silence which nothing will be able to reach any longer, that your imagination has been definitively disciplined and that you are master of it. No, the gift which is given you is fragile. You have to carry it with fear and trembling if you are not to break its charm. Do not think either that you have succeeded, that you have reached the point, by yourself, of reducing imaginations and dreams to silence. For your part all you have done is lend your being, the heart of your being, to the work of Another: it is he who has pacified your mind, almost without you. If you receive it truly as a fragile gift, it will be able gradually to bear fruit. As for you, you do your part by avoiding absorbing or futile preoccupations, by often taking the way to your heart again. Often, that is to say, not only when you have decided to pray, often in the course of the day, very often, as often as you possibly can. An interior and attentive look is enough, although it lasts but an instant.

In this way the way to your heart becomes familiar to you. You need but little effort to sink into it, far from things and noise. And the more you plunge thus into the heart of yourself, the more also silence is confirmed in you and you acquire the taste for it. Not for the silence itself, but because that silence enables you to taste a little more closely your Father's presence in the utmost depths of yourself, there, in the secret place, in the silence which he has given you and in which he lives.

You will know (perhaps) periods of easy silence and others, at times very long, during which the combat will be unending. What does it matter? Interior silence is a free gift. You cannot demand it as your due nor complain if it is withdrawn from you. Be content with coming back to it unceasingly, because your Father does not weary of being present in the heart of your being, at the root of yourself. The rest, in the last resort, does not count any longer.

3. The void of my heart

The way to my heart. I have had to find it again in my own heart, in those depths inside one of which one often knows nothing. Have you had the experience of living on the outside of yourself, almost without roots, like those blades of grass on the rocks which have found a scrap of soil and have taken root in it. If you pull at them just a bit, everything comes out, plant and soil, and there remains just bare rock, without even a scar. This is a precarious, superficial life.

Nothing was happening in my life. Things were happening, but nothing remained from them or almost nothing, like the grass in the cleft of the rock. People also passed by without entering, without pushing the door, fugitive shadows which left no trace in me, still less any scar. For there was no wound in me that I admitted to: I had made myself invulnerable.

As for myself, I did not go inside or very little. I was living on the outside, skilfully avoiding what would have wounded me. The days and the months and the years passed, monotonously. I retained some impression from them, for you cannot avoid the wrinkles of time, but I did not change. I was living on the surface, invulnerable. One is not invulnerable without a breastplate. It is made of indifference, insensibility, chilly precaution. And soon your breastplate is sheltering only an empty heart. Your interior becomes strange to you. You no longer find yourself at home there; you are ill at ease. You scarcely venture in. You become an empty shell, just like those old willows at the edge of streams, with gnarled and dishevelled head, on a hollow trunk, a mere covering for emptiness. An empty heart is not only an insensitive heart, it becomes progressively an absence of heart, a void in the place of the heart.

Do not deceive yourself. There are quite a few other ways of living like that, on the outside of yourself. As for me, it came about as I have just told you. For others, the experience is different, but the result can be the same. In the place of invulnerability, you may cultivate another person, as an alibi. Then he becomes for you a thing, a means of asserting yourself. You use him, make him serve you. You are vaguely aware of that void in your own heart and you seek to fill it up. More exactly to stuff it, for you will not succeed in filling it. Others are then material for stuffing. You pump them, pursue them with an obstructive attentiveness which you baptise as altruism, generosity, the feeling and the need for others. Now they serve only to stuff that void in yourself, but in vain. For the void resists and does not let itself be inhabited. You try then to multiply your contacts. Still in vain. The void is still empty, the hollow becomes even hollower.

Then you reach the point of accusing others, interiorly at first, then out loud, of not responding to the advances of your 'friendship', of your 'generosity'. You make them responsible for your own interior emptiness, as if they were not interested in you. But in fact, you just increase your own solitude, because no other person can fill the void in your heart.

Escaping into things is another way of avoiding the issue. And you tend to escape into the most banal things. You possess them simply for possession's sake. You project yourself into them and they take the place of a reason for living. You accumulate, you collect, a consenting and exploited victim of the consumer society. The difference is not so great between an empty heart and one that is crammed with things. The sign is inverted, as in mathematics, but the reality is the same. You still imagine that what you do not yet possess is alone able to fill up your empty heart. This is an illusion. Things cram your heart without being able to fill it.

Do you know the ancient myth of the Danaids? They had been condemned by Zeus to fill up a bottomless jar – an impossible and derisory task. The only difference is that you are not condemned to it: it is you yourself who condemn yourself to it. You have become that empty and bottomless jar, and you are trying desperately to fill it up with things. You think that you possess them, whereas it is they that possess you and they conspire to close the way to your heart.

A little bit of poverty could set you free, but you are not aware of that. How then could you begin to desire it?

A void instead of a heart – and you do not realise it. You would have to enter into yourself for an instant, undertake a sort of interior exploration, in order to become aware of the emptiness which is in you. But the hour for that has not yet arrived. This superficial life is enough for you. You have not known any other, or you have forgotten it, once the rather ridiculous generosities of youth were over.

I did not so much have the impression of an empty heart, I had inured myself to vulnerability. I was living in things which possessed me, busy, at times engrossed. It was almost a satisfying life. I enjoyed the pleasures of the passing moment, warding off boredom and criticism with a wave of my hand. Confusedly I dreaded that return to myself, the best thing being still not to think about it.

And then a day came, in the course of one of those retreats of which I have spoken.

That day we were invited to an examination of conscience. It was not the first. To be sure what I knew as examination of conscience resembled for the most part an inspection of an iceberg with a telescope. You can only see the bit above the surface of the water. You don't reach the depths and what you think you are seeing is only the reflection of what is above the surface.

And so, I made an examination of conscience. It was

quite painless, and very respectful of secret recesses. It was a question of each person asking pardon, in a fraternal meeting, for the mistakes of his apostolic life. I looked for something that I could say. Certainly prayer had already penetrated into my life to some slight extent. But not to the point of bringing that void in me to the light of day. I wished to express myself honestly. And so I was rather looking for the happy phrase, the apt and well turned formula. And then it came to me and I said in my turn: 'Lord, I ask your forgiveness for all the facile statements which have hidden the emptiness of my heart.'

Now, today, I realise it was actually nothing to do with my apostolic life. This statement, this cry thrown out to mercy, went much deeper: it did not so much tell of my activity, as reveal my own heart. It would not be an exaggeration to say that it revealed it to me. For at the same time as the words were forming themselves on my lips, I was becoming aware, to the point of dizziness, of the void in my heart. Never yet had it appeared to me so plainly. Until then I had kept it thoroughly tamed. I was experiencing it suddenly. I am not exaggerating when I speak of felling dizzy. When the void surprises you thus, suddenly, unexpectedly, you do not have time to prepare yourself for it, to inure yourself to it. It attacks you brutally, the more so that in an instant it brings home to you the inanity, the inconsistency of all the rubbish by which you were letting yourself be ensnared and on which you were resting your security, indeed your well-being.

It is a painful discomfort, which lasts and reduces to nothing the structure of alibis which until then served as a skeleton. Illusions are shattered and you are left alone with yourself, that is to say, confronting that void which appears where you thought you were finding your heart. This shattering is salutary: it establishes you in the truth about yourself and allows you to take off your breastplate with your illusions. It is a grace which is given you and which you have to take hold of. Perhaps, by the normal ways of reflection and of self-examination one may arrive at the same result, but that would doubtless take years. There, on the contrary, I was having the experience of that sudden light which was given to me and which was taking hold of me to a depth which I would never have attained by my own powers. That light is both painful and good. It clears away false appearances and lays bare 'that which is', in truth. It is a harsh truth. And if at the outset, I was experiencing a giddy void, of which until then I had been unconscious, at least the way was now free. At the very least, although a little cluttered up, the way to my heart was opening to me a little more.

4. The head and the heart

The way to your heart does not pass through your head. A curious way of putting it, you are no doubt thinking. It is not however a taste for paradox but a profound reality, which is not easy to talk about, because the things of the head are spoken about more easily than those of the heart.

Suppose for a moment that Bernard declares his love for Sylvia by speaking to her with his head. The conversation might go something like this: 'Sylvia, I have a declaration to make to you. Reflecting the other day on our meeting, I sought to analyse what we said to one another. There are deep forces in us which seem to be bringing us together. Our desires are, in part, similar. In any case, it seems to me that we can reconcile them. I find that the moments that we pass together are positive. Our exchanges reach what is central in each of us. And physical attraction plays its part likewise. The type of woman I had in mind up to that time corresponds quite well with what you are. I can then conclude: it seems to me that I love you.'

This is clearly idiotic. You don't make a declaration of love with your head. A look, a smile, a feeling of joy, an awkward 'I love you', say so much more and say it so much better. 'Pierre is too intellectual', a youngster, now baptised, said of me not long ago, before his conversion. And another: 'You talk and you talk; you are constantly on show.' I was like that. In fact, I'm still like that to some extent, too much, perhaps.

When my head was functioning, I was quite at ease in the land of knowledge, as it were. The head in fact likes abstractions. It turns smoothly in them like a motor swimming in oil, but it is turning in the abstract. And abstraction is what is left when life has gone off somewhere else. There are people like that, who reason (excuse me, I was going to write 'like a clanging cymbal': see St. Paul, 1 Cor. 13, 1) on the things of God. I was one of them, to a large extent, and that took up quite a large part of my life, at the risk even of leading me astray. It gave me the illusion of contact with God. I was talking about God. As a priest I was even talking about him quite often: that was my job, almost my *raison d'être*. And I used to say, it seems to me (I am duly ashamed of my vanity), quite good things about

59

him. My head spoke, and I let myself be carried along by it. After all, the 'subject' was God, what better thing could one hope for?

I am reminded now (but then I was not aware of it) of the passage from the prophet Isaiah quoted by Jesus: 'This people honours me with its lips, but its heart is far from me' (Is. 29, 13; Mk 7, 6). The head may talk about God without the heart drawing near to him.

So we must pass from the head to the heart. It is not a question of sentimentality, which is no better than using the head. You don't enter into prayer with your head but with your heart; not with what you know, but with what you are living; not with ideas or words, but with your own person. It is you who pray. Then you let go of your reasoning, your fine ideas, your learned deductions, preferring silence to facile words. The value of prayer is not judged by the words you say, for your words do not always carry with them the deepest part of yourself. On the contrary, it may be that they are a means of avoiding involving yourself in what you are saying, a loophole. Ideas and words are things that you project outside of yourself. Your lips utter them, but they may prevent the other person having access to your intimacy. They may prevent you yourself from having access to it. They become a protective screen, like the smoke screens which hide a ship from enemy eyes. Words give security and lead astray. They divert from the essential and thus create illusion.

In this way, your lips may be functioning without your heart being involved. It remains a stranger, it keeps itself in reserve, it preserves itself, it refuses to give itself. The refusal is not explicit, perhaps not even conscious: it is camouflaged by words which lose themselves in their very brilliance. But the refusal is there nonetheless, and it shuts you up in a defence system which you do not acknowledge. Finally you keep your heart for yourself, even when you think that you are giving it. Words, your head with its reasoning, close up your heart.

That is where I was. Once more, I was in need of liberation. Fortunately for me, I was often put on my guard, and, quite simply, I tried to silence my brain. At the beginning, you do not know how to set about it. I was continuing to cultivate, drawn on by my favourite devil, fine phrases and well turned formulae. Nonetheless, each time I caught myself doing it, I used to stop short: 'Forgive me, Lord, for coming back to that. Open my heart and take hold of it!'

In fact, you have to pass like this from a prayer that you 'make' to a prayer which you 'receive', which is 'given' to you, a prayer for which you no longer have to make 'your meanings work'. I was content then with halting each time my head went off again. You may have seen trotting races on television. At certain moments the horse, abandoning the mastery it has acquired in training, passes suddenly from a trot, which is not natural to it, to a gallop, which is much easier. Then the driver pulls on the reins, forces the animal's neck to leave the upright position, moderates it, brings it back to that trot which is so difficult to keep up, and the horse resumes the rhythm imposed by the hand of man, until the next deviation. It is a long and thankless breaking in, and one which is never perfectly accomplished. But what does it matter? In the same way we must not kill ourselves trying to keep silent, if not, the result would be worse than the evil to be cured.

Like the driver keeping his horse under control, you learn from day to day to pray with your heart, with much silence and many silences.

Matthew's Gospel says: 'Do not go babbling on like the heathens who imagine that the more they say the more likely they are to be heard' (Mt. 6, 7). For us, the term 'babbling on' means repeating things unceasingly. People often say that an elderly person who is losing his memory is babbling on. But this is not what is meant here. Jesus means that the number of words is of no importance in prayer, on the contrary, it becomes an ill-considered and loquacious business which is trying to influence God. It is basically heathen and barren, for it counts more on humans, on the human capacity to convince, than on God and on his love. 'Your Father knows what you need, before you ask him for it' (Mt. 6, 8).

But there is a quiet and calm sort of repetition which helps to enter into true prayer. A word, a saying, a phrase, a memory, can speak to your heart. You repeat them, within you, to extract from them slowly all their spiritual savour. They cannot, on a single occasion, yield all the sap which they contain for you. It must be squeezed out to the last drop. You come back to them, you let the word or the phrase resound deeply within you for as long as is necessary for them to bear all their fruit, for them to nourish your heart: you 'ruminate' on them. And while the word spoken to you is penetrating, let its last echoes fall silent. Then take it up again. As long as it speaks to your heart, as long as it feeds and holds your attention, stay there, profit by it.

You do not have to react to it. Don't look for explanations for it. Do not draw conclusions from it. Turn away from any developments. Be content with repeating the word in the depths of your heart, it alone, slowly. Do not add anything to it. It is the word which accomplishes its work in you. If it is a Word of God, drawn from the Bible, it penetrates into you to the very depths of your being, finding again the Spirit who inspired it originally and who is guiding you in order that it may bear the fruit of truth in you.

In the end you will see that you need few words to animate a long prayer. But from these few words, which have nourished your heart and your prayer, you will have drawn all that God had put into them for you. So, gradually, I was training myself to pass from head to heart. And I was noticing at the same time that I no longer had to 'make' a prayer (to 'manufacture' it myself), but to 'receive' it, as a gift which leaves you marvelling and confused. You learn more quickly than you would believe. It is not difficult, precisely because there is nothing to 'make'. But it still has to be learnt.

If I tell you these things, through the experience which has been given to me, it is in order that you in your turn may have this experience, and not be content to 'know' things simply through reading them. Read, have the experience yourself, prolong it for the time necessary, and then pass on to what follows and, again live the experience. Perhaps it will take you some time to reach the end of this book. What does it matter? What does it matter even if you decide to stop in the middle, if you have succeeded in entering into prayer, if the moment has come at which prayer is given to you, as it was given to me?

5. In the furthest depths of your heart

The way to your heart. You must go deep, very deep. Enter into interiority, into the intimacy of yourself. It is not a matter of a complacent look. But through travelling towards the deepest part of yourself, there is created in you, as it were, a complicity. The way to your heart becomes familiar to you. It is easier for you to take it, and its course (going back into yourself) becomes quicker. You arrive more speedily at the heart of yourself, with that new quality of recollection which is given to you. The preliminaries to prayer are simplified, the entry into prayer calls for a less intensive effort. And on the way to your heart, that beloved way, on which you are advancing with joy, peace comes to meet you. The peace of the heart's depths, where the surface waves, as for a submarine that has submerged, no longer reach and are stilled. The experience of peace of heart was given to me suddenly, as if a wave of a magic wand had in an instant changed the whole of my interior set-up.

I had just been experiencing that void in my heart which facile utterances had covered over for a moment, that dizziness, that unfathomable abyss, where it seemed to me that I was perishing. Suffering, crippled, at a loss, I no longer had any resource left but to plunge into prayer, desperately, and to shout my cry of distress. It was an arid and desolate prayer, such as I had never known before. Yet at the same time, it was a haven of hope in which I regained life. For a long time I stayed thus, before the void in my heart which God himself, in my prayer, was not filling up. All at once, in that cold which was freezing my heart, there rises, as it were, a gust of warmth which wraps me round and submerges me. A word makes itself heard to me, clear, distinct, luminous, obvious: 'You have not abandoned me to the power of death!' A lightning impression: everything in me capsizes. The light is too strong, too sudden, too unhoped for. Like the shockwave that carries away everything in its path, a sob rises to my throat: tears of infinite gratitude, of joyful confusion, overflowing from a heart that has passed in the twinkling of an eye from the giddy void to total plenitude. A sudden experience of that love of the Father which had not ceased to seek me out and which was reaching me in the furthest depths of my infidelities. Instantaneously I understood that the Father's love was snatching me from the power of death which had begun to weigh upon me, stifling my half-formed desires, blocking my attempts to rise. Never had I seen so clearly the ruins which had accumulated. With lucidity I saw also from what sort of ruins I was being saved. At the very instant my heart was filled with peace, the peace of God which passes all understanding and which was keeping my heart and my thoughts in Christ Jesus (Phil. 4, 7).

Since then it has never left me. When it seems to withdraw to a distance and when worry or cares besiege it, it is enough for me now to take again the 'way to my heart', the way to that depth in which the Father's love manifests itself, for it to be born anew and for the eddies to be stilled.

It does not suppress suffering: it is the peace of God which helps one to bear it. It does not resolve problems: it relativises them and simplifies them, reducing them to more modest proportions. It is not a conquest, as a psychotherapy might be which would gum up the anguish: it is a free gift, fragile and wonderful, which truly surpasses all that one can imagine. It is the peace of God, always within reach. Yet you cannot take hold of it: it takes hold of you and comes to dwell in you.

It was rising from a depth that had nothing in common with anything I knew; a depth which was at once radical intimacy and secret paradise, inaccessible to my unaided efforts; a depth which was being offered to me by the good pleasure of him who was residing there. A depth which reaches to the root of being, to that level at which the soul is joined to the body, at which the flesh is united with the spirit. At that depth a presence is revealed and radiates, but not a strange and disturbing presence like that of an intruder. Quite the contrary, it is the presence at once familiar and mysterious of a guest whom one discovers to the extent that he has disclosed himself.

A comparison, a very weak one, it is true, comes to mind. In *The Mysterious Island,* Jules Vernes' shipwrecked sailors become aware, again and again, with some anxiety, of a 'presence' which is an invisible protection for them, which deals with desperate situations, frees them from insurmountable dangers. Some considerable time later they find out that it is the mysterious Captain Nemo, watching over this handful of men from the depths of the cave in which the 'Nautilus' has come to rest. But what a distance between this protective presence and the presence in the depth of myself of him who thus, but with an incomparable delicacy, protects and pacifies, upholds and animates, of him whom one finds at the heart of being, because he creates being and creates life: of him who establishes his dwelling in each of us (cf. Jn 14, 23).

And one understands Augustine's saying, transmitting his own experience of the interior guest: *Intimior intimo meo*, more interior than my own inmost depths. It is at such a depth that God dwells in the heart of a person and no one can force his way into its citadel unless God himself reveals his presence and opens the access to that mystery. An enclosed garden, a sealed fountain, which no human industry can attain: the place of the presence. Formerly, for the people of the Old Covenant, that place was the Temple at Jerusalem, where God made his name dwell, where the cloud had marked that presence and hidden it from sight (1 Kgs 8, 11). In three days, in his death and resurrection, Jesus had destroyed that temple to rebuild another, not made by human hands. 'And he was speaking of the temple of his body' (Jn 2, 21). To those who 'are not born of any human stock or by the fleshly desire of a human father', but are the offspring of God himself (Jn 1, 13), through faith in him whom God the Father had sent, Jesus proclaims: 'If anyone loves me they will keep my word, and my Father will love them, and we shall come to them and make our dwelling with them' (Jn 14, 23). It is humankind now who is the place of the presence, for 'you are the temple of God' (1 Cor. 2, 17).

There is a depth at which God reveals himself and yields himself: as the Creator, at the root of being, but especially as the Father, at the origin of filial adoption, where we become son in the Son. A mysterious image buried deep in an interior world of which the features have been obscured by the ravages of time and the power of evil, like those old photographs which have faded over the years through the action of light. It is an image rediscovered in the heart to heart of prayer which purifies and renews the resemblance; an image in which no narcissism comes to turn back in upon itself in proud feelings of complacency; an image which is also a real presence, a presence which grows, while human sufficiency diminishes.

God present in the heart of humankind. Thus prayer is no longer a monologue or introspection. The way to my heart becomes a quest of Someone, of him who brings me into being and loves me to the point of making himself more intimate to myself than I myself am. Thus the desire for the meeting grows, in that deepest part of myself, where God speaks to my heart.

The angel with the flaming sword no longer guards the garden gate to forbid you entry to it. You yourself are that garden, in which the intimacy of your Father is offered to you as he walks once again with you at the time of the evening breeze (Gen. 3, 8; 24). Or rather, that garden, the existence of which in the utmost depths of your heart you were ignorant of, is revealed to you and opens itself to your desire. Your Father is with you, and he sees in the secret place.

III

Prayer is a gift of God

1. Do you not know how to pray?

'Lord, teach us to pray,' the disciples asked Jesus (Lk. 11, 1). I found it easy to understand their request. But Jesus' answer, to some extent, puzzled me: 'When you pray, say: Father, who art in heaven...' As if it could be enough to use a fixed formula, however fine, to be able to pray. For me, I must admit, it had become somewhat mechanical. I knew it by heart, all too well, and its words were worn, like those familiar objects, rounded at the corners through much use. I was not unaware that I had to search beyond the formula and that Jesus' words were intended to direct the spirit, giving it a framework, guiding it in prayer, not enclosing it in the straitjacket of a sacrosanct formula. Certainly, at that moment, I had not yet found 'the way to my heart' again. But in the end the difficulty left me nonplussed and with little confidence. How could I hope to persevere in prayer if I did not know how to pray? At once the undertaking appeared to me doomed to failure. And that, in part, was a pretext for postponing all attempts to make a fresh entry into prayer: the chances of success were too slender, I thought. What was the point of making an attempt, an effort which I did not think would last very long?

What then was the timetable of my rediscovered prayer? Had I suddenly 'found out how to pray? No, and I would have found it very awkward to give an account of it, to explain how I set about praying. Yet, for all that, I was praying…

The paradox was real: I was praying, but I did not know how to pray. So, what was happening? At that time I did not have a clear understanding of my experience, but now, looking back, I think I can say something about it.

What were the words of my prayer? I scarcely remember, certainly they were not remarkable. They were quite simple words, poor, without poetry, everyday words, words that I repeated at leisure. I relied on them to some extent, they upheld me, gave me some assurance. For the weak man, or one who is subject to vertigo, a small support is enough to strengthen his steps or to ensure his equilibrium. Such then were the words of my prayer: a small support, sufficient and fragile, indispensable and without importance.

I have forgotten them. What does it matter? It is not the words that count. It is not the words that make prayer. They are not even its framework. They were for me like the tailor's needle. It's not the needle that holds the garment together. Once the job is completed the needle is put away and forgotten. So it is with words. Words have no importance. It is even better to forget them, otherwise they could take the place of prayer. Words will never enable you to pray.

Bodily position? Far be it from me to neglect that. It has some importance, for you are also body and you have to pray with your body. Without it you exhaust yourself trying to pray 'against' it. Then it rebels and becomes a hindrance to prayer. When one makes good use of it on the other hand it helps and favours it. It is good to know that and to make one's body a good servant of prayer. But I had not yet learnt to make good use of it. It helped me hardly at all. It frequently distracted my attention, interrupting a recollection, calling for a change of position. I found it difficult to stay put. If I prayed, it was not because of my bodily position, that came from elsewhere, in due course. If you want to pray, don't begin by learning postures. That is not the right way.

Methods certainly have some advantages, for some people at least. They are precise, they propose an ordered procedure, a sort of plan of action, more or less systematic: firstly, secondly, thirdly... But, more often than not, I found them an obstacle. You risk being more attentive to the method than to prayer, or again, and this is more serious, you believe that it is the method which makes prayer, and you find yourself more hindered than helped. The lighter the methods are, the more they let themselves be forgotten, the more they leave you free and hence the better they are. Perhaps the best method is not to have any.

Recourse to oriental methods, such as yoga or transcendental meditation is also recommended. They are physical and psychological techniques. They can favour a certain self-mastery, a certain 'concentration', a certain recollection. But they are not in any position to accord entry into prayer. Prayer comes from elsewhere. Taken as an external aid, like crutches, they can help some people. I myself have tried yoga (after I had found prayer again), and then I stopped doing it. I became aware of the danger of ascribing prayer to a human effort, a natural process, in the way that laboratory techniques make it possible nowadays to learn a foreign language. But that is not the way one learns prayer.

There will always be a gulf, a hiatus, a leap to be made, for entry into prayer: God is never on the same level as you. Even if you find this presence at the end of the way to your heart, it remains a fragile presence and one that is but little understood. It is given to you and it escapes you if you try to grasp it, to possess it. Nonetheless you have to 'learn' to pray! Certainly, but the word itself is ambiguous, equivocal. You have to 'learn', but not so as to 'know how to'. The moment you think that you 'know how' to pray, you run the risk of seeing everything collapse. You become the actor, you take things into your hands, you steer the ship. Then that 'enterprise' of yours will meet with the fate of many others: failure, and you will find yourself once again back at the beginning. The more you 'do' yourself, the less you 'receive'. The more you think you possess and know, the more also the essential thing eludes you. And the illusion takes a long time to dispel.

When you have become the craftsman of your prayer, you see your desire itself gradually being blunted. And this time the experience is destructive: failure, discouragement, abandonment. The process is familiar. It is not illusory, and the fall is all the harder. It seems to me today that not having known how to pray helped me to enter into prayer. I had neither recipe nor method nor plan. I had the good fortune of not raising the question for myself, but of simply throwing myself into it, just as things came. So, I was flexible, open to all that might come. I was in a position to receive. I did not know what, to tell the truth. But I did receive, much, much more than I could have hoped for. Don't seek to 'know how' to pray. Keep your ignorance. Pray, simply, in poverty. And prayer will be given to you.

2. Let yourself be loved

For a long time I had stood at the door of prayer, and then, all at once, the door was opened to me. I had gone in, step by step, with many backward moves, but never had the door to it been shut to me on that account, leaving me once again outside after one of my escapades. I felt like a convalescent, still very close to a relapse, still quite incapable of the simplest actions, dependent on the kind offices of those who surround him and do everything for him. A gentle hand does more in this way than all the declarations in the world, even the most ardent.

In the past I had had a very forthright spiritual director. He had shaken me, pointing out my numerous deficiencies, my infidelities, condemning my lack of resolution. He was no doubt right, and deep within me I was well aware of it. But curiously, the effect produced was the opposite. Instead of yielding to his reprimands, his invitations, justified though they were, I found that I was gradually closing up again, like the shellfish which senses danger or the snail that withdraws into its shell.

The sick man that I was needed a gentle and compassionate hand. Without that, relapse would have been inevitable. The sinner needs to feel mercy rather than judgement. He has no great need to be condemned, for his sin to be denounced: he knows it well enough and suffers from it secretly. Is humility necessary? Yes, indeed. But that is his own business. No one else has received the mission to do it for him, to humiliate him. That is not God's way. That is not the way of conversion. There is only one way: that of love. 'Who are you to pass judgement on your brother?' (cf. Rom. 3, 14).

By grace, I had always believed strongly in the love of God for us, for me. This conviction remained in the deepest part of my being like a backdrop, whatever the scene might be 'on stage'. In that rediscovery of prayer, I truly experienced God's tenderness, as an atmosphere which bathed my days. I entered into it with all my heart, with joy, with hope. The face of God's tenderness revealed itself to me and it is that face which I learnt to contemplate, to recognise. Doubtless I would not have been able to contemplate a face of severity or even of justice.

I was well able then to look at the way I had travelled, my wanderings like those of the prodigal son, my timid returns, usually followed by other occasions of infidelity. I was not proud of myself, but I did not feel crushed. I did not feel judged by God's gaze upon me. In the face of the poverty and the sin that I knew so well, there stood not the inflexible judge, not the avenging hand of the magistrate, but the smile and the tenderness of God's heart. I recognised myself in the oracle of the prophet Hosea (2, 16; 21-22):

> But look, I am going to seduce her
> and lead her into the desert
> and speak to her heart
> …
> I shall betroth you to myself forever,
> I shall betroth you in uprightness and justice,
> and faithful love and tenderness.
> Yes, I shall betroth you to myself in loyalty
> and in the knowledge of the Lord.

I was ashamed before other people and I carefully hid my interior state, disguising reality without making too much of a pretence. Before God I was not ashamed; it was sorrow that I felt and it was nourished by the hope of mercy. I did not fear God's vengeance. I had told others quite enough about the mercy and love of the Father. As a priest I had been his instrument for the forgiveness and the rescue of many. I was left with something from that. Yes, the conviction of God's tenderness has always been with me. I would more easily have abused his goodness than I would have doubted it. 'Judgement' itself did not make me afraid: I knew that mercy is the form of justice which adapts itself to wretchedness and I looked for, and was certain of, a mercy in proportion to my wretchedness. More even, for if my wretchedness was great, it was not infinite, while the mercy of God was infinite.

I came across an old man many years ago. He was an upright man with a deep faith and he had brought his children up admirably. He had brought them up both as good human beings and Christians. He told me more than once, and his words have long been imprinted on my heart: 'I have always lived in the terror of God!' And never, right up to his last hour, was I able to deliver him from it...

How many young people of the previous generation were troubled like him, indeed, terrorised, at the time of their retreats in preparation for First Holy Communion for example. Preachers thought it good practice to ground faith on fear, fear of sin, fear of Hell, fear of God's terrible judgement. May God forgive them! Already, I am sure, mercy has covered over their mistakes and they have seen the true face of the God of tenderness and pity, such as Jesus shows us in the Gospel, he who scandalised the virtuous by his preference for the poor and for sinners. Yes, my friend, the Lord has his preferences. They go to the poor, and to sinners. And if you happen to feel unworthy, a sinner, if you disgust yourself, then, lift up your head: the more you think you are falling off and sinking, the nearer also you will be to the love and the tenderness of God, the more you will have his preferential love. Yes, let yourself be loved! How could you 'seek the face' of one you dread, how could you want to live with someone you are afraid of?

The fear of God, which often derives from obscure feelings of guilt, hides itself at times in deep recesses. It is difficult to clear them out. The submerged part of an iceberg of self-condemnations, the fear of God destroys being and shuts it up, beneath the false pretext of rendering justice. Jesus teaches us that the only justice is love. Banish from your heart all fear of God, even if it has a stranglehold on you. Do not accept even the merest suggestion of it, react straightaway, violently. Throw yourself into the heart of God, plunge into his love. Refuse every other standpoint, for on this level nothing is true but love. And if you hesitate, cry with all your strength to God that he may drive this demon of fear out of you. Tell yourself, again and again of the love of God, repeat it, let it penetrate into you by all your pores, let it bathe you and set you at peace.

Cultivate the deep and calm conviction of God's tenderness. Let yourself be loved! Then you will be in a position to dare to contemplate his beloved face and his light will stream into your life in peace and joy.

'For if our heart accuses us, God is greater than our heart' (1 Jn 3, 20). He certainly has the right to love you and to open to your heart the door of prayer.

3. Make room for the Spirit

To pray, without 'knowing how' to pray, entails a great fragility: no reliable support, no security, no stability. One is always at one's limit, at breaking point. The tiniest thing is enough to break the charm and everything collapses. I was gradually becoming aware of this fragility, with some surprises. It was almost unbelievable that it should last. It seemed to me that it could not come from me, that it was the work of Another who, in the wings, was putting everything in its proper place.

I was experiencing, in fact, what St Paul said: 'Likewise the Spirit helps us in our weakness; for we do not know how to pray as we ought, but that very Spirit intercedes with sighs too deep for words' (Rom. 8, 26). Yes, that was it. The very words of the apostle seemed to me all at once the perfect illustration of what I was in the process of living. Normally, humanly speaking, given the poor hand I held, prayer in my life could not last, ought not to last. But it was lasting. Another was praying in me. I was lending him my being. He was besieging my heart, my spirit. He was holding my attention; he was stretching the string of the desire which his presence was increasing in me. I only had to follow the path traced out, to hear the appeal which was addressed to me and that voice which was becoming mine and dwelling in me.

Was it a new facility that was given to me? In a certain sense, yes, without doubt. Effectively, the process of prayer was becoming easier for me, less burdensome. I was experiencing the desire for and the joy of praying. Devoting time to it was becoming natural and prayer for me was like an appointment eagerly looked forward to. To miss it or to prefer something else to it was beginning to seem impossible. Generally I began my day with it and from my awakening that meeting enlightened my heart. I was taken up with it. I did not prepare my prayer, I prepared myself for it. It is prayer which came to me, smiling and happy, and I waited for it as one waits for the joy of a friend's visit.

Neither laziness nor wanderings of the imagination nor at times the sleep which overpowers you, had disappeared, but they were no longer obstacles, insurmountable impediments. No, at the most they were passing inconveniences, reminders of that fragility which remained. At the same time, there was that calm strength, that assurance coming from elsewhere, that humble confidence in the Other who was living in me, to whom I owed all. 'The Spirit of truth ... You know him, for he dwells with you and is in you' (Jn 14, 17). The experience of the Spirit is indeed astounding!

I was beginning to understand why I had no need to 'know how' to pray. The Holy Spirit had no use for my spiritual skills. He was in me, a living competence, beyond all knowledge, in proportion to my welcome. It was enough for me to welcome him; better: to be a welcome. I did not have to look for words for my prayer. The words were given to me, full of nourishment and savour, rich and life-giving, their sap inexhaustible; everyday words, simple and unpretentious. They were words which resounded in the depth of the heart and their echo fed my prayer for a long time. They rose to my heart, all alone, as a jet of water wells up from the sand and never dries up, or they spoke suddenly to my heart, coming from a psalm, from a verse of the Gospel, from a memory, and their light radiated, became life and prayer. They were words which no longer had the banality of human words, but the unfathomable meaning which they drew from the Spirit, that meaning to which only the Spirit of God can introduce you, grant you access, beyond yourself, by grace.

I could not repeat those words to you, for they only be misleading streams, cut off from their source, emptied of their life. They would no longer be anything but words which 'I' spoke. They can only be the words of the Spirit if it is the Spirit who utters them in you and makes them live for you. 'He who believes in me … streams of living water shall flow out from within him' (Jn 7, 38).

To be a welcome. I no longer had to guide my prayer as one might try to guide a line of reasoning, a speech, a debate. I had to let myself be led, receiving prayer from Another, without closing my hand over the gift which was being given to me. Now the temptation is there, and it spares no one: that of ascribing the gift to one's own efforts, of saying to oneself: 'I've got it now, it's going very well.' But at the mere touch of your vanity, of your conceit, everything collapses and falls to dust. Never begin to think that you 'possess' prayer: you would only close your hand over empty air.

Let yourself be guided by the Spirit: 'They are sons of God who are led by the Spirit of God' (Rom. 8, 14). Jesus was led into the desert by the Spirit. The desert is the place without path or highway, without landmarks or footprints. And the Spirit breathes where he wills, you do not know whence he comes nor whither he goes. Be content with listening to his voice (Jn 3, 8). If it is to the desert that he leads you, do not forget that the desert is also the place of the presence, of the silence in which the voice of God is heard and one is freed from all encumbrances.

Let yourself be led by the Spirit. What does that mean in the context of prayer?

For me, it came about almost by itself, since, thanks be to God, I did not 'know how' to pray. Without experience, I could not have preconceived ideas. I had begun with silence, calm and peace: not doing anything, not saying anything, having no plan. I fixed my interior gaze on that Other in the deepest part of myself, to find his presence again and let it impose itself gradually on my spirit. I waited for it to be the first to speak, in some way, attentive and trusting. Take note, it was not a question of tension of spirit or of sustained effort, no, but a great interior flexibility, smiling and relaxed, in peace and patience, without haste. One has to take one's time, know how to wait, be happy to wait, without taking any initiative, until the Spirit has tamed your heart and you are able to welcome him, ready and available. That is necessary for the Spirit to begin to lead you.

A thought, a word, rises to your heart. Welcome them, savour them, make them your food and your sufficiency. Be content with what has been given to you. Do not go to look elsewhere, further afield, for something else – ruminate. Let things resound deeply in your heart. Come back to them. Repeat the word, the phrase which has been given to you.

Each repetition will awaken in your heart a new echo, an unsuspected life. That is what your Father has prepared for you today: your bread, your prayer for this day. The Spirit is leading you by the way which is his own. He is forming prayer in you: that is his aid to your weakness, you who do not know how to pray as you ought. You who will never pray as you ought. For the Spirit does not come to teach you to pray, in order that you may free yourself and grow proud of your knowledge. He comes to pray in you and he testifies to your spirit that you are a child of God (Rom. 8, 16). He makes you an adoptive child and through him you cry out: Abba, Father! (Rom. 8, 15). It is your voice, they are your words. But they have become the voice, the words of the Spirit in you, the prayer which he gives you.

4. The whole truth

I have never been very keen on 'meditation'. By that I mean the form of prayer in which the imagination constructs series of representations, the reason strings together a more or less coherent discourse in accordance with the various schemes which the 'method' proposes. In a word, it is a procedure in which the person is the craftsman of their prayer, calling upon the resources of their faculties to set it in motion. Is it a deficiency in my mind that it tires of such constraint? Is it a lack of taste for what more or less resembles a pious dissertation? I had indeed, at one time or another in my life, tried to make a meditation in writing. I rarely kept it up for any length of time. I believe that I derived but slight benefit from it, too little, in any case, to convince me.

Certainly the time which I devoted to it could be considered as spiritual activity; but I had the feeling, in a confused way, of not finding sufficient nourishment in it. At least my mind was working, so it was better than nothing. But I cannot say that it led me into prayer. It is impossible to compare this 'activity' to what, subsequently, the gift of prayer allowed me to experience. One cannot compare such disparate realities.

Far be it from me to disparage a way of praying, still less to dissuade those who find it suits them. I believe simply that there is nothing in common between human endeavour and the gift of God. Who could be content with human endeavour when the gift of God is offered? Does one use the stairs when the lift is available? St Thérèse of Lisieux was the first to make this comparison: 'The lift which is to raise me to heaven is your arms, Jesus' (MS C, folio 3). This is an experience which is not reserved for 'great souls' but which is the lot of 'little souls', yours and mine, as Thérèse often repeats. It is offered to everyone if they want it.

What is to be done? Nothing. Above all, do not do anything. Do not seek to 'encroach upon Providence', according to Monsieur Vincent's felicitous expression. Do not foresee ways, do not form plans. Let what comes come.

Of course, I was not praying without any starting point. You cannot pray without some starting point. You need fullness and not emptiness. At the very least, you must find that presence again deep within you and hold to it. It is with that that you must always begin: the way to your heart, of which I have spoken at length. All the rest, and yourself in the first place, your own small person, you will try to forget. That presence, found again deep within you, can be enough to fill up a long prayer, a long time of prayer. Two lovers can very well remain for hours without saying anything, simply present to one another. It is enough for them to be together and their heart is filled to overflowing. After all, why should you blush at being a lover of God?

Let his presence invade you like a jet of water which

84

rises and brings new life. Above all, do not say anything. He is there for you, with you, in you. That is enough for you. Stay with him, for as long as you can, motionless, silent, attentive, present. Do not expect to hear his voice either. You have no more to hear than you have to speak. The Spirit of God is not talkative. And the presence which he reveals to you has no need of words to invade you. What more can you desire?

The fruits? Be patient, they will come in good time. Trees also have to wait to bear their fruit. Let the tree and the fruit ripen in you. Whatever you do, you will not hasten their ripening. But, if you live by that presence deep within you, something is bound to happen. The moment will come, impossible to foresee, when you are least expecting it. What does it matter if you have to wait a long time? God is not in a hurry, but he will not fail you. Often I used to pray over a phrase that had touched me, even over a simple word. How often did St Thérèse of Lisieux see her young prayer take its flight over that simple phrase which Abbé Arminjon put on God's lips in the book which nourished her faith for a long time: 'Now it is my turn!' Thérèse quivered with fervour and joy over that. The imprint which that phrase made on her heart, in her utmost depths, did not come from any human emotion. The support for it was too slight. The Spirit of God in her was shedding his warm light on the treasures which the love of God reserves for his elect (1 Cor. 2, 9). And the flame which was burning the heart of the adolescent girl was a divine flame. Who knows what Thérèse received from God through that simple phrase? What inexhaustible riches she found there!

Sometimes a phrase, a word, irrupts into your life like a

clap of thunder in a serene sky. I have already told you of the extent to which I felt the resonance of that verse: 'You have not abandoned me to the power of death.' Without being so overwhelming, other verses, other words, can in their turn feed your prayer. And not only your prayer but your spiritual life, your life in its entirety. The benefit they impart does not come in the first place from the fact that you have understood them well. On the contrary they often remain obscure, and it is with difficulty that your intelligence exercises itself in pondering them: they remain closed, like a door of which you have not got the key. In spite of their obscurity you perceive confusedly the wealth they have to yield for you and you ruminate on them, slowly, patiently, at length, simply, in the depths of your heart, and at the same time as you repeat their words, a humble desire, the call to the light, rises.

For months on end, I remember, I prayed that cry of Jesus on the Cross: 'My God, my God, why have you forsaken me?' Doubtless I understood the human meaning of those words quite well: they are simple enough for that. But I did not attain to the heart of their mystery, to the heart of what Jesus had wished to say and live in that experience of abandonment. For months I stayed there, and those words and that experience of Jesus, alone, fed my prayer and my life. I knew that I had to stay there, obstinately, as a shipwrecked man holds on to the floating spar. I did not grow weary of that prayer ceaselessly begun afresh, ceaselessly repeated. I had an intuition that there was hidden treasure in it for me and that one day, perhaps, it would be disclosed to my patience, to my persistence.

And one day in fact, the light comes. Like a curtain one

pulls back, like the sun emerging from a cloud. 'When the Spirit of truth comes, he will introduce you to the truth in its entirety' (Jn 16, 13). That gift of the Spirit does not make you any more learned, or a better theologian. I am not any more able now than before to explain the abandonment of Christ. But my heart and my life have perceived something of it, have received from it a light which leads me on. I would be quite incapable of explaining it to you. Doubtless I could tell you some tiny scrap of it, humble and poor, by disclosing to you what has become a part of my life. But to enter fully into it there is only one way, and that consists in receiving the light which the Spirit of the Lord will, in the end, make rise in your heart, like a morning star. An incomparable light, impossible to speak about, but which, in you, becomes life.

You will not have gone all through the Gospel and the other Scriptural texts without the Spirit renewing in your heart the inspiration and the meaning which brought them into being. So it is that man lives, by the Word which comes forth from the mouth of God (Mt. 4, 4).

5. The name of the Lord

'Whoever calls upon the name of the Lord will be saved' (Rom. 10, 13). Everyone invokes the name of the Lord when he prays. What prayer is there which does not begin with an address, by an appeal to God, to the Father, to Jesus? The Gospel shows it in the cry of the lame, of the blind, of the sick: 'Jesus, son of David, have pity on me!' (Mk 10, 47). Calling for help, attracting the attention of the Lord, by naming him, renews the awareness of God's presence in us, sets us face to face with him. Already a certain familiarity is necessary to call upon the name of the Lord. That call is an act of faith in the living God and in providence, in the Father who 'knows what you need before even you ask him for it' (Mt. 6, 8).

However I would like to speak about another experience here. It is a deeper experience of the name of the Lord, an experience for which the West has perhaps somewhat lost the attraction, or at least it has rather lost the habit. It was at the time of a recent retreat. I have retained the habit of long retreats, eight days every year. For me it is a necessary breathing-space, one of those breaks which have become indispensable. It is essentially a time devoted to prayer. In it I had the experience of nocturnal prayer. Not of course that there is anything exceptional in that. I never decide to wake up at night. I never set the alarm with that in view. But if I wake up, spontaneously, it seems to me that then it is, as it were, a call and a gift from the Lord. Then you get up and join him who is calling you, in the silence of the night. There is nothing heroic in that: I have never felt tired as a result the next day, nor have I had heavy eyelids. When it is the Lord himself who calls you, he takes care that you do not suffer any disadvantage from it, or tiredness. In a word, on that evening I had said to the Lord: 'I would be glad if you would invite me tonight and I had a bit of time for you.' And I went to sleep without the least worry, without the least preoccupation. I would have given thanks just as much if I had slept right through the night. It was not for me to decide. However at one o'clock in the morning, that night, I was woken up, fresh, ready, wide awake. The call was clear. I answered it, with that interior joy at having been heard, at having been invited.

I had desired, in the solitude and silence of the night, that the Spirit would lead me into the truth of the Lord and that he would introduce me into the mystery of Jesus' Passion. That is something which takes time, but it was offered to me. I had not foreseen anything but that desire to welcome the movement of the Spirit, of entering into the mystery of Christ. I had not brought anything, no book, not even the Gospel. I was preparing myself to receive what the Lord had prepared for me. And then the name of the Lord Jesus rose to my heart. That was not something new: how many times, like so many other people, had I not begun my prayer by invoking his name? But the name of Jesus, having risen to my heart, did not leave it again, 'Jesus, Jesus, Jesus.' There had been previous occasions on which I had repeated the name several times, but never in that way, never with that continuity. It was coming back unceasingly, and I was uttering it silently in the night. It was taking up the whole of my attention, it was filling me. What else could have occupied me? That name was dwelling in my heart, my spirit, my being. It was taking hold of me, entering into possession of me, enfolding me entirely: 'Jesus, Jesus, Jesus.'

I was not seeking it, I was not holding on to it, I was not trying to repeat it. It was imposing itself on me, taking up the whole field of my consciousness, like a marvellous and unexpected incantation. At every instant it was being given to me and I was receiving it ever new and living. It seemed to me that I could no longer utter any other word, any other name but that of Jesus. But I would never have known such intensity in this if I had sought for it, wished for it, if I had deliberately kept up its movement.

For more than two hours I repeated the name of Jesus within myself, nothing else. I found subsequently that during those two hours it had been given to me approximately at the rhythm of my heartbeats, thousands of times. And it was a great wonder: no weariness, no desire to stop, to pass on to something else. I would almost say no possibility of saying anything else. No other word attracted me or interested me. The name of Jesus was being given to me by the Spirit, as an inexhaustible spiritual food, a source of life and joy in me. No sensible image accompanied it, no particular thought. No, the name alone: 'Jesus, Jesus, Jesus.' But 'there is no other name by which we can be saved' (Acts 4, 12).

On other occasions I have known a similar prayer, never for so long, but always with that joy and that plenitude which one knows only on such occasions. Then the name of Jesus is not a cry, your cry, which you raise to him. It is not an appeal which comes from your will, from your desire of going towards him. You may try to repeat his name in the same way. You will truly succeed only if it is given to you. Saying it of yourself is in fact something quite different from receiving it from the Spirit. You must have had the experience of it to understand it, to grasp the difference. That does not mean that one must not try, quite the contrary.

For this 'manducation', this incessant repetition of the name of Jesus, there exists a long and venerable oriental tradition, that of the 'Jesus Prayer'. In it the unwearying repetition of the name of Jesus is generally associated with the very meaning of his name: 'The Lord saves'. It is an act of faith, unceasingly flowering into prayer. It is a putting into effect of Jesus' recommendation to his disciples to 'pray unceasingly' (Lk. 18, 1). It consists in repeating, at every moment at which the mind is at liberty: 'Jesus, Son of God, Saviour, take pity on me a sinner', or even, more briefly, 'Lord Jesus, have pity on me.' The formula matters little: the only thing that matters is the repeated invocation of the name of Jesus. The rest is only ornament.

But how is it possible to pray unceasingly? Is it an illusion, and, on the part of Jesus who has asked us for it, an inconsiderate requirement? 'It has been given to you,' says the starets[1] to the Russian pilgrim who is seeking perpetual prayer, 'to understand that it is not the wisdom of this world nor a vain desire of knowledge which is leading you to heavenly light, perpetual interior prayer, but on the contrary, poverty of spirit and active experience in simplicity of heart'.[2]

One thing is certain, that if you wish to succeed by yourself, relying on your own strength, in 'praying unceasingly', as Jesus asks for, you are doomed to failure, to weariness, to discouragement. Even invoking the name of Jesus is not possible without the inspiration and the help of the Holy Spirit: 'No one can say "Jesus is Lord" except by the Holy Spirit' (1 Cor. 12, 3). But you can begin to train yourself to fill your heart with the name of the Lord, with perseverance, with faith, tasting all its savour. Gradually the

---

[1] A spiritual director or religious teacher (not necessarily a priest) in the Eastern Orthodox Church.
[2] The Story of a Russian Pilgrim.

Spirit of God will take over and give you the prayer. He 'will come to the aid of your weakness' (Rom. 8, 26) and open you to that dwelling on the name of Jesus in you.

> *'No word can tell,*
> *nor any word translate,*
> *only one who has lived it can understand,*
> *what it is to love Jesus. '[3]*

---

[3] A verse of the hymn *Jesus dulcis memoria.*

IV

Go out from yourself

Go out from yourself

I have explored with you at length the 'way to my heart'. We have followed it to its deepest point, where the presence of the Other who is the Lord is revealed. Must we now then turn back, retrace our footsteps and take another road? Will the way to my heart turn out to be a cul-de-sac or a track leading nowhere? After all the distance traversed to enter into oneself again, why must one 'go out from oneself'? Is it not contradictory? No, the contradiction is only apparent. It does not exist in reality. And if there really is a paradox, it is that of the Gospel, that of the beatitudes, that of the cross which one resolves only by living them.

Rather than another way, it is another landscape which I invite you to explore. At times it is austere, but after the fashion of the bare landscape which is presented to the mountaineer and grows in grandeur the higher he climbs. Already, here and there, as the road has twisted and turned, some aspects of it have appeared to us. Shall we take a closer look at it?

1. Like little children

The vision of a little child moves and charms us: calling a little child, Jesus set it in the midst of his disciples and said: 'In truth I tell you, unless you change and become like children, you shall not enter into the kingdom of heaven' (Mt. 18, 2). For us, childhood is synonymous with innocence and purity. It bears the promise of flowers and disarms older people, softens their hearts. People like to see themselves become little children again, delivered from their load of miseries and of nastiness, renewed as it were: a return to innocence.

But this image of the child is of recent origin. Do you know what the child evoked at the time of Jesus? Not all those poetic scenes. The child did not then possess any value in society. It was a being without importance, a symbol of fragility, of poverty, of powerlessness; unable to speak, obliged to receive everything from others. That is the child which Jesus brings forward as an example for his disciples.

The adult has taken on importance. Socially, professionally, he has weight. He has acquired knowledge and power. One has to reckon with him, and other people, often, depend on him to some extent. And that is what prevents him from entering into the kingdom of heaven. That is what one has to lose to become once again the insignificant child which Jesus had before his eyes. For it can happen that older people take themselves seriously before God! That they show off their 'personage' before him.

I myself was like that: the temptation to it is quite subtle. It is only now that I am becoming aware of it, after having let myself be caught in its trap for a long time. But could I have borne the revelation of it? Once again, I am having the experience that God only reveals the recesses of the heart to a person when they can profit from it: when they are able to accept themselves as such, selfish, proud, pretentious, and to welcome it without drama, without discouragement.

Entering into prayer, I was introduced to that path, step by step. It is a long path. You never come to the end of it. You do not begin by choosing to live the spirit of childhood. Or at least you may well choose it, but that hardly lets you make any progress. That comes from elsewhere, from the very practice of prayer, like the tide that rises inexorably and ruins the best constructed sandcastles, levelling the sand and restoring it in a few assaults to that flat stretch of beach on which nothing remains of the contours or the heights your hands had created.

All you need to do is to enter into prayer in truth. Face to face with God, you soon perceive that it is not you who is the main contributor. You are deflated, like a goldbeater's skin, and the goldbeater's skin owes its volume only to the wind which fills it. Thus, gradually, you take on more reasonable proportions before God. The wind, the void, the vanities on which you prided yourself, free you of their encumbrance and deflate you to the extent that they leave you. But you must be before God in truth. That is to say, ready to receive the truth about yourself which you were not willing to see, which you were not able to see. Nevertheless, how many times have I spoken about the spirit of childhood! How many times have I commented on the kingdom of God reserved for little children! How then can one both talk about these things and remain unaffected by them oneself, without even becoming aware of them?

I was very much helped by the gift of God which in me became desire for prayer. But I found myself empty of words again, voiceless to some extent, not because I had lost my voice, but through incapacity of spirit and of heart. Words, as I have already said, are so poor and inept. They betray you so quickly, so totally. They fly from you and not one is left to come to your aid. In prayer I was becoming 'the child', one who cannot speak, who does not know what to say. While, in the affairs of life, in normal relations, my brain was functioning normally, there it seemed to have broken down, to be derelict.

In fact, the child is one who does not know how to speak, who has never known, who is only beginning to catch a few words, without yet being able to use them. Never yet had I known how to 'speak' as one ought to speak when one addresses God. My derelict brain no longer served me. It was more of a nuisance, for it persisted in trying to formulate phrases which sounded hollow in that new language which was still strange to me! If only I could silence it! If only I could stay dumb like a child! Accept only words coming from elsewhere, from Another, from that tongue which is still strange to me. You learn it only day by day, for true prayer does not lend itself to a human flow of words, to the music of apt phrases. It is built up in silence, attentive to something beyond oneself, to that presence which reveals itself at the end of the way to your heart.

The child is wholly dependent. He receives everything from another, his very survival. The myth of the wolf-child is probably legendary: what child could survive without a human being, without a mother or someone to take her place? At his birth the human child is without question the most helpless of beings, the most naked in regard to life. Prayer leads one back to the nakedness of birth. It strips one to the full extent of that poverty. It disarms one and lays one bare to the very root of the heart, with a stubborn gentleness, a long patience.

For our part, we are tempted to take drastic measures, in order, so we think, not to prolong the pain. Prayer does not resort to surgical operations, because it is the work of God who leads us 'with strings of love' (Hos. 11, 4). Brutality, as is often the case, would keep us far from the goal that is sought. God knows what it costs us to see ourselves thus stripped. Then he leaves us the time to inure ourselves to it and to acquire the habit of it. He bides his time, waiting, before he calls us to the following steps. Slowly, we will progress towards that rediscovered childhood and towards our birth. We will perceive that Nicodemus was right to some extent and that it is a work much greater and much more mysterious than entering into our mother's womb again (cf. Jn 3, 4).

Our incapacity, our dependence, will be lightened by the smile of God's love. Our nakedness will no longer involve the shame which Adam and Eve experienced but that joy which obliges God, if one may so put it, to show some maternal solicitude and love for us. In our prayer and in our life, we will depend on him, we will look to him for everything, we will receive everything from him. Thus is born the love of a child for his father, with the joy of being filled. Filled in nakedness, in the stripping of ourselves which opens a space in which the rediscovered child can gambol in peace and serenity, where the lost garden is opened again to the beloved presence: God talks with us in the evening breeze, a

Father with his child who no longer seeks to hide away. It is the greatness of the childhood that can be recognised in the features of the child in Mary's arms, wealth of her poverty, which it is given to us to be taught and to know. Happy the child that prayer brings to birth in you.

2. A bit of humility

I believed that I possessed a certain degree of humility. At times I experienced reactions of modesty which sufficed to deceive me. A certain mask of modesty does in fact embellish one's personality and shows it in a favourable light. But this modesty for external use, as I noticed much later, is coupled with a secret complacency for internal use. It surfaces for example, when we feel aggrieved when congratulations (entirely deserved, we thought, obviously) are slow in coming. You discover then that you possess an unbelievable skill for bringing the subject up again and presenting matters in such a way that the one who does not compliment you can no longer appear as anything but ignorant. And then, when the compliment comes, you hasten to deprecate it, in order to manifest your exemplary modesty.

One day someone was telling me about his career, and how he had reached the position he now occupied. We had been sharing confidences for a moment and he had told me about himself. I was astonished by what he said. Such an admiration for himself, such complacency, such self-satisfaction, such pleasure in boasting his skills, his strategy, even his double-dealing, it all left me stupefied. I would never have believed such a display of vanity possible: it was nothing less than grotesque. A touch of contempt, almost disgust, took hold of me, for I believed myself immune from these vauntings.

Here the parable of the prophet Nathan to king David comes to mind (2 Sam. 12, 1-7), the anger of the king who desires prompt justice and the prophet's conclusion: 'You are that man!' Yes, the same thing happened to me, is happening to me, and will happen to me for a long time to come, as St Francis de Sales says: 'conceit will die half an hour after our death.'

It is so very easy to pride oneself on one's humility and thus let oneself be blown away by every gust of flattery. Pride, vanity, conceit burn up any wood. Everything suits their purpose, everything is grist for their mill, everything an occasion, everything provides them with food. And you (probably) are the only one not to notice it. For in this domain, lucidity is difficult and rare. The trap closes even on your good will, even on your desire to walk in the ways of humility, even on the endeavours you make to forget yourself. How difficult it is to describe the pride there is in taking the last place, one's unawareness of certain vanities, the secret enjoyment in being remarked, for all that one modestly lowers one's eyes. 'I know what I am worth and believe what I heard about it,' Corneille said. Is there any attitude, any effort, any word or gesture, which is not liable to this? It is a vicious circle which encloses you and which it is very difficult to break.

Thus I became aware one day of the pride which was hidden in my rediscovered prayer: I, at least, was praying and God was very fortunate to find a man like me to do him the favour of concerning himself with him! The Pharisee who slumbered in me had long appropriated the gesture and the humble protestation of the publican to assert his sufficiency.

If matters have reached this point, to which saint should one turn? Is there any hope of escaping from it? To tell the truth, I don't think so. And it is much better so. Just imagine if you were to become truly humble and that you noticed the fact: at that very moment you would have to begin all over again. No, you will never be humble. Let it be enough for you to become aware of your pride. That already will be quite an achievement.

So it is that prayer dismantles your self-sufficiency, stone by stone. Not however that you can hope to come to the end of it. Prayer acts in the same way like a photographic developer – slowly, in stages. First the darkest shadows appear: they are sketched out confusedly, as a slight shadow, scarcely visible, then they grow stronger to the extent that the developer acts, until they take on all their intensity. Gradually other shadows come to light, more and more dense, with a variety of shades. Finally the photograph is composed, made up of shadows and lights. The picture is revealed in all its plain truth: the developer does not invent anything, it does not improvise, it does not yield to any fantasy. It discloses what is there, without false show or adornment. It does not spare your susceptibility, for the portrait is rarely flattering. How can we stay before God in truth without his light showing up the shadows in which conceit and vanity have established their lair?

Look carefully: you will find them everywhere and you will never come to the end of dislodging them. You have a fine voice: you pride yourself on it and you make full use of it in order that no one may be ignorant of it. Or on the other hand, you have a poor voice: you make the best of it, like the fox in the fable, you confide to anyone who will listen to you that it is much better like that, so that the grapes which are out of your reach are simply 'too sour and only good for rogues'. You have some gifts of intellect or of dexterity: the gallery is there and you play to it, making sure it admires you. It is your social position which gives you confidence and bolsters you: you pose, always 'modestly', and you end up by identifying yourself with your position. A position besides which others envy you, and their flatteries last only as long as your splendour. A minute later nothing is left of you: you are forgotten, besmirched, taunted.

How many human subjects of pride there are, giving out a hollow sound, blowing hither and thither by every breath of air, dressing themselves up in all the gaudy and shifting tints of a soap bubble! And the soap bubble boasts before God! It congratulates itself upon it if need be. And believes that it has succeeded! Indeed you are fortunate if you do not expect God to thank you for it! But God is not like a courtesan who crushes you after having flattered you. Certainly, his light brings the sewer of your vanities into broad daylight. But he does not despise the blind man who at length opens his eyes upon his miserable vanities, on his hidden pride, on that conceit which sticks fast to him. It is enough for him that the blind man should see, without attempting any longer to turn his eyes away and deny his pathetic conceits. It is enough for him that the proud person should recognise their pride, the vain person their vanity, the pretentious person their pretentiousness. Such a truth is already hard to admit. What purpose is there in seeking to drive it in any further?

That is the humility which is built up in you by the daily meeting of prayer. It does not make you no longer proud, it does not make you humble. It convinces you, with gentleness, that in fact you are proud, vain and all the rest. It opens your heart to recognising it, to accepting the fact that you are not humble, to smiling at times at the subterfuges of your vanity. For it teaches you above all not to be aggrieved or saddened or discouraged, but serene and confident.

And you will begin to ask the Lord that that light may be given to you every day, that it may illuminate the darkest corners of yourself. Pride fears nothing so much as the light which shows it up. And if he wishes, and when he wishes, God will give you a bit of humility, and it will grow up in your heart like a mustard plant.

3. The sinner that I am

A banal sinner, like thousands of others. A sinner without originality or imagination, who commits silly sins and is always committing the same ones over and over again. Who has taken a thousand resolutions 'with the help of your holy grace, never to offend you again...' A sinner who is always coming back to his past weaknesses, as the water of a stream always follows the path of the steepest slope, and hollows out its bed a little more all the time.

Humanly speaking, the situation of the sinner is desperate. Habit begets a certain prejudice. Weariness of making any effort and discontent are liable to bring about a relapse: one more, one less, what does it matter at the point I have reached? This line of reasoning, which is a surrender to evil, brings about a progressive blinding, a sort of numbing of the conscience. It now reacts only weakly and consoles itself cheaply by repeating that after all, we are no saints. Examination of conscience, that refuge of lucidity, grows infrequent, it is dreaded and fled from.

That is more or less the point I had reached, with some momentary revivals, followed by further desertions. It is not necessary either that the sins be serious. A little girl who came back to confess shortly after having received absolution answered the priest's surprise: 'It is not that they are serious, but that they are too many!' Marvellous wisdom. With me too, they were too many, but I was troubling myself less and less about that. I usually began a retreat by making a confession which set everything in order... for some time, things then started off again, as of their own accord, in the direction of the greatest slope, quietly, no drama, no uproar. It is what some people call, with some complacency, 'a decent mediocrity', and which is rather a 'quiet indifference'. One hardly cares any longer for anything but the facade, which may still disguise reality, but which only hides ruins. 'It is not that they are serious, but that they are too many.' The ruins also were too many.

'You have not abandoned me to the power of death!' Why did this verse, and not some other, disturb me, as I have said, to the very depths of my heart? What interior experience did it express? All at once, in that long arid and desolate prayer, the evidence of salvation was bursting upon my heart: God was revealing to me that his love was saving me, had saved me. It was not a question of salvation in general, nor of a theological theory of salvation, nor of the answers which are given to the problem of salvation. No, what was happening was that I myself, in the exact situation in which I found myself, was receiving the gift of a precise and appropriate salvation, made to measure for me. All at once I knew that it was true, that I was truly saved. And a flood of gratitude had risen to my heart with a sob that had shaken me. And peace, that peace which is beyond all expectation, had invaded me and never again left me. 'Joy, joy, tears of joy,' Pascal would have said. I did not say that, but I had lived the reality of it then.

'Today salvation has come to this house' (Lk. 19, 9), Jesus said to Zachaeus, the thieving tax-collector, who had just seen himself as a sinner at the moment at which he was receiving both Jesus and salvation. Being saved brings awareness of the fact that you were lost. But this brutal revelation does not provoke a sense of despair: you know that you were lost only at the moment at which you know you are saved. A wonderful delicacy of the Lord.

St Teresa of Avila tells in her autobiography how one day she had the clear vision of the place which was destined for her in hell, or rather of the place which would have been hers: she saw what she was escaping from. She expressed herself according to the consecrated phrases and the customs of her age. But it seems to me that, the experience of being saved, which is inseparable from the experience of being lost, is of the same order: the love of God has intervened and shows you where your path was leading. It is a powerful revelation which sets your heart singing with an immense gratitude and introduces you to the path of conversion and of life.

This first experience of perdition and of salvation was

for me only global. I did not see the detail of the sins which filled my life, but only sin at work. In the light of the Love which was giving me salvation, my sin appeared as what it was: power of death, spiritual death, a quiet and slow death, imperceptible, at work in me, almost without my knowing it. I had died and I was coming back to life, I had been lost and I was found again, saved (cf. Lk. 15, 32).

For all that, I did not feel any desire to dwell upon my sin. My heart was entirely taken up with gratitude: only that mattered to me. I had no wish to turn on my self, by scrutinising the details of my sins, the gaze which a deep gratitude had concentrated on God, on him who had not 'abandoned me to the power of death'. Of course I wanted to live according to God's will. I had been conquered by the delicacy of his love and by the deep impression that the experience of being saved had left in me. I did not want to let go of it, not even to concern myself with the way in which I needed to struggle against sin and temptation.

So, for some time, there dwelt together in me tension towards God who was filling my heart, and the continuance of my weakness and poverty. I was still a sinner, almost to the same extent, but I was content to forge ahead without worrying about the load of wretchedness I was still carrying. To tell the truth, frontal attack on temptation had so often appeared ineffective to me that I felt little inclination to waste time over it. I tended rather, thanks to the whole of the experience already lived through, to look to God for liberation which I felt myself quite incapable of.

In a word I was waiting for prayer – which had already given me the deep need to pray – to continue its work of slow purification in me. The presence and the love of God which had been given to me seemed much more effective weapons than the hand-to-hand struggle that I had so often tried: your hands slip and do not keep their hold on anything, or hardly anything, and you exhaust yourself in vain. God's alluring me had other effects, deeper and surer.

Yet one does not live for long years in carelessness and facility without some enduring effects. Habits dig deep ruts in you which are not obliterated at a stroke. For a long time, in spite of yourself, they twist your road and lead you where you no longer want to go. Imperceptibly, as the days pass, the inclination of your heart becomes more marked, a certain attachment to sin: to the sin of weakness – you would need a courage which you no longer possess; to the sin of omission – it is so easy to be inattentive, forgetful, or to take the other side of the road; to the sin of misery – why should you deny yourself so many passing joys which do not do anyone much harm?

It takes time to straighten out your heart's inclination, so that it automatically tends, as by its own weight, with a joyful eagerness, towards what you now desire, since the love of God has entered into you. A calm and slow struggle, stubborn and assiduous, which fights against sin without frontal attack, but taking the bypass of loving more and loving better. When all is said and done, if you love truly, you will be well able to do all you want to, for prayer will have taught you also never to want anything any longer but to love.

Fix the gaze of your heart on the Lord, since it is he who delivers you from evil, and prayer will be for you an inexhaustible source of purification and of fidelity, a spring of water welling up into eternal life.

4. Enter into praise

'I bless you, Father, Lord of heaven and earth, because you have hidden these mysteries from the wise and the learned and revealed them to little children' (Mt. 11, 25).

Very quickly, from the beginning of my rediscovery of prayer, that cry to his Father on the part of Jesus made a strong impression on me. Those words came back to me incessantly, and they remained for me the best expression of what I had lived through. I made that cry of Jesus my own: I repeated it often and I desired to insert myself into that wondering praise of the Son to his Father. An inner joy was awakening, as if in echo, and was impelling me to repeat it again and again. 'I bless you, Father…'

It seemed to me then that I was living in the very prayer of Jesus, making my heart his heart and my lips his lips. I was son in him and I did not tire of entering into his praise: 'I bless you, Father ...'

How many times those simple words served me as support for my prayer! They sufficed to fill up the time which I devoted to it. I had no need of anything else. In them I found plentiful food and especially that contact with God, with his Father, which was gradually shaping and moulding my spiritual being. A new relationship was being created in me, made up of admiration, love and gratitude, adoration. The simple thought of finding again the joy of that presence of the Father and of repeating, with Jesus, his praise, maintained my desire to pray and made me look forward to the moment of it with impatience. A joyful apprenticeship, all simplicity, in which you see yourself filled, almost without doing anything, in any case without any merit, because everything is given to you, even the desire which inclines you to be still more a well-loved son of the Father, to the praise of his tenderness. Then praise breaks out automatically on your lips, it dwells in your heart and suffices to fill it, as the heart of the bride in the Song of Songs is full of admiration for him whom she loves.

Praise is the prayer of love. It knows nothing of the gaze turned back upon itself in which so many spiritual courses dry up. It makes you no longer your own master and takes away even the taste for coming back to yourself, for wasting your time in examining your own petty affairs.

God alone is God. What would be only a truism for the mathematical mind is a marvelling, an intense joy, for one whose heart has been shaped by praise. You never stop admiring him and every instant offers you a fresh discovery which leads you on and lifts you up. I am not afraid of telling you, like Didier Decoin[4] and so many others who have lived it in secret: I was falling in love with God. With love full of infinite respect, a sentiment of adoration in which you are glad to disappear because nothing else has truly any importance. You have no need to ask in order to receive and you receive what you would not even dare to ask for, so much is the measure of God's heart beyond the measure of your own heart.

Everything causes praise to well up in you, for life itself becomes the place of God's tender affection, of his countless delicate attentions, which wait neither for your

---

[4] In *Il fait Dieu.*

desire nor for your appeal. How could you then find words for anything else? What plans, what hopes could you formulate which are not already fulfilled? At every moment God precedes you and his love forestalls you, calling forth the praise which breaks out spontaneously on your lips. 'I bless you, Father!'

Praise is enough then to fill up the time of prayer, as it is to fill your heart, in spite of poverty in words. What have the Gospels preserved for us of the praise of Jesus? Some words the richness of which nourish you for a moment but then die away on your lips, for they are only a little star in the infinite constellations of praise in which the Son spoke of the beauty of his Father and of his love and his goodness and his greatness and so many other things, in which words fail to speak of God in truth. But that little star brings to birth in you, inextinguishably, an ardent thirst for praising God, for praising him beyond your words, beyond all words; a thirst for praising God with inexhaustible words, infinitely more expressive than all human words, the words of God himself.

One day when some of us were meeting together fraternally in prayer, and thirst for praise was animating my prayer, I surprised myself saying deep within me: 'Other words would have to be invented to praise you, Lord!' so convinced was I of the immense poverty of my praise and that God deserved infinitely more and better. Scarcely had I uttered that word, which no one could have heard, when at my side there rose up, out loud, unexpectedly, impressive, from the mouth of a brother, a long chant of praise, an ardent utterance which went beyond words, making them burst, escaping from the language of men to say something else in a different way. It was an astonishing answer to my unexpressed prayer, in which God himself seemed to be making a sign to me by granting my absurd request. 'The Spirit himself intercedes for us in inexpressible groaning,' St Paul tells us (Rom. 8, 26). A gift of praise in which man has only his lips to offer, and his voice, to the initiatives of the Holy Spirit who has taken hold of him and makes him say what human speech cannot say and which has not even risen to the heart of humans (cf. 1 Cor. 2, 9). It is called improperly the 'gift of tongues' and it leaves many 'reasonable' people astonished and wary, at times with good reason. Certainly one can 'speak with the tongues of men and of angels' and be only, 'if we lack love, a resounding gong and clanging cymbals' (1 Cor. 13, 1). But the absolute primacy of love does not, for all that, tie down the gifts of the Spirit, who 'breathes where he wills' (Jn 3, 8) and distributes his gifts according to his good pleasure. 'One who speaks in tongues does not speak to humans but to God. No one understands him: his spirit utters mysterious things' (1 Cor. 14, 2). But the Spirit of God in us is free to meet the Spirit of God in him who speaks thus and utters mysterious things, to the praise of the glory of the Father. In this domain also, possible illusions do not extinguish the Spirit and do not sterilise his freedom and his power.

Why should the Spirit not take hold of you in your turn, to raise your heart and your lips to a praise which you could not attain of yourself? St Paul declares that it was so with him: 'Thanks be to God, I speak in tongues more than all of you' (1 Cor. 14, 18). May God deign, in accordance with his good pleasure, to open your heart and your lips, and many other hearts and many other lips, to that inexpressible praise which is a gift of the Spirit. But it is never you who makes the decision and you cannot elicit it. Gratuitous, this gift comes and goes according to the liberty of the Spirit.[5]

The important thing is praise, whatever form it may take, spontaneous or received, expressed or inexpressible.

Following the promptings of the Spirit I was trying to welcome the prayer which was being given me. Thus I knew long periods of which the greater part of my prayer was praise and others in which it opened my prayer and helped me enter into it, others finally in which it had a more reduced place. Whatever in fact its richness and its spiritual efficacy, the stripping of self which it effects, praise does not exhaust the forms of prayer. Other forms also are good and fruitful. But from time to time – and the Spirit takes care to bring me back to it – I experience the desire and the need to come back to pure praise, to restore my strength and to find again in it, more total and more true, that orientation of the whole being towards God which takes you out of yourself

---

[5] To tell the truth it is not indispensable to prayer. It seems that great Saints themselves did not receive it: neither Teresa of Avila nor John of the Cross allude to it. Frequent in the first days of the Church, this gift, this charism was gradually eclipsed, partly on account of its disturbing and irrational character. Its decline, besides, accompanied the progressive eclipse of the Spirit himself in Christian consciousness, at least in the West. It is being manifested anew today, especially in the wake of the Charismatic Renewal: but it does not belong to it. Neither, again, is it a criterion of the authenticity of prayer. If you receive it, so much the better, but it is never anything more than an extra which cannot be demanded as of right.

and roots you in him. A beneficial cure which puts many things back in their proper place and revives in you the thirst for the essential.

5. Thank you, again and again

Look back at the path that has been travelled, neither for vain complacency nor a turning back upon oneself, but to become aware of the grace that has been given to you.

If anyone had tried to foretell what has been given to me to live, I would have reacted with an incredulous smile, indeed outright dismissal. Probably fear also would have taken hold of me then: the unknown element in a new path creates apprehension, urges one to refuse it.

And precisely what I was no longer hoping for and did not even desire, became a reality in my life by the favour of Another. I knew that God gives without ceasing: at my lowest ebb his gifts had never failed me. But what were they then in comparison with what I have received since?

Then, words of gladness rose up in my heart, an interior song which is fed by pure joy: 'You have not abandoned me to the power of death!' Those words, which sum up the whole of my experience and which had overwhelmed me, were singing in me. You have given me back life and, every day, life does its work in what was my death, my unsuspected death. 'He was dead and he has come back to life...' Joy of the Father for his returned son. Joy of the prodigal son for the Father he has found again. Joy which breaks forth in infinite gratitude. A hymn of gratitude, which never comes to an end, for the gifts of God never run dry:

you never exhaust their wealth and God does not weary of filling you still more.

I would have to go back over everything, day by day, read everything again, as the fiancé reads and rereads the letter of his beloved to nourish his love and his gratitude. Each word for him is a whole speech, a whole slice of life, and he receives it as a gift which embellishes accordingly. The words form for him as it were a litany which speaks of the beloved, details her beauty, her wit, her love. Memories abound and take on fresh life, bathing the whole of lived experience in a joyful light. The heart is filled and overflows with gladness. Troubles melt away, difficulties vanish. Life breaks forth like buds too swollen with sap in rich springtimes. How can such a joy be mine? What can I have done to deserve it? But, I know, God does not measure his gifts by our merits. My hands are empty and they are filled only with what I receive. Everything is gift, 'everything is grace'.

'Everything is grace.' This saying of the little Thérèse, which is echoed by the Curé of Torcy in Bernanos' *Diary of a Country Parish Priest*, suddenly takes on a new meaning. Until then it had been for me, like so many other essential sayings, a hackneyed phrase, familiar to all, like a consecrated expression that is used unthinkingly, without awareness of its depths. It had meaning only in my head. But now it was becoming, beneath the impact of experience, a saying full and overflowing with life, with manifold resonances, with indefinite evocations. I could recite the unending litany of the gifts of God.

'Everything is grace.' Where I saw formerly only banal happening, without interest and without value, there was being revealed to the eyes of my faith, to that interior sense which prayer gives, the loving attention of the heart of God. A love incessantly at work, in great things and in small, in those everyday and routine matters which so often wear out enthusiasm. As if God had only you to love and were spending his time in presenting to you on a dish what will bring pleasure to that depth in you which seeks him and recognises him. A serene and quiet confusion which is only the discreet form of the gratitude which dwells in you.

'Everything is grace.' I say 'everything' advisedly. The joy of knowing oneself loved, and that pang of the heart at the sight of wretchedness. The intimacy of prayer and the dispersion of human responsibilities. The meeting with a brother and the difficulty of being together. The desire to love and the inability of attaining it. The brightness which illuminates the heart and fulfils the whole of a hope, and the long nights of doubt and uncertainty. The wink of God's love and the slow ripenings which seem never to reach their completion. Yes, everything, absolutely everything, is grace.

All that remains then is to live in 'thanksgiving'. That is your part, the choice part which falls to you. That part which is so often forgotten because everything seems natural and proceeding from cause to effect. You could follow that path which is traced out for you like a blind man, making out only the obstacles, whereas it is a path of love prepared for you: the obstacles themselves are a springboard for you and each step speaks to you of him who has already, for you, smoothed out the highway. Soon, distracted indifference is no longer possible for you, for every instant opens your heart and your eyes to the wonders of love with which you are filled.

Thus your life sails from praise to thanksgiving and from thanksgiving to praise, both of them responses, related and disinterested, to the gifts you receive and which you have learnt to recognise: the most gratuitous praise, the thanksgiving to which you devote yourself through the gifts you have received.

There also, however, you can stop on the way and close your hand again over God's gifts, make them your own property, your wealth, your treasure. And once again your heart goes astray and turns back upon its selfish comfort. God, whom you believed you were taking hold of and possessing, escapes from you and his gifts themselves dry up in your hand, which no longer grasps anything but thin air. A brusque and sometimes mortal disappointment, after a fervent hope. A new sterility, more serious and more terrible than the first for which your wretchedness alone was responsible.

Yes, even the gifts of God must leave you poor. If you are attached to them as one is avidly attached to gain, you make a dead thing of what is a work of love. Yes, even the gifts of God must leave you humble, small, fragile. If you take pride in them, you distort and corrupt them. Like insipid salt they are no longer good for anything but to be trodden under foot. You run the risk of experiencing that to your cost.

On the other hand, thanksgiving, with a refusal of all consideration of yourself, makes them bear fruit beyond all human measure, and calls forth fresh boons. True prayer and incessant thanksgiving preserve you from the subtle temptation of complacency in those riches. They prevent you from being content with the gifts of God, however wonderful they may be, whereas in truth it is God whom you desire and who alone can fill your heart. 'At all times, for everything, give thanks to God the Father in the name of our Lord Jesus Christ' (Eph. 5, 20). It is a whole interior attitude: a life, as it were, in the form of thanksgiving. That after all was Jesus' way: he had received everything from the Father, he owed everything to him and he sent up to him without ceasing the hymn of love of his thanksgiving.

By giving thanks in this way, you appreciate better, at every moment, the gift which is being given to you. And the days spell out for you the wonders of God and each one of those wonders in its turn impels you towards him, humbly, lovingly, with that infinite gratitude which leads you to give thanks even for such suffering as may fall to your lot. Then, looking back over the path that has been travelled, you perceive that it is a path strewn with flowers for you by the love of your Father. The very stones of the path, transfigured by your thanksgiving, form in your eyes the rich mosaic of a love which has always gone before you and which accompanies your singing.

And then, in conclusion, let me give thanks gratuitously, for nothing, or rather for all: because God is God, because God is Love, because he is life, mercy, because he is humble and patient, because he is, and I love him.

6. Ask and you shall receive

Between praise and thanksgiving is there a space free for the simple prayer of petition? Coming unbidden to the heart of simple folk, does it disappear, giving way to nobler forms, when one progresses further in prayer? It is to be feared, however, that the said nobility is then only pretension and spiritual pride.

In the course of my life I, like everyone else, have asked for the cure of friends or loved ones. It seems to me today, I must admit, that I used to do so without much hope in efficacy of prayer. So many people have died who had been prayed for so much. Was it just a sort of experiment, as after all it can never do anyone any harm? I have very seldom asked, except in my childhood, for success in exams. I do not think I have ever asked for those purely material things of which popular prayer is fond at times, as is witnessed to by so many spontaneous and naive intentions.

In any case God is something other than the almighty provider of our daily needs, the stop-gap for our shortages and our failures, the universal (and free, or almost free) garage mechanic, always available, to whom one may resort in the least trouble. To put God thus at one's service is to lose sight of essential reality, and turns our heart back upon itself: God is not a utility.

To the extent that I was entering into prayer, I was feeling, as it were, an instinctive repugnance, more and more pronounced, to treating God in this way. Thus I came to dispense with petition to some extent. Discovering praise and thanksgiving sufficed to fill my heart and God himself made it his business to fill me. What could I have asked for?

A simple presence, attentive and silent, a praise scarcely voiced on the tip of the tongue, on the brink of the heart, were feeding my prayer quite sufficiently. A relationship was being established with God, intimate, deep, silent, alive. It was extinguishing petition in my heart. I was not seeking this, properly speaking. It just happened so, quite simply. For a certain time, I did not ask for anything.

And then, little by little, petition came back, all alone, without calculation on my part, without any particular decision. But it had changed. I didn't feel there was much to ask for, for myself, apart from the gifts of God. I was aware, for example, that prayer was being given to me, that it was not the result of my own efforts. Often, then, I used to ask (and I still ask): 'Lord, give me today's prayer'. Such a petition, far from centring me on myself, helped me to go out of myself and to sink myself in God to whom I looked for everything.

I also became aware of petition, frequently made – but without impatience and without fixing any time limit – of arriving at some understanding, simple and heartfelt, of the mysteries of God and of Jesus, into which only the Spirit can introduce you. But it was still the desire for God, in one way or another, that it was expressing. Until then I scarcely prayed for others, except in a very general way and when I learnt about some especially serious or sad situation. It was not lack of interest, but rather a reaction of a somewhat disembodied 'spiritualism' (for all that I was then living a life so little 'spiritual'!). I was reacting, mainly on the intellectual level, against the vision of God as a stop-gap. But in the very idea which I was forming for myself then of intercessory prayer, I realise now, there was, as it were, a lack of faith. I reached the point of thinking that we do not have to weary God with our petty affairs.

It is true that certain petitions, too interested, at times too materialistic, must indeed 'weary God'. But I was attributing to God too much of my own thinking, for I myself quickly tired of the requests of others. Those too human petitions irritated me. But does God let himself be irritated by our 'earthly' petitions? Doesn't his heart know how to discern, behind the poverty of the request, the trust of the heart which has recourse to him? And whose fault is it if so many people know only how to ask for simple things? Have they been told enough about God and his love? Have they any other means of witnessing that they believe in his love?

It is simple people who are right, not intellectuals. Doesn't asking the love of the beloved for what, prosaically, one could obtain oneself, mark an absolute trust, and a deep desire for receiving one's own life from the hands of another? How false the proverb which declares that one is never so well served as by oneself! I am never so well served as by the one who loves me.

From day to day the desire to receive everything from the love of my Father was rising in me: for then everything takes on the colour of love and the humblest thing becomes a treasure. Possessing hardly has any further interest. Petition that has been granted does not make you richer, more comfortable or more powerful, but only more loved and more aware of the fact. And that is much more important than things. Thus prayer of petition has come back to dwell in my heart.

Then, to your great astonishment, you notice that your petitions, your loving petitions, are heard, often, almost always. You didn't notice it before for you were judging what was granted you by the standard of the things that you could grasp and turn to profit. But now, the important thing is the weight of love that you receive: the only value which truly counts. You no longer have as much need for things as for the love of him who gives them to you.

Intercession for one's brothers and sisters finds here its true significance. 'The good God grants me more or less all that I ask him for,' the Curé d'Ars said, 'except when I pray to him for myself.' And it is a great wonder which will also be worked for you. Asking for others will fill your heart better than all that you could obtain for yourself. Certainly you will have nothing for yourself (and rightly so) but love, lived, will fill you, and that things never succeed in doing.

When you ask on behalf of others you find yourself with full hands: not in order to close them upon what you have received, for you only receive in order to give. You will be surprised that you always have something in your hands, at your disposal, something that your brother needs. Do not be afraid of exhausting his reserves, for it is not you who are giving: you distribute what you receive from Another.

I came also to ask for myself. Not what I needed in order to live: as for that, your Father knows what you need and he gives it to you, in good measure, without your even asking him for it. I have then no desire to ask for things. I do not know what to do with them and sometimes I am cluttered up with them. I no longer seek to have but to be. That is what I ask for today: what I need in order to be. You will tell me that in this also your Father knows what you need even before you ask. However, in this regard things are somewhat different. The want that you feel at that deep level of being, far beyond all psychological hollows, is already revealed to you by your Father, as his pardons reveal, in contrast, the miseries which exhaust you. Thus light is given to you in order that you may know, in truth, what you must ask for. And it is the Spirit who, in you, formulates the petitions: 'Through our inarticulate groans the Spirit himself is pleading for us, and God who searches our inmost being knows what the Spirit means, because he pleads for God's people as God himself wills' (Rom. 8, 26-27).

Quite naturally then there emerge on the surface of your heart, like those bubbles which come from the furthest depths of the pond to burst in the open air, words which you recognise because you have uttered them a hundred times, a thousand times: 'Father, give us our daily bread. Forgive, since you also give us at the same time the ability to forgive. Do not subject your servant to temptation or to trial which would prevail over him, but stay with him to be strength in his weakness. Deliver from evil and from the Malignant One him whom you save by your love. May I be not as I wish, but as you will, your will be done.'

Ask and you will receive. Not to enrich yourself, but to live that true poverty which knows only how to receive.

7. Our sister suffering

I have hesitated much over speaking about this. All that can be said about it leaves as it were an impression of awkwardness. Has any one ever grasped in depth, shared in truth, the suffering of another? One can form some idea of it only in relationship to one's own suffering. One may describe the suffering of one's brother or sister, one may speak of it, say something about it, but can only ever bear it partially, poorly. And in the presence of the suffering of others, you can accompany them, walk with them, but that is about all. One tires so quickly of the heavy silence which is compassion, and words often tire those whom they are intended to console.

I will say nothing or almost nothing of the suffering of others. Of my own, I will, rather, remain discreet: what can one say about it oneself? I will speak about prayer and that shifting of centre which it effects gradually in us. It is from that angle only that I will allude to suffering.

'Something happened to death when Jesus underwent it,' Romano Guardini said. What I would like to say is that something happens to suffering when prayer takes hold of it. Even after having been lived by Jesus, death has remained death, savage and derisory. Even lived in prayer, suffering remains suffering, a trial which at times is incomprehensible and which poses the most bewildering problems. Suffering defies every answer: none is adequate to justify it. But, in prayer, something happens to it.

I don't think that one should ever ask for suffering. I did ask for it once. I must have been sixteen or seventeen years old, the age at which one is a bit silly and presumptuous (but it is good also to pass through that stage). If others have asked for it, why shouldn't I? And I was heard, only a very little, like when parents let their child undergo some painful experience, but without going the whole way, so as not to involve serious risk. I waited several years and I had completely forgotten my petition. And then it came one day, in an unexpected way, quite differently from what I had imagined. Almost at once I remembered what I had asked for... and I promised myself never to do it again.

It is enough to welcome the suffering which comes. In

that you find less occasion for feelings of pride. For even in suffering we find grounds for pride: especially from suffering which you have planned out yourself, or from that which you welcome as a means of proving your strength of soul or because it is the only way of demonstrating to yourself for the present that you exist. The human soul has such twists!

Suffering hurts. Too sensitive, we are easily crushed. In order to avoid suffering we create for ourselves an armour-plating which makes us less vulnerable, 'tougher', in regard to suffering. We make ourselves inaccessible to suffering and to many other things at the same time. Because we are tougher, we believe ourselves more human. Invulnerable, we ourselves do not realise that we have exchanged our heart for a breastplate. I have already spoken of that invulnerability in which I had encased myself. It hid, even from my own eyes, the emptiness of my heart.

To the extent that, through prayer, I was coming back to dwell in my own heart, I was becoming more vulnerable, more sensitive. The breastplate was falling apart and coming away piece by piece. But at the same time suffering was reaching more deeply into me, it was stinging a new sensitivity, like those scars scarcely closed over and still painful to the least touch. I was not undergoing more sufferings than previously, but I was suffering more from them, they were hurting me more, with nothing to protect me.

At times we have the impression that the Saints, who often underwent many sufferings, did not really suffer from them, that they had, so to speak, tamed suffering to the point of no longer feeling it painfully in their soul or in their flesh. The truth is just the opposite: holiness gave them a much more refined sensitivity than ours, a greater capacity for suffering, and probably it also multiplied the occasions for it. Their superiority to us lay elsewhere. For them suffering had already taken on the face of love. 'I want to suffer for love,' 'I have suffered much since I have been on earth, but if in my childhood I suffered with sadness, it is no longer thus that I suffer now, it is in joy and peace, I am truly happy to suffer,' St Thérèse of Lisieux tells us.[6] It is along the same path that the Spirit leads us, even if we never land on such distant shores.

God begins then by softening your heart. For me the beginnings of prayer were, to keep to Theresian comparisons, a path carpeted with flowers. The Lord draws and holds a soul with gentleness and kindness. Before the bareness of autumn and the harshness of winter he gives you a taste of the brightness and the joys of spring, the certitudes of spring. Otherwise how would you acquire the taste for his company?

But suffering is also a daily companion. And your heart having become more sensitive, you feel its sting more deeply. Perhaps it is a deficiency in me, but suffering has never appeared to me as a punishment, a chastisement, I was almost going to say, a revenge. Suffering is something too serious to be spoken of lightly.

Suffering produces sadness when you bear it with self-pity, when you spend your time complaining or comparing yourself with happy people. Then it becomes a cancer which gnaws at you. It destroys you.

---

[6] *Story of a Soul*, MS B, fol. 4, verso; MS C, fol. 4, verso.

With prayer, trust in the Lord and in his love was growing in my heart. How could it be possible that a God of tenderness, tenderness which I was experiencing at every instant, could take pleasure in seeing us suffer? Better, according to a dolorist vision that was, until recently, quite widespread, how could he cultivate the suffering, find satisfaction in it (even in its 'expiatory' aspect)? No, that God was not mine, he could never become that. And yet how can suffering be removed from our lives?

The Gospel itself... 'Let him take up his cross and follow me' (Mk 8, 34). That often obtruded itself on my prayer; a stumbling block on which many come to grief.

And then one day... I was keeping my eyes too fixed on myself. I was feeling too sorry for myself, looking at the cross that I had to bear. I had simply forgotten the essential thing, the second part of the saying: 'and follow me'. It was a question for me of looking somewhere else, of going out from myself at last and from that self-pity which was exasperating the evil.

I was learning to look at Jesus. I was becoming aware that I had never, so to speak, looked straight at Jesus on the cross. I thought that I knew and was moved sufficiently. It is not a question of emotion. I had never truly meditated on the passion and the death of Jesus. I know that this might seem outrageous, exaggerated, unbelievable, that it could make me appear utterly abnormal. So much the worse, since it is true. I did not find it easy to remain contemplating Christ on the cross for a long time. Very quickly I would turn aside or make my escape. I found a justification for myself in the joy of the resurrection, a divine answer to accepted death. But the cross of Jesus remained a side-issue in my life, in my faith. Fundamentally, it was too dangerous.

It took weeks and months for prayer to take me into the mystery of Jesus' death and abandonment; for suffering in my life to take on his face, the disfigured face of 'the fairest among the sons of men'. It took a long time for suffering, contemplated on the face of Jesus dead and abandoned, to take on for me the features of love. I am still, even now, on this journey of discovery.

But I understood one thing and the Lord is rooting it gradually in my heart: neither the saints nor any 'sane' man has ever loved suffering or desired to carry the cross for love of suffering or of the cross. However, for us, there no longer exists a cross which is not a crucifix, nor suffering which does not take on the face of Jesus' love.

In itself the cross is only an instrument of punishment, something abominable, and suffering is an evil to be fought against. Only Jesus on his cross, Jesus suffering, dying, abandoned, can be loved even in what makes us like him, in our sister suffering.

8. Welcoming the love of one's brothers and sisters

Brothers and sisters have taken up very little space in this narrative. It's true. I had to choose, and concentrate on the prayer I received from God.

On this point of fraternal charity, prayer has however allowed me to travel, I believe, a considerable distance. I can't tell the whole story, it would need another book!

I had a long way to go. I hardly dare to write it down.

'People annoy me,' I said one day to a friend. Not that I live like a savage or a recluse. But it often seemed to me very meritorious to listen to them, or to waste time outright. I was quite happy in solitude, even when surrounded by people, and it was repugnant to me to have to break it. I left it without enthusiasm, even if, subsequently, I rarely regretted the time spent together. But I tried not to multiply the occasions for it: those which simply occurred were quite enough by themselves.

But you can't find a new contact with God in prayer without something happening elsewhere and your attitude towards your brothers and sisters being changed somewhat. Prayer, received as a gift, as was the case with me, reveals the love which is given to you. It impels you to love in return. And love, by itself, rejects limits and frontiers, just as a gas occupies all the space that you are prepared to give it.

One evening, just after I had returned from a retreat, full of new life, I was coming back home after a meeting. A tramp was sleeping in the yard. Rain was beginning to fall. He had no shelter. I felt a pang in my heart. For my part I was returning to warmth, to find a comfortable interior and to sleep without care. He was sleeping there, accustomed no doubt to bad weather, but even so! I could not leave him there without doing anything. I thought for a moment of taking him into the house with me, giving him a bed, a room: I didn't even need to give him my own. I drew back at the prospect of the protests to be expected from the others who lived in the house, who would have feared some damage. Perhaps I should have moved on. I woke the man up and gave him the money to go and sleep elsewhere, under shelter. But that evening I wept over it! I had never wept over a tramp, nor had I ever given away so much money! But my heart told me that I was far from having done all that I ought to have done. This was one of the first breaches by which love for others, entered into me. Until that point I had given money to tramps with commiseration and often with impatience, the impatience of the man who has been disturbed: what affronts have to be endured when one lives on public charity! And how many humiliating steps are required to attain the necessary minimum! And so, until then, I gave them alms, but I did not love them. That evening I began, to a very slight extent, awkwardly, still very selfishly, to love, a tramp, my brother, over whom I wept, from powerlessness and shame.

So, I had some slight traces of fraternal love. And in any case, the solitude in which I was shutting myself up to preserve my independence, started to seem hollow to me. I was in need of someone, in need of being with others, especially – and this desire came on me suddenly – in need of prayer together with brothers and sisters. A shared prayer, fraternal, simple like the Spirit of God, but rich with the contribution of others, that becomes for you the word of God. And the poverty, and nakedness, and dryness of your own prayer find in that fraternity encouragement and a depth hitherto unknown. I did not say anything very much, but my very silence, rarely broken, no longer weighed on me, and was not an emptiness. In a wonderful exchange, the prayer of others was giving me God and feeding my heart. Today, when I have been deprived of it for a long time, I need to go back, as if to an oxygen tent, to the prayer of others. I do not have to choose them, provided that they welcome me into their prayer and that

I welcome them into mine. The prayer itself makes us fraternal and creates bonds of a depth which is different from those of blood or friendship: 'Where two or three are gathered together in my name, I am in the midst of them,' Jesus said (Mt. 18, 20). He is himself the common heart which unites brothers and sisters in their simple prayer. How should fraternal love not find an inexhaustible source there? How can one fail to love those whose prayer gives God to you? Perhaps it may seem a bit selfish to feed oneself on the prayer of others, but each receives from the other because no one keeps anything for themselves of their prayer or their joy.

However, day by day, I was becoming aware, in prayer, of the smallness of the love of which I was capable. I had good reasons, or at least I thought so (other people always have, to your mind, so many incurable failings!) for setting limits to my love... Was there so much need for me to do that? Those limits existed in me, bound up with the narrowness of my heart. It was in vain that I made efforts and experiments in the endeavour to love, in vain that I asked the Lord incessantly to teach me to love. There was an inbuilt resistance which seemed beyond my control.

The first thing you become aware of, that prayer and the proximity of God bring before you, is that you do not love. Yet I believed that I loved, at least certain persons. I had done much for them, was that not loving them? With others, it was more difficult; the distance was greater, the differences more marked, which sometimes broke out into forms of animosity, even thought they might be spiced with those smiles which fail to convince, despite your efforts to disguise your feelings.

I often asked myself: how do I set about loving? How can I love such and such a person in whom everything repels me, who represents more or less all that I reject, to the point that he appears to me like a living contradiction? I cannot love those faults, those idiosyncrasies. So, how do I set about loving?

It took years for a dawn to break in my heart. A little light which was the answer to the insistent prayer so many times repeated: 'Lord, give me fraternal love! Teach me to love!'

A strong light lays bare the secret recesses in which are hidden the anguish of living, the fear of dying and that desperate fear of not being oneself. I would never have believed that in me, beneath such 'logical' reasons, there lay the irrational fear of disappearing. But our self-defence mechanisms are so very sophisticated and so well camouflaged. I was only dimly aware of the extent to which I was frustrating myself. I was going on about the difficulty of loving, blaming others for my inability to love, whereas the problem was in me.

If you do not love someone, if you do not succeed in loving them, it isn't their fault; God loves them just as they are and he knows much more about their faults and shortcomings. If he loves them it is because they are lovable. The obstacle to love is in you, not in the other person. You are so ready to judge and to blame the other. I understood that in prayer, gradually, and gradually, the grace of the Lord freed me from it. Contrary to the story of the garden (Gen. 3, 7), my eyes were opened, not to the distress of my unbearable nakedness, but to my neighbour, a neighbour who was completely new for me. What did their faults or limitations matter? What did even their attacks or aggressiveness (a replica of my own!) or annoying little mannerisms matter? My neighbour had not changed. It was my attitude towards him which was no longer the same and I was beginning to love him, truly, simply, without much difficulty.

I was beginning to understand the statement of John in his Epistle (I liked that epistle, to be sure, but I had not truly 'entered into' it): 'It is by this that we know what love is: that Christ laid down his life for us. And we in our turn are bound to lay down our lives for our brothers' (1 Jn 3, 16). And that other statement: 'God is love: he who dwells in love is dwelling in God, and God in him' (1 Jn 4, 16). Prayer had introduced me into the abode of God and God into my abode. And now he was introducing me, himself, to love, in order that I might dwell also in the love of my brothers and sisters. It was a poor, humble, fragile love, the fruit of the path of prayer which I received from God.

SO IT IS PRAYER GOES

So it is that prayer goes, a river which flows throughout life, in a variety of landscapes, making its bed in all sorts of terrains. Along its course it shapes new, unknown and contrasting landscapes. It is water which makes the river. It doesn't invent itself nor cause itself to rise. The water comes to it always from elsewhere, from what is not itself; it is given to it at every instant. Do you even grasp why it comes to rise at that moment, in that place? The source is not the river. It brings it to birth and feeds it. Thus from source to source, from rivulet to brook, from stream to river, its waters swell and flow.

The source is a mystery of which you see only the effect. Like the breath of the Spirit which you do not know from where it comes or to where it goes. Without that water, which is given to you welling up to life eternal, your life would be only a parched terrain, an arid land. You cannot lay commands on the source to make it well up or to increase its volume. You take what is given to you. You are never master of the sources, but you can sing about them and drink of their freshness and of their poetry.

It is a mystery long in the making, like those glaciers from which ravines and torrents come to birth. Snow fell, slow and stubborn on the heights. It lay, frozen and hardened under the impact of winter. It pursued its path down the centuries, a petrified torrent, monstrous and tranquil. Beneath the strip of ice, blue water filtered, witness of ancient rains. When then did it fall, by what paths does it reach you, this water which provides you with drink today?

There are the mysteries of enclosed banks, too narrow, in which the river no longer breathes and hurls itself forward, panting, in a fight which breaks and bruises it. From one edge to the other it rebounds, falls back, returns and shatters itself again, breaking out into foam, into droplets in which the light itself is broken up and radiates. There is the fierceness of the struggles along the paths of life, of the temptations in which one reels, drunk and disabled. There are wounds which bleed and which cost the blood of your heart. You must go on, jostled by the fury of the waters. It is God who is breaking you.

There are the mysteries of the nights in which the river loses itself in dark crevasses, in the belly of the earth. The nights in which nothing any longer seems to exist but darkness and human anguish: 'My God, my God, why have you forsaken me?' Yet the water is always there, invisible, imperceptible, making its way in the hidden depths of the earth. Walk on, pursue your journey. The water you can't see is not lost: it is only veiled from your sight and snatched for a moment from your thirst. Walk on and hope. Soon it will rise up again for you, at that bend in the road where you were no longer looking for it. See how fresh and pure it is, and how it offers itself to your joy.

There is the mystery of the boundless plains. The river parades the laziness of its waters there and each of its meanders takes you back two steps from where you set out. Time drags on for you and you seem not to be making any progress in this world which is so featureless and without landmarks. Nothing happens and your steps become heavy. 'My soul thirsts for the living God: when shall I see him face to face?'

There is the mystery of springtime: flowers and birds make the meadow sing, nature smiles at the rising sap, at the sun growing warm again. Life is resplendent and joy rises in your heart, like early morning mists by tranquil waters. A quiet joy, a secret harmony which reconciles you with the world, with others, with yourself, and which murmurs to your ear the name of your Lord.

There are the mysteries of estuaries. The river spreads itself there, but it is in order better to lose itself. It can only become ocean if it is willing to die to the river which it was and if it gives back with joy all the waters it received, to which it owed its existence. 'Father, into your hands I commit my spirit... my life.' Beyond all death.

Lord, you know the secret of hearts.
You know what is in humankind:
Wretchedness, distress, sin.
My wretchedness, my distress, my sin.
You sought me, when I was no longer seeking you.
You were hoping when I was despairing of myself.
You took hold of me when I was running away.
You did not abandon me to the power of death.
You have showered tenderness upon me and filled me
        with your gifts.
That is our common story
Yours and mine,
Mine in yours,

The history of your mercies.
Here it is, for your sole glory.
Here it is, for you also, my brother, my sister,
'If you knew the gift of God...'

Paris, December 8, 1980,
on the Feast of Mary Immaculate.

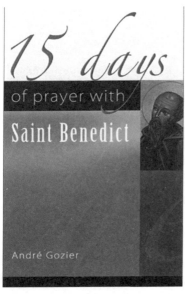

ISBN: 978-1-56548-304-0
PB 136 pp   £8.95

Born in 480 to a distinguished family in Nursia, Benedict as a young man abandoned his studies and gave up his inheritance to pursue a monastic life. He lived for several years as a hermit in Subiaco, where a group of monks seeking a spiritual leader joined him. After an attempt on his life he moved to Monte Cassino, where he founded the abbey considered the birthplace of the Benedictine order. At Monte Cassino Benedict wrote his Rule, and died there in 547. Benedict required of himself and his monastic brothers a life of work, prayer, and spiritual reading – a pattern that anyone may reproduce in some form today.

Not everyone is called to the monastic ideal of poverty, chastity, and obedience, but even the busiest person may draw nearer to God and live humbly and prayerfully, in the spirit of Saint Benedict.

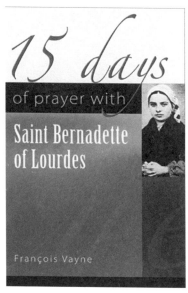

15 days
of prayer with
Saint Bernadette
of Lourdes

François Vayne

ISBN: 978-1-56548-314-9
PB 136 pp £8.95

Born into a humble family which fell into extreme poverty, Saint Bernadette of Lourdes was only four-teen when the Blessed Virgin Mary appeared to her for the first of eighteen visits near Lourdes, in southern France. A woman of faith and purity, Saint Bernadette maintained a state of childlike innocence throughout her short life and believed that God is Love and that he never stops calling us from our sin.

Although Bernadette endured the painful disease of tuberculosis of the bone, she served a faithful life as a Sister of Notre Dame until her death in 1879.

Enjoy your time with Saint Bernadette of Lourdes in this book and be prepared to be surprised as you journey with one of the most engaging spiritual figures of our time.